The Best American Mystery Stories 2016

GUEST EDITORS OF
THE BEST AMERICAN MYSTERY STORIES

1997 ROBERT B. PARKER
1998 SUE GRAFTON
1999 ED MCBAIN
2000 DONALD E. WESTLAKE
2001 LAWRENCE BLOCK
2002 JAMES ELLROY
2003 MICHAEL CONNELLY
2004 NELSON DEMILLE
2005 JOYCE CAROL OATES
2006 SCOTT TUROW
2007 CARL HIAASEN
2008 GEORGE PELECANOS
2009 JEFFERY DEAVER
2010 LEE CHILD
2011 HARLAN COBEN
2012 ROBERT CRAIS
2013 LISA SCOTTOLINE
2014 LAURA LIPPMAN
2015 JAMES PATTERSON
2016 ELIZABETH GEORGE

The Best American Mystery Stories™ 2016

Edited and with an Introduction
by **Elizabeth George**

Otto Penzler, *Series Editor*

A Mariner Original
HOUGHTON MIFFLIN HARCOURT
BOSTON • NEW YORK

www.hmhco.com

ISSN 1094-8384
ISBN 978-0-544-52718-8

Printed in the United States of America
DOC 10 9 8 7 6 5 4 3 2
4500642152

"Christians" by Tom Franklin. First published in *Murder under the Oaks,* edited by Art Taylor. Copyright © 2015 by Tom Franklin. Reprinted by permission of Tom Franklin.

"A Death" by Stephen King. First published in *The New Yorker,* March 9, 2015. From *The Bazaar of Bad Dreams* by Stephen King. Copyright © 2015 by Stephen King. Reprinted with the permission of Scribner, a division of Simon & Schuster, Inc. All rights reserved.

"For Something to Do" by Elmore Leonard. First published in *Charlie Martz and Other Stories: The Unpublished Stories of Elmore Leonard.* Copyright © 2015 by Elmore Leonard, Inc. Reprinted by permission of HarperCollins Publishers.

"The Continental Opposite" by Evan Lewis. First published in *Alfred Hitchcock's Mystery Magazine,* May 2015. Copyright © 2015 by David Evan Lewis. Reprinted by permission of Evan Lewis.

"Street of the Dead House" by Robert Lopresti. First published in *nEvermore!,* edited by Nancy Kilpatrick and Caro Soles, July 1, 2015. Copyright © 2015 by Robert Lopresti. Reprinted by permission of Robert Lopresti.

"Lafferty's Ghost" by Dennis McFadden. First published in *Fiction,* no. 61. Copyright © 2015 by Dennis McFadden. Reprinted by permission of the author.

"The Tank Yard" by Michael Noll. First published in *Ellery Queen's Mystery Magazine,* July 2015. Copyright © 2015 by Michael Noll. Reprinted by permission of Michael Noll.

"Trash" by Todd Robinson. First published in *Last Word* by the editors of Joyride Press, August 2015. Copyright © 2015 by Todd Robinson. Reprinted by permission of Todd Robinson.

"Christmas Eve at the Exit" by Kristine Kathryn Rusch. First published in *Ellery Queen's Mystery Magazine,* January 2015. Copyright © 2015 by Kristine K. Rusch. Reprinted by permission of Kristine K. Rusch.

"The Mountain Top" by Georgia Ruth. First published in *Fish or Cut Bait: A Guppy Anthology,* April 7, 2015. Copyright © 2015 by Georgia Wilson. Reprinted by permission of Georgia Wilson.

"Mailman" by Jonathan Stone. First published in *Cold-Blooded,* edited by Clay Stafford and Jeffery Deaver, October 27, 2015. Copyright © 2015 by Jonathan Stone. Reprinted by permission of Jonathan Stone.

"Rearview Mirror" by Art Taylor. First published in *On the Road with Del & Louise* by Art Taylor, September 15, 2015. Copyright © 2015 by Art Taylor. Reprinted by permission of Henery Press, LLC.

"Border Crossing" by Susan Thornton. First published in the *Literary Review,* vol. 58, no. 3, Summer 2015. Copyright © 2015 by Susan R. Thornton. Reprinted by permission of Susan R. Thornton.

"Entwined" by Brian Tobin. First published in *Alfred Hitchcock's Mystery Magazine,* June 2015. Copyright © 2015 by Brian Tobin. Reprinted by permission of Brian Tobin.

"God's Plan for Dr. Gaynor and Hastings Chiume" by Saral Waldorf. First published in *Southern Review,* Spring 2015. Copyright © 2015 by Saral Waldorf. Reprinted by permission of Saral Waldorf.

Contents

Foreword ix

Introduction xiii

MEGAN ABBOTT
The Little Men 1

STEVE ALMOND
Okay, Now Do You Surrender? 35

MATT BELL
Toward the Company of Others 54

BRUCE ROBERT COFFIN
Fool Proof 61

LYDIA FITZPATRICK
Safety 71

TOM FRANKLIN
Christians 82

STEPHEN KING
A Death 102

ELMORE LEONARD
For Something to Do 116

EVAN LEWIS
The Continental Opposite 130

ROBERT LOPRESTI
Street of the Dead House 154

DENNIS McFADDEN
Lafferty's Ghost 173

MICHAEL NOLL
The Tank Yard 185

TODD ROBINSON
Trash 204

KRISTINE KATHRYN RUSCH
Christmas Eve at the Exit 214

GEORGIA RUTH
The Mountain Top 237

JONATHAN STONE
Mailman 249

ART TAYLOR
Rearview Mirror 265

SUSAN THORNTON
Border Crossing 286

BRIAN TOBIN
Entwined 298

SARAL WALDORF
God's Plan for Dr. Gaynor and Hastings Chiume 311

Contributors' Notes 333

Other Distinguished Mystery Stories of 2015 346

lowing a merger of these two honored houses, both with long histories of excellence. The editor in chief has changed twice during those two decades. The publishing landscape has changed, with more and more mergers, though there is less impact on readers than one might have expected. The bookselling landscape has changed even more. Twenty years ago, Amazon was just beginning to emerge as a major force; today it dominates the bookselling world. Whereas the giant book emporiums of Barnes & Noble and Borders had forced many independent bookshops out of business, the marketplace dominance of Amazon has forced Borders out of existence and seriously threatens Barnes & Noble, while further crippling the independent bookstore. The ray of light is that more independent bookstores have opened in America during the past three years than closed their doors.

Similarities? I am still the series editor, and the methodology of determining which stories make the cut remains the same. My invaluable associate Michele Slung reads and evaluates thousands of stories every year, culling those that clearly do not belong on a short list—or a long one either, for that matter—to determine if they have mystery or criminal content, frequently impossible to know merely by reading the title, as well as whether they have any literary merit. I then read the stories that need to be considered in order to arrive at the fifty best (or at least those I like the most). Those are sent to the guest editor, who selects the twenty stories that make it into the book; the remaining thirty receive honorable mention. The best writing makes it into the book. Fame, friendship, original venue, reputation, subject—none of it matters. It isn't only the qualification of being the best writer that will earn a spot in the table of contents; it also must be the best story.

Another similarity from the first book to the twentieth has been the quest to have the right person serve as the guest editor. Willingness to do this is an act of generosity. Every guest editor for this series has been a national bestseller, and therefore these are authors who are asked to do something virtually every day of their lives: write a story, make a speech, sign a book, visit a bookshop or library, provide a quote for a dust jacket, offer advice about how to be a better writer or a more successful one, attend a conference or convention—the list goes on.

It is with deep gratitude, then, that I applaud Elizabeth George for agreeing to serve in this role for the 2016 edition. She is a

Foreword

THIS IS THE twentieth edition of *The Best American Mystery Stories* of the year, a very gratifying milestone. The series began when my agent, Nat Sobel, and I were having lunch, as we have every month for the past thirty years. In the middle of a sentence about who knows what he said, "I have an idea." This is common in our relationship, as I would argue that he is the best and most creative agent on the planet.

Nat had represented the longtime series editor of Houghton Mifflin's prestigious *The Best American Short Stories* of the year, an annual event that began in 1915. He suggested that it was time for a similar mystery series and thought I should be the editor. I agreed. He went back to his office, called the editor in chief of Houghton Mifflin, and they came to an agreement in two minutes.

For my first guest editor, I wanted someone who was an accomplished author, not just in the mystery category but one who brought serious literary credentials to the table as well. Being a bestseller was not a requirement but was certainly a desirable element. I aimed high and called my friend Robert B. Parker, who agreed to take on the job without hesitation. To this day, his introduction to the 1997 edition remains the most erudite and comprehensive essay in the history of the series. The book went on to make the bestseller list in Boston and sold enough copies nationally to make Houghton Mifflin happy.

Reflecting on the past twenty years reminds me of how much has changed but also how much has remained the same.

Changes? The publisher is now Houghton Mifflin Harcourt, fol-

number-one best-selling writer, an American whose detective novels are set in England, best known for her superb series featuring Detective Inspector Thomas Lynley, actually Lord Asherton, privately educated (Eton College and Oxford University), and his partner, Detective Sergeant Barbara Havers, who comes from a working-class background—both from Scotland Yard. George's first novel, *A Great Deliverance,* was published in 1988, and there have been eighteen further adventures of Lynley and Havers, as well as four young adult novels and two short story collections.

I also am in debt to previous guest editors; my thanks continue to resonate for James Patterson, Laura Lippman, Lisa Scottoline, Robert Crais, Harlan Coben, Lee Child, Jeffery Deaver, George Pelecanos, Carl Hiaasen, Scott Turow, Joyce Carol Oates, Nelson DeMille, Michael Connelly, James Ellroy, Lawrence Block, Donald E. Westlake, Ed McBain, Sue Grafton, and, of course, Robert B. Parker.

While it is redundant to write it again, since I have already done it in each of the previous nineteen volumes of this series (although it is painful to acknowledge, I do recognize that not everyone reads and memorizes my annual forewords), it is fair warning to state that many people erroneously regard a "mystery" as a detective story. The detective story is important but is only one subgenre of a much bigger literary category, mystery fiction, which I define as any work of fiction in which a crime, or the threat of a crime, is central to the theme or the plot. While I love good puzzles and tales of pure ratiocination, few of these are written today, as the mystery genre has evolved (or devolved, depending on your point of view) into a more character-driven form of literature, with more emphasis on the "why" of a crime's commission than a "who" or "how." The line between mystery fiction and general fiction has become more and more blurred in recent years, producing fewer memorable detective stories but more significant literature.

While I engage in a relentless quest to locate and read every mystery/crime/suspense story published, I live in terror that I will miss a worthy story, so if you are an author, editor, or publisher, or care about one, please feel free to send a book, magazine, or tearsheet to me c/o The Mysterious Bookshop, 58 Warren Street, New York, NY 10007. If the story first appeared electronically, you must submit a hard copy. It is vital to include the author's contact information. No unpublished material will be considered, for what should be obvious reasons. No material will be returned. If you distrust the postal service, enclose a self-addressed, stamped postcard and I'll let you know your submission was received.

To be eligible for next year's edition, a story must have been written by an American or a Canadian and first published in an American or Canadian publication in the calendar year 2016. The earlier in the year I receive the story, the more fondly I regard it. For reasons known only to the dunderheads who wait until Christmas week to submit a story published the previous spring, this occurs every year, causing serious irritableness as I read a stack of stories while friends trim Christmas trees, shop, meet for lunches and dinners, and otherwise celebrate the holiday season. It had better be a damned good story if you do this. I am being neither arrogant nor whimsical when I state that the absolute firm deadline for me to receive a submission is December 31; it is due to the very tight production schedule for the book. If the story arrives one day later, it will not be read. Sorry.

O.P.

Introduction

When I was asked to choose the twenty best mystery stories published in 2015 and then to write an introduction to the volume that would contain them, I had to think about whether I wanted to take on the task. Not only is it always difficult to choose one peer-written story over another, but it's also tough to decide whether a tale actually constitutes a mystery story in the first place.

I've always seen the mystery as a very particular kind of story, quite distinguishable from a tale of crime. A mystery story, to me, has always been about the game, and the game has always pitted the writer against the reader. The rules of the game are simple. A mystery is unfolded by the writer, and during the unfolding all the clues are set into the various scenes, as are the red herrings. The private investigator, police detective, or amateur sleuth explores the circumstances surrounding some sort of act of malfeasance, possibly experiencing the crime scene itself through photos or a personal encounter with it. Ultimately this investigator arrives at a conclusion that concerns the guilty party, the resolution of the crime, or whatever else will bring the story to a satisfactory close. Part of the denouement of this kind of tale is, of course, an explanation from the investigator, to include an interpretation of the clues and the red herrings. Between the writer and the reader, the game involved is a contest in which the reader attempts to discern the clues, to distinguish them from the red herrings, and to reach a conclusion about the guilty party in advance of the author's unveiling it all. In the mystery story, neither clues nor red herrings are explained as the story goes along. Frequently they're not even identified as clues or red herrings. When they're seen by the fictional investigator, they are noted in passing but never dwelt upon. Because of this, the reader must be astute enough to recognize them for what they are as the writer mentions them in passing. Should the reader sort everything out and identify the killer or thief or kidnapper or whatever, then she wins the game and the author loses. A clever author can keep a reader guessing throughout, but because no explanation of clues and red herrings is necessary in a mystery, not an enormous amount of cleverness on the writer's part is actually required.

An example of this would be the most infamous mystery novel of all time, written by none other than the grand dame of the Golden Age of Mystery, Agatha Christie. In her controversial novel *The Murder of Roger Ackroyd,* she certainly reveals the clues to the reader. Hercule Poirot sees them and he makes careful note of them. But in every case the reader is left in the dark as to what they are or what they mean. The reader has no way of knowing, for example, that the glittering object that Poirot scoops up from the pond is a wedding ring with the initials of two characters engraved upon it, just as the reader doesn't know that the stranger who came to the house in the days prior to the victim's murder was a salesman offering a Dictaphone to the soon-to-be-done-away-with Roger Ackroyd. What makes the story so maddening—and so infamous—has to do with the narrator of the piece. He admits in the novel's conclusion that had he only put an ellipsis instead of a period at the end of a certain sentence, the game would have been up shortly after Mr. Ackroyd's demise. But he did not do that, Agatha Christie did not do that, and the argument has raged for nearly one hundred years about whether the novel plays fair with the reader.

For me, the larger question has always been this: ellipsis or not, does the novel actually offer an opportunity for the reader to solve the crime in the first place? The answer has to be decidedly no. The reader can certainly guess at it (or, as one of my students once did, write the name of the killer in the margin of his book to spoil the experience for any student following him), but compared to Hercule Poirot, the reader has no real opportunity to work things out, because until the final moments of revelation (along with Poirot's suggestion that the killer politely commit suicide so as not to disturb people significant in his life), the reader doesn't have all the information. The reader may be able to sort clues from red herrings, but as to what they mean? As it is said in some parts of the U.S., fuhgeddaboutit.

Not so the crime story. I've always seen crime stories as different altogether from mysteries. Crime stories, in my point of view, are stories in which the writer all along reveals the clues to the reader. Of course, the writer reveals the red herrings as well. Both are presented in their absolute fullness. In other words, a glittering object drawn out of a pond by the detective in a crime novel would have been identified at once as a ring, and if there were engraved initials upon it, the reader would at once know what they were. That a salesman had been on the dead man's property peddling Dictaphones would also be discovered openly and in the fullness of time. What would occur post *any* discovery of anything at all is a discussion, a meditation, a reflection, or an argument, the subject being the clue or the red herring that had been discovered, uncovered, unearthed, or tripped over.

The art of the crime story derives from exactly that point: the discussion, meditation, reflection, or argument. For it is here that the writer must position the reader to believe the wrong thing. Thus the reader knows from the get-go every single thing the investigator knows or learns. The reader is also present as the investigator and her cohorts try to work out how their piece of information fits or does not fit into the overall puzzle of the crime. Not a single thing is withheld from the reader. And if the crime story is beautifully constructed and artfully written, the reader remains in the dark until the end.

Both approaches to this form of literature are perfectly legitimate. One is generally more lighthearted than the other. One is grittier and possesses more social commentary. Both can be a pleasure to read. But make no mistake: they are very different creatures indeed.

The short story is a tough form to select when a writer wishes to deal either with mystery or with crime. The main stricture is one of length. It's a difficult proposition for the author to lay out both crime and resolution to crime if the author also wishes to play absolutely fair with the reader. Generally one has to cut a corner here or there. One has to make a decision about each fundamental of the writing craft:

How much of a setting can a writer employ? Setting in a crime novel especially often functions as a virtual character.

Which of the many viewpoints available to her will best serve the writer's intent in the story?

How much attitude can be conveyed within the point of view chosen?

Can suspense be developed?

Can suspicion fall on more than one character?

Is there enough time for atmosphere and tone, for any kind of theme, to be developed, for clues to be planted, for the inclusion of red herrings to mislead the reader?

A novella would allow for all of this, but unfortunately, a short story must fight to stay short. This makes things difficult and often results in some elements of the craft being given decidedly short shrift.

In this collection, what I've tried to do is first of all to include both mystery stories and crime stories, the latter being more challenging to find because of fairness to the reader. Since a short story cannot possibly contain every element that I've already mentioned as belonging within a longer work, I've looked for stories that best reflect at least one of those elements.

Thus, what you'll find in this volume are stories that demonstrate a mastery of plotting; stories that compel you to keep turning the pages because of plot and because of setting; stories that wield suspense like a sword; stories of people getting their comeuppance; stories that utilize superb point of view; stories that plumb one particular and unfortunate attribute of a character. You will read the traditional hard-boiled detective story; you will also read the literary crime story. You'll see the screws of madness or misunderstanding or avarice tighten upon characters; you'll read endings that you foresaw from the first and endings that perfectly surprise you.

Each story was chosen, then, because it reflects at least one of the elements that constitute fine writing within the genre. One of the stories was chosen because, with remarkable wit and discipline, it actually reflects them all. I'm not going to tell you which story it is, though.

That's a mystery you'll have to work out on your own.

Elizabeth George

The Best American Mystery Stories 2016

MEGAN ABBOTT

The Little Men

FROM *Bibliomysteries*

AT NIGHT, THE sounds from the canyon shifted and changed. The bungalow seemed to lift itself with every echo and the walls were breathing. Panting.

Just after two, she'd wake, her eyes stinging, as if someone had waved a flashlight across them.

And then she'd hear the noise.

Every night.

The tapping noise, like a small animal trapped behind the wall.

That was what it reminded her of. Like when she was a girl, and that possum got caught in the crawlspace. For weeks they just heard scratching. They only found it when the walls started to smell.

It's not the little men, she told herself. *It's not.*

And then she'd hear a whimper and startle herself. Because it was her whimper and she was so frightened.

I'm not afraid I'm not I'm not

It had begun four months ago, the day Penny first set foot in the Canyon Arms. The chocolate and pink bungalows, the high arched windows and French doors, the tiled courtyard, cosseted on all sides by eucalyptus, pepper, and olive trees, miniature date palms—it was like a dream of a place, not a place itself.

This is what it was supposed to be, she thought.

The Hollywood she'd always imagined, the Hollywood of her childhood imagination, assembled from newsreels: Kay Francis in silver lamé and Clark Gable driving down Sunset in his Duesenberg, everyone beautiful and everything possible.

That world, if it ever really existed, was long gone by the time she'd arrived on that Greyhound a half-dozen years ago. It had been swallowed up by the clatter and color of 1953 Hollywood, with its swooping motel roofs and the shiny glare of its hamburger stands and drive-ins, and its descending smog, which made her throat burn at night. Sometimes she could barely breathe.

But here in this tucked-away courtyard, deep in Beachwood Canyon, it was as if that Old Hollywood still lingered, even bloomed. The smell of apricot hovered, the hush and echoes of the canyons soothed. You couldn't hear a horn honk, a brake squeal. Only the distant *ting-ting* of window chimes somewhere. One might imagine a peignoired Norma Shearer drifting through the rounded doorway of one of the bungalows, cocktail shaker in hand.

"It's perfect," Penny whispered, her heels tapping on the Mexican tiles. "I'll take it."

"That's fine," said the landlady, Mrs. Stahl, placing Penny's cashier's check in the drooping pocket of her satin housecoat and handing her the key ring, heavy in her palm.

The scent, thick with pollen and dew, was enough to make you dizzy with longing.

And so close to the Hollywood sign, visible from every vantage, which had to mean something.

She had found it almost by accident, tripping out of the Carnival Tavern after three stingers.

"We've all been stood up," the waitress had tut-tutted, snapping the bill holder at her hip. "But we still pay up."

"I wasn't stood up," Penny said. After all, Mr. D. had called, the hostess summoning Penny to one of the hot telephone booths. Penny was still tugging her skirt free from its door hinges when he broke it to her.

He wasn't coming tonight and wouldn't be coming again. He had many reasons why, beginning with his busy work schedule, the demands of the studio, plus negotiations with the union were going badly. By the time he got around to the matter of his wife and six children, she wasn't listening, letting the phone drift from her ear.

Gazing through the booth's glass accordion doors, she looked out at the long row of spinning lanterns strung along the bar's windows. They reminded her of the magic lamp she had had when she was small, scattering galloping horses across her bedroom walls.

You could see the Carnival Tavern from miles away because of the lanterns. It was funny seeing them up close, the faded circus clowns silhouetted on each. They looked so much less glamorous, sort of shabby. She wondered how long they'd been here, and if anyone even noticed them anymore.

She was thinking all these things while Mr. D. was still talking, his voice hoarse with logic and finality. A faint aggression.

He concluded by saying surely she agreed that all the craziness had to end.

You were a luscious piece of candy, he said, *but now I gotta spit you out.*

After, she walked down the steep exit ramp from the bar, the lanterns shivering in the canyon breeze.

And she walked and walked and that was how she found the Canyon Arms, tucked off behind hedges so deep you could disappear into them. The smell of the jasmine so strong she wanted to cry.

"You're an actress, of course," Mrs. Stahl said, walking her to Bungalow Number Four.

"Yes," she said. "I mean, no." Shaking her head. She felt like she was drunk. It was the apricot. No, Mrs. Stahl's cigarette. No, it was her lipstick. Tangee, with its sweet orange smell, just like Penny's own mother.

"Well," Mrs. Stahl said. "We're all actresses, I suppose."

"I used to be," Penny finally managed. "But I got practical. I do makeup now. Over at Republic."

Mrs. Stahl's eyebrows, thin as seaweed, lifted. "Maybe you could do me sometime."

It was the beginning of something, she was sure.

No more living with sundry starlets stacked bunk-to-bunk in one of those stucco boxes in West Hollywood. The Sham-Rock. The Sun-Kist Villa. The smell of cold cream and last night's sweat, a brush of talcum powder between the legs.

She hadn't been sure she could afford to live alone, but Mrs. Stahl's rent was low. Surprisingly low. And if the job at Republic didn't last, she still had her kitty, which was fat these days on account of those six months with Mr. D., a studio man with a sofa in his office that wheezed and puffed. Even if he really meant what he said, that it really was kaput, she still had that last check he'd given her. He must have been planning the brushoff, because it was the biggest yet, and made out to cash.

And the Canyon Arms had other advantages. Number Four, like all the bungalows, was already furnished: sun-bleached zebra-print sofa and key-lime walls, that bright-white kitchen with its cherry-sprigged wallpaper. The first place she'd ever lived that didn't have rust stains in the tub or the smell of mothballs everywhere.

And there were the built-in bookshelves filled with novels in crinkling dust jackets.

She liked books, especially the big ones by Lloyd C. Douglas or Frances Parkinson Keyes, though the books in Number Four were all at least twenty years old, with a sleek, high-toned look about them. The kind without any people on the cover.

She vowed to read them all during her time at the Canyon Arms. Even the few tucked in the back, the ones with brown paper covers.

In fact, she started with those. Reading them late at night, with a pink gin conjured from grapefruit peel and an old bottle of Gilbey's she found in the cupboard. Those books gave her funny dreams.

"She got one."

Penny turned on her heels, one nearly catching on one of the courtyard tiles. But, looking around, she didn't see anyone. Only an open window, smoke rings emanating as if from a dragon's mouth.

"She finally got one," the voice came again.

"Who's there?" Penny said, squinting toward the window.

An old man leaned forward from his perch just inside Number Three, the bungalow next door. He wore a velvet smoking jacket faded to a deep rose.

"And a pretty one at that," he said, smiling with graying teeth. "How do you like Number Four?"

"I like it very much," she said. She could hear something rustling behind him in his bungalow. "It's perfect for me."

"I believe it is," he said, nodding slowly. "Of that I am sure."

The rustle came again. Was it a roommate? A pet? It was too dark to tell. When it came once more, it was almost like a voice shushing.

"I'm late," she said, taking a step back, her heel caving slightly.

"Oh," he said, taking a puff. "Next time."

That night she woke, her mouth dry from gin, at two o'clock. She had been dreaming she was on an exam table and a doctor with an enormous head mirror was leaning so close to her she could smell his gum: violet. The ring light at its center seemed to spin, as if to hypnotize her.

She saw spots even when she closed her eyes again.

The next morning the man in Number Three was there again, shadowed just inside the window frame, watching the comings and goings in the courtyard.

Head thick from last night's gin and two morning cigarettes, Penny was feeling what her mother used to call "the hickedty-ticks."

So when she saw the man, she stopped and said briskly, "What did you mean yesterday? 'She finally got one'?"

He smiled, laughing without any noise, his shoulders shaking.

"Mrs. Stahl got one, got you," he said. "As in, Will you walk into my parlor? said the spider to the fly."

When he leaned forward, she could see the stripes of his pajama top through the shiny threads of his velvet sleeve. His skin was rosy and wet-looking.

"I'm no chump, if that's your idea. It's good rent. I know good rent."

"I bet you do, my girl. I bet you do. Why don't you come inside for a cup? I'll tell you a thing or two about this place. And about your Number Four."

The bungalow behind him was dark, with something shining beside him. A bottle, or something else.

"We all need something," he added cryptically, winking.

She looked at him. "Look, mister—"

"Flant. Mr. Flant. Come inside, miss. Open the front door. I'm harmless." He waved his pale pink hand, gesturing toward his lap mysteriously.

Behind him, she thought she saw something moving in the

darkness over his slouching shoulders. And music playing softly. An old song about setting the world on fire, or not.

Mr. Flant was humming with it, his body soft with age and stillness but his milky eyes insistent and penetrating.

A breeze lifted and the front door creaked open several inches, and the scent of tobacco and bay rum nearly overwhelmed her.

"I don't know," she said, even as she moved forward.

Later she would wonder why, but in that moment she felt it was definitely the right thing to do.

The other man in Number Three was not as old as Mr. Flant but still much older than Penny. Wearing only an undershirt and trousers, he had a mustache and big round shoulders that looked gray with old sweat. When he smiled, which was often, she could tell he was once matinee-idol handsome, with the outsized head of all movie stars.

"Call me Benny," he said, handing her a coffee cup that smelled strongly of rum.

Mr. Flant was explaining that Number Four had been empty for years because of something that happened there a long time ago.

"Sometimes she gets a tenant," Benny reminded Mr. Flant. "The young musician with the sweaters."

"That did not last long," Mr. Flant said.

"What happened?"

"The police came. He tore out a piece of the wall with his bare hands."

Penny's eyebrows lifted.

Benny nodded. "His fingers were hanging like clothespins."

"But I don't understand. What happened in Number Four?"

"Some people let the story get to them," Benny said, shaking his head.

"What story?"

The two men looked at each other. Mr. Flant rotated his cup in his hand.

"There was a death," he said softly. "A man who lived there, a dear man. Lawrence was his name. Larry. A talented bookseller. He died."

"Oh."

"Boy, did he," Benny said. "Gassed himself."

"At the Canyon Arms?" she asked, feeling sweat on her neck

despite all the fans blowing everywhere, lifting motes and old skin. *That's what dust really is, you know,* one of her roommates once told her, blowing it from her fingertips. "Inside my bungalow?"

They both nodded gravely.

"They carried him out through the courtyard," Mr. Flant said, staring vaguely out the window. "That great sheaf of blond hair of his. Oh, my."

"So it's a challenge for some people," Benny said. "Once they know."

Penny remembered the neighbor boy who fell from their tree and died from blood poisoning two days later. No one would eat its pears after that.

"Well," she said, eyes drifting to the smudgy window, "some people are superstitious."

Soon Penny began stopping by Number Three a few mornings a week, before work. Then the occasional evening too. They served rye or applejack.

It helped with her sleep. She didn't remember her dreams, but her eyes still stung with light spots most nights.

Sometimes the spots took odd shapes and she would press her fingers against her lids, trying to make them stop.

"You could come to my bungalow," she offered once. But they both shook their heads slowly, and in unison.

Mostly they spoke of Lawrence. Larry. Who seemed like such a sensitive soul, delicately formed and too fine for this town.

"When did it happen?" Penny asked, feeling dizzy, wishing Benny had put more water in the applejack. "When did he die?"

"Just before the war. A dozen years ago."

"He was only thirty-five."

"That's so sad," Penny said, finding her eyes misting, the liquor starting to tell on her.

"His bookstore is still on Cahuenga Boulevard," Benny told her. "He was so proud when it opened."

"Before that he sold books for Stanley Rose," Mr. Flant added, sliding a handkerchief from under the cuff of his fraying sleeve. "Larry was very popular. Very attractive. An accent soft as a Carolina pine."

"He'd pronounce *bed* like *bay-ed.*" Benny grinned, leaning against the windowsill and smiling that Gable smile. "And he said *bay-ed* a lot."

"I met him even before he got the job with Stanley," Mr. Flant said, voice speeding up. "Long before Benny."

Benny shrugged, topping off everyone's drinks.

"He was selling books out of the trunk of his old Ford," Mr. Flant continued. "That's where I first bought *Ulysses*."

Benny grinned again. "He sold me my first Tijuana Bible. *Dagwood Has a Family Party*."

Mr. Flant nodded, laughed. "*Popeye in The Art of Love*. It staggered me. He had an uncanny sense. He knew just what you wanted."

They explained that Mr. Rose, whose bookstore had once graced Hollywood Boulevard and had attracted great talents, used to send young Larry to the studios with a suitcase full of books. His job was to trap and mount the big shots. Show them the goods, sell them books by the yard, art books they could show off in their offices, dirty books they could hide in their big gold safes.

Penny nodded. She was thinking about the special books Mr. D. kept in his office, behind the false encyclopedia fronts. The books had pictures of girls doing things with long, fuzzy fans and peacock feathers, a leather crop.

She wondered if Larry had sold them to him.

"To get to those guys, he had to climb the satin rope," Benny said. "The studio secretaries, the script girls, the publicity office, even makeup girls like you. Hell, the grips. He loved a sexy grip."

"This town can make a whore out of anyone," Penny found herself blurting.

She covered her mouth, ashamed, but both men just laughed.

Mr. Flant looked out the window into the courtyard, the *flip-flipping* of banana leaves against the shutter. "I think he loved the actresses the most, famous or not."

"He said he liked the feel of a woman's skin in *bay-ed*," Benny said, rubbing his left arm, his eyes turning dark, soft. "Course, he'd slept with his mammy until he was thirteen."

As she walked back to her own bungalow, she always had the strange feeling she might see Larry. That he might emerge behind the rosebushes or around the statue of Venus.

Once she looked down into the fountain basin and thought she could see his face instead of her own.

But she didn't even know what he looked like.

Back in the bungalow, head fuzzy and the canyon so quiet, she thought about him more. The furniture, its fashion at least two decades past, seemed surely the same furniture he'd known. Her hands on the smooth bands of the rattan sofa. Her feet, her toes on the banana silk tassels of the rug. And the old mirror in the bathroom, its tiny black pocks.

In the late hours, lying on the bed, the mattress too soft, with a vague smell of mildew, she found herself waking again and again, each time with a start.

It always began with her eyes stinging, dreaming again of a doctor with the head mirror, or a car careering toward her on the highway, always lights in her face.

One night she caught the lights moving, her eyes landing on the far wall, the baseboards.

For several moments she'd see the light spots, fuzzed and floating, as if strung together by the thinnest of threads.

The spots began to look like the darting mice that sometimes snuck inside her childhood home. She never knew mice could be that fast. So fast that if she blinked, she'd miss them, until more came. Was that what it was?

If she squinted hard, they even looked like little men. Could it be mice on their hind feet?

The next morning she set traps.

"I'm sorry, he's unavailable," the receptionist said. Even over the phone, Penny knew which one. The beauty marks and giraffe neck.

"But listen," Penny said, "it's not like he thinks. I'm just calling about the check he gave me. The bank stopped payment on it."

So much for Mr. D.'s parting gift for their time together. She was going to use it to make rent, to buy a new girdle, maybe even a television set.

"I've passed along your messages, Miss Smith. That's really all I can do."

"Well, that's not all I can do," Penny said, her voice trembling. "You tell him that."

*

Keeping busy was the only balm. At work it was easy, the crush of people, the noise and personality of the crew.

Nights were when the bad thoughts came, and she knew she shouldn't let them.

In the past she'd had those greasy-skinned roommates to drown out thinking. They all had rashes from cheap studio makeup and the clap from cheap studio men and beautiful figures like Penny's own. And they never stopped talking, twirling their hair in curlers and licking their fingers to turn the magazine pages. But their chatter-chatter-chatter muffled all Penny's thoughts. And the whole atmosphere—the thick muzz of Woolworth's face powder and nylon nighties when they even shared a bed—made everything seem cheap and lively and dumb and easy and light.

Here, in the bungalow, after leaving Mr. Flant and Benny to drift off into their applejack dreams, Penny had only herself. And the books.

Late into the night, waiting for the light spots to come, she found her eyes wouldn't shut. They started twitching all the time, and maybe it was the night jasmine, or the beach burr.

But she had the books. All those books, these beautiful, brittling books, books that made her feel things, made her long to go places and see things—the River Liffey and Paris, France.

And then there were those in the wrappers, the brown paper soft at the creases, the white baker string slightly fraying.

Her favorite was about a detective recovering stolen jewels from an unlikely hiding spot.

But there was one that frightened her. About a farmer's daughter who fell asleep each night on a bed of hay. And in the night the hay came alive, poking and stabbing at her.

It was supposed to be funny, but it gave Penny bad dreams.

"Well, she was in love with Larry," Mr. Flant said. "But she was not Larry's kind."

Penny had been telling them how Mrs. Stahl had shown up at her door the night before, in worn satin pajamas and cold cream, to scold her for moving furniture around.

"I don't even know how she saw," Penny said. "I just pushed the bed away from the wall."

She had lied, telling Mrs. Stahl she could hear the oven damper popping at night. She was afraid to tell her about the shadows and lights and other things that made no sense in daytime. Like the mice moving behind the wall on hind feet, so agile she'd come to think of them as pixies, dwarves. Little men.

"It's not your place to move things," Mrs. Stahl had said, quite loudly, and for a moment Penny thought the woman might cry.

"That's all his furniture, you know," Benny said. "Larry's. Down to the forks and spoons."

Penny felt her teeth rattle slightly in her mouth.

"He gave her books she liked," Benny added. "Stiff British stuff he teased her about. Charmed himself out of the rent for months."

"When he died she wailed around the courtyard for weeks," Mr. Flant recalled. "She wanted to scatter the ashes into the canyon."

"But his people came instead," Benny said. "Came on a train all the way from Carolina. A man and woman with cardboard suitcases packed with pimento sandwiches. They took the body home."

"They said Hollywood had killed him."

Benny shook his head, smiled that tobacco-toothed smile of his. "They always say that."

"You're awfully pretty for a face-fixer," one of the actors told her, fingers wagging beneath his long makeup bib.

Penny only smiled, and scooted before the pinch came.

It was a western, so it was mostly men, whiskers, lip bristle, three-day beards filled with dust.

Painting the girls' faces was harder. They all had ideas of how they wanted it. They were hard girls, striving to get to Paramount, to MGM. Or they'd started out there and hit the Republic rung on the long slide down. To Allied, AIP. Then studios no one ever heard of, operating out of some slick guy's house in the Valley.

They had bad teeth and head lice and some had smells on them when they came to the studio, like they hadn't washed properly. The costume assistants always pinched their noses behind their backs.

It was a rough town for pretty girls. The only place it was.

Penny knew she had lost her shine long ago. Many men had rubbed it off, shimmy by shimmy.

But it was just as well, and she'd just as soon be in the war-paint business. When it rubbed off the girls, she could just get out her brushes, her powder puffs, and shine them up like new.

As she tapped the powder pots, though, her mind would wander. She began thinking about Larry bounding through the back lots. Would he have come to Republic with his wares? Maybe. Would he have soft-soaped her, hoping her bosses might have a taste for T. S. Eliot or a French deck?

By day she imagined him as a charmer, a cheery, silver-tongued roué.

But at night, back at the Canyon Arms, it was different.

You see, sometimes she thought she could see him moving, room to room, his face pale, his trousers soiled. Drinking and crying over someone, something, whatever he'd lost that he was sure wasn't ever coming back.

There were sounds now. Sounds to go with the 2 a.m. lights, or the mice or whatever they were.

Tap-tap-tap.

At first she thought she was only hearing the banana trees brushing against the side of the bungalow. Peering out the window, the moon-filled courtyard, she couldn't tell. The air looked very still.

Maybe, she thought, it's the fan palms outside the kitchen window, so much lush foliage everywhere, just the thing she'd loved, but now it seemed to be touching her constantly, closing in.

And she didn't like to go into the kitchen at night. The white tile glowed eerily, reminded her of something. The wide expanse of Mr. D.'s belly, his shirt pushed up, his watch chain hanging. The coaster of milk she left for the cat the morning she ran away from home. For Hollywood.

The mousetraps never caught anything. Every morning, after the rumpled sleep and all the flits and flickers along the wall, she moved them to different places. She looked for signs.

She never saw any.

One night, 3 a.m., she knelt down on the floor, running her fingers along the baseboards. With her ear to the wall, she thought the tapping might be coming from inside. A *tap-tap-tap.* Or was it a *tick-tick-tick?*

"I've never heard anything here," Mr. Flant told her the following day, "but I take sedatives."

Benny wrinkled his brow. "Once I saw pink elephants," he offered. "You think that might be it?"

Penny shook her head. "It's making it hard to sleep."

"Dear," Mr. Flant said, "would you like a little helper?"

He held out his palm, pale and moist. In the center, a white pill shone.

That night she slept impossibly deeply. So deeply she could barely move, her neck twisted and locked, her body hunched inside itself.

Upon waking, she threw up in the wastebasket.

That evening, after work, she waited in the courtyard for Mrs. Stahl.

Smoking cigarette after cigarette, Penny noticed things she hadn't before. Some of the tiles in the courtyard were cracked, some missing. She hadn't noticed that before. Or the chips and gouges on the sculpted lions on the center fountain, their mouths spouting only a trickle of acid green. The drain at the bottom of the fountain, clogged with crushed cigarette packs, a used contraceptive.

Finally she saw Mrs. Stahl saunter into view, a large picture hat wilting across her tiny head.

"Mrs. Stahl," she said, "have you ever had an exterminator come?"

The woman stopped, her entire body still for a moment, her left hand finally rising to her face, brushing her hair back under her mustard-colored scarf.

"I run a clean residence," she said, voice low in the empty, sunlit courtyard. That courtyard, oleander and wisteria everywhere, bright and poisonous, like everything in this town.

"I can hear something behind the wainscoting," Penny replied. "Maybe mice, or maybe it's baby possums caught in the wall between the bedroom and kitchen."

Mrs. Stahl looked at her. "Is it after you bake? It might be the dampers popping again."

"I'm not much of a cook. I haven't even turned on the oven yet."

"That's not true," Mrs. Stahl said, lifting her chin triumphantly. "You had it on the other night."

"What?" Then Penny remembered. It had rained sheets and she'd used it to dry her dress. But it had been very late and she didn't see how Mrs. Stahl could know. "Are you peeking in my windows?" she asked, voice tightening.

"I saw the light. The oven door was open. You shouldn't do that," Mrs. Stahl said, shaking her head. "It's very dangerous."

"You're not the first landlord I caught peeping. I guess I need to close my curtains," Penny said coolly. "But it's not the oven damper I'm hearing each and every night. I'm telling you, there's something inside my walls. Something in the kitchen."

Mrs. Stahl's mouth seemed to quiver slightly, which emboldened Penny.

"Do I need to get out the ball peen I found under the sink and tear a hole in the kitchen wall, Mrs. Stahl?"

"Don't you dare!" she said, clutching Penny's wrist, her costume rings digging in. "Don't you dare!"

Penny felt the panic on her, the woman's breath coming in sputters. She insisted they both sit on the fountain edge.

For a moment they both just breathed, the apricot-perfumed air thick in Penny's lungs.

"Mrs. Stahl, I'm sorry. It's just—I need to sleep."

Mrs. Stahl took a long breath, then her eyes narrowed again. "It's those chinwags next door, isn't it? They've been filling your ear with bile."

"What? Not about this, I—"

"I had the kitchen cleaned thoroughly after it happened. I had it cleaned, the linoleum stripped out. I put up fresh wallpaper over every square inch after it happened. I covered everything with wallpaper."

"Is that where it happened?" Penny asked. "That poor man who died in Number Four? Larry?"

But Mrs. Stahl couldn't speak, or wouldn't, breathing into her handkerchief, lilac silk, the small square over her mouth suctioning open and closed, open and closed.

"He was very beautiful," she finally whispered. "When they pulled him out of the oven, his face was the most exquisite red. Like a ripe, ripe cherry."

Knowing how it happened changed things. Penny had always imagined handsome, melancholy Larry walking around the apartment, turning gas jets on. Settling into that club chair in the living room. Or maybe settling in bed and slowly drifting from earth's fine tethers.

She wondered how she could ever use the oven now, or even look at it.

It had to be the same one. That Magic Chef, which looked like the one from childhood, white porcelain and cast iron. Not like those new slabs, buttercup or mint green.

The last tenant, Mr. Flant told her later, smelled gas all the time.

"She said it gave her headaches," he said. "Then one night she came here, her face white as snow. She said she'd just seen Saint Agatha in the kitchen, with her bloody breasts."

"I . . . I don't see anything like that," Penny said.

Back in the bungalow, trying to sleep, she began picturing herself the week before. How she'd left that oven door open, her fine, rain-slicked dress draped over the rack. The truth was, she'd forgotten about it, only returning for it hours later.

Walking to the closet now, she slid the dress from its hanger, pressing it to her face. But she couldn't smell anything.

Mr. D. still had not returned her calls. The bank had charged her for the bounced check, so she'd have to return the hat she'd bought, and rent was due again in two days.

When all the other crew members were making their way to the commissary for lunch, Penny slipped away and splurged on cab fare to the studio.

As she opened the door to his outer office, the receptionist was already on her feet and walking purposefully toward Penny.

"Miss," she said, nearly blocking Penny, "you're going to have to leave. Mac shouldn't have let you in downstairs."

"Why not? I've been here dozens of—"

"You're not on the appointment list, and that's our system now, miss."

"Does he have an appointment list now for that squeaking starlet sofa in there?" Penny asked, jerking her arm and pointing at the leather-padded door. A man with a thin mustache and a woman in a feathered hat looked up from their magazines.

The receptionist was already on the phone. "Mac, I need you . . . Yes, that one."

"If he thinks he can just toss me out like street trade," she said, marching over and thumping on Mr. D.'s door, "he'll be very, very sorry."

Her knuckles made no noise in the soft leather. Nor did her fist.

"Miss," someone said. It was the security guard striding toward her.

"I'm allowed to be here," she insisted, her voice tight and high. "I did my time. I earned the right."

But the guard had his hand on her arm.

Desperate, she looked down at the man and the woman waiting. Maybe she thought they would help. But why would they?

The woman pretended to be absorbed in her *Cinestar* magazine.

But the man smiled at her, hair oil gleaming. And winked.

The next morning she woke bleary but determined. She would forget about Mr. D. She didn't need his money. After all, she had a job, a good one.

It was hot on the lot that afternoon, and none of the makeup crew could keep the dust off the faces. There were so many lines and creases on every face—you never think about it until you're trying to make everything smooth.

"Penny," Gordon, the makeup supervisor, said. She had the feeling he'd been watching her for several moments as she pressed the powder into the actor's face, holding it still.

"It's so dusty," she said, "so it's taking a while."

He waited until she finished. Then, as the actor walked away, he leaned forward.

"Everything all right, Pen?"

He was looking at something—her neck, her chest.

"What do you mean?" she said, setting the powder down.

But he just kept looking at her.

"Working on your carburetor, beautiful?" one of the grips said as he walked by.

"What? I . . ."

Peggy turned to the makeup mirror. That was when she saw the long grease smear on her collarbone. And the line of black soot across her hairline too.

"I don't know," Penny said, her voice sounding slow and sleepy. "I don't have a car."

Then it came to her: the dream she'd had in the early morning hours. That she was in the kitchen, checking on the oven damper. The squeak of the door on its hinges, and Mrs. Stahl outside the window, her eyes glowing like a wolf's.

"It was a dream," she said now. Or was it? Had she been sleepwalking the night before?

Had she been in the kitchen . . . *at the oven* . . . in her sleep?

"Penny," Gordon said, looking at her squintily. "Penny, maybe you should go home."

It was so early, and Penny didn't want to go back to the Canyon Arms. She didn't want to go inside Number Four, or walk past the kitchen, its cherry wallpaper lately giving her the feeling of blood spatters.

Also, lately she kept thinking she saw Mrs. Stahl peering at her between the wooden blinds as she watered the banana trees.

Instead she took the bus downtown to the big library on South Fifth. She had an idea.

The librarian, a boy with a bow tie, helped her find the obituaries.

She found three about Larry, but none had photos, which was disappointing.

The one in the *Mirror* was the only one with any detail, any texture.

It mentioned that the body had been found by the "handsome proprietress, one Mrs. Herman Stahl," who "fell to wailing" so loud it was heard all through the canyons, up the promontories and likely high into the mossed eaves of the Hollywood sign.

"So what happened to Mrs. Stahl's husband?" Penny asked when she saw Mr. Flant and Benny that night.

"He died just a few months before Larry," Benny said. "Bad heart, they say."

Mr. Flant raised one pale eyebrow. "She never spoke of him. Only of Larry."

"He told me once she watched him, Larry did," Benny said. "She watched him through his bedroom blinds. While he made love."

Instantly Penny knew this was true.

She thought of herself in that same bed each night, the mattress so soft, its posts sometimes seeming to curl inward.

Mrs. Stahl had insisted Penny move it back against the wall. Penny refused, but the next day she came home to find the woman moving it herself, her short arms spanning the mattress, her face pressed into its appliqué.

Watching, Penny had felt like the peeping Tom. It was so intimate.

"Sometimes I wonder," Mr. Flant said now. "There were rumors. Black widow, or old maid."

"You can't make someone put his head in the oven," Benny said. "At least not for long. The gas'd get at you, too."

"True," Mr. Flant said.

"Maybe it didn't happen at the oven," Penny blurted. "She found the body. What if she just turned on the gas while he was sleeping?"

"And dragged him in there, for the cops?"

Mr. Flant and Benny looked at each other.

"She's very strong," Penny said.

Back in her bungalow, Penny sat just inside her bedroom window, waiting.

Peering through the blinds, long after midnight, she finally saw her. Mrs. Stahl, walking along the edges of the courtyard.

She was singing softly and her steps were uneven and Penny thought she might be tight, but it was hard to know.

Penny was developing a theory.

Picking up a book, she made herself stay awake until two. Then, slipping from bed, she tried to follow the flashes of light, the shadows.

Bending down, she put her hand on the baseboards, as if she could touch those funny shapes, like mice on their haunches. Or tiny men, marching.

"Something's there!" she said out loud, her voice surprising her. "It's in the walls."

In the morning it would all be blurry, but in that moment clues were coming together in her head, something to do with gas jets and Mrs. Stahl and love gone awry and poison in the walls, and she had figured it out before anything bad had happened.

It made so much sense in the moment, and when the sounds came too, the little *tap-taps* behind the plaster, she nearly cheered.

Mr. Flant poured her glass after glass of Amaro. Benny waxed his mustache and showed Penny his soft shoe.

They were trying to make her feel better about losing her job.

"I never came in late except two or three times. I always did my job," Penny said, biting her lip so hard it bled. "I think I know who's responsible. He kited me for seven hundred and forty dollars and now he's out to ruin me."

Then she told them how, a few days ago, she had written him a letter.

> Mr. D.—
>
> I don't write to cause you any trouble. What's mine is mine and I never knew you for an indian giver.
>
> I bought fine dresses to go to Hollywood Park with you, to be on your arm at Villa Capri. I had to buy three stockings a week, your clumsy hands pawing at them. I had to turn down jobs and do two cycles of penicillin because of you. Also because of you, I got the heave-ho from my roommate Pauline who said you fondled her by the dumbwaiter. So that money is the least a gentleman could offer a lady. The least, Mr. D.
>
> Let me ask you: those books you kept beneath the false bottom in your desk drawer on the lot—did you buy those from Mr. Stanley Rose, or his handsome assistant Larry?
>
> I wonder if your wife knows the kinds of books you keep in your office, the girls you keep there and make do shameful things?
>
> I know Larry would agree with me about you. He was a sensitive man and I live where he did and sleep in his bed and all of you ruined him, drove him to drink and to a perilous act.
>
> How dare you try to take my money away. And you with a wife with ermine, mink, lynx dripping from her plump, sunk shoulders.
>
> Your wife at 312 North Faring Road, Holmby Hills.
>
> Let's be adults, sophisticates. After all, we might not know what we might do if backed against the wall.
>
> —yr lucky penny

It had made more sense when she wrote it than it did now, reading it aloud to Mr. Flant and Benny.

Benny patted her shoulder. "So he called the cops on ya, huh?"

"The studio cops. Which is bad enough," Penny said.

They had escorted her from the makeup department. Everyone had watched, a few of the girls smiling.

"Sorry, Pen," Gordon had said, taking the powder brush from her hand. "What gives in this business is what takes away."

When he'd hired her two months ago, she'd watched as he wrote on her personnel file "Mr. D."

"Your man, he took this as a threat, you see," Mr. Flant said, shaking his head as he looked at the letter. "He is a hard man. Those men are. They are hard men and you are soft. Like Larry was soft."

Penny knew it was true. She'd never been hard enough, at least not in the right way. The smart way.

It was very late when she left the two men.

She paused before Number Four and found herself unable to move, cold fingertips pressed between her breasts, pushing her back.

That was when she spotted Mrs. Stahl inside the bungalow, fluttering past the picture window in her evening coat.

"Stop!" Penny called out. "I see you!"

And Mrs. Stahl froze. Then, slowly, she turned to face Penny, her face warped through the glass, as if she were under water.

"Dear," a voice came from behind Penny. A voice just like Mrs. Stahl's. *Could she throw her voice?*

Swiveling around, she saw the landlady standing in the courtyard, a few feet away.

It was as if she were a witch, a shapeshifter from one of the fairy tales she'd read as a child.

"Dear," she said again.

"I thought you were inside," Penny said, trying to catch her breath. "But it was just your reflection."

Mrs. Stahl did not say anything for a moment, her hands cupped in front of herself.

Penny saw she was holding a scarlet-covered book in her palms.

"I often sit out here at night," she said, voice loose and tipsy, "reading under the stars. Larry used to do that, you know."

She invited Penny into her bungalow, the smallest one, in back.

"I'd like us to talk," she said.

Penny did not pause. She wanted to see it. Wanted to understand.

Walking inside, she realized at last what the strongest smell in the courtyard was. All around were pots of night-blooming jasmine, climbing and vining up the built-in bookshelves, around the window frame, even trained over the arched doorway into the dining room.

They drank jasmine tea, iced. The room was close and Penny had never seen so many books. None of them looked like they'd ever been opened, their spines cool and immaculate.

"I have more," Mrs. Stahl said, waving toward the mint-walled hallway, some space beyond, the air itself so thick with the breath of the jasmine, Penny couldn't see it. "I love books. Larry taught me how. He knew what ones I'd like."

Penny nodded. "At night I read the books in the bungalow. I never read so much."

"I wanted to keep them there. It only seemed right. And I didn't believe what the other tenants said, about the paper smelling like gas."

At that, Penny had a grim thought. What if everything smelled like gas and she didn't know it? The strong scent of apricot, of eucalyptus, a perpetual perfume suffusing everything—how would one know?

"Dear, do you enjoy living in Larry's bungalow?"

Penny didn't know what to say, so she only nodded, taking a long sip of the tea. Was it rum? Some kind of liqueur? It was very sweet and tingled on her tongue.

"He was my favorite tenant. Even after . . ."—she paused, her head shaking—"what he did."

"And you found him," Penny said. "That must have been awful."

She held up the red-covered book she'd been reading in the courtyard.

"This was found on . . . on his person. He must've been planning on giving it to me. He gave me so many things. See how it's red, like a heart?"

"What kind of book is it?" Penny asked, leaning closer.

Mrs. Stahl looked at her but didn't seem to be listening, clasping the book with one hand while with the other she stroked her neck, long and unlined.

"Every book he gave me showed how much he understood me. He gave me many things and never asked for anything. That was when my mother was dying from Bright's, her face puffed up like a carnival balloon. Nasty woman."

"Mrs. Stahl," Penny started, her fingers tingling unbearably, the smell so strong, Mrs. Stahl's plants, her strong perfume—sandalwood?

"He just liked everyone. You'd think it was just you. The care he took. Once he brought me a brass rouge pot from Paramount studios. He told me it belonged to Paulette Goddard. I still have it."

"Mrs. Stahl," Penny tried again, bolder now, "were you in love with him?"

The woman looked at her, and Penny felt her focus loosen, like in those old detective movies, right before the screen went black.

"He really only wanted the stars," Mrs. Stahl said, running her fingers across her décolletage, the satin of her dressing robe, a dragon painted up the front. "He said their skin felt different. They smelled different. He was strange about smells. Sounds. Light. He was very sensitive."

"But you loved him, didn't you?" Penny's voice more insistent now.

Her eyes narrowed. "Everyone loved him. Everyone. He said yes to everybody. He gave himself to everybody."

"But why did he do it, Mrs. Stahl?"

"He put his head in the oven and died," she said, straightening her back ever so slightly. "He was mad in a way only southerners and artistic souls are mad. And he was both. You're too young, too simple, to understand."

"Mrs. Stahl, did you do something to Larry?" This is what Penny was trying to say, but the words weren't coming. And Mrs. Stahl kept growing larger and larger, the dragon on her robe, it seemed, somehow, to be speaking to Penny, whispering things to her.

"What's in this tea?"

"What do you mean, dear?"

But the woman's face had gone strange, stretched out. There was a scurrying sound from somewhere, like little paws, animal claws, the sharp feet of sharp-footed men. A gold watch chain swinging and that neighbor hanging from the pear tree.

She woke to the purple creep of dawn. Slumped in the same rattan chair in Mrs. Stahl's living room. Her finger still crooked in the teacup handle, her arm hanging to one side.

"Mrs. Stahl," she whispered.

But the woman was no longer on the sofa across from her.

Somehow Penny was on her feet, inching across the room.

The bedroom door was ajar, Mrs. Stahl sprawled on the mattress, the painted dragon on her robe sprawled on top of her.

On the bed beside her was the book she'd been reading in the courtyard. Scarlet red, with a lurid title.

Gaudy Night, it was called.

Opening it with great care, Penny saw the inscription:

To Mrs. Stahl, my dirty murderess.
Love, Lawrence.

She took the book, and the teacup.

She slept for a few hours in her living room, curled on the zebra-print sofa.

She had stopped going into the kitchen two days ago, tacking an old bath towel over the doorway so she couldn't even see inside. The gleaming porcelain of the oven.

She was sure she smelled gas radiating from it. Spotted blue light flickering behind the towel.

But still she didn't go inside.

And now she was afraid the smell was coming through the walls.

It was all connected, you see, and Mrs. Stahl was behind all of it. The light spots, the shadows on the baseboard, the noises in the walls, and now the hiss of the gas.

Mr. Flant looked at the inscription, shaking his head.

"My god, is it possible? He wasn't making much sense those final days. Holed up in Number Four. Maybe he was hiding from her. Because he knew."

"It was found on his body," Penny said, voice trembling. "That's what she told me."

"Then this inscription," he said, reaching out for Penny's wrist, "was meant to be our clue. Like pointing a finger from beyond the grave."

Penny nodded. She knew what she had to do.

"I know how it sounds. But someone needs to do something."

The police detective nodded, drinking from his Coca-Cola, his white shirt bright. He had gray hair at the temples and he said his name was Noble, which seemed impossible.

"Well, miss, let's see what we can do. That was a long time ago. After you called, I had to get the case file from the crypt. I can't say I even remember it." Licking his index finger, he flicked open the file folder, then began turning pages. "A gas job, right? We got a lot of them back then. Those months before the war."

"Yes. In the kitchen. My kitchen now."

Looking through the slim folder, he pursed his lips a moment, then came a grim smile. "Ah, I remember. I remember. The little men."

"The little men?" Penny felt her spine tighten.

"One of our patrolmen had been out there the week before on a noise complaint. Your bookseller was screaming in the courtyard. Claimed there were little men coming out of the walls to kill him."

Penny didn't say anything at all. Something deep inside herself seemed to be screaming and it took all her effort just to sit there and listen.

"DTs. Said he'd been trying to kick the sauce," he said, reading the report. "He was a drunk, miss. Sounds like it was a whole courtyard full of 'em."

"No," Penny said, head shaking back and forth. "That's not it. Larry wasn't like that."

"Well," he said, "I'll tell you what Larry was like. In his bedside table we found a half-dozen catcher's mitts." He stopped himself, looked at her. "Pardon. Female contraceptive devices. Each one with the name of a different woman. A few big stars. At least they were big then. I can't remember now."

Penny was still thinking about the wall. The little men. And her mice on their hind feet. Pixies, dancing fairies.

"There you go," the detective said, closing the folder. "Guy's a dipso, one of his high-class affairs turned sour. Suicide. Pretty clear-cut."

"No," Penny said.

"No?" Eyebrows raised. "He was in that oven waist deep, miss. He even had a hunting knife in his hand for good measure."

"A knife?" Penny said, her fingers pressing her forehead. "Of course. Don't you see? He was trying to protect himself. I told you on the phone, detective. It's imperative that you look into Mrs. Stahl."

"The landlady. Your landlady?"

"She was in love with him. And he rejected her, you see."

"A woman scorned, eh?" he said, leaning back. "Once saw a jilted lady over on Cheremoya take a clothes iron to her fellow's face while he slept."

"Look at this," Penny said, pulling Mrs. Stahl's little red book from her purse.

"*Gaudy Night,*" he said, pronouncing the first word in a funny way.

"I think it's a dirty book."

He looked at her, squinting. "My wife owns this book."

Penny didn't say anything.

"Have you even read it?" he asked wearily.

Opening the front to the inscription, she held it in front of him.

"'Dirty murderess.'" He shrugged. "So you're saying this fella knew she was going to kill him, and instead of going to, say, the police, he writes this little inscription, then lets himself get killed?"

Everything sounded so different when he said it aloud, different from the way everything joined in perfect and horrible symmetry in her head.

"I don't know how it happened. Maybe he was going to go to the police and she beat him to it. And I don't know how she did it," Penny said. "But she's dangerous, don't you get it?"

It was clear he did not.

"I'm telling you, I see her out there at night, doing things," Penny said, her breath coming faster and faster. "She's doing something with the natural gas. If you check the gas jets maybe you can figure it out."

She was aware that she was talking very loudly, and her chest felt damp. Lowering her voice, she leaned toward him.

"I think there might be a clue in my oven," she said.

"Do you?" he said, rubbing his chin. "Any little men in there?"

"It's not like that. It's not. I see them, yes." She couldn't look him in the eye or she would lose her nerve. "But I know they're not really little men. It's something she's doing. It always starts at two. Two a.m. She's doing something. She did it to Larry and she's doing it to me."

He was rubbing his face with his hand, and she knew she had lost him.

"I told you on the phone," she said, more desperately now. "I think she drugged me. I brought the cup."

Penny reached into her purse again, this time removing the teacup, its bottom still brown-ringed.

Detective Noble lifted it, took a sniff, set it down.

"Drugged you with Old Grandad, eh?"

"I know there's booze in it. But detective, there's more than booze going on here." Again her voice rose high and sharp, and other detectives seemed to be watching now from their desks.

But Noble seemed unfazed. There even seemed to be the flicker of a smile on his clean-shaven face.

"So why does she want to harm you?" he asked. "Is she in love with you too?"

Penny looked at him and counted quietly in her head, the dampness on her chest gathering.

She had been dealing with men like this her whole life. Smug men. Men with fine clothes or shabby ones, all with the same slick ideas, the same impatience, big voice, slap-and-tickle, fast with a backhanded slug. Nice turned to nasty on a dime.

"Detective," she said, taking it slowly, "Mrs. Stahl must suspect that I know. About what she did to Larry. I don't know if she drugged him and staged it. The hunting knife shows there was a struggle. What I do know is there's more than what's in your little file."

He nodded, leaning back in his chair once more. With his right arm he reached for another folder in the metal tray on his desk.

"Miss, can we talk for a minute about *your* file?"

"My file?"

"When you called, I checked your name. S.O.P. Do you want to tell me about the letters you've been sending to a certain address in Holmby Hills?"

"What? I . . . There was only one."

"And two years ago, the fellow over at MCA? Said you slashed his tires?"

"I was never charged."

Penny would never speak about that, or what that man had tried to do to her in a back booth at Chasen's.

He set the file down. "Miss, what exactly are you here for? You got a gripe with Mrs. Stahl? Hey, I don't like my landlord either. What, don't wanna pay the rent?"

A wave of exhaustion shuddered through Penny. For a moment she did not know if she could stand.

But there was Larry to think about. And how much she belonged in Number Four. Because she did, and it had marked the beginning of things. A new day for Penny.

"No," Penny said, rising. "That's not it. You'll see. You'll see. I'll show you."

"Miss," he said, calling after her. "Please don't show me anything. Just behave yourself, okay? Like a good girl."

Back at Number Four, Penny lay down on the rattan sofa, trying to breathe, to think.

Pulling Mrs. Stahl's book from her dress pocket, she began reading.

But it wasn't like she thought.

It wasn't dirty, not like the brown-papered ones. It was a detective novel, and it took place in England. A woman recently exonerated for poisoning her lover attends her school reunion. While there, she finds an anonymous poison-pen note tucked in the sleeve of her gown: "You Dirty Murderess . . . !"

Penny gasped. But then wondered: Had that inscription just been a wink, Larry to Mrs. Stahl?

He gave her books she liked, Benny had said. *Stiff British stuff that he could tease her about.*

Was that all this was, all the inscription had meant?

No, she assured herself, sliding the book back into her pocket. It's a red herring. To confuse me, to keep me from finding the truth. Larry needs me to find out the truth.

It was shortly after that she heard the click of her mail slot. Looking over, she saw a piece of paper slip through the slit and land on the entryway floor.

Walking over, she picked it up.

Bungalow Four:
You are past due.
—Mrs. H. Stahl

"I have to move anyway," she told Benny, showing him the note.

"No, kid, why?" he whispered. Mr. Flant was sleeping in the bedroom, the gentle whistle of his snore.

"I can't prove she's doing it," Penny said. "But it smells like a gas chamber in there."

"Listen, don't let her spook you," Benny said. "I bet the pilot light is out. Want me to take a look? I can come by later."

"Can you come now?"

Looking into the darkened bedroom, Benny smiled, patted her forearm. "I don't mind."

Stripped to his undershirt, Benny ducked under the bath towel Penny had hung over the kitchen door.

"I thought you were inviting me over to keep your bed warm," he said as he kneeled down on the linoleum.

The familiar noise started, the *tick-tick-tick.*

"Do you hear it?" Penny said, voice tight. Except the sound was different in the kitchen than in the bedroom. It was closer. Not inside the walls but everywhere.

"It's the igniter," Benny said. "Trying to light the gas."

Peering behind the towel, Penny watched him.

"But you smell it, right?" she said.

"Of course I smell it," he said, his voice strangely high. "God, it's awful."

He put his face to the baseboards, the sink, the shuddering refrigerator.

"What's this?" he said, tugging the oven forward, his arms straining.

He was touching the wall behind the oven, but Penny couldn't see.

"What's what?" she asked. "Did you find something?"

"I don't know," he said, his head turned from her. "I . . . Christ, you can't think with it. I feel like I'm back in Argonne."

He had to lean backward, palms resting on the floor.

"What is it you saw back there?" Penny asked, pointing behind the oven.

But he kept shaking his head, breathing into the front of his undershirt, pulled up.

After a minute, both of them breathing hard, he reached up and turned the knob on the front of the oven door.

"I smell it," Penny said, stepping back. "Don't you?"

"That pilot light," he said, covering his face, breathing raspily. "It's gotta be out."

His knees sliding on the linoleum, he inched back toward the oven, white and glowing.

"Are you . . . are you going to open it?"

He looked at her, his face pale and his mouth stretched like a piece of rubber.

"I'm going to," he said. "We need to light it."

But he didn't stir. There was a feeling of something, that door open like a black maw, and neither of them could move.

Penny turned, hearing a knock at the door.

When she turned back around, she gasped.

Benny's head and shoulders were inside the oven, his voice making the most terrible sound, like a cat, its neck caught in a trap.

"Get out," Penny said, no matter how silly it sounded. "Get out!"

Pitching forward, she leaned down and grabbed for him, tugging at his trousers, yanking him back.

Stumbling, they both rose to their feet, Penny nearly huddling against the kitchen wall, its cherry-sprigged paper.

Turning, he took her arms hard, pressing himself against her, pressing Penny against the wall.

She could smell him, and his skin was clammy and goose-quilled.

His mouth pressed against her neck roughly and she could feel his teeth, his hands on her hips. Something had changed, and she'd missed it.

"But this is what you want, isn't it, honey?" the whisper came, his mouth over her ear. "It's all you've ever wanted."

"No, no, no," she said, and found herself crying. "And you don't like girls. You don't like girls."

"I like everybody," he said, his palm on her chest, hand heel hard.

And she lifted her head and looked at him, and he was Larry.

She knew he was Larry.

Larry.

Until he became Benny again, mustache and grin, but fear in that grin still.

"I'm sorry, Penny," he said, stepping back. "I'm flattered, but I don't go that way."

"What?" she said, looking down, seeing her fingers clamped on his trouser waist. "Oh. Oh."

*

Back at Number Three, they both drank from tall tumblers, breathing hungrily.

"You shouldn't go back in there," Benny said. "We need to call the gas company in the morning."

Mr. Flant said she could stay on their sofa that night, if they could make room under all the old newspapers.

"You shouldn't have looked in there," he said to Benny, shaking his head. "The oven. It's like whistling in a cemetery."

A towel wrapped around his shoulders, Benny was shivering. He was so white.

"I didn't see anything," he kept saying. "I didn't see a goddamned thing."

She was dreaming.

"You took my book!"

In the dream she'd risen from Mr. Flant's sofa, slick with sweat, and opened the door. Although nearly midnight, the courtyard was mysteriously bright, all the plants gaudy and pungent.

Wait. Had someone said something?

"Larry gave it to me!"

Penny's body was moving so slowly, like she was caught in molasses.

The door to Number Four was open, and Mrs. Stahl was emerging from it, something red in her hand.

"You took it while I slept, didn't you? Sneak thief! Thieving whore!"

When Mrs. Stahl began charging at her, her robe billowing like great scarlet wings, Penny thought she was still dreaming.

"Stop," Penny said, but the woman was so close.

It had to be a dream, and in dreams you can do anything, so Penny raised her arms high, clamping down on those scarlet wings as they came toward her.

The book slid from her pocket, and both of them grappled for it, but Penny was faster, grabbing it and pushing back, pressing the volume against the old woman's neck until she stumbled, heels tangling.

It had to be a dream because Mrs. Stahl was so weak, weaker than any murderess could possibly be, her body like that of a yarn doll, limp and flailing.

There was a flurry of elbows, clawing hands, the fat golden beetle ring on Mrs. Stahl's gnarled hand against Penny's face.

Then, with one hard jerk, the old woman fell to the ground with such ease, her head clacking against the courtyard tiles.

The rat-a-tat-tat of blood from her mouth, her ear.

"Penny!" A voice came from behind her. It was Mr. Flant, standing in his doorway, hand to his mouth.

"Penny, what did you *do*?"

Her expression when she'd faced Mr. Flant must have been meaningful, because he had immediately retreated inside his bungalow, the door locking with a click.

But it was time anyway. Of that she felt sure.

Walking into Number Four, she almost felt herself smiling.

One by one, she removed all the tacks from her makeshift kitchen door, letting the towel drop onto her forearm.

The kitchen was dark, and smelled as it never had. No apricots, no jasmine, and no gas. Instead, the tinny smell of must, wallpaper paste, rusty water.

Moving slowly, purposefully, she walked directly to the oven, the moonlight striking it. White and monstrous, a glowing smear.

Its door shut.

Cold to the touch.

Kneeling down, she crawled behind it, to the spot Benny had been struck by.

What's this? he'd said.

As in a dream, which this had to be, she knew what to do, her palm sliding along the cherry-sprig wallpaper down by the baseboard.

She saw the spot, the wallpaper gaping at its seam, seeming to breathe. Inhale, exhale.

Penny's hand went there, pulling back, the paper glue dried to fine dust under her hand.

She was remembering Mrs. Stahl. *I put up fresh wallpaper over every square inch after it happened. I covered everything with wallpaper.*

What did she think she would see, breathing hard, her knees creaking and her forehead pushed against the wall?

The paper did not come off cleanly, came off in pieces, strands, like her hair after the dose Mr. D. passed to her, making her sick for weeks.

A patch of wall exposed, she saw the series of gashes, one after the next, as if someone had jabbed a knife into the plaster. A hunting knife. Though there seemed a pattern, a hieroglyphics.

Squinting, the kitchen so dark she couldn't see.

Reaching up to the oven, she grabbed for a kitchen match.

Leaning close, the match lit, she could see a faint scrawl etched deep.

> The little men come out of the walls. I cut off
> their heads every night. My mind is gone.
> Tonight, I end my life.
> I hope you find this.
> Goodbye.

Penny leaned forward, pressed her palm on the words.

This is what mattered most, nothing else.

"Oh, Larry," she said, her voice catching with grateful tears. "I see them too."

The sound that followed was the loudest she'd ever heard, the fire sweeping up her face.

The detective stood in the center of the courtyard, next to a banana tree with its top shorn off, a smoldering slab of wood, the front door to the blackened bungalow on the ground in front of him.

The firemen were dragging their equipment past him. The gurney with the dead girl long gone.

"Pilot light. Damn near took the roof off," one of the patrolmen said. "The kitchen looks like the Blitz. But only one scorched, inside. The girl. Or what's left of her. Could've been much worse."

"That's always true," the detective said, a billow of smoke making them both cover their faces.

Another officer approached him.

"Detective Noble, we talked to the pair next door," he said. "They said they warned the girl not to go back inside. But she'd been drinking all day, saying crazy things."

"How's the landlady?"

"Hospital."

Noble nodded. "We're done."

It was close to two. But he didn't want to go home yet. It was a long drive to Eagle Rock anyway.

And the smell, and what he'd seen in that kitchen—he didn't want to go home yet.

At the top of the road he saw the bar, its bright lights beckoning.

The Carnival Tavern, the one with the roof shaped like a big top.

Life is a carnival, he said to himself, which is what the detective might say, wryly, in the books his wife loved to read.

He couldn't believe it was still there. He remembered it from before the war. When he used to date that usherette at the Hollywood Bowl.

A quick jerk to the wheel and he was pulling into its small lot, those crazy clown lanterns he remembered from all those years ago.

Inside, everything was warm and inviting, even if the waitress had a sour look.

"Last call," she said, leaving him his rye. "We close in ten minutes."

"I just need to make a quick call," he said.

He stepped into one of the telephone booths in the back, pulling the accordion door shut behind him.

"Yes, I have that one," his wife replied, stifling a yawn. "But it's not a dirty book."

Then she laughed a little in a way that made him bristle.

"So what kind of book is it?" he asked.

"Books mean different things to different people," she said. She was always saying stuff like that, just to show him how smart she was.

"You know what I mean," he said.

She was silent for several seconds. He thought he could hear someone crying, maybe one of the kids.

"It's a mystery," she said finally. "Not your kind. No one even dies."

"Okay," he said. He wasn't sure what he'd wanted to hear. "I'll be home soon."

"It's a love story too," she said, almost a whisper, strangely sad. "Not your kind."

After he hung up, he ordered a beer, the night's last tug from the bartender's tap.

Sitting by the picture window, he looked down into the canyon, and up to the Hollywood sign. Everything about the moment felt familiar. He'd worked this precinct for twenty years, minus three to Uncle Sam, so even the surprises were the same.

He thought about the girl, about her at the station. Her nervous legs, that worn dress of hers, the plea in her voice.

Someone should think of her for a minute, shouldn't they?

He looked at his watch. Two a.m. But she won't see her little men tonight.

A busboy with a pencil mustache came over with a long stick. One by one, he turned off all the dingy lanterns that hung in the window. The painted clowns faced the canyon now. Closing time.

"Don't miss me too much," he told the sour waitress as he left.

In the parking lot, looking down into the canyon, he noticed he could see the Canyon Arms, the smoke still settling on the bungalow's shell, black as a mussel. Her bedroom window, glass blown out, curtains shuddering in the night breeze.

He was just about to get in his car when he saw them. The little men.

They were dancing across the hood of his car, the canyon beneath him.

Turning, he looked up at the bar, the lanterns in the window, spinning, sending their dancing clowns across the canyon, across the Canyon Arms, everywhere.

He took a breath.

"That happens every night?" he asked the busboy as the young man hustled down the stairs into the parking lot.

Pausing, the busboy followed his gaze, then nodded. "Every night," he said. "Like a dream."

STEVE ALMOND

Okay, Now Do You Surrender?

FROM *Cincinnati Review*

LOOMIS WAS HEADED out of work, or out of his *workplace,* which is what you were supposed to call it now, so that later when the TV vans showed up and disgorged their heartbroken androids they would be able to utter sentences such as "The suspect was a familiar and friendly presence in his workplace . . ." Anyhoo, he was done for the day—done whoring himself to the hipster lords of Marketing, done creating *content*—and just a few steps from his car when two men appeared in his path. They wore vintage suits. The larger of the two had a furrowed scar that curled across one cheek. "You gotta minute here?" he said.

"What?" said Loomis.

"We were hoping for a few words." The men were suddenly very close to him, smelling of matches and Brut.

Loomis had taken off early to beat traffic and was parked in the back of the building. Bobito the Security Guard was doubtless sprawled out in the smoker alcove, flirting with HR specialists who were going to fuck him only if their lives took a harrowing turn.

"A few words about what?" Loomis said.

The pair scanned the parking lot.

"Are you guys FBI or something?"

The one with the scar winced. "Afraid not."

"It's about the thank-you notes," said the smaller one. He had the velvety rasp of Tony Bennett and a Roman nose that had been derailed a few times.

"What thank-you notes?"

"For the kid's party," Scarface said.

"The kid?"

"*Your* kid. The older one. Isabelle."

"Isadora?"

"Right."

"How the hell do you know the name of my daughter?"

Scarface set a hand on Loomis's shoulder. It was a tender gesture that suggested profound brutality. "Settle down," he said. "There's no reason for this to turn in the wrong direction."

Tony Bennett patted his coat in the way of an ex-smoker. "Quicker we clear this thing up, quicker we're out of your hair."

"What thing?" Loomis couldn't figure out how frightened he should be. He had to pee rather ardently.

"A beautiful day like this," Scarface said. He gestured toward the sky as if the director of a community theater production had just stage-whispered at him to gesture toward the sky. "Who wants to be standing around in a parking lot? Not me."

"To review," Tony Bennett said. "You throw this party, what, two weeks ago? All these kids bringing your daughter gifts and whatnot. So then, just as a common—"

"How do you know what's going on in my house?" Loomis said. "Have you been spying on us?"

Scarface exhaled through his nose, as if he'd been expecting Loomis to behave this way and it bored him. "Nobody's spying on anybody. You're missing the point, Mr. Loomis. Just *listen.*"

"As a courtesy," Tony Bennett continued, "your wife went out and bought some nice thank-you cards. And you, Mr. Loomis, told her there was no need to waste good money on such an extravagance. Then you threw the cards straight into the *garbagio.*"

"I didn't throw them in the garbage," Loomis said. "I dropped them into a wastepaper basket. I was making a point."

Scarface ran a thumb down his nose. "What exact point would that be, Mr. Loomis?"

"That it was overkill. We'd already thrown these kids a whole party with lunch and two art activities and gift bags, and I was just sick and tired of feeding into this never-ending arms race of bourgeois pieties."

Tony Bennett yawned. "I don't understand what you just said,

Mr. Loomis. But I didn't like the tone." He stretched in such a way as to make visible the outline of something gun-buttish against his sport coat.

Loomis felt the flutter in his gut go spastic. The air took on a sour radiance. Scarface's hand was on his shoulder again, again very gently. "Calm down, Mr. Loomis."

"I feel like you're threatening me."

"Nobody's threatening anybody."

"We're having a conversation."

"Who *are* you? What do you want from me?"

"You don't ask the questions," Tony Bennett said quietly. "That's not how this relationship works." He slipped his hand inside his jacket and let it stay there. "How it works is you go get in your car there and drive home and kiss your wife and send those thank-you notes."

"And you do one more thing," Scarface said. "You play it smart and keep your mouth shut."

Loomis drove straight to Taco Bell and ordered three chalupas and a Diet Pepsi and ate them in his car, like an American, then fished a Camel Light from the pack hidden in the wheel well. Later he would vomit or have the runs, perhaps both, perhaps simultaneously.

The police officer he spoke to on the phone was a female who sounded black, which was fine.

"When you say *accosted,* can you be more specific?"

"They approached me in a threatening manner. They spoke about my wife and daughter, about intimate details of our life."

"Intimate details being what?"

"Just, you know, domestic issues between my wife and I."

"Are you in the midst of a dispute with your wife?"

"No," Loomis said. "That's not the point. Wait a second. Are you accusing me—"

"Nobody's accusing you, sir."

"I'm practically gunned down in broad daylight by a couple of mooks who've been surveilling my family, and your response is to suggest that I beat my wife?"

The officer took some time to absorb this. "What do you mean by *mook?*" she said finally.

Loomis closed his eyes and whispered, just in his mind, *Nigger, kike, spic.*

"Did either of these gentlemen make an explicit threat?"

"They didn't say, *We're going to kill you.* We were in a parking lot. One of them had a *gun!*"

"Did he aim the gun at you, sir?"

"He stretched in a way that made it obvious he had a gun."

"So you didn't actually see the gun?"

"I saw the clear outline of a gun."

"Did they demand money or property?"

"No."

"What did they want, exactly?"

Loomis flashed to the thank-you cards, which were in the shape of little ice cream cones, no doubt hand-cut by an order of incorporated monks. Fourteen bucks for a pack of twelve—the sort of quaint corruption upon which American capitalism now relied.

"I can't help you if you don't tell me everything, you know," the cop said in her patient, insinuating tone. "Let me ask you this: Have there been problems in your marriage recently?"

"For fuck's sake," Loomis said. "I'm the *victim.*"

Kate had made her virtuous stir-fry. She was feeling fat, though she weighed only five pounds more than the day they married, whereas Loomis, upon reaching forty, had bloated up like a tick. He stared down the soggy broccoli florets and tempeh chunks and felt a surge of empathy for his children, Izzy, age ten, and four-year-old Trevor, who had once referred to this meal, in a phrase appropriated from Izzy, who had appropriated it from Loomis, as "Mommy's shit-fry."

Everything was fine. He was home, his drafty little home on the outskirts of Boston. Kate ate like she always ate, mauling her food, punishing it for her hunger. She asked everyone to say their Favorite Part of the Day. It was part of her Gratitude Agenda. Izzy said reading Harry Potter. Trevor said building a cave for his Uhmoomah. Kate said snuggling with her Uhmoomahs before school. Loomis said being here with all of you right now. He looked round the table and felt the truth of it punch his throat.

"Awwww," Kate said.

"Dad's being sweet," Izzy said suspiciously.

Trevor farted. "Broccoli fart," he observed.

They'd been married a decade: met in grad school for library science, danced to the wretched bands then being danced to, broke up, found new people, backslid. Then Kate announced her move to Boston, do or die, and Loomis did, in a small Vermont ceremony officiated by Kate's best friend, The Lesbian Anita. It was a modern arrangement.

When Trevor came along, Kate quit her position at Widener Library to become a full-time mom, and Loomis was suddenly the sole breadwinner. He bid farewell to his post at the branch library reference desk and made for the ergometric wards of biotech, where remarkable things were being done to override our loser genetic material.

After dinner Kate read a story to Trevor while Loomis forked at the crud in the toaster oven and tried to figure his approach.

In the bedroom, Kate was rubbing coconut butter into her ankles. "What's with you?" she said. "You seem tense."

"What's with me," Loomis said, "is that your goons came and talked to me."

Kate's expression landed somewhere between bewilderment and mirth. "My what?"

Loomis saw his error at once. Kate didn't hire goons to resolve marital issues. She communicated. She lit candles and acknowledged the underlying conflict, and sometimes later they screwed in some mildly raunchy yoga way, though not so much recently because Loomis was fat and often failed to be present in the moment.

"Did you say goons?"

"Did I say what?"

"Goons."

"I said," Loomis said slowly, experimentally, "that I'm sick of the balloons. I feel like they're stalking me. We had this thing at work—"

"Balloons?"

"Just listen, honey. We had this thing at work, one of these team-building exercises, and they ordered everyone to blow up huge balloons with, like, foot pumps, and the balloons had all these, like, Buddhist affirmations on them, like *Tranquility is the ultimate dividend.* And after a while with these balloons, it was like they were stalking me."

Kate stared at him for several seconds. "That's not what you said, Todd."

"Yeah, it is," Loomis said. He despised his imagination; it was a retarded psychopath. "I'm sorry, sweetie. It is what I said. About the balloons. It was a strange experience. I don't know if I can explain it, really."

Kate inspected her buttered ankles. The room smelled like a Caribbean island they would never visit for ethical reasons. "Why are you smoking again?"

"I'm not smoking. I had one cigarette. It was a long day."

"What with the balloons and all?"

Kate was being an asshole, but only because he had been an asshole first. This was their dynamic.

"Hey. Remember those thank-you cards? For Izzy's party?"

Kate closed her eyes in forbearance. "We settled that. She'll make homemade cards next time and put them in school cubbies."

"Right. No. Of course. That's a great plan. I meant the ones for the party we just had."

"Do we have to go over this right now?"

"No. We don't *have* to."

"Good."

Izzy appeared in the doorway. "Why are you guys fighting?"

"We're not fighting," Loomis said.

"Yes, you are. I heard you."

"Nobody's fighting, sweetie. I promise you."

"You better not be," she said.

Kate rose from the bed and hug-steered their daughter back toward her room. She was a tough kid, beating boys in soccer and letting them know about it. But she was in a fragile phase. Kate said it was because her best friend, Maya, had moved away after her parents split. Loomis was putting his money on early puberty and bracing himself.

Later, in the dark, Loomis said, "I just wondered if those cards ever got sent out. Because I'd be cool with that. I'd even send them out myself. I feel like I might have overreacted before."

"Are you trying to apologize for throwing the cards in the garbage?"

"More or less."

"Which is it?"

"I'm apologizing."

He reached out and touched his wife's hip.

She hummed noncommittally. "I already sent them out."

After lunch Loomis did a cigarette consult with Bobito the Security Guard.

"Hold up, chief," Bobito said. "Someone stepping up on you with heat? In *my* parking lot? That shit is gangfucked."

"Pretty gangfucked," Loomis agreed.

"That shit is raped, man. What was they hassling you about?"

"Some fight I had with my wife."

Bobito rapped his skull (shaved, bluish) with his knuckles; this was how he applauded. "Oh, shit. You got a pig on the side, chief? That what this is about? I ain't making value judgments, man. Shit. I fucked half the bitches in this building on my fianceé's *fu*ton."

"There were two of them," Loomis explained. "Sort of *Godfather* types. Like the movie."

"'Take the cannoli,'" Bobito said. "That shit is classic."

"One had a huge scar on his cheek."

"Naw. That's a fake. Ain't nobody profiling you with some scar."

"It looked real."

"That's how you *know* it's fake." Bobito scratched his neck tattoo with a scythelike pinkie nail. "I'll make sure they're not creeping round here. That's the easy part, chief. What I'd be asking is who hired them."

"Yeah?"

"Mos def. Villains gotta make rent in a recession too, bro. Now along comes the Internet, Angie's List, all that direct-sales shit. It's got so easy to bring heat a fucking bonobo could do it." Bobito held his cigarette like a dart and poked out little rings of wisdom. "You gotta think about your enemies, chief. 'Cause they're sure as shit thinking about you."

Bobito now began narrating his own criminal record and the various OG motherfuckers with whom he had compiled this record.

"You've been in prison?" Loomis said.

"Oh, hell yeah," Bobito said. "I'm a ex-con. Did a dog's year in Pondville. That's like seven on the outside, chief."

"What'd they get you for?"

"Felony two. Check fraud. Tried to buy some body spray for my boo at Bed, Bath & Beyond, where, by the way, I fucking *worked.* The whole thing was a reverse sting. These corporate lawyers do not fuck around. They flat-out gangster." Bobito finished his cigarette and flicked the butt into the koi pond. "I been thinking about your situation," he said. "I'm prepared to help you out in the form of personal security services." He produced a crisp business card with the image of a rooster in boxing trunks. "Check out the website."

"Thank you," Loomis said. "I'll do that."

"Cheap and deep, chief. That's how I do what got to get done."

Loomis spent the afternoon compiling suspects. He came up with two: his father-in-law, Kent, and The Lesbian Anita.

Kent was a soft-spoken Kansan who sang in a barbershop quartet and had the mustache to prove it. He had grown up on a farm but worked at a car dealership now, sweet-talking gullible sophomores into sleek Korean shitboxes. Kate was his only daughter; she looked almost exactly like his late wife, Mindy. He'd called her "Mindy" the previous Christmas, then wept without embarrassment, a practice endorsed by his men's group. Kent despised Loomis in that affable midwestern manner that often passed for affection on the coasts.

"Well hello there, stranger," he said when Loomis greeted him. "To what do I owe the pleasure of this call?"

"No reason. Kate mentioned you had a little surgery."

"Oh, jiminy. I wouldn't call a colonoscopy surgery. They just run a thingamabob up your bottom and broadcast your guts on a little TV."

"Still."

"There's only three things that can kill a farmer," Kent said. "Lightning. Rolling a tractor. And old age."

Loomis wanted to say, *What about cancer?* This was how his mind worked. It had made him popular in college. "Hey, by the way, thanks for sending Izzy that birthday check. It was very generous."

"Nonsense."

"Between you and my mom she's gonna bank her first million by twelve."

"It's a good thing to save with the economy the way it is."

Loomis cleared his throat. "I hope you got the thank-you card Izzy sent along."

"I did. Lovely. I'm going to put it on the wall here." Kent gestured at his wall over there in Kansas.

"Good," Loomis said. "Because I wouldn't want you to be angry *on account of a thank-you card.*"

After a pause, Kent said, "Why are you talking like that?"

"Like what?" Loomis said.

"Like a dimwit. Like someone sounding out the words."

"I'm just saying that I hope you'd tell me if you were angry at me, Kent."

"For what?"

"Or disappointed."

"I don't get it. Is everything okay with you and Kate?"

"Why? Did she say something to you?"

"This is a very odd conversation, Todd. I have to wonder if you've been drinking."

So this was Loomis now: sowing panic among the elderly. The beers had been a mistake—the last two, anyway. "I'm sorry. Work's been tough. They're downsizing our group. I've lost a lot of buddies." He was thinking about Kent, alone in his ranch house, tying bass lures, making cups of Maxwell House. It was some ginned-up notion he had about loneliness, being left behind. He heard Kent release a half sob into the phone, then realized it was him.

"I understand," his father-in-law said. "You wouldn't believe the stories I hear on the lot."

"Don't say anything to Kate. It's just nice sometimes to talk to another dad, you know?"

Downstairs, Izzy was caressing her iPad like a lover. Kate was at a spinning class.

"Where's Trevor?"

"In the bath," Izzy said.

"The bath?"

"Don't stress. I'm monitoring him. You smell like beer. Are you, like, an alcoholic now?"

And what if he was? He wasn't. But what if? It wasn't every day that a guy's persecution complex came true.

After Kate and the kiddies conked out, he paced the perimeter of his darkened home debating the merits of gun control. He scanned the street for suspicious vehicles. A red Scion had tailed him home from work. Possibly twice. Later that night a loud thumping bolted him awake. "What the hell was that?"

"Trevvie," Kate murmured. "Kicks the wall." She laughed drowsily. "You're so jumpy. It's cute."

Jumpy? Cute? He felt like slugging her in the kidney, wherever that might be.

On Saturday she returned from her weekly sojourn to Trader Joe's with nine recyclable sacks full of festive yuppie kibble: tandoori chicken skewers, chipotle hummus, trail mix brimming with mystical Mayan seeds intended to charm his cholesterol. Loomis was busy thrashing Izzy at Monopoly, which would eventually build her character. He had no intention of wandering into the kitchen to audit his wife's purchases. That was something the Old Loomis would have done, a petty pleasure wrung from the fluke of his economic prerogative.

No, all Loomis wanted was to see if there might be a little something he could nosh on while Izzy was in the bathroom. He even offered to help Kate put the groceries away, an offer she politely declined, a declination he politely ignored. Loomis was going to be helpful because it was the right thing to do. He held to this conviction until the precise moment his eyes fell upon a small container of Greek yogurt.

He and Kate had discussed this product at length. They had *agreed* it was an unnecessary luxury. He tamped down his urge to speak, then realized he was tamping down his urge to speak, then glared at Kate, who was reaching into the fridge to put the almond milk away and humming—humming, of all things! Her ass looked delish. This made Loomis wish he had not seen the yogurt. But it was too late. He was going to say something now, something awful and thrilling—he'd had enough of muzzling himself, of kowtowing, of groveling, which is probably how Kate had got the idea that the fucking Greek yogurt was back in play. She turned from the fridge. Her eyes followed his. He suffered an exquisite moment of pre-regret, of wanting to fall to his knees in some kind of spiritual silence. Then his vile mouth began to speak.

On Monday morning, having forgotten to pretend to have an early meeting, Loomis walked Trevor to preschool. They bonded. This consisted of listening to Trevor hold forth on the Uhmoomah, a species of his own invention that appeared to embody all the vital Freudian archetypes. (Pale wormy body? Check. Damp cave habitat? Check. Humps that squirt white lava? Check.)

They passed all the landmarks Izzy had loved: the tree with the tiny door at the bottom, the doghouse shaped like an igloo. Trevor droned sweetly on. Loomis missed the days of one child. The math was so complicated now. Someone always had a cold. They all fought too much. Loomis was fat and unhappy and lonely in his unhappiness. That was why he picked fights. What did one do with such insights?

They were standing in front of the church basement where Trevor was being taught to clean up glue spills and use his words. Loomis crouched down to hug his little weirdo goodbye. Over Trevor's shoulder he spotted a red Scion parked down the street. The vehicle pulled a U-ie and raced off. Loomis jumped up and waved his arms and started yelling, "Hey! Hey!"

A number of kids and parents were by now staring at him. Loomis fell silent. Trevor regarded his father with the solemn majesty of one burdened by too many secrets. He held a pink finger to his lips. "The Uhmoomah don't like yelling," he whispered. "It hurts their tentacles."

The interview with The Lesbian Anita was brief. It had to be, because The Lesbian Anita was extremely busy. She was a rabbi and a tenured scholar of transgender literature, a kind of Venn-diagram celebrity. She had three offices, two secretaries, a solar system of overly sexualized graduate assistants. Loomis ambushed her outside her synagogue.

"Look at you," she said. "You've gotten fat, Toddy. It gives me real pleasure. Your hairline's fucked too."

They stood, not hugging.

The Lesbian Anita wore a flowing white robe and Pocahontas braids. She looked like a Manson Girl back from rehab.

"I'll cut to the chase," Loomis said. "Two armed men approached me in a threatening manner regarding a dispute I had with Kate. I believe you hired these men because you're in love with my wife and hope to drive us apart."

The Lesbian Anita roared like a pirate. "Is this what happens when you turn forty and start turning tricks for the man?"

"If you come clean, I'll let this go without involving the police."

"Omigod! Let's by all means involve the police. Let's call them *right now.* I want to see how this plays out. It's so awesomely unhinged." She pulled out her iPhone and dialed 911.

On speaker, a dispatcher asked, "Is this an emergency?"

The Lesbian Anita stared at Loomis. "Yes."

"Okay. Point made." He tried to grab the phone, but The Lesbian Anita caught his hand and gave it a quick crushing. She'd been an Olympic finalist in the hammer throw.

Loomis looked around to make sure no one had seen him physically subdued by The Lesbian Anita. It had happened before, on a vacation to Squam Lake long ago. Loomis was the new suitor, seeking the approval of Kate's brilliant best friend. They drank a lot and smoked weed and skinny-dipped, and somehow the subject of Indian leg wrestling came up, as it often does among the drunk and erotically agitated. So there was Loomis with a confused half-chub and a bota bag of sangria, slathered in mud like an Iroquois. He stepped forward to fell The Lesbian Anita. Down he went, like Foreman in Zaire.

He had squirmed in the muck, not unhappily. "Okay, now do you surrender?" he howled. Kate was doubled over on the porch. The Lesbian Anita cupped her mons pubis in a gesture whose precise meaning Loomis declined to interpret. Instead he adopted the accent of a Native American person imitating English. "I, Him Who Pisses Self at Dawn, bow down before you, the mighty warrioress She Who Munches Squaws!" and they all whooped and the loons whooped back and later, in front of the fire, Kate whispered that she loved him. Why not? He was man enough to take his licking with good humor, and he gave it right back that same night, between Kate's sturdy thighs, the region he called Sweet Valley in tribute to her Kansan youth.

The Lesbian Anita had pocketed her phone. She squinted rabbinically. "Whatever you've gotten yourself into, get out of it."

"I haven't gotten into anything."

"I'd hate to think I was right about you all these years," The Lesbian Anita said. "Pull it together, Toddy. Have a little faith in yourself."

Faith. Right. That was what Loomis needed—a little taste of the ancient codes, the chance to maybe slaughter an animal with sanctioned hooves. He settled for the local Unitarian Universalist Church, tagging along with Kate and the kiddos. "My little atheist wingman," Kate called him, and he pretended the "little" part didn't offend him. He made fruit salad for the potluck, sang the ungendered hymns. It was nice: holding hands, participating in the sudden vulnerability of human voices lifted together, letting the ponchoed crones fawn over his kids. Later he wolfed French toast stuffed with cream cheese and tried to forgive himself.

He did his weekend time with the kids, the playground, the drop-offs, the dizzy itinerary of domestic duties that now passed for foreplay. Why was he so angry at his wife all the time? It was as if he'd come to the end of his decency. Kate herself was done arguing, into some ominous new phase.

"What?" Loomis found himself saying defensively, standing in the middle of an empty room with some useless implement in his fist, a paint scraper or egg whisk. Then, with a note of scorn, *"What?"*

Trevor had spent weeks building an elaborate home for his Uhmoomah out of construction paper, glitter glue, Legos, popsicle sticks. He carried it to the back porch and stomped on it with a sudden al-fresco wrath.

Loomis burst through the back door. "What are you doing?"

"It's ruined," Trevor explained.

"It's not ruined!" Loomis shrieked.

"Yes it is," Trevor said calmly. "There was a volcano that exploded. Why are you yelling, Dad?"

A few days later Loomis was standing in back of the Dunkin' Donuts across the street from Izzy's soccer practice. She wouldn't be done for another half hour, so he ordered a dozen Munchkins, half for the kid, but she didn't need the sugar and he did, because he worked for a living and she didn't. He finished the last one and sky-hooked the box into the dumpster.

"Those are gonna go straight to your breadbasket." Tony Bennett had materialized beside him, spiffy as a dime.

Loomis felt the bolt of his hypothalamus. His bloodstream flushed with epinephrine. His soft muscles clenched. His plaqued heart thudded. A million years ago, or even, like, ten, he would have done something useful with all these panic hormones—fought, or more likely fled. But he was a modern domesticated human, a suburban kvetcher unversed in the protocols of genuine danger.

Scarface appeared on the other side of Loomis and set a paw on his trembling shoulder. "This is what I'm wondering, friend: if my wife, God rest her soul, if she came back from shopping—"

"Please don't touch me without my permission," Loomis managed.

"She finally gets everything unloaded," Scarface said, unperturbed, "but here I come, Big Mister Hubby Man, and I see something I don't approve of on that kitchen island. Does this give me the right to . . ."

"Demean," Tony Bennett said.

"Right."

"Insult."

"Sure."

"Hector."

"Listen to this guy. Friggin' Roget."

"Is this about the Greek yogurt?"

Tony Bennett reached into his hip pocket and left his hand there. "Yeah, let's address the yogurt thing."

They were standing side by side, a brief, miserable chorus line.

"I have a right to know how my money's being spent," Loomis said.

"You don't trust your wife?" Scarface made his tongue go *tut.* "The mother of your children?" He said something in Italian, and they both laughed.

"What do you want me to say? That I'm a tyrant? Okay, I'm a tyrant."

"We don't want you to say anything," Tony Bennett said. "That's the goal we're pursuing here."

Loomis needed to shut up. He knew that. But the portion of his brain responsible for shutting up had lost function. "A buck seventy-nine for a single yogurt," he said slowly. "Eight fucking ounces. How is that in any way reasonable? They put a little pod of strawberry jam next to the yogurt, like it's so fucking sacred it requires its own habitat, like American consumers are so stupid as to think, 'Wow, in Greece they're *sophisticated* about their yogurt! They don't put fruit at the bottom! No, Greeks assemble each yogurt themselves, as in the days of the ancient Athenian democracy, when Plato sat upon the steps of the Parthenon and stirred a brace of fresh berries into his single-serving portion!'"

His interrogators said nothing. What could they say? Loomis had dazzled them into silence.

"You really think like this?" Scarface asked finally.

Tony Bennett turned to face Loomis. His breath smelled of sirloin and Altoids. "Do you work hard, Mr. Loomis?"

"I do," Loomis said, though he wanted to say something a bit more elastic, something like *Define hard.* Because the truth is he had offered a single good idea early in his tenure, a phrase uttered in jest at the end of a brainstorm, which had become a slogan, then a logo, then a campaign. He was a one-hit wonder. He was Men Without Hats. Did Men Without Hats work hard? Define hard.

"So this hard work," Scarface said, "it entitles you to a certain respect, am I correct?"

Loomis nodded wearily.

"And your wife, as the primary caretaker for your children, she works hard too, right?"

"I respect my wife," Loomis said.

"Your behavior," Tony Bennett said.

"Not respectful," Scarface said.

"Because respectful would be to thank her for going shopping."

"Give her a kiss. Say, *Thanks, honey.*"

"Then later, if you got a problem, away from the kids."

"You find a nice way."

"You don't jump down her throat about the yogurt, the applesauce."

"That fucking applesauce!" Loomis barked. "You tell me, you guys are so reasonable, does it make sense to put an ounce of fruit-based paste into a brightly colored polyurethane pouch with a screw top, a pouch no doubt assembled by underaged slaves on the outskirts of some toxic Asian megalopolis—"

Scarface nudged Loomis. He gestured with his chin toward Tony Bennett, who brushed open his coat to reveal an elaborate holster, out of which peeked the black butt of a pistol.

Loomis's knees went to jelly. He tried to take a step and stumbled, and his brow struck something.

"You got a decision to make," Tony Bennett said from somewhere up above. "We don't want to have to keep doing this. It's not to our liking."

"A decision," Loomis said woozily. Then he was on the ground next to the dumpster, and his ribs hurt.

Now many things were happening simultaneously, and Loomis was struggling to process each of them. Scarface stood over him, looking spooked. The scar itself—and this made no sense—seemed to be peeling off at one end. The red Scion was parked across the street, and a figure stepped out of it and began twirling a baton. Someone was yelling at a much higher, feminine pitch. Loomis could feel an itchy trickling down his cheek. It was unclear how much time had passed.

The scene began to resolve: The guy from the red Scion was Bobito. He was working a pair of nunchucks (not a baton!) and instructing Tony Bennett to "Step off." Tony Bennett appeared unsure what to do. With some difficulty, he removed the gun from his holster, which brought Bobito up short. Scarface had his hands out, palms up. This was all taking place behind a Dunkin' Donuts, in what one might call a low-traffic asphalt area.

Then a fourth figure became visible: his daughter Izzy in orange soccer shorts and shin guards; Izzy, who had inherited his big dumb nose—he felt terrible about it—what in God's name had he ensnared her in? She was marching toward Scarface and Tony Bennett from behind, at such an angle that she couldn't see the basic standoff scenario. "I told you guys, no being rough!" she yelled. Then, catching sight of the weapons, she shrieked: "Omigod-omigod-omigod!"

Loomis concurred. He did not ponder why his daughter had been shouting at Scarface and Tony Bennett. He did not think about anything but Izzy, who was still wearing her cleats, which he'd expressly told her not to do because nongrass surfaces wore the plastic down, but what did it matter, what did any of it matter? She was his baby girl, his number one; he had caught her at birth, her tender bluish body coated in hot slop. He rose up and staggered toward her, right through the line of fire. He was going to possibly die a hero, and this felt, for a gorgeous fraction of a second, true and good. He lunged and knocked Izzy to the ground and lay on top of her like a soggy rug, bellowing, "Please don't shoot oh god she's my baby daughter please don't shoot I beg you oh god I'm begging."

This went on for a while.

Scarface gestured toward Bobito. "Who the hell is this guy?"

"Mr. Loomis's personal security detail is who I am, bitch."

Loomis was too terrified to mention that this was not technically true.

"Drop the Chink sticks," Tony Bennett said. He was trying to sound tough, but his voice strained for the effect, and Loomis, cowering below him, could see his hands trembling, as if the gun clasped between them weighed next to nothing.

"You first," Bobito said.

"Please do it," Loomis whimpered. "Please, Bobito. Please please."

Bobito sneered and dropped the nunchucks. "For the girl."

Tony Bennett had just lowered his weapon when a siren sounded. Suddenly all three men were yelling *shit* and *fuck* and glaring at Loomis as if this were all his fault. Bobito tossed his nunchucks in the dumpster. To Tony Bennett he said, "Ditch the piece, dammit."

"Wait," Tony Bennett said. "Wait wait."

"Ditch it," Bobito snarled.

The gun landed on the pavement with a hollow plasticky clatter. Loomis could see that the weapon, which lay a few feet away, had a tiny plug in back, to keep the water inside.

"What the fuck?" Bobito said.

"Here's the thing," Scarface said. His cheeks had become damp with sweat; the scar now dangled.

"Let's just get out of here," Tony Bennett murmured.

"Oh no you don't," Bobito said. "You been terrorizing my client. You ain't going nowhere."

"He was never in any danger," Scarface said.

"Tell that to my man," Bobito said. "He's on the ground, crushing his little girl, his head all bleeding."

"Bleeding?" Loomis said. "Crushing?" He rolled off Izzy and wiped his temple with the back of his hand. The red made him gag. Scarface hurried over and offered a handkerchief. "Direct pressure," he said with genuine remorse. "Head wounds bleed."

Loomis struggled to process the new data. The gun was a toy.

The scar was a fake. He was not going to die heroically, which was great news, terrific really, but also a little disappointing. Izzy seemed to be in some kind of shock. She kept sobbing that she was sorry, which was not a word he associated with her. The cops, yipping through red lights, were closing in on all of them.

Tony Bennett and Scarface began walking backward, toward the alley behind the dumpster.

"Don't you dare," Bobito said.

"We were just doing a job," Tony Bennett said.

"I got your license plate," Bobito said. "I'll track you down."

"Cut us some slack," Scarface said, sounding notably less Italian. "We got downsized. You got any idea how hard it is to find work when you're over fifty and can't operate Excel?"

"I got three teenagers at home to feed," Tony Bennett said in an imploring tone. "Let's forget this ever happened, okay? Okay?"

But no, it was not okay. A cop car pulled up behind them, and a black female officer stepped out, her stout partner emerging from the other side of the car. The officers spotted Izzy, Loomis, the blood, and drew their weapons. Everyone raised their hands in unison, like a dance troupe.

"This gentleman fell," Tony Bennett called out. "He had some kind of seizure."

"Is that true, sir?" the black cop demanded.

"My dad's a diabetic," Izzy said suddenly. "He gets dizzy when he gets low blood sugar." She squeezed his hand and looked at Bobito imploringly.

Loomis made his head nod. "I came here to get a doughnut, but I got lightheaded. I guess I fell."

"We got a report of a dispute," the other cop said.

"That was me, officer," Izzy said tearfully. "Because, you know, it's my dad. These guys came by to help me. I was sort of panicking."

The black cop lowered her weapon. "I'm going to call an ambulance."

"Omigod," Izzy said. "Are you taking him to the hospital?"

"Please, officer," Loomis said. "I'm fine. These gentlemen have been very kind. We'd really just like to walk home. It's only a few blocks, and my daughter is quite upset."

The officer cocked her head.

Loomis stood up and smiled and showed her that the wound

was no big deal, just a small gash. The sun was drawing their shadows across the parking lot. Loomis felt a strange elation, a sense of things cohering, of some larger force having summoned him to this moment. It made no sense, but he wanted to thank everyone: Bobito for watching over him without his permission, Tony Bennett for keeping a cool head, Scarface for the handkerchief, the black lady cop for, in her own way, trying to warn him.

He lifted his daughter and hugged her to him as the others walked back into their own lives. But there was something amiss —a hard object pressed against his tender ribs, and he knew at once what it was: the toy pistol, which Izzy had stashed inside her shirt to conceal it from the cops. He thought of how she had spoken to Tony Bennett and Scarface when she first appeared, and he realized what she had done, and then why. Izzy must have sensed his revelation because she began to weep again. And then he was weeping too, because she was right, she had seen it more clearly than he had, how fragile their little family was, how easily daddies lost faith in themselves, and how this made families fall apart. And this made him think (for whatever blessed reason) of those first few seconds of her life, how slippery she had been, how easily he might have dropped her, and up above, Kate, her lovely face smeared red with joy.

They'd have to explain to her that he'd fallen and hit his head. Or maybe they'd confess to the whole crazy thing. It didn't matter. He'd ask forgiveness too. But that was the easy part: finding the right words. The hard part, the part he'd been fighting all along, would be facing who he'd become. How did one find a way back to grace?

Loomis held on—to the memory of Izzy and the truth of her, lashed between rage and mercy like the rest of humankind, precious, alive, his number-one girl smelling of grass and bubblegum.

MATT BELL

Toward the Company of Others

FROM *Tin House*

THE MORNING OF the first snow, Kelly drove an unexplored length of the zone, coasting the truck slowly from driveway to driveway, assessing doors left open, windows missing, porches collapsed by the removal of their metal supports. Some of the houses had been scrapped already, but he knew he would find one more recently closed, with boards in the windows and an intact door. A space empty but not yet shredded. The farther he moved toward the center of the city, the more the neighborhoods sagged, all the wood falling off of brick, most every house uninhabited, the stores a couple thousand square feet of blank shelves, windows barred against the stealing of the nothing there. Paint scraped off concrete, concrete crumbled, turned to dust beneath the weather. Wind damage, water damage. Fire and flood. Before the zone, Kelly had never known rain alone could turn a building to dust. But rain had flooded the Great Lakes, ice had sheered Michigan's cliffs, had shaped the dunes he'd dreamed of often after he'd left the state, before he'd returned to find these fading city streets, the left-behind houses abandoned to this latest age of the state's greatest city.

As Kelly drove he saw how the zone sprawled beneath the falling snow, casting its imperfection wider than he could accept, but eventually he chose a house—two floors, blue paint on the siding, gray boards over the windows, a yellow door, surrounded on both sides by vacant lots, with only a burnt shell standing watch across the street—then went to the door and knocked, yelled greetings loaded with question marks.

He waited, yelled again.

He raised his hood, returned to the truck for a pry bar. He moved out of the front yard and along the side of the house, the brown grass crunching beneath the snow. Beside the blue house was a metal gate in a chain-link fence, but the gate wasn't latched. At the first window he pulled back the covering board, found the glass gone. He peeked in, searched for furniture, a television or a radio. Instead, stained carpet, signs of water damage, a kitchen with no dirty dishes but an intact gas range, a sink and faucet he could wrench from the countertops.

He lifted himself through the window. Leading away from the kitchen was a staircase to the second floor and also a basement door, closed and latched with a padlock. He'd cut the lock later, after the other work was done. Upstairs, the bedrooms were small, their ceilings sloped to fit beneath the peaked roof, but there was enough room to swing a sledge. Back downstairs he opened the front door—the door not even locked, but he hadn't thought to check before climbing in the window—then crossed the snowy yard to the truck for the rest of his tools. Already his first footprints were buried beneath the accumulation and afterward he wouldn't be able to convince himself there had been others, no matter how insistently he was asked.

In the master bedroom he flicked the light switch to check the power, then aimed above the outlets and swung. He took what other scrappers might have left behind. With a screwdriver he removed each metal junction box from the bedroom, then in the bathroom he cut free the old copper plumbing from under the sink and inside the walls. He smoked and watched the snowfall through a bedroom window, the world quiet and wet under its weight. In the South he'd forgotten the feeling of a house in winter, the unexpected nostalgia of watching the world disappear under snowfall. He put his forehead to the cool glass, watched the stillness fill the pane.

Downstairs, he dismantled the kitchen, disconnected the stove from the wall, cut the steel sink from the counter. He worked quietly in what he thought was the wintry hush of the house, but later he would be told about the amateur soundproofing in the basement, about the mattresses nailed to the walls, about the eggshell foam pressed between the basement rafters.

The soundproofing meant the boy screaming in the basement

wasn't screaming for Kelly but for anyone. There would be talk of providence, but what was providence but a fancy word for luck? If the upstairs of the blue house had been plumbed with PVC, Kelly might not have gone down into the basement. But then copper in the bathroom, but then the copper price.

It wasn't until he cut the padlock's loop and opened the basement door that he heard the boy's voice, the boy's hoarse cry for help rising out of the dark.

As soon as Kelly heard the boy's voice the moment split, and in the aftermath of that cry Kelly thought he lived both possibilities in simultaneous sequence: there was an empty basement or else there was a basement with a boy in a bed, and it seemed to Kelly he had gone into both rooms. Kelly thought if he had fled and left the boy there and disappeared into the night he might never have had to think about it again, couldn't be held responsible for everything that followed. Instead he had acted, and now there would be no knowing where this action would stop.

Kelly climbed downward, descending the shaft of light falling through the basement door. His clothes clung to the nervous damp of his skin as he stepped off the stairs toward the bed at the back of the low room, toward the boy restrained there, all skin and skinny bones, naked beneath a pile of blankets and howling in the black basement air.

One by one each element of the scene came into focus, the room's angles resolving out of the darkness, each shape alien in the moment, the experience too unexpected for sense: the humidity under the earth, the musky heat of trapped breath and sweat, piss in a bucket; the smell of burrow or warren, then the filth of the mattress as Kelly slid to his knees beside the bed, his headlamp unable to light the whole scene; the boy atop the stained and stinking sheets, confusing in his nudity, half hidden by the pile of covers, a nest of slick sleeping bags and rougher fabrics partially kicked off the bed, and beside the pile of blankets a folding metal chair.

The boy's screaming stopped as soon as Kelly lit his features, but Kelly knew the boy couldn't see him through the glare. He shut off the headlamp, removed the glow between them, let their eyes readjust to the dimmer light. He leaned closer, close enough to hear the boy's rasping breath, to smell his captivity, to touch the boy's hand. To try to bring the boy out of abstraction into the sensible world.

Kelly's body was moving as if disconnected from thought, but if he could retouch the connections he would begin to speak. He tried to say his name, pointed to himself, failed to speak the word. He shook his head, reached down for the boy. The boy flinched from Kelly's touch, but Kelly took him in his arms anyway, gathered him against his chest and lifted quick—and then the boy crying out in pain as Kelly jerked him against the metal cuffs shackling the boy's feet to the bed, hidden beneath the bunched blankets.

The sound of the boy's voice, naming his hurt into the black air: this was not the incomprehensible idea of a boy abducted but the presence of such a boy, real enough. And how had Kelly come to hold him, to smell the boy's sweat, then the sudden stink of his own, their thickening musk of fear? Because what if he had not left the South. If he had been able to find work instead of resorting to scrapping. If there had not been the fire in the plant so that afterward he worked alone. If he had not met the girl with the limp. If she had not been working today. If she hadn't had another attack the night before, keeping him from drinking so much he couldn't scrap. Providence or luck, it didn't matter. He told himself he believed only in the grimness of the world, the great loneliness of the vacuum without end to come. You could be good but what did it buy you. You could be good and it meant more precisely because it bought you nothing.

Kelly cursed, lowered the boy back onto the bed, felt the boy's heat linger on his chest like a stain. He touched the place where the boy had been, felt the thump of his heart pounding beneath the same skin, listened to their bodies huffing in the dark as he relit the narrow beam of the headlamp, its light scattering the boy's features into nonsense.

I have to go back upstairs, Kelly said. *I'll be right back.*

No, the boy whispered, his voice swallowed by the muted room. *Please.*

Kelly quickly removed his coat and wrapped it around the boy to cover the boy's nakedness, then moved toward the stairs as fast as he could, trying to outdistance the increasing volume of the boy's cries. But there was no way of freeing the boy without his saw, no way of getting the saw without leaving the boy. The basement door opened into the kitchen, and in every direction Kelly saw the destruction he'd brought, the walls gutted, the counters opened, the stove dragged free from the wall, waiting for the handcart. The day was ending fast, the light fading as Kelly moved across the dirty tile, looking for his backpack, the hacksaw inside.

Outside the opened window the wet whisper of snow fell, quieting the world beyond the house's walls, while inside the air was charged and waiting. When Kelly turned back to the basement he saw the door was closed, the boy and the boy's sound trapped again. It was a habit to close a door when he left a room, but this time it was a cruelty too. Back downstairs Kelly found the boy sitting with his bare knees curled into his naked chest, all of his body cloaked under Kelly's coat. Kelly raised the saw so the boy could see what it was, what Kelly intended. *I'm here to help you,* Kelly said, or thought he did, the boy was nodding, or Kelly thought the boy was, but after he switched the headlamp on again he couldn't see the whole boy anymore, only the boy in parts. The boy's terrified face. The boy's clammy chest. The boy's clenched hands and curled toes. He ran the beam along the boy's dirty bony legs, inspected the cuffs, the bruised skin below.

Kelly put a hand on the boy's ankle and they both recoiled at the surprise. *Hold still,* Kelly said. He lifted the chain in one hand and the saw in the other and as he cut he had to turn his face away from the boy's rising voice, speaking again its awesome need.

The boy was heavier than Kelly expected, a dead weight of dangling limbs. He asked the boy to hold on and the boy said nothing, did less. When Kelly looked down at the boy he saw the boy wasn't looking at anything. Out of the low room, up the stairs, into the dirty kitchen. All the noise the boy had made in the basement was gone, replaced by something more ragged, a threatened hissing. The front door was close to the truck but the back door was closer to where they stood, and more than anything else Kelly wanted out of the blue house, out into the fresh snow and the safety of the truck, its almost escape.

Other scenarios emerged. Other uses for the basement, what might happen to Kelly if they were caught there. What might happen to the boy for trying to escape. Outside, the wind was louder than Kelly had expected and the thick wet snow would bury his newest footprints but there wouldn't be any hiding what he'd done. Kelly carried the boy around the house to the truck, adjusted the boy's weight across his shoulder so he could dig in his pocket for the keys. The boy was shoeless and Kelly couldn't put him down. The boy was limp and shoeless in his arms, but Kelly thought if he put the boy down the boy might run.

Kelly lowered the boy into the passenger seat, then stripped off his own flannel shirt. His arms were bare to the falling snow, but he wasn't cold as he helped the boy stick his arms into the shirt, its fabric long enough to cover most of the boy's nakedness. He bundled the boy back into the coat too, but the truck was freezing and the boy's legs were bare and Kelly wasn't sure the boy's shivering would stop no matter how warm he made the cab.

Kelly walked around to the driver's side, opened the door. Without climbing inside he reached under the steering wheel, put the key in the ignition, started the engine. He punched the rear defrost, cranked the heat, hesitated.

I have to go, he said. *I have to go back into the house, but I will be back for you.*

The boy didn't speak, didn't look in his direction. It wasn't permission. He didn't know if the boy understood. This was shock, trauma. The boy needed to go to a hospital, he needed Kelly to call the police, an ambulance. He needed Kelly to act, to keep rescuing him a little longer.

However many minutes it took—moving back into the kitchen to gather his tools into his backpack, then down into the basement for the hacksaw he'd left behind—each minute was its own crime. In the basement Kelly knew the bed was unoccupied, but when he entered the low room there appeared a vision of the boy still chained to the bed, an afterimage burning before him. He knew he'd saved the boy, but when he made it back to the truck the doors were locked, the boy gone. A new panic fluttered in Kelly's chest—but then he looked again, saw the boy hidden in the dark of the snow-covered cab, crouched down in the space near the floorboards beneath the passenger seat—a space, Kelly remembered, as a kid he had called the pit.

The boy wouldn't come out of the pit, wouldn't unlock the doors or turn his terrified face toward Kelly. Kelly waited until he was sure the boy was looking away, then pulled his undershirt sleeve over his bare elbow and shattered the truck's driver-side window. Before he drove the boy to the hospital he had to clear the safety glass from the boy's seat, from the thick scrub of the boy's hair.

When Kelly pulled into the hospital parking lot he maneuvered the truck under the emergency sign, the snow turned heavier than at the blue house, then stepped outside into the unplowed parking lot. He walked around the truck, opened the passenger door, lifted the boy's limpness into his arms, said his own name to the boy for the first time. The snow fell on Kelly's face and on the boy's face, and neither said anything else as Kelly carried the boy across the parking lot. The boy didn't look at Kelly, and Kelly thought he had to stop looking at the boy, had to watch where he was going instead of taking in every feature, every eyelash and pimple and steaming exhale, had to concentrate on making his body move. *A few more steps,* he said to the boy. A few more steps and they would be inside, passing through the bright and sterile and inextinguishable light of the hospital, toward the company of others, where they would be safer than they were now, alone.

BRUCE ROBERT COFFIN

FROM *Red Dawn*

BILLY FIRKIN KNELT quietly in the dark, steadying himself with his hands, as the container rocked from side to side. The claustrophobic feeling was bad but the odor was far worse. His feet slipped on the barrel's slick bottom. *Three more miles to freedom.*

Billy had professed his innocence from the start, lying to his attorney, denying any involvement in the murder of his unfaithful girlfriend Tina and her new beau, even after the cops found his bloody shoes in the trash. Lying had always been second nature, and he was extremely convincing. As a young boy, he'd displayed an innate ability to manipulate others. His mother had cautioned friends, "That boy has the face of an angel. Just remember to check his pockets before you go."

His string of successful cons ended abruptly the day a Portland jury, comprised of his so-called peers, spent less than two hours deliberating his fate. "Guilty," they'd said.

During his sentencing, Justice Stratham rebuked him. "Anyone capable of inflicting as much pain and suffering as you did on that poor couple deserves to die. You, sir, are an abomination to mankind. Were it within my purview, I'd sentence you to death."

Billy caught a lucky break by committing his crime in a state devoid of capital punishment. Stratham sentenced him to life without the possibility of parole. He was shackled and carted off to the Maine State Prison in Thomaston, eleven months ago, in the summer of '61.

*

On the eve of his planned escape, he'd barely slept a wink. The excitement and promise of the coming day were nearly intolerable. All he could think about was rising early and dressing for breakfast, but he'd forced himself to wait, having learned the value of patience.

"A successful scam artist has to have patience," his father once told him. "Takes time to gain a person's confidence, son. You gotta earn their trust, slowly. But once you get it, you can do anything, anything at all."

Everything had to appear status quo. The last thing he needed was for his cellmate to start asking questions or, worse still, some nosy bull like Jeeter smelling a rat. Bull was convict-speak for prison guard.

The seeds of his plan had been sown during his first month inside. One afternoon he'd been out in the recreation yard smoking a cigarette when he saw his cousin—second cousin, actually, and only by marriage—driving a flatbed truck through the prison gates. Cousin Frank was employed by Milo Trucking, a company the State of Maine contracted to remove prison refuse.

Armed bulls, carrying rifles, removed Frank from the truck while they searched the cab, the payload, and the undercarriage using mirrors. After they had finished, Frank drove around to the rear of the chow hall. Billy noted that the back of the Dodge was loaded with both red and white fifty-five-gallon drums, the same white drums that the kitchen detail used to depose of the waste grease from the fryolators. Discreetly, he continued to monitor the event until finally the truck reappeared. When Frank reached the main gate, the bulls repeated their search. They searched everything, everything except the barrels. It was on that very afternoon that he began to plan his escape.

The first step was getting assigned to the kitchen detail, but it hadn't been easy. Prison trustees were required to stay out of trouble for their first six months, no fights, no bad disciplinary reports, and no contraband. Several times he'd turned the other cheek, when what he really wanted was to drive a homemade shiv through the guts of another convict. Six excruciatingly long months of "yes boss, no boss, thank you boss," until finally his request had been approved. He'd spent the remaining months meticulously planning each and every aspect, even conducting research by reading books from the prison library.

The cost of putting his plan into action had only been six cartons of cigarettes for Mel, the head of the kitchen detail, and a promise of four thousand dollars to Cousin Frank. Billy didn't actually have four thousand dollars "hidden away from a scam," but Frank didn't know that and had readily agreed to help.

Like all of his best schemes, this one was simple. With Mel's help, Billy planned to seal himself inside one of the waste containers. The barrel in question would only contain a small quantity of grease, allowing plenty of room for him and making the overall weight seem about right, should anyone become suspicious.

The truck lurched over a pothole, slamming Billy's head against the inside of the barrel. *Dammit all to hell, Frank. Take it easy, would ya.* The pavement smoothed. He resumed his shallow breathing.

He'd waited until the other inmates began to rise and prepare for their morning duties before sliding out of his own bunk. Silently he dressed in his prison gray shirt, blue cargo pants, and black shoes. He shaved, brushed his hair and teeth, everything as normal. He stood waiting by the cell door as the bull appeared.

"Morning, Firkin," Barrett had said.

As bulls went, Barrett was a good one. He'd been professional and pleasant since the day Billy first arrived. The same could not be said of all the bulls.

Barrett's boss Jeeter, a horse's ass of the highest order, was small in stature but big on bullying. Being a bully was Jeeter's favorite pastime, frequently caving in some convict's skull with the hardwood club he carried. He'd even named the club, carving MABEL into the side of it. Billy didn't know if "little man's syndrome" was a real malady or not, but if so, old Jeeter the Bull was in the advanced stages. Rumor had it that he was also king of the swirlies, the name given to Jeeter's practice of taking a con's toothbrush and swirling it around inside the toilet bowl before replacing it undetected. As far as Billy was concerned, having Barrett on duty today rather than Jeeter only meant that the god of good fortune was smiling down upon him once more.

"Morning, boss," Billy replied, needing every ounce of his self-control not to push past Barrett and run down the hall shouting, "I'm free, I'm free." He studied the bull's face for any indication that his excitement had been detected, but saw nothing. Billy was escorted down the corridor to the other detailees. The entire group then walked to the kitchen, where they prepared the day's first meal.

Breakfast was always served at seven o'clock sharp. Members of the kitchen detail ate first, at quarter till. This morning's meal had consisted of chipped beef and gravy on toast, scrambled eggs, canned peaches, and of course black coffee. Billy despised chipped beef and gravy, or what the inmates fondly referred to as "shit on a shingle," but today was his stepping-out day and he ate a double helping that tasted more like the ambrosia his grandma Josephine used to make. Viewpoint is everything, and Billy had come to believe that his cup would soon runneth over.

Following breakfast, under the watchful eye of the bulls, the kitchen crew cleaned up. Dishes, utensils, and cookware were scrubbed, dining tables cleared, and floors were swept and mopped. The cycle began anew as they prepared for the noontime meal. Billy worked quietly alongside the others, not wanting to draw any attention to himself, no matter how slight. He'd just finished mopping the chow hall when Jeeter appeared.

"Well, well, well, what do we have here?" Jeeter asked with a sneer.

Billy's heart skipped a beat. Not having seen Jeeter until that very moment, he'd foolishly assumed the bull wasn't working. The other inmates, grateful that Jeeter wasn't targeting them, stopped to watch.

"Just cleaning up, boss," Billy said.

"Just cleaning up, boss," Jeeter said, mocking him in falsetto. "Think you got it all, convict?"

Billy nodded in the affirmative.

"You sure?"

"Yes, boss."

Billy knew what was coming, having witnessed this sadistic game before, but was powerless to stop it. Jeeter hooked his highly polished black military boot under the bucket, upending it, sending a wave of dirty water cascading across the previously clean concrete floor.

"Oops," Jeeter said. "Looks like you missed some after all. You'd best clean that up, convict."

"Yes, boss."

Jeeter laughed, then walked away, spinning Mabel and whistling a happy tune.

Billy hated Jeeter. Sometimes he'd daydream about slicing the bull's throat, giving him that nice below-the-chin grin. The same grin he'd denied carving into the throats of Tina and her boyfriend.

Two-thirty couldn't come soon enough.

Another pothole jarred the Dodge violently. Billy's barrel bounced up, momentarily losing contact with the bed of the truck, then landed hard, nearly tipping over. He struggled to maintain both his balance and his composure. His legs were beginning to cramp from being bent so long. *Only a couple more miles.* He closed his eyes, repositioned his legs, and resumed his shallow breathing.

Twenty minutes, according to the prison library book about Harry Houdini, is the amount of time an average-sized person can survive if sealed in a fifty-five-gallon drum, before running out of air. Houdini had been handcuffed, sealed in a metal barrel, and then submerged in ten feet of water. Twenty minutes later, he escaped. Afterward, when asked how he had been able to continue breathing for so long, Houdini explained that he took shallow breaths and willed himself to remain calm. Billy practiced shallow breathing every night before falling asleep.

Billy's brother Darryl came to see him at the prison once a month. Darryl was also very adept at getting people to do what he wanted, although he used a gun and had done time for armed robbery. It was during one of these visits that Darryl agreed to help his brother. The two men were very careful when discussing the details of the plan, as the bulls were always watching, but not always listening.

Darryl lived in Portland, over seventy miles south of the prison, and wasn't all that familiar with Thomaston. Billy asked his brother to reconnoiter the surrounding area for anything abandoned with a loading dock. The only additional requirement was that it needed to be within close proximity to the prison, as Billy would only have a limited supply of oxygen.

Darryl located an abandoned warehouse exactly 3.1 miles from the prison, according to his odometer. It couldn't be seen from the road, had no guards and no gate. What it did have was a cement platform, perfect for offloading a barrel.

Billy, who'd always been good with numbers, calculated that it would take seven or eight minutes, depending upon traffic, for Frank to reach the warehouse after leaving the prison. He knew that the bulls only spent two to three minutes conducting the exit search, leaving him nine minutes. Nine minutes for Frank to load the barrel onto the truck, drive to the prison gate, then roll the barrel off the truck and onto the platform at the warehouse. If everything went according to plan, he'd have a window of four and a half minutes. Two hundred and seventy seconds were all that stood between glorious freedom and death by suffocation.

During the months that followed, Billy had Darryl go over the plan with Cousin Frank repeatedly until he was confident that both men had it memorized.

Mel, the kitchen chief, was a friend to Billy. He'd taken him under his wing immediately upon joining the detail. Because of Mel, Billy always got plenty to eat and was only rarely assigned to P and P duty, convict-speak for pots-and-pans detail, considered the nastiest of all kitchen work. The slop sinks were deep, making it tough on the back, and the water was scalding. When Billy first broached the subject of trying to escape, Mel's eyes sparkled with excitement. It had actually been Mel's idea to mark Billy's container.

"It should be something ironic," Mel said. "A big F.U. to the bulls."

Billy liked the idea initially, but worried that it might be foolhardy. He couldn't risk anything that might be detected during the exit search. In the end, he'd instructed Mel to mark a large letter *B* on the lid of the barrel. The marking would enable Frank to know which of the barrels to offload at the warehouse.

The temperature inside the container was rising quickly. Billy was just beginning to feel the first prickles of fear. He willed them away like swatting at flies. Nothing to worry about. Everything was proceeding exactly as he'd planned. Less than a mile now. Shallow breathing.

*

Lunch was uneventful. The menu had consisted of tuna salad, stale bread, soup, and fries. Billy's stomach was in knots, partially because of his earlier run-in with Jeeter but mostly because the hour of his escape was nearly at hand. He wasn't hungry but he'd forced himself to eat, it was a necessary part of the ruse. It wouldn't do to have one of the bulls notice he wasn't eating, especially Jeeter.

All of the remaining details had been worked out during Darryl's last visit. Billy told him to pick up a sandwich, then park out behind the warehouse. If anyone inquired why he was there, he'd simply say he was eating his lunch. Billy instructed him to hang back as the barrel was unloaded, waiting until Frank drove off before making his approach.

"How will Frank know which barrel to unload?" Billy asked, testing his brother.

"He'll know because there will be a big letter *B* written on the top, in black marker."

"What do you do as soon as he drives off?"

"I hightail it to the loading dock, pry off the lid, and get you the hell outta there."

"What else?"

"I'm to bring you a change of clothes and a trash bag for the stuff you'll be wearing."

They'd been over the plan again and again, until Billy was confident that everyone knew exactly what to do. Frank knew to be at the warehouse by two-forty-five. If he hadn't made it by then, he would scrap the plan and get Billy out of the barrel. Billy promised that Frank would get his money either way. Greed is the best insurance.

At two-twenty, Billy and Mel were working in the kitchen along with several other inmates. Mel was cleaning out the fryolators while Billy assisted. The rest of the crew had begun to prep for supper. Billy could hear several of the bulls laughing about something, just beyond the kitchen door. At two-twenty-five, Billy and Mel moved into the back room. They were standing at the loading-dock doors when Jeeter walked into the kitchen and began hassling one of the workers.

"Dammit," Billy whispered. "Not now."

"Stay here," Mel said, wiping his hands on his apron. "I'll take care of this."

Billy waited nervously, beside an open barrel. A loud crash came from the adjoining room.

"Why don't you watch what the hell you're doing, convict!" Jeeter yelled. "Clean that mess up."

Mel hastily returned through the doorway, just as the truck was backing up to the loading platform.

"Now," Mel said. "Let's go, we've only got a second."

Billy climbed into the barrel and crouched down just as he had practiced. "Wish me luck."

Mel picked up the lid and looked down at Billy one last time. "See you on the other side."

Then there was only darkness.

All of his senses were dampened by the enclosure. It was like being blind. He was aware of movement and heard the muffled banging of other barrels being loaded onto the truck, but aside from those things he was effectively cut off from the outside world. After a minute or so he felt the truck begin moving toward the main gate, toward freedom.

He knew the bulls would realize he was missing by suppertime; he only hoped they wouldn't notice beforehand. His only regret was not being around to see the look on their faces. If all went according to plan, he and Darryl would be across the state line into New Hampshire by the time the inmates sat down to eat.

Billy knew they were close. Frank had made an unmistakable right-hand turn. Judging by the way his barrel was bouncing, they were now traveling on the dirt drive which led to the warehouse. The air had become noticeably thinner. He felt lightheaded. Concentration was more difficult, and the leg cramps were almost unbearable. *Just a little longer.* The truck came to a stop.

Darryl was parked exactly where he was supposed to be when the blue Dodge came into view. He checked his watch: two-forty-six. They'd done it. He threw the rest of his half-eaten sub out the window and turned the key. Nothing but a click. "Shit!" *This can't be happening. Not now.* He'd forgotten about the Merc's temperamental starter. He knew it had a bad spot, but it hadn't acted up for some time. He turned the key in the ignition again. This time he heard a loud screech. "Come on. Come on." He watched anxiously as Frank backed the truck into position and got out.

As Frank wrestled with the barrel, he tried the key a third time. "Come on, baby." The engine roared to life. He let out a sigh of relief. Frank got back in the cab and began driving away. Darryl shifted into drive and sped toward the loading dock. He jumped out of the car, pry tool in hand, and hopped onto the concrete platform, where a single white barrel stood. On the lid in black marker was a big letter *B*. "I gotcha, Bill," he said as he pried off the lid.

Frank was one happy camper. "I'm rich!" he yelled out the window to a passing car. "Goddamn, I'm rich! Four thousand buckaroos." He reached down and cranked up the volume on the AM radio and began to sing along with Elvis. "Let's rock, everybody let's rock."

Billy wasn't sure if the lack of oxygen was muddling his thoughts or if the truck really was moving again. It couldn't be. They'd stopped and Frank had moved his barrel. He was positive. *What if he only moved your barrel to get at another one? What if he unloaded the wrong barrel?* No, it couldn't be. The barrel was clearly marked. But muddled thoughts or no, they were definitely moving again. As if to punctuate this thought, his barrel bounced up and down on the flatbed. He opened his mouth to scream but couldn't draw any air into his lungs. Panic set in, and unlike the little flies of fear he'd shooed away earlier, these were huge and had sharp teeth. He beat on the inside of the drum with his fists, but his arms grew heavy and the pounding ceased. With his last bit of strength, he pushed his entire body up against the lid.

Darryl stared dumbfounded into the open barrel. It was full to the top with foul-smelling brownish lard. He checked the lid again, confirming the letter *B*. He checked his watch: two-fifty. His brother Billy had been locked in a barrel, some other barrel, for twenty minutes. In desperation he drove his arm into the grease, hoping to feel his brother's head, but felt nothing.

He leapt off the loading dock and back into his car. He floored the accelerator. Spinning tires threw gravel everywhere. *I've got to catch up with Frank.* He locked the brakes. In a cloud of dust the

Mercury skidded to a stop at the main road. Darryl looked both ways. Frank's truck was nowhere in sight. They'd never discussed where he was headed after unloading the barrel. It wasn't part of the plan. Darryl figured he had a fifty-fifty chance at guessing correctly. He spun the steering wheel hard left and screeched out onto the pavement.

Darryl guessed wrong.

The two men stood out on the loading dock, enjoying the warm afternoon sun and smoking cigarettes. One wore a greasy white apron over his inmate clothing, the other a spotless prison guard uniform.

"Well, I guess he'll think twice before he murders the nephew of a bull again," Mel said.

The guard took a long drag off what remained of his cigarette before dropping it onto the loading platform and twisting it under his highly polished boot. "I'm sure you're right," Barrett said with a chuckle. "I'm sure you're right."

LYDIA FITZPATRICK

Safety

FROM *One Story*

IN THE GYM, the children are stretching in rows. Their arms are over their heads, their right elbows cupped in left palms. Class is almost over, and this is the wind-down—that is what the gym teacher calls it—though the children move constantly, flexing their toes inside their sneakers, shifting their feet, canting their hips, biting their lips, because they are young, and their bodies are still new to them, a constant experiment. The gym teacher counts softly, *one, two, three, four,* and before *five* there is a sound that reminds a boy in the back row of the sound a bat makes when it hits a baseball perfectly. In the front row, a girl thinks it is the sound of lightning, not lightning in real life, because it is sunny out and because she can't remember ever hearing real lightning, but like lightning on TV, when the storm comes all at once. Next to her, her best friend thinks it is a sound like when her mother drives her into the city and the car first enters the tunnel, only this sound is sharper than that one and stays within its lines, and she is not inside it. One boy recognizes the sound. He has been to the range with his father and brother, and he has worn headphones and stood a safe distance and watched the sound jerk his father's arm and push his brother off-balance. This boy is the first to let his elbow drop.

The gym teacher is thinking *five,* and then he knows. He looks to the door that leads to outside, to the ESL trailers, to the walkway that connects the elementary school to its middle school, because that is where the shot has come from, and there is this throb of hope for the girl who teaches ESL, who has just moved here and still bakes brownies for the teachers' lounge. The gym teacher is calm, and in his wind-down voice he tells the children to be quiet, completely quiet, and to run into the boys' locker room. The gym teacher is old, has been at this school for decades, and with each passing year the children like him more and listen to him less, but they know to be afraid from the carefulness in his voice—they are not talked to carefully, except when they ask questions about death and divorce—and at first their fear is only for the tone of his voice, but then they remember the sound. They run, and their sneakers are the sort that light up with each footfall and their shoelaces whip against polished wood, and the gym teacher is not worried that they will trip but that they will stop—because they are that age when rules are God and shoelaces must be tied—but they don't stop, and they don't trip. There are eighteen of them. They are as fast and graceful as he has ever seen them.

When they reach the locker room, one boy grabs the gym teacher's sleeve. It is September, and he has not yet memorized their names, but he knows that the boy's brother was a student of his years ago and that the boy's father is back from the war. The boy whispers, "Gun." He is the one who recognized the sound and he has worried, as he sprinted across the basketball court, that the gym teacher might not know. The gym teacher nods, puts a finger to his lips. He is thinking means of egress. He is thinking police, hide, gun. He is thinking of his cell phone, which was a present from his son last Christmas, a tongue-in-cheek present, a comment on character, and it is in the pocket of his windbreaker on the back of the ladder chair in his kitchen at home.

The children have gathered around him when usually they scatter, and he can see in their eyes that they want to be picked up and held. One girl has forgotten the sound. She smiles and raises her hand. She has a question. She wants to know whether they should change out of their uniforms, but before she can ask, the gym teacher points to his office, which is in the middle of the locker room, and he tells them to lie on the floor behind his desk and to be quiet, and the carefulness drops from his voice—he can't help it, there are more shots, inside the school now, and a yell cut short.

As the children file into his office, the gym teacher turns out the lights in the locker room and looks out into the lighted gym. The floor is perfectly bare, perfectly clean, glowing like the surface of a planet seen from afar. The cones and Frisbees and hula hoops are back in their bins, and there is nothing to show that a class meets this period. Through the windows of the double doors he sees pale yellow wall tiles (they are the color of butter, of winter sun, but the tiles are more a constant in his world than butter or pale suns, and so when he sees those things he thinks that they are the color of the school). The boy whose father is just back from the war, the one who recognized the sound, watches the gym teacher look to the doors, and he wishes that the gym teacher were his father, because the gym teacher is old and afraid, and his father has only been afraid twice and both times were at the war, never at home, because here, he says, is paradise compared to there. This boy is the last into the office, and as he lies down next to the girl who thought of lightning, he goes on wishing for his father in the fervent way that children wish for things because they think those things are almost in their grasp.

On the teacher's desk is the blue parachute that the children play with on Fridays. On Fridays, they grip the silk and make it ripple and buck, they run underneath it and around it, but one of its seams is split, and the gym teacher meant to take it home to his wife, who would stitch it up as she has dozens of times before. Behind his desk, the children are lying in two neat rows, and he has seen children lie this way before, on the news, in other countries, but not these children, his children, and he almost tells them to get up, that it is tempting fate to lie this way, but there are more shots, closer, in the cul-de-sac of classrooms across from the gym, and the gym teacher grabs the parachute and spreads it over them, and they are so small that it covers all eighteen of them easily, and at the thought of them—of how many and how small—his chest seizes, and he thinks that he will be the one to make a noise, but then he hears the clang of the gym doors opening and the long sigh of them swinging shut and his fear becomes the biggest thing he's ever felt. It is so much bigger than him that for a second it eclipses him entirely.

The gym teacher cannot think, and then, just as suddenly, he can. He turns out the lights in his office and the parachute is not quite as dark as the shadows around it—the silk has a gleam—but it is the best he can do. He crouches under his desk. He is between the children and the door, and he whispers to them one more time, "Do not make a sound. Do not move." Under the parachute, a girl pees without thinking of holding it. She feels it hot and soaking the seat of her gym shorts, and the parachute is light on her face. On Fridays this is the best feeling, and she thinks of that, of how she is getting to feel it today even though it is not a Friday. There are footsteps moving across the gym. A boy thinks, Dad. A girl thinks, Mom, Mom, Mom. One boy thinks it is the principal, because the principal is the only one who walks through the halls when they're empty. One girl begins to count silently. She panics sometimes—when she sees the road disappearing too fast under the car's tires; when the train cuts through their town, its whistle blaring; when she is in the swing at the park and finds herself too high—and her parents tell her to count, to breathe, to count and breathe, and they count with her, lead her from one number to the next.

The footsteps are slow. The gym teacher knows that this means it is the man with the gun and it means something about him too. The gym teacher is curled around his own knees. He has never made himself so small. Behind him, the parachute moves with each of their breaths.

There is a new noise. A clang of metal on metal. The boy who recognized the shot does not know what this sound is, and he realizes now that there was comfort in knowing. He does not love Fridays and the parachute. He does not love anything that hems him in, and his mother tells him that even as a baby he did not like to be held. He edges out from under the parachute. He is between the wall and the girl who thought of lightning, and it is dark, but he can see the gym teacher's coat rack branching over him and he can see the windows that line the walls of the office and look out into the locker room. Deep in the dark there is a red haze from the exit sign over the door that leads to outside, to the ESL trailers, and to the walkway to the middle school where his brother is, and the boy could run that walkway in twenty-two seconds—he has timed himself on a watch that is both waterproof and a calculator—but his brother does not like him to come to the middle school. Instead his brother meets the boy on the hill above the soccer field, where there is a tree with peeling bark and a path that leads through the woods to their house.

The clanging noise shakes in the air and gives way to the footsteps. The girl counts thirty, thirty-one. The man with the gun is close, the gym teacher thinks, by the showers, whose dripping is the metronome of his days. The showers are separated from the office by three banks of lockers, and as he thinks of the lockers, he realizes that that was the clanging sound, metal on metal—the butt of the gun or the muzzle. The children's things are inside the lockers and strewn around them, their backpacks and jackets and lunch bags and dioramas—they are that age, when teachers tell them to pick their favorite place in the world and fit it in a shoebox and they can—and the man with the gun will see these things, and he will know that they are here. The gym teacher shifts into a squat and one of his ankles cracks. He doesn't know what he'll do when the door opens, but he keeps his eye on the dark square of the window next to the door. The footsteps are closer and closer and closer and far away there are screams, and a girl—the youngest in the class—has heard these screams before, at the hospital, when she was having an arm set and down the hall someone else was having something worse. Next to her, a boy wishes for something to hold on to. His palms burn with the need, and he finds the girl's hand next to his and grabs it, and she thinks this is like the hospital too, where everyone was holding hands.

He is here. There is a change in the darkness in the window that the gym teacher feels more than sees (just as he feels his wife's absence some nights, when she is sleepless and moves through the house below him), and then the change is clearer: he can see the man's glasses catch the red light of the exit sign. He can see the nose of the gun moving toward the window. There is a clink, a knife on a plate. Fifty-six, the girl counts, and the gym teacher knows the glass will splinter, he knows how this ends, but behind him the boy crouched under the coat rack sees something different: a half foot down the gun's barrel, where the shoulder strap attaches, there is a dangling medal, a slim silver oval barely bigger than a thumbnail, but big enough for the boy to recognize it. It is a saint medal, the saint whose job it is to protect soldiers, and the boy knows the saint's name because it is the same as his own, and he knows the medal because his mother gave it to his father years ago, before you were born, she tells him, before your brother was born, when your father left for the first time.

The gun drops from the window, and the boy does not hesitate. He is up. He opens the door and slips through it, his body filled with the certainty of it, with a wish fulfilled, his father, and as he turns the gun is ready for him. It is inches from him. Dad, the boy thinks, even as he realizes that the man is not tall enough to be his father, is not tall enough to be a father at all. In life, the boy has been fearless—he trusts the dark, trusts the slimmest branch, trusts that he alone can fly—but he looks at the gun and his mind goes cold and cavernous.

"Where's your class?" the man says, his voice muffled by a ski mask.

The boy hesitates for a moment—he does not think of protecting his class, of protecting the girl who is his favorite, who is under the parachute, trying to remember the prayer that her grandmother mumbles in Polish each night—for a moment he hesitates because he cannot speak. Then that moment is over, and he is still alive, and he says, "Outside."

"Outside," the gym teacher hears, and he thinks that this might save them, but the silence grows long and he does not know what it means. He is listening for sirens, wishing for sirens in the fervent way that children wish, as though his chest is opening to dispatch some part of him that will find the sirens and usher them here. Behind him, the children know that for the first time they are hiding without wanting to be found.

The boy raises his eyes and looks up the long line of the gun to the medal. It *is* his father's gun. The boy can see it here, and he can see it locked in the case in the hall between the door to his room and the door to his brother's room, where it glows in the way things precious and forbidden glow—the grandfather clock with the damp brass gears and the ostrich egg with foreign letters inked on its curves and the tiny crystal bottle on his mother's dresser—and the constellation of these things is as sacred and eternal as anything up in the sky, and the boy cannot believe that the gun is here and that its case is empty.

"Let's go," the man says, and his voice is muffled, but there is something strained in it that the boy recognizes. The boy looks up, past the medal, to the mask, which is a ski hat with holes cut for the mouth and nose and eyes, and over the eyeholes are glasses that could be anyone's, except that they are his brother's. They are across the table from him every morning, slanted toward a book whose pages are dusted with the crumbs of the toast his mother makes. They were across the table from him this morning.

The boy reaches out and puts a finger to the nose of the gun, and it is warm. He has never touched the gun before, and his brother yanks it away, and the medal jingles, this tiny silver noise, and his brother grabs his hand.

Under the desk, the gym teacher listens to them walk away and he begins to cry. He has always thought that you could *know,* that right and wrong were like bones beneath the skin—hidden but there, waiting to be laid bare—and his hands are empty and he cannot weigh the one against the seventeen. The girl who is counting hits a hundred and starts over again at one, and the boy's brother pulls him toward the emergency exit, and the boy has dreamed of this, in certain stretches of homeroom, when he is filling a sheet with cursive *L*'s, he has dreamed of his brother taking him out of class and letting him sit on the back of his bike as they coast down the hill into the town to the store with the miniature models of helicopters and tanks and dragons that are all the color of flour, waiting to be painted with brushes whose bristles are thin as eyelashes, but even as he has dreamed this, he has known it will not happen because his brother prefers to be alone, likes to have space, though their mother says that as a baby his brother was the one who liked to be held.

They are at the door, and his brother pushes it open with a hip so that he can keep one hand on the gun. The gym teacher watches a wedge of light stretch across the locker room, the benches, the bookbags, and he is waiting for a child to speak, to cough—it is that season, when their noses run and their lips chap—but they are silent, and the light recedes, and he tells the children to stay quiet and that he will be back.

Outside, the air is cool and sweet. The light is too bright—it makes the boy think of Sundays, when their mother takes them to the movies, and the boy loves the movies, cannot sit close enough to the screen, and when the movie is over and they step out of the theater, the fact of the world outside is a shock to him, an insult. The boy's brother lets go of his hand, and the bell rings, blaring from loudspeakers in the corridors and classrooms, from speakers mounted on the corners of the ESL trailer. It is time for lunch, but no one comes out of the trailer, and the school is still. There is the soccer field. The grass arches away from the wind, and they cross the parking lot to the field, and the boy looks back over his shoulder and sees a girl lying on the sidewalk next to the ESL trailer. She has fallen with one ear against the pavement, and the boy recognizes the girl. She is two grades above him, with dark hair and a red birthmark on her cheek in the shape of a cloud. Her face has gone so pale that even the birthmark is drained of color, and beyond her, on the steps of the trailer, there is a woman, and from the way she is lying the boy can tell that her face will look the same.

Under the parachute, the girl who thought of lightning is thinking of her grandfather, who is the only person she knows to have died—his heart had been good but turned bad—and her own chest hurts, and she wonders if it is her heart turning inside her. A boy begins to shake. His teeth are chattering and he puts a finger between them because the teacher said not to make a sound. He has never thought of himself as truly separate from his mother, and yet he is sure that at her desk in the office in the city she does not know what is happening to him and cannot feel his fear. In the years to come, he will think of this over and over, of how she did not know.

The boy's brother is breathing fast behind the mask, and the boy knows that he shot the girl and the woman. The tip of the gun was warm, but the boy cannot make sense of it or of why he is following his brother, crossing the field at the same angle he does every afternoon. From the door to the locker room, the gym teacher watches the two boys—they are both boys, he can see that now—as they walk up the hill toward the woods. There is a dead girl on the pavement and on the steps of the trailer a woman moans, and when the boys are far enough away the gym teacher runs to the woman. It is the ESL teacher, and he puts his fingers to her neck and says, *Please, please, please.* Under the parachute the girl counts, her lips careful with the numbers: eighty-eight, eighty-nine. The silk is so hot that it begins to stick to them, to foreheads and noses and knees.

At the top of the hill, where there is the tree with the peeling bark and where the path to the boy's home begins, there is a cross stuck in the ground. It is two pieces of a yardstick that the boy recognizes because his mother used it to stir a can of paint—one end is the blue of their kitchen—and now it has been broken in two and nailed together. The boy's brother stops at the cross and says, "They'll ask you why." Every word comes out like a splinter, like he is in pain, and the boy says, "Are you crying?"

The gym teacher hears sirens, faint as wind chimes, as he puts his mouth to the woman's and exhales.

"Listen to me," the boy's brother says, and he gets down on his knees. "They're going to ask you why."

His brother's glasses are fogged. The ski hat is their mother's. It is the one she wears when she shovels snow and it smells of a dog, though they've never had one, and he does not know how to square these ordinary things with the way his brother is shaking—not gently, but wildly—as he pulls the gun over his shoulder and points it at him.

"Are you going to shoot me?" the boy says.

The girl counting reaches one hundred and stops, because her fear has dissolved, is a memory now. The gym teacher puts his fingers to the woman's neck again, and this time there is nothing. Another girl hears the sirens and thinks of her dog and the way he howls with his throat arched whenever he hears a siren and of how he will be howling now, in her house, which is nearby, pacing the halls and filling the empty rooms with that sound.

The boy begins to cry. Not because he is afraid of being shot—he cannot think what that might feel like, though he has seen it in games and on TV, though he has seen the holes burned through the paper targets at the range—but because he is afraid that his brother hates him, has always hated him. That must have been why, one time, his brother held his palm open and ran the blade of a knife across it.

The gym teacher looks up the hill and he sees that the boys are the same height—the boy with the gun is kneeling—and he sees where the gun is pointed, and he gets up and begins to run across the soccer field. The seventeen are safe, under the parachute, but already he knows that it won't matter against this one, that that is not how the scales work.

"I'm not going to shoot you," the boy's brother says, "because I'm not crazy. You tell them that. That I'm not crazy."

The boy nods, but he will not tell anyone what his brother said, not his mother, not his father, not ever. He will insist that his brother was silent, that his brother was crazy, and he will dream of the girl with the cloud-shaped birthmark. With the gun, the boy's brother motions for him to turn toward the tree with the peeling bark, and the boy turns. He is facing the path that leads home and he has timed himself on this path too. In two minutes and seven seconds he can be home, where his mother is pulling clothes from the dryer. She straightens, hearing the sirens, and it takes her a moment to unravel the sound, to register how many and how close, and she thinks there must be a fire—it has been a dry summer, a dry fall—and she goes to the window and looks toward the school. The boy can't tell if the sirens are getting closer. They seem to be carried on the wind, like they are coming from the trees, and even though he knows this isn't so, he looks up at the leaves that are red and brown and thrashing.

The gym teacher is halfway across the soccer field, and in two months, when the school reopens, his wife will walk from goal to goal for hours, eyes on the grass, looking for the gleam of a bullet in the dirt. Under the parachute, the children think of lightning and tunnels. They think of the gym teacher who said he'd come back and of mothers and fathers and of the sound of the man's voice when he said, "Let's go," and how you are never supposed to go. Later, when the policeman finds them, when he pulls up the parachute and tells them they are safe, he will not be able to forget it: how still the children were, how silent, how they didn't move a muscle.

The boy looks from the trees to the school. The gym teacher is running across the field, and he is old and slow, and from this high on the hill it seems like he is barely moving. The gym teacher's heart is battering at his lungs, his chest is burning, and the boy only watches him for a second, but it is too long—his brother turns toward the field. The sirens are everywhere now. His brother is breathing in the way that means you're hurt. The gym teacher is across the field, and he is afraid, but with his next breath his fear goes, and he does not know why, because the gun is aimed at him now, but he thinks of a morning years ago, when his son got a shoelace caught in the mower, and the gym teacher cut the lace with a pocket knife and watched the panic roll out of his son's eyes, and an hour later, in the hospital, he will die, whispering to his wife about a knife through cotton.

The boy hears the shot. He begins to run, and the leaves slide under his sneakers and he keeps his eyes on the path because there is a root up ahead that tripped him once, walking home, and his knee had bled, and his brother had looked at him and kissed his knee and said, "What's the point in crying?" The boy leaps over the root. He is running fast enough that the trees blur around him, and the gym teacher feels the hot rip of the bullet, and up on the hill there is another shot.

TOM FRANKLIN

Christians

FROM *Murder under the Oaks*

1887

IT WAS AUGUST, so she had to bury him quick. Soon she would be able to smell him, a thing she didn't know if she could endure —not the live, biting odor he brought in from a day in the fields but a mixture of turned earth and rot, an odor she associated with decaying possum and coon carcasses, the bowl of a turtle she'd overturned as a girl and then tumbled away from, vomiting at the soup of maggots pulsing inside.

It was late afternoon. He lay on his back on the porch, covered by a sheet stained across the torso with blood, the sheet mapped with flies and more coming, as many flies as she'd seen gathered in one place, a revival of them, death calling like the Holy Spirit. In her left hand she held his hat, which the two men had thrown to the ground after they'd rolled him off the wagon and left him in the dirt.

She hadn't wailed at the sight. Hadn't flung herself on the body or swiped her fingernails at their implacable faces as they watched, the two of them, one young, one old. She hadn't even put her hand over her mouth.

They told her they'd kept his gun. Said they meant to give it to the sheriff. Said, *Like father, like son.*

"Leave," is all she'd said.

And she herself had dragged him up the steps, holding him under his arms. She herself had draped him with their spare bed sheet and turned her rocking chair east to face him and sat rocking and gazing past him—past the corpse of him and its continents of flies—to the outreaching cotton so stark and white in the sun she could barely look at it, cotton she'd have to pick herself now that her son was dead.

Sheriff Waite came. He got down off his horse and left the reins hanging and stood in the yard. He studied the drag marks, the stained dirt. His green eyes followed the marks and paused at the blood on the plank steps and the gritty line of blood smeared across the porch. He watched the boy under the sheet for nearly a minute before he moved his eyes—it seemed such an effort for him to look at country folks—to her face. In the past she'd always had trouble meeting town men's eyes, the lust there or the judgment (or both), but now she sat rocking and staring back at him as though she understood a secret about him not even his wife knew. His hand went toward his nose, an unconscious gesture, but he must've considered it disrespectful for he lowered the hand and cleared his throat.

"Missus Freemont."

"It was that Glaine Bolton," she said. "Him and Marcus Eady."

Waite stepped closer to the porch. Behind him his tall handsome horse had sweat tracks down through the dust caked on its coat. It wiggled its long head and blinked and sighed at the heat, flicked the skin of its back and the saddle and the rifle in its scabbard.

"I know," Waite said. "They already come talked to me. Caught me over at Coffeeville." He moved his hand again, as if he didn't know what to do with it. "How I was able to get here so quick."

She folded her arms despite the heat, nestled her sweating breasts between them.

"They give me his pistol," Waite said.

She waited, and his face became all lines as he got himself ready to say it out loud. That there would be no justice. Not the kind she wanted, anyway.

Since it was so easy to look at him now, she did it, reckoning him in his late forties. If she hadn't been so brimming with hate, she'd have still considered him fine-looking, even all these years later. His shirt fit well at the shoulders, his pants snug at the hips.

He was skinnier than before. One thing she noticed was that his fingers weren't scarred from cotton, where nail met skin, the way hers and her son's were. Had been.

"You see," Waite began, "it's pretty generally known where your boy was going." He flapped a hand at her son. "When they stopped him."

"'Stopped him'? That's what you call what they done?"

"Yes'm."

She waited.

"He was going to shoot Glaine's daddy."

She waited. She realized she'd quit rocking and pushed at the porch boards with her bare feet until she was moving again, whisper of wind on the back of her neck, beneath her bun of brown hair. She heard her breath going in and out of her nose.

Waite suddenly took off his hat and began to examine the brim, the leather band sweated through, then turned it over and looked into the dark crown shaped by his head. "Way I hear it," he said, "is your boy and Travis Bolton had some words at the Coffeeville Methodist last week. I wasn't there, see. I'd been serving a warrant down in Jackson." When Waite came forward she heard his holster creak. He set a foot on the bottom step, careful not to touch the blood, and bent at the waist and rested his elbows on his knee. "But I got me a long memory, Missus Freemont. And the thing I told you back then, well, it still stands."

Bess had a long memory too.

She'd been sixteen years younger. Sixteen years younger and almost asleep when that *other* wagon, the first one, had rattled up outside. She rose from where she'd been kneeling before the hearth, half in prayer, half for warmth. Another cold December day had passed, she remembered, rain coming, or snow. It was dark out, windy at intervals, the rocking chair on the porch tapping against the front wall. A pair of sweet potatoes on the rocks before her all the food they had left.

A horse nickered. She pulled her shawl around her shoulders and held it at her throat. Clay, not two years old then, had been asleep under a quilt on the floor beside her. Now he got up.

"Stay here, boy," she told him, resting a hand on top of his head. He wore a tattered shirt and pants given by church women from the last county they'd lived in, just over a week before. Barefooted, he stood shivering with his back to the fire, hands behind him, the way his father liked to stand.

On the porch, she pulled the latch closed behind her and peered into the weakly starred night. Movement. Then a lantern raised and a man in a duster coat and derby hat seemed to form out of the fabric of darkness. He wore a beard and spectacles that reflected the light he held above him.

"Would you tell me your name, miss?" he asked her.

She said it, her knuckles cold at her throat. She heard the door open behind her and stepped in front of it to shield Clay.

"This is my land you're on," the man said, "and that's one of my tenant houses y'all are camped out in."

Bess felt relief. *He's only here about the property.*

"My husband," she said. "He ain't home."

"Miss," the man said, "I believe I know that."

Fear again. She came forward on the porch, boards loose beneath her feet, and stopped on the first step. The horse shook its head and stamped against the cold. "Easy," the man whispered. He set the brake and stepped from the seat into the back of the wagon, holding the lantern aloft. He bent and began pushing something heavy. Bess came down the first step. Behind her, Clay slipped out the door.

The man climbed from the tailgate of the wagon and took a few steps toward her. He was shorter than she was, even with his hat and in his boots. Now she could see his eyes.

"My name is Mister Bolton," he said. "Could you walk over here, miss?"

She seemed unable to move. The dirt was cold, her toes numb. He waited a moment, gazing past her at Clay. Then he looked down, shaking his head. He came toward her and she recoiled as if he might hit her, but he only placed a gloved hand on her back and pushed her forward, not roughly but firmly. They went that way to the wagon, where she looked in and, in the light of his lantern, saw her husband.

E. J. was dead. He was dead. His jacket opened and his shirtfront red with blood. His fingers were squeezed into fists and his head thrown back, mouth open. His hair covered his eyes.

"He was stealing from me," Bolton said. "I seen somebody down in my smokehouse and thought it was a nigger. I yelled at him to stop but he took off running."

"Stealing what?" she whispered.

"A ham," Bolton said.

Bess's knees began to give way; she grasped the wagon edge. Her shawl fell off and she stood in her thin dress. Bolton steadied her, his arm going around her shoulders. He set the lantern on the floor of the wagon, by E. J.'s boot.

"I am sorry, miss," Bolton said, a hand now at each of her shoulders. "I wish . . ."

Clay had appeared behind her, hugging himself, his toes curling in the dirt.

"Go on in, boy," she told him. "Now."

He didn't move.

"Do like your momma says," Bolton ordered, and Clay turned and ran up the stairs and went inside, pulling the door to.

Bolton led Bess back to the porch and she slumped on the steps. He retrieved her shawl and hung it across her shoulders.

"My own blame fault," he said. "I knew y'all was out here. Just ain't had time to come see you. Run you off."

No longer able to hold back, Bess was sobbing into her hands, which smelled of smoke. Some fraction of her, she knew, was glad E. J. was gone, glad he'd no longer pull them from place to place, only to be threatened off at gunpoint by some landowner again and again. No more of the sudden rages or the beatings he gave her or Clay or some bystander. But, she thought, for all his violence, there were the nights he got only half drunk and they slept enmeshed in one another's limbs, her gown up high where she'd pulled it and his long johns around one ankle. His quiet snoring. The marvelous lightness between her legs and the mattress wet beneath them. There were those nights. And there was the boy, her darling son, who needed a stern hand, a father, even if what he got was one like E. J., prone to temper and meanness when he drank too much whiskey. Where would they go now, she asked herself, the two of them?

"Miss?" Bolton tugged at his beard.

She looked up. It had begun to rain, cold drops on her face, in her eyes.

"You want me to leave him here?" Bolton asked her. "I don't

know what else to do with him. I'll go fetch the sheriff directly. He'll ride out tomorrow, I expect."

"Yeah," Bess said. She blinked. "Would you wait . . . ?" She looked toward the window where Clay's face ducked out of sight.

"Go on ahead," he said.

Inside, she told the boy to take his quilt into the next room and wait for her.

When she came out, Bolton was wrestling E. J. to the edge of the wagon. Bess helped him and together they dragged him up the steps.

"You want to leave him on the porch?" Bolton huffed. "He'll keep better."

"No," she said. "Inside."

He looked doubtful but helped her pull him into the house. They rolled him over on a torn sheet on the floor by the hearth. In the soft flickering firelight, her husband seemed somehow even more dead, a ghost, the way the shadows moved on his still features, his flat nose, the dark hollows under his eyes that Clay would likely have as well. She pushed his hair back. She touched his lower jaw and closed his mouth. Tried to remember the last thing he'd said to her when he left that afternoon. His mouth had slowly fallen back open, and she put one of the sweet potatoes under his chin as a prop.

Bolton was gazing around the room, still wearing his gloves, hands on his hips. Abruptly he walked across the floor and went outside, closing the door behind him. When he came back in, she jumped up and stared at him.

In one arm he held a bundle.

"This is the ham," he said, casting about for somewhere to set it. When nowhere seemed right, he knelt and laid it beside the door. "Reckon it's paid for."

He waited a few moments, his breath misting, then went outside, shutting the door. She heard it latch. Heard the wagon's brake released and the creak of hinges and the horse whinny and stamp and the wheels click as Mr. Bolton rolled off into the night. She went to the window and outside was only darkness. She turned.

Her fingers trembling, Bess unwrapped the cloth sack from around the ham, a good ten-pounder, the bone still in it. A pang of guilt turned in her chest when her mouth watered. Already its smoked smell filled the tiny room. She touched the cold, hard surface, saw four strange pockmarks in its red skin. Horrified, she used a fingernail to dig out a pellet of buckshot. It dropped and rolled over the floor. She looked at her husband's bloody shirt.

"Oh, E. J.," she whispered.

The next morning, as Bolton predicted, Waite arrived. She left Clay in the back, eating ham with his fingers.

"I'm the sheriff," he said, walking past her into the cold front room. He didn't take off his hat. His cheeks were clean-shaven and red from wind and he wore a red mustache with the ends twisted into tiny waxed tips. The silver star pinned to his shirt was askew, its topmost point aimed at his left shoulder.

Moving through the room, he seemed angry. When he saw E. J.'s old single-barrel shotgun he took it up from the corner where it stood and unbreeched it and removed the shell and dropped it in his pocket. He snapped the gun closed and replaced it. The door to the back room was shut, and glancing her way, he pushed aside his coat to reveal the white wood handle of a sidearm on his gun belt. Pistol in hand, he eased open the door and peered in. The little boy he saw must not have seemed threatening, because he closed the door and holstered his pistol. He brushed past Bess where she stood by the window and clopped in his boots to the hearth and squatted by E. J. and studied him. He patted the dead man's pockets, withdrew a plug of tobacco, and set it on the hearthstones. Watching, she felt a sting of anger at E. J., buying tobacco when the boy needed feeding. In E. J.'s right boot the sheriff found the knife her husband always carried. He glanced at her and laid it on the rocks beside the plug but found nothing else.

Waite squatted a moment longer, as if considering the height and weight of the dead man, then rose and stepped past the body to be closer to her. He cleared his throat and asked where they'd come from. She told him Tennessee. He asked how long they'd been here *illegally* on Mr. Bolton's property and she told him that too. Then he asked what she planned to do now.

She said, "I don't know."

Then she said, "I want my husband's pistol back. And that shotgun shell too."

"That's a bold request," he said. "For someone in your position."

"My 'position.'"

"Trespasser. Mr. Bolton shot a thief. There are those would argue that sidearm belongs to him now."

Unable to meet his eyes, she glared at his boots. Muddied at the tips, along the heels.

"I'll leave the shell when I go," he said, "but I won't have a loaded gun while I'm here."

"You think I'd shoot you?"

"No, I don't. But you won't get the chance. The undertaker will be here directly. I passed him back yonder at the bridge."

"I can't afford no undertaker."

"Mr. Bolton's already paid him."

Bess felt her cheeks redden. "I don't understand."

"Miss," he said, folding his arms, "the fact is, some of us has too little conscience, and some has too much." He raised his chin to indicate E. J. "I expect your husband yonder chose the right man to try and rob."

She refused to cry. She folded her arms over her chest and wished the shawl could swallow her whole.

"I have but one piece of advice for you," the sheriff said, lowering his voice, "and you should take it. Travis Bolton is a damn good man. I've known him for over ten years. If I was you I would get the hell out of this county. And wherever it is you end up, I wouldn't tell that young one of yours who pulled the trigger on his daddy. 'Cause if this thing goes any farther, even if it's ten years from now, fifteen, twenty years, I'll be the one that ends it." He looked at E. J. as he might look at a slop jar, then turned to go.

From the window, she had watched him toss the shotgun shell onto the frozen dirt and swing into his saddle and spur his horse to a trot, as if he couldn't get away from such business fast enough. From such people.

"Travis Bolton's a good man," Waite repeated now, these years later, putting his hat back on. "And it ain't that he's my wife's brother. Which I reckon you know. And it ain't that he's turned into a preacher, neither. If he needed hanging, I'd do it. Hanged a preacher in Dickinson one time—least he said he was a preacher. Didn't stop him from stealing horses. Hanged my second cousin's oldest boy once too. A murderer, that one. Duty's a thing I ain't never shied from, is what I'm saying. And what I said back then, in case you've forgot, is that you better not tell that boy who killed his daddy. 'Cause if you do, he'll be bound to avengement."

"Wasn't me told him," she said. So quietly he had to lean in and ask her to repeat herself, which she did.

"Who told him, then?"

"The preacher's son hisself did."

Waite straightened, his arms dangling. Fingers flexing. He looked at her dead boy. He looked back at her. "Well, Glaine ain't the man his daddy is. I'm first to admit that. Preacher's sons," he said, but didn't finish.

"Told him at school, sheriff. Walked up to my boy in the schoolyard and said, 'My daddy kilt your daddy, what'll you say about that, trash.' It was five years ago it happened. When my boy wasn't but thirteen years old. Five years he had to live with that knowing and do nothing. Five years I was able to keep him from doing something. And all the time that Glaine Bolton looking at him like he was a coward. Him and that whole bunch of boys from town."

Waite took off his hat again. Flies had drifted over and he swatted at them. He rubbed a finger under his nose, along his mustache, which was going gray. "Thing is, Missus Freemont, that there ain't against the law. Young fellows being mean. It ain't fair, it ain't right, but it ain't illegal, either. What is illegal is your boy taking up that Colt that I never should've give you back and waving it around at the church like I heard he done last Sunday. Threatening everbody. Saying he was gone kill the man killed his daddy, even if he is a preacher."

Last Sunday, yes. Clay'd gone out before dawn without telling her. Soon as she'd awakened to such an empty house, soon as she opened the drawer where they kept the pistol and saw nothing but her needle and thread there, the box of cartridges gone too, she'd known. Known. But then he'd come home, come home and said no, he didn't kill nobody, you have to be a man to kill somebody, and he reckoned all he was was a coward, like everybody said.

Thank God, she'd whispered, hugging him.

Waite dug a handkerchief from his back pocket and wiped his forehead. "Only thing I wish," he said, "is that somebody'd come told me. If somebody did, I'd have rode out and got him myself. Put him in jail a spell, try to talk some sense into him. Told him all killing Bolton'd do is get him hanged. Or shot one. But nobody warned me. You yourself didn't come tell me. Travis neither. And I'm just a fellow by hisself with a lot of county to mind. One river to the other. Why I count on folks to help me. Tell me things."

He looked again at her son, shook his head. "If he'd had a daddy, might've been a different end. You don't know. But when a fellow says—in hearing of a lot of witnesses, mind you—that he's gone walk to a man's house and shoot him, well, that's enough cause for Glaine Bolton and Marcus Eady to take up a post in the bushes and wait. I'd have done the same thing myself, you want the truth. And if your boy come along, toting that pistol, heading up toward my house, well, miss, I'd a shot him too."

A fly landed on her arm, tickle of its air-light feet over her skin. Waite said other things but she never again looked up at him and didn't answer him further or take notice when he sighed one last time and turned and gathered the reins of his mount and climbed on the animal's back and sat a spell longer and then finally prodded the horse with his spurs and walked it away.

She sat watching her hands. There was dried blood on her knuckles, beneath her nails, that she wouldn't ever wash off. Blood on her dress front. She'd have to bury her boy now, and this time there'd be no undertaker to summon the preacher so it could be a Christian funeral. She'd have to find the preacher herself. This time there was only her.

She walked two miles along unfenced cotton fields wearing Clay's hat, which had been E. J.'s before Clay took it up. She didn't see a person the whole time. She saw a tree full of crows, spiteful loud things that didn't fly as she passed, and a long black snake that whispered across the road in front of her. She carried her family Bible. For no reason she could name she remembered a school spelling bee she'd almost won, except the word *Bible* had caused her to lose. She'd not said, "Capital *B*" to begin the word, had just recited its letters, so her teacher had disqualified her. Someone else got the ribbon.

Her Bible was sweaty from her hand so she switched it to the other hand, then carried it under her arm for a while. Later she read in it as she walked, to pass the time, from her favorite book, Judges.

Her pastor, Brother Hill, lived with his wife and eight daughters in a four-room house at a bend in the road. Like everyone else, they grew cotton. With eight sets of extra hands, they did well at it, and the blond stepping-stone girls, less than a year apart and all blue-eyed like their father, were marvels of efficiency in the field, tough and uncomplaining children. For Bess it was a constant struggle not to covet the preacher and his family. She liked his wife too, a tiny woman named Elda, and more than once had had to ask God's forgiveness for picturing herself in Elda's frilly blue town dress and bonnet with a pair of blond girls, the youngest two, holding each of her hands as the group of them crossed the street in Coffeeville on a Saturday. And once—more than once—she'd imagined herself to be Elda in the sanctity of the marriage bed. Then rolling into her own stale pillow, which took her tears and her repentance. How understanding God was said to be, and yet how little understanding she had witnessed. Even he, even God, had only sacrificed once.

Girls. Everyone thought them the lesser result. The lesser sex. But to Bess a girl was something that didn't have to pick up his daddy's pistol out of the sideboard and ignore his mother's crying and push her away and leave her on the floor as he opened the door, checking the pistol's loads. Looking back, looking just like his daddy in his daddy's hat. A girl was something that didn't run down the road and leap sideways into the tall cotton and disappear like a deer in order to get away and leave you alone in the yard, trying to pull your fingers out of their sockets.

She stopped in the heat atop a hill in the road. She looked behind her and saw no one. Just cotton. In front of her the same. Grasshoppers springing through the air and for noise only bird whistles and the distant razz of cicadas. She looked at her Bible and raised it to throw it into the field. For a long time she stood in this pose, but it was only a pose, which God saw or didn't, and after a time she lowered her arm and walked on.

At Brother Hill's some of his girls were shelling peas on the porch. Others were shucking corn, saving the husks in a basket. Things a family did in the weeks the cotton was laid by. When they saw her coming along the fence, one hopped up and went inside and returned with her mother. Bess stopped, tried in a half panic to remember each girl's name but could only recall four or five. Elda stood on the steps with her hand leveled over her eyes like the brim of a hat, squinting to see. When Bess didn't move, Elda came down the steps toward her, stopping at the well for a tin cup of water, leaving the shadow of her house to meet Bess so the girls wouldn't hear what they were going to say.

"Dear, I'm so sorry," Elda whispered when Bess had finished. She reached to trace a finger down her face. She offered the tin.

"I thank you," Bess said, and drank.

Elda touched her shoulder. "Will you stay supper with us? Let us go over and help you prepare him? I can sit up with you. Me and Darla."

Bess shook her head. "I can get him ready myself. I only come to see if Brother Hill would read the service."

The watchful girls resumed work, like a picture suddenly alive, when their mother looked back toward them.

"Oh, dear," Elda said. "He's away. His first cousin died in Grove Hill and he's there doing that service. He won't be back until day after tomorrow, in time for picking. Can you wait, dear?"

She said she couldn't, the heat was too much. She'd find someone else, another preacher. Even if he wasn't a Baptist.

It was after dark when she arrived at the next place, a dogtrot house with a mule standing in the trot. There was a barn off in the shadows down the sloping land and the chatter of chickens everywhere. This man was a Methodist from Hattiesburg, Mississippi, but he was prone to fits and was in the midst of one then, his wife said, offering Bess a cup of water and a biscuit, which she took but didn't eat. Though Bess couldn't recall her name, she knew that here was a good woman who'd married the minister after her sister, his first wife, had died of malaria. Been a mother to the children.

In a whisper, casting a glance at the house, the woman told Bess that her husband hadn't been himself for nearly a week and showed no sign of returning to his natural, caring state. She'd sent the young ones to a neighbor's.

As Bess walked away, she heard him moaning from inside and calling out profane words. A hand seemed to clamp her neck and she felt suddenly cold, though her dress was soaked with sweat. God above was nothing if not a giver of tests. When she thought to look for it, the biscuit was gone; she'd dropped it somewhere.

The last place to go was to the nigger preacher, but she didn't do that. She walked toward home instead. She thought she smelled Clay on the wind on her face before she came in sight of their house. For a long time she sat on the porch holding his cold hand in hers, held it for so long it grew warm from her warmth, and for a spell she imagined he was alive. The flies had gone wherever flies go after dark and she fell asleep, praying.

She woke against the wall with a pain in her neck like an iron through it. The flies were back. She gasped at their number and fell off the porch batting them away. In the yard was a pair of wild dogs, which she chased down the road with a hoe. There were buzzards smudged against the white sky, mocking things that may have been from God or the devil, she had no idea which. One seemed the same as the other to her now as she got to her knees.

Got to her knees and pushed him and pulled him inside and lay over him crying. With more strength than she knew she possessed, she lifted him onto the sideboard and stood bent and panting. He was so tall his ankles and feet stuck out in the air. She waved both hands at the flies, but most were outside; only a few had got in. She closed the door, the shutters, and moved back the sheet to look at his face. For a moment it was E. J. she saw. Then it wasn't. She touched Clay's chin, rasp of whisker. It was only a year he'd been shaving. She built a little fire in the stove, heated some water, found the straight razor, and soaped his cheeks. She scraped the razor over his skin, rubbing the stiff hairs onto the sheet that still covered his body, her hand on his neck, thumb caressing his Adam's apple. She talked to him as she shaved him and talked to him as she peeled back the stiff sheet and unlaced his brogans and set them side by side on the floor. She had never prepared anyone for burial and wished Elda were here and told him this in a quiet voice, but then added that she'd not want anybody to see him in such a state, especially since she'd imagined that he and Elda's oldest daughter would someday be wed. Or the second oldest. You could've had your pick of them, she said. We would've all spent Christmases together in their house and the sound of a baby laughing would be the sound of music to my ears. His clothes stank, so she unfastened his work pants and told him she'd launder them as she inched them over his hips, his knees, ankles. She removed his underpants, which were soiled, and covered his privates with the sheet from her bed. She unbuttoned his shirt and spread it and closed her eyes, then opened them to look at the wounds. Each near his heart. Two eye-socket holes—she could cover them with one hand and knew enough about shooting to note the skill of the marksman—the skin black around them. She flecked the hardened blood away with her fingernails and washed him with soap and water that turned pink on his skin. Then, with his middle covered, she washed him and combed his hair. She had been talking the entire time. Now she stopped.

She snatched off the sheet and beheld her boy, naked as the day he'd wriggled into the world of air and men. It was time for him to go home and she began to cry again. "Look what they did," she said.

The Reverend Isaiah Hovington Walker's place seemed deserted. The house was painted white, which had upset many of the white people in the area, that a nigger man would have the gall to doctor up his house so that it no longer had that hornet's nest gray wood the rest of the places in these parts had. He'd even painted his outhouse, which had nearly got him lynched. So many of the white folks, Bess and Clay included, not having privies themselves. If Sheriff Waite hadn't come out and made him scrape off the outhouse paint (at gunpoint, she'd heard), there'd have been one less preacher for her to consult today.

"Isaiah Walker," she called. "Get on out here."

Three short-haired yellow dogs kept her at the edge of the yard while she waited, her neck still throbbing from the crick in it. She watched the windows, curtains pulled, for a sign of movement. She looked over at the well, its bucket and rope, longing for a sup of water, but it wouldn't do for her to drink here. "Isaiah Walker," she called again, remembering how, on their first night in the area, E. J. had horse-whipped Walker for not getting his mule off the road fast enough. Though the preacher kicked and pulled the mule's halter until his hands were bloody, E. J. muttered that a nigger's mule ought to have as much respect for its betters as the nigger himself. He'd snatched the wagon's brake and drawn from its slot the stiff whip. She'd hoped it was the mule he meant to hit, but it hadn't been.

The dogs were inching toward her, hackles flashing over their backs, taking their courage from each other, smelling the blood on her hands, her dress. She wished she'd brought a stick with her. She'd even forgotten her Bible this time, saw it in her mind's eye as it lay splayed open on the porch with the wind paging it. She hadn't eaten since they'd brought Clay back, and for a moment she thought she might faint.

She stamped at the dogs and they stopped their approach but kept barking.

In all, it must have been half an hour before Walker's door finally opened, the dogs never having quit. She lowered her hand from her neck. The reverend came out fastening his suspenders and put a toothpick in his mouth. He looked up at the sky as if seeking rain. A man entirely bald of hair but with a long white beard and white eyebrows and small rifle-barrel eyes. He whistled at the dogs, but they ignored him and ignored him when he called them by name.

She thought it proper for him to come down and meet her, but he never left the porch.

"This how you treat white folks?" she croaked at him.

"I know you," he said. "Heard why you here too. And you might try tell me the Lord God, he expect me to forgive. But I been in there praying since you first step in my yard, Missus Freemont, since them dogs first start they racket, and I been intent on listen what God say. But he ain't say nothing 'bout me saying no words over your boy soul. If he wanted me to, he'd a said so. Might be them dogs stop barking. That would tell me. The Lord, he ain't never been shy 'bout telling me what to do and I ain't never been shy for listening."

But she had turned away before he finished, and by the time the dogs stopped their noise she had rounded a curve and another curve and gone up a hill and then sat in the road and then lay in it.

Lay in it thinking of her past life, of her farmer father, widowed and quick to punish, overburdened with his failing tobacco farm and seven children, she the second oldest and a dreamer of daydreams, possessed he said by the demon Sloth. Thinking of the narrow-shouldered, handsome man coming on horseback seemingly from between the round mountains she'd seen and not seen all her life, galloping she thought right down out of the broad purple sky onto her father's property. The young man taking one look at her and campaigning and working and coercing and at last trading her father that fine black mare for a battered wagon, a pair of mules, and a thin eighteen-year-old wife glad to see someplace new. Of crossing steaming green Tennessee in the wagon, of clear cool rainless nights with the canvas top drawn aside, lying shoulder to shoulder with her husband, the sky huge and intense overhead, stars winking past on their distant, pretold trajectories, the mules braying down by the creek where they were staked and she falling asleep smelling their dying fire, his arms around her.

E. J. Ezekiel Jeremiah. No living person knows what them letters stands for but you, he'd said.

Ezekiel, she'd repeated. *Jeremiah.*

Out of the wagon to jump across the state line (which he'd drawn in the dirt with his shoe), laughing, holding hands, and going south through so much Alabama she thought it must spread all the way from Heaven to Hell. Slate mountains gave way to flatland and swamp to red clay hills, and they ferried a wide river dead as glass, then bumped over dry stony roads atop the buckboard pulled by the two thinning mules. Then the oldest mule died: within two months of their wedding.

E. J. not saying anything for a long time, staring at the carcass where it lay in the field, hands on his hips, his back to her; and then saying why the hell didn't she tell him her daddy was trading a bum mule.

For days and mostly in silence they paralleled a lonely railroad until it just stopped and there were nigger men hammering alongside white ones and the ring of metal on metal and tents speckling the horizon and octoroon whores hanging their stockings on what looked to be a traveling gallows.

For two months he laid crossties and flirted (and more) with the whores. Then they departed on a Sunday at dawn when he was still drunk from the night. She had a high fever and from inside her hot lolling head it seemed they were slipping off the land, ever south into an ooze of mud.

Then clabbertrap railroad or river towns on the landscape, she expecting a baby and sick each afternoon, staying with the wagon and reading in her Bible while he walked to town or rode aback the remaining mule to find a game of blackjack or stud and coming out more often than not with less money than he'd gone in with, her little dowry smaller and smaller and then things traded, the iron skillet from her grandmother for cornmeal and her uncle's fiddle—which she could play a little—for cartridges. E. J. had begun to sleep with the pistol by his head and his arms around his coat, the wagon always covered at night now, as if he'd deny her the stars. Waking one morning to a world shelled in bright snow and that evening giving birth to the squalling boy they called Clay, after her father, who, despite herself, she missed.

Where we going? she'd asked E. J., and he'd said, *To a place I know of.*

Which, eventually, was here. The cabin that belonged to Travis Bolton. Who lived in a large house four miles away and who killed E. J. for a ham and then said she and Clay could stay on in the cabin if they wanted to, and not pay rent, and pick cotton for him when harvest time came.

Some thoughtful part of her knew it was killing E. J. that had let Travis Bolton hear God's call. That made him do whatever a man did, within his heart and without—papers, vows—to become a preacher of the gospel. She imagined him a man of extravagant gestures, who when he gave himself to Christ gave fully and so not only allowed her and her boy to work and live on his land, in his house, but did more. On the coldest days she might find a gutted doe laid across the fence at the edge of the property. Or a plucked turkey at Christmas. Not a week after E. J. had been committed to the earth by Brother Hill, a milk cow had shown up with the Bolton brand on it. She'd waited for Mr. Bolton or his hand Marcus Eady to come claim it, but after a day and a night no one had and so she'd sheltered it in the lean-to back of the house. Aware she could be called a thief, she'd wrapped Clay in E. J.'s coat (buckshot holes still in it) and carried him to the Bolton place. Instinct sent her to the back door, where a nigger woman eyed her down a broad nose and fetched Mrs. Bolton, who told her Mr. Bolton meant for her to use the cow so that the boy might have milk. Then she shut the door. Bess understood that Mrs. Bolton disapproved of her husband's decision to let them live in the cabin. To let them pick cotton alongside the other hired hands and tenant farmers, to pay them for the work of two people even though she was a sorry picker at first and Clay did little work at all in his early years. Nights in the cabin's bed with Clay asleep against her body, Bess imagined arguments between the Boltons, imagined them in such detail that she herself could hardly believe Mr. Bolton would let *those people* stay in their house, bleed them of milk and meat and money. Bess's own father would never have let squatters settle in one of his tenant houses, had in fact run off families in worse shape than Bess's. If you could call her and Clay a family.

When she woke, she knew God had spoken to her through Jesus Christ. In a dream, he had appeared before her in the road with a new wagon and team of strong yellow oxen behind him, not moving, and he had knelt and pushed back the hair from her eyes and lifted her chin in his fingers. She couldn't see his face for the sun was too bright, but she could look on his boots and did, fine dark leather stitched with gold thread and no dust to mar them. She heard him say, *Walk, witness what man can do if I live in his heart.*

She rose, brushing away sand from her cheek, shaking sand from her dress, and started toward Coffeeville.

She had walked for two hours talking softly to herself when she heard the wagon behind her and stepped from the road into the grass to give way to its berth. The driver, a tall man dressed in a suit, tie, and derby hat, whoaed the mules pulling it and touched the brim of the hat and looked at her with his head tilted. He glanced behind him in the wagon. Then he seemed to arrive at a kind of peace and smiled, said she looked give out, asked her would she like a ride to town. She thanked him and climbed in the back amid children, who frowned at one another at her presence, the haze of flies she'd grown used to. A young one asked was she going to the doctor.

"No," she said, "to church."

She slept despite the wagon's bumpy ride and woke only when one of the children wiggled her toe.

"We here," the child said.

Her neck felt better, but still she moved it cautiously when she turned toward the Coffeeville Methodist Church, a simple sturdy building painted white and with a row of tall windows along its side, the glasses raised, people sitting in them, their backs to the world, attention focused inside. In front of the building, buggies, horses, and mules stood shaded by pecan branches. Women in hats were unrolling blankets on the brown grass that sloped down to the graveyard, itself shaded by magnolias. From out of the windows she heard singing:

Are you weak and heavy laden?
Cumbered with a load of care?

Precious Savior still our refuge,
Take it to the Lord in prayer.

The children parted around her and spilled from the wagon, as if glad to be freed of her. The man stood and set the brake, then climbed down. He had a cloth-covered dish in his hand. "Here we are," he said, and put down his plate, which she could smell —fried chicken—and offered his hand. She took it, warm in hers, and the earth felt firm beneath her feet.

Tipping his hat, he began to make his way through the maze of wagons and buggies and up the steps and inside. She stood waiting. The song ended and more women—too busy to see her—hurried out a side door carrying cakes, and several children ran laughing down the hill, some rolling in the grass, and from somewhere a dog barked.

Two familiar men stepped out the front door, both dressed in dark suits and string ties. They began rolling cigarettes. When the young one noticed her he pointed with a match in his hand and the other looked and saw her too. They glanced at one another and began to talk, then Glaine Bolton hurried back inside. Marcus Eady stayed, watching her. His long gray hair swept back beneath his hat, his goatee combed to a point, and his cheeks shaved clean. He lit his cigarette, and trailing a hand along the wall, he moved slowly down the steps and off the side of the porch and along the building. When he got to his horse he stroked its mane and spoke softly to it, all the while watching her.

The front door opened and the man who stepped out putting on his hat was Sheriff Waite, wearing a white shirt and thin black suspenders. He stood on the porch with his hands on his hips. She was holding on to the side of the wagon to keep from falling, and for a moment Waite seemed to stand beside his own twin, and then they blurred and she blinked them back into a single sheriff.

He had seen her. He glanced over at Marcus Eady and patted the air with his hand to stay the man as he, Waite, came down the steps and through the wagons and buggies and horses and mules, laying his hands across the necks and rumps of the skittish animals nearest her to calm them. When he stood over her, bent as she was, she came only to his badge.

"Missus Freemont," he said. "What are you doing?"

"My boy needs burying," she said. "The Lord led me here."

For a moment, as he watched her, Waite held in his eyes a look that doubted that such a Lord existed anymore. What did he see in her face that made his own face both dreadful and aggrieved? What a sight she must be, bloodied, rank, listing up from the camp of the dead to here, the sunlit world of the living, framed in God's view from the sky in startling white cotton. She clung to the wagon's sideboard and felt her heart beat against it, confused for a moment which of her men it held. More people had come onto the porch in their black and white clothes and were watching, stepping down into the churchyard. A woman put her hand over her mouth. Another hid a child's face. Marcus Eady had drawn his rifle and levered a round into its chamber. Glaine Bolton emerged red-faced from the church, pushing people aside, and pointed toward Bess and Waite, the sheriff reaching to steady her. The man last out was the preacher, Travis Bolton, and now she remembered why she had come. It was for her boy. It was for Clay. At the church Bolton raised his Bible above his eyes to shade them so he might see. Then he pushed aside the arm of his son trying to hold him back and left the boy frowning and came through the people, toward her.

STEPHEN KING

A Death

FROM *The New Yorker*

JIM TRUSDALE HAD a shack on the west side of his father's gone-to-seed ranch, and that was where he was when Sheriff Barclay and half a dozen deputized townsmen found him, sitting in the one chair by the cold stove, wearing a dirty barn coat and reading an old issue of the *Black Hills Pioneer* by lantern light. Looking at it, anyway.

Sheriff Barclay stood in the doorway, almost filling it up. He was holding his own lantern. "Come out of there, Jim, and do it with your hands up. I ain't drawn my pistol and don't want to."

Trusdale came out. He still had the newspaper in one of his raised hands. He stood there looking at the sheriff with his flat gray eyes. The sheriff looked back. So did the others, four on horseback and two on the seat of an old buckboard with HINES MORTUARY printed on the side in faded yellow letters.

"I notice you ain't asked why we're here," Sheriff Barclay said.

"Why are you here, sheriff?"

"Where is your hat, Jim?"

Trusdale put the hand not holding the newspaper to his head as if to feel for his hat, which was a brown plainsman and not there.

"In your place, is it?" the sheriff asked. A cold breeze kicked up, blowing the horses' manes and flattening the grass in a wave that ran south.

"No," Trusdale said. "I don't believe it is."

"Then where?"

"I might have lost it."

"You need to get in the back of the wagon," the sheriff said.

"I don't want to ride in no funeral hack," Trusdale said. "That's bad luck."

"You got bad luck all over," one of the men said. "You're painted in it. Get in."

Trusdale went to the back of the buckboard and climbed up. The breeze kicked again, harder, and he turned up the collar of his barn coat.

The two men on the seat of the buckboard got down and stood either side of it. One drew his gun; the other did not. Trusdale knew their faces but not their names. They were town men. The sheriff and the other four went into his shack. One of them was Hines, the undertaker. They were in there for some time. They even opened the stove and dug through the ashes. At last they came out.

"No hat," Sheriff Barclay said. "And we would have seen it. That's a damn big hat. Got anything to say about that?"

"It's too bad I lost it. My father gave it to me back when he was still right in the head."

"Where is it, then?"

"Told you, I might have lost it. Or had it stoled. That might have happened too. Say, I was going to bed right soon."

"Never mind going to bed. You were in town this afternoon, weren't you?"

"Sure he was," one of the men said, mounting up again. "I seen him myself. Wearing that hat too."

"Shut up, Dave," Sheriff Barclay said. "Were you in town, Jim?"

"Yes sir, I was," Trusdale said.

"In the Chuck-a-Luck?"

"Yes sir, I was. I walked from here, and had two drinks, and then I walked home. I guess the Chuck-a-Luck's where I lost my hat."

"That's your story?"

Trusdale looked up at the black November sky. "It's the only story I got."

"Look at me, son."

Trusdale looked at him.

"That's your story?"

"Told you, the only one I got," Trusdale said, looking at him.

Sheriff Barclay sighed. "All right, let's go to town."

"Why?"

"Because you're arrested."

"Ain't got a brain in his fuckin' head," one of the men remarked. "Makes his daddy look smart."

They went to town. It was four miles. Trusdale rode in the back of the mortuary wagon, shivering against the cold. Without turning around, the man holding the reins said, "Did you rape her as well as steal her dollar, you hound?"

"I don't know what you're talking about," Trusdale said.

The rest of the trip continued in silence except for the wind. In town, people lined the street. At first they were quiet. Then an old woman in a brown shawl ran after the funeral hack in a sort of limping hobble and spat at Trusdale. She missed, but there was a spatter of applause.

At the jail, Sheriff Barclay helped Trusdale down from the wagon. The wind was brisk, and smelled of snow. Tumbleweeds blew straight down Main Street and toward the town water tower, where they piled up against a shakepole fence and rattled there.

"Hang that baby-killer!" a man shouted, and someone threw a rock. It flew past Trusdale's head and clattered on the board sidewalk.

Sheriff Barclay turned and held up his lantern and surveyed the crowd that had gathered in front of the mercantile. "Don't do that," he said. "Don't act foolish. This is in hand."

The sheriff took Trusdale through his office, holding him by his upper arm, and into the jail. There were two cells. Barclay led Trusdale into the one on the left. There was a bunk and a stool and a waste bucket. Trusdale made to sit down on the stool, and Barclay said, "No. Just stand there."

The sheriff looked around and saw the possemen crowding into the doorway. "You all get out of here," he said.

"Otis," the one named Dave said, "what if he attacks you?"

"Then I will subdue him. I thank you for doing your duty, but now you need to scat."

When they were gone, Barclay said, "Take off that coat and give it to me."

Trusdale took off his barn coat and began shivering. Beneath he was wearing nothing but an undershirt and corduroy pants so worn the wale was almost gone and one knee was out. Sheriff Barclay went through the pockets of the coat and found a twist of tobacco in a page of an R. W. Sears Watch Company catalogue, and an old lottery ticket promising a payoff in pesos. There was also a black marble.

"That's my lucky marble," Trusdale said. "I had it since I was a boy."

"Turn out your pants pockets."

Trusdale turned them out. He had a penny and three nickels and a folded-up news clipping about the Nevada silver rush that looked as old as the Mexican lottery ticket.

"Take off your boots."

Trusdale took them off. Barclay felt inside them. There was a hole in one sole the size of a dime.

"Now your stockings."

Barclay turned them inside out and tossed them aside.

"Drop your pants."

"I don't want to."

"No more than I want to see what's in there, but drop them anyway."

Trusdale dropped his pants. He wasn't wearing underdrawers.

"Turn around and spread your cheeks."

Trusdale turned, grabbed his buttocks, and pulled them apart. Sheriff Barclay winced, sighed, and poked a finger into Trusdale's anus. Trusdale groaned. Barclay removed his finger, wincing again at the soft pop, and wiped his finger on Trusdale's undershirt.

"Where is it, Jim?"

"My hat?"

"You think I went up your ass looking for your hat? Or through the ashes in your stove? Are you being smart?"

Trusdale pulled up his trousers and buttoned them. Then he stood shivering and barefoot. An hour earlier he had been at home, reading his newspaper and thinking about starting a fire in the stove, but that seemed long ago.

"I've got your hat in my office."

"Then why did you ask about it?"

"To see what you'd say. That hat is all settled. What I really want to know is where you put the girl's silver dollar. It's not in your house, or your pockets, or up your ass. Did you get to feeling guilty and throw it away?"

"I don't know about no silver dollar. Can I have my hat back?"

"No. It's evidence. Jim Trusdale, I'm arresting you for the murder of Rebecca Cline. Do you have anything you want to say to that?"

"Yes, sir. That I don't know no Rebecca Cline."

The sheriff left the cell, closed the door, took a key from the wall, and locked it. The tumblers screeched as they turned. The cell mostly housed drunks and was rarely locked. He looked in at Trusdale and said, "I feel sorry for you, Jim. Hell ain't too hot for a man who'd do such a thing."

"What thing?"

The sheriff clumped away without any reply.

Trusdale stayed there in the cell, eating grub from Mother's Best, sleeping on the bunk, shitting and pissing in the bucket, which was emptied every two days. His father didn't come to see him, because his father had gone foolish in his eighties, and was now being cared for by a couple of squaws, one Sioux and the other Cheyenne. Sometimes they stood on the porch of the deserted bunkhouse and sang hymns in harmony. His brother was in Nevada, hunting for silver.

Sometimes children came and stood in the alley outside his cell, chanting, "Hangman, hangman, come on down." Sometimes men stood out there and threatened to cut off his privates. Once Rebecca Cline's mother came and said she would hang him herself, were she allowed. "How could you kill my baby?" she asked through the barred window. "She was only ten years old, and 'twas her birthday."

"Ma'am," Trusdale said, standing on the bunk so that he could look down at her upturned face, "I didn't kill your baby nor no one."

"Black liar," she said, and went away.

Almost everyone in town attended the child's funeral. The squaws went. Even the two whores who plied their trade in the Chuck-a-Luck went. Trusdale heard the singing from his cell, as he squatted over the bucket in the corner.

Sheriff Barclay telegraphed Fort Pierre, and after a week or so the circuit-riding judge came. He was newly appointed and young for the job, a dandy with long blond hair down his back like Wild Bill Hickok. His name was Roger Mizell. He wore small round spectacles, and in both the Chuck-a-Luck and Mother's Best proved himself a man with an eye for the ladies, although he wore a wedding band.

There was no lawyer in town to serve as Trusdale's defense, so Mizell called on George Andrews, owner of the mercantile, the hostelry, and the Good Rest Hotel. Andrews had got two years of higher education at a business school back east. He said he would serve as Trusdale's attorney only if Mr. and Mrs. Cline agreed.

"Then go see them," Mizell said. He was in the barbershop, tilted back in the chair and taking a shave. "Don't let the grass grow under your feet."

"Well," Mr. Cline said, after Andrews had stated his business, "I got a question. If he doesn't have someone to stand for him, can they still hang him?"

"That would not be American justice," Andrews said. "And although we are not one of the United States just yet, we will be soon."

"Can he wriggle out of it?" Mrs. Cline asked.

"No, ma'am," Andrews said. "I don't see how."

"Then do your duty and God bless you," Mrs. Cline said.

The trial lasted through one November morning and halfway into the afternoon. It was held in the municipal hall, and on that day there were snow flurries as fine as wedding lace. Slate-gray clouds rolling toward town threatened a bigger storm. Roger Mizell, who had familiarized himself with the case, served as prosecuting attorney as well as judge.

"Like a banker taking out a loan from himself and then paying himself interest," one of the jurors was overheard to say during the lunch break at Mother's Best, and although nobody disagreed with this, no one suggested that it was a bad idea. It had a certain economy, after all.

Prosecutor Mizell called half a dozen witnesses, and Judge Mizell never objected once to his line of questioning. Mr. Cline testified first, and Sheriff Barclay came last. The story that emerged was a simple one. At noon on the day of Rebecca Cline's murder, there had been a birthday party, with cake and ice cream. Several of Rebecca's friends had attended. Around two o'clock, while the little girls were playing pin the tail on the donkey and musical chairs,

Jim Trusdale entered the Chuck-a-Luck and ordered a knock of whiskey. He was wearing his plainsman hat. He made the drink last, and when it was gone he ordered another.

Did he at any point take off the hat? Perhaps hang it on one of the hooks by the door? No one could remember.

"Only I never seen him without it," Dale Gerard, the barman, said. "He was partial to that hat. If he did take it off, he probably laid it on the bar beside him. He had his second drink, and then he went on his way."

"Was his hat on the bar when he left?" Mizell asked.

"No, sir."

"Was it on one of the hooks when you closed up shop for the night?"

"No, sir."

Around three o'clock that day, Rebecca Cline left her house at the south end of town to visit the apothecary on Main Street. Her mother had told her she could buy some candy with her birthday dollar, but not eat it, because she had had sweets enough for one day. When five o'clock came and she hadn't returned home, Mr. Cline and some other men began searching for her. They found her in Barker's Alley, between the stage depot and the Good Rest. She had been strangled. Her silver dollar was gone. It was only when the grieving father took her in his arms that the men saw Trusdale's broad-brimmed leather hat. It had been hidden beneath the skirt of the girl's party dress.

During the jury's lunch hour, hammering was heard from behind the stage depot and not ninety paces from the scene of the crime. This was the gallows going up. The work was supervised by the town's best carpenter, whose name, appropriately enough, was Mr. John House. Big snow was coming, and the road to Fort Pierre would be impassable, perhaps for a week, perhaps for the entire winter. There were no plans to jug Trusdale in the local calaboose until spring. There was no economy in that.

"Nothing to building a gallows," House told folks who came to watch. "A child could build one of these."

He told how a lever-operated beam would run beneath the trapdoor, and how it would be axle-greased to make sure there wouldn't be any last-minute holdups. "If you have to do a thing like this, you want to do it right the first time," House said.

In the afternoon, George Andrews put Trusdale on the stand.

This occasioned some hissing from the spectators, which Judge Mizell gaveled down, promising to clear the courtroom if folks couldn't behave themselves.

"Did you enter the Chuck-a-Luck Saloon on the day in question?" Andrews asked when order had been restored.

"I guess so," Trusdale said. "Otherwise I wouldn't be here."

There was some laughter at that, which Mizell also gaveled down, although he was smiling himself and did not issue a second admonition.

"Did you order two drinks?"

"Yes, sir, I did. Two was all I had money for."

"But you got another dollar right quick, didn't you, you hound!" Abel Hines shouted.

Mizell pointed his gavel first at Hines, then at Sheriff Barclay, sitting in the front row. "Sheriff, escort that man out and charge him with disorderly conduct, if you please."

Barclay escorted Hines out but did not charge him with disorderly conduct. Instead he asked what had got into him.

"I'm sorry, Otis," Hines said. "It was seeing him sitting there with his bare face hanging out."

"You go on downstreet and see if John House needs some help with his work," Barclay said. "Don't come back in here until this mess is over."

"He's got all the help he needs, and it's snowing hard now."

"You won't blow away. Go on."

Meanwhile, Trusdale continued to testify. No, he hadn't left the Chuck-a-Luck wearing his hat, but hadn't realized it until he got to his place. By then, he said, he was too tired to walk all the way back to town in search of it. Besides, it was dark.

Mizell broke in. "Are you asking this court to believe you walked four miles without realizing you weren't wearing your damn hat?"

"I guess since I wear it all the time I just figured it must be there," Trusdale said. This elicited another gust of laughter.

Barclay came back in and took his place next to Dave Fisher. "What are they laughing at?"

"Dummy don't need a hangman," Fisher said. "He's tying the knot all by himself. It shouldn't be funny, but it's pretty comical, just the same."

"Did you encounter Rebecca Cline in that alley?" George Andrews asked in a loud voice. With every eye on him, he had discovered a heretofore hidden flair for the dramatic. "Did you encounter her and steal her birthday dollar?"

"No, sir," Trusdale said.

"Did you kill her?"

"No, sir. I didn't even know who she was."

Mr. Cline rose from his seat and shouted, "You did it, you lying son of a bitch!"

"I ain't lying," Trusdale said, and that was when Sheriff Barclay believed him.

"I have no further questions," Andrews said, and walked back to his seat.

Trusdale started to get up, but Mizell told him to sit still and answer a few more questions.

"Do you continue to contend, Mr. Trusdale, that someone stole your hat while you were drinking in the Chuck-a-Luck, and that someone put it on, and went into the alley, and killed Rebecca Cline, and left it there to implicate you?"

Trusdale was silent.

"Answer the question, Mr. Trusdale."

"Sir, I don't know what *implicate* means."

"Do you expect us to believe someone framed you for this heinous murder?"

Trusdale considered, twisting his hands together. At last he said, "Maybe somebody took it by mistake and throwed it away."

Mizell looked out at the rapt gallery. "Did anyone here take Mr. Trusdale's hat by mistake?"

There was silence, except for the snow hitting the windows. The first big storm of winter had arrived. That was the winter townsfolk called the Wolf Winter, because the wolves came down from the Black Hills in packs to hunt for garbage.

"I have no more questions," Mizell said. "And due to the weather we are going to dispense with any closing statements. The jury will retire to consider a verdict. You have three choices, gentlemen—innocent, manslaughter, or murder in the first degree."

"Girlslaughter, more like it," someone remarked.

Sheriff Barclay and Dave Fisher retired to the Chuck-a-Luck. Abel Hines joined them, brushing snow from the shoulders of his coat. Dale Gerard served them schooners of beer on the house.

"Mizell might not have had any more questions," Barclay said, "but I got one. Never mind the hat. If Trusdale killed her, how come we never found that silver dollar?"

"Because he got scared and threw it away," Hines said.

"I don't think so. He's too bone-stupid. If he'd had that dollar, he'd have gone back to the Chuck-a-Luck and drunk it up."

"What are you saying?" Dave asked. "That you think he's innocent?"

"I'm saying I wish we'd found that cartwheel."

"Maybe he lost it out a hole in his pocket."

"He didn't have any holes in his pockets," Barclay said. "Only one in his boot, and it wasn't big enough for a dollar to get through." He drank some of his beer. The tumbleweeds blowing up Main Street looked like ghostly brains in the snow.

The jury took an hour and a half. "We voted to hang him on the first ballot," Kelton Fisher said later, "but we wanted it to look decent."

Mizell asked Trusdale if he had anything to say before sentence was passed.

"I can't think of nothing," Trusdale said. "Just I never killed that girl."

The storm blew for three days. John House asked Barclay how much he reckoned Trusdale weighed, and Barclay said he guessed the man went around one-forty. House made a dummy out of burlap sacks and filled it with stones, weighing it on the hostelry scales until the needle stood pat on one-forty. Then he hanged the dummy while half the town stood around in the snowdrifts and watched. The trial run went all right.

On the night before the execution, the weather cleared. Sheriff Barclay told Trusdale he could have anything he wanted for dinner. Trusdale asked for steak and eggs, with home fries on the side soaked in gravy. Barclay paid for it out of his own pocket, then sat at his desk cleaning his fingernails and listening to the steady clink of Trusdale's knife and fork on the china plate. When it stopped, he went in. Trusdale was sitting on his bunk. His plate was so clean Barclay figured he must have lapped up the last of the gravy like a dog. He was crying.

"Something just come to me," Trusdale said.

"What's that, Jim?"

"If they hang me tomorrow morning, I'll go into my grave with steak and eggs still in my belly. It won't have no chance to work through."

For a moment Barclay said nothing. He was horrified not by the image but because Trusdale had thought of it. Then he said, "Wipe your nose."

Trusdale wiped it.

"Now listen to me, Jim, because this is your last chance. You were in that bar in the middle of the afternoon. Not many people in there then. Isn't that right?"

"I guess it is."

"Then who took your hat? Close your eyes. Think back. See it."

Trusdale closed his eyes. Barclay waited. At last Trusdale opened his eyes, which were red from crying. "I can't even remember was I wearing it."

Barclay sighed. "Give me your plate, and mind that knife."

Trusdale handed the plate through the bars with the knife and fork laid on it, and said he wished he could have some beer. Barclay thought it over, then put on his heavy coat and Stetson and walked down to the Chuck-a-Luck, where he got a small pail of beer from Dale Gerard. Undertaker Hines was just finishing a glass of wine. He followed Barclay out.

"Big day tomorrow," Barclay said. "There hasn't been a hanging here in ten years, and with luck there won't be another for ten more. I'll be gone out of the job by then. I wish I was now."

Hines looked at him. "You really don't think he killed her."

"If he didn't," Barclay said, "whoever did is still walking around."

The hanging was at nine o'clock the next morning. The day was windy and bitterly cold, but most of the town turned out to watch. Pastor Ray Rowles stood on the scaffold next to John House. Both of them were shivering in spite of their coats and scarves. The pages of Pastor Rowles's Bible fluttered. Tucked into House's belt, also fluttering, was a hood of homespun cloth dyed black.

Barclay led Trusdale, his hands cuffed behind his back, to the gallows. Trusdale was all right until he got to the steps, then he began to buck and cry.

"Don't do this," he said. "Please don't do this to me. Please don't hurt me. Please don't kill me."

He was strong for a little man, and Barclay motioned Dave Fisher to come and lend a hand. Together they muscled Trusdale, twisting and ducking and pushing, up the twelve wooden steps.

Once he bucked so hard all three of them almost fell off, and arms reached up to catch them if they did.

"Quit that and die like a man!" someone shouted.

On the platform, Trusdale was momentarily quiet, but when Pastor Rowles commenced Psalm 51, he began to scream. "Like a woman with her tit caught in the wringer," someone said later in the Chuck-a-Luck.

"Have mercy on me, O God, after thy great goodness," Rowles read, raising his voice to be heard above the condemned man's shrieks to be let off. "According to the multitude of thy mercies, do away with mine offenses."

When Trusdale saw House take the black hood out of his belt, he began to pant like a dog. He shook his head from side to side, trying to dodge the hood. His hair flew. House followed each jerk patiently, like a man who means to bridle a skittish horse.

"Let me look at the mountains!" Trusdale bellowed. Runners of snot hung from his nostrils. "I'll be good if you let me look at the mountains one more time!"

But House only jammed the hood over Trusdale's head and pulled it down to his shaking shoulders. Pastor Rowles was droning on, and Trusdale tried to run off the trapdoor. Barclay and Fisher pushed him back onto it. Down below, someone cried, "Ride 'em, cowboy!"

"Say amen," Barclay told Pastor Rowles. "For Christ's sake, say amen."

"Amen," Pastor Rowles said, and stepped back, closing his Bible with a clap.

Barclay nodded to House. House pulled the lever. The greased beam retracted and the trap dropped. So did Trusdale. There was a crack when his neck broke. His legs drew up almost to his chin, then fell back limp. Yellow drops stained the snow under his feet.

"There, you bastard!" Rebecca Cline's father shouted. "Died pissing like a dog on a fireplug. Welcome to Hell." A few people clapped.

The spectators stayed until Trusdale's corpse, still wearing the black hood, was laid in the same hurry-up wagon he'd ridden to town in. Then they dispersed.

Barclay went back to the jail and sat in the cell Trusdale had occupied. He sat there for ten minutes. It was cold enough to see his breath. He knew what he was waiting for, and eventually it came. He picked up the small bucket that had held Trusdale's last drink of beer and vomited. Then he went into his office and stoked up the stove.

He was still there eight hours later, trying to read a book, when Abel Hines came in. He said, "You need to come down to the funeral parlor, Otis. There's something I want to show you."

"What?"

"No. You'll want to see it for yourself."

They walked down to the Hines Funeral Parlor & Mortuary. In the back room, Trusdale lay naked on a cooling board. There was a smell of chemicals and shit.

"They load their pants when they die that way," Hines said. "Even men who go to it with their heads up. They can't help it. The sphincter lets go."

"And?"

"Step over here. I figure a man in your job has seen worse than a pair of shitty drawers."

They lay on the floor, mostly turned inside out. Something gleamed in the mess. Barclay leaned closer and saw it was a silver dollar. He reached down and plucked it from the crap.

"I don't understand it," Hines said. "Son of a bitch was locked up a good long time."

There was a chair in the corner. Barclay sat down on it so heavily he made a little *woof* sound. "He must have swallowed it the first time when he saw our lanterns coming. And every time it came out he cleaned it off and swallowed it again."

The two men stared at each other.

"You believed him," Hines said at last.

"Fool that I am, I did."

"Maybe that says more about you than it does about him."

"He went on saying he was innocent right to the end. He'll most likely stand at the throne of God saying the same thing."

"Yes," Hines said.

"I don't understand. He was going to hang. Either way, he was going to hang. Do you understand it?"

"I don't even understand why the sun comes up. What are you going to do with that cartwheel? Give it back to the girl's mother and father? It might be better if you didn't, because . . ." Hines shrugged.

Because the Clines knew all along. Everyone in town knew all along. He was the only one who hadn't known. Fool that he was.

"I don't know what I'm going to do with it," he said.

The wind gusted, bringing the sound of singing. It was coming from the church. It was the Doxology.

ELMORE LEONARD

For Something to Do

FROM *Charlie Martz and Other Stories*

1955

PAST HOWELL, HE kept the speedometer needle at seventy for almost six miles, until he was in sight of the mailbox. Then he eased his foot from the accelerator, braked, and turned off the highway onto the road that cut back through the trees. The road was little wider than his car, a dim, rutted passageway that twice climbed into small clearings, but through most of its quarter of a mile kept to tree-covered dimness until it opened onto the yard and the one-story white farmhouse. He left the car in the gravel drive and went in the side door. It was almost seven o'clock in the evening.

"Ev?"

He heard Julie's voice and passed through the kitchen to see his wife at the end of the hall coming out of the bedroom. She went to him quickly, kissing him and holding herself against him for a moment before looking up.

"I was starting to worry—"

"They haven't been here?" Evan asked.

His wife's hair, smooth dark, parted on the side and clipped with a silver barrette, hung almost to her shoulders, where it turned up softly and moved as she shook her head. She was twenty-three, with a slight, boyish figure, a perhaps too-thin face, though her features were delicately small and even, and with freckles she did not try to conceal because her husband liked them.

"Did they call?" asked Evan.

"Not a word since Cal telephoned this morning."

"If they left Detroit at two . . ." Evan paused. "Isn't that what Cal said?"

Julie nodded. "He was picking up Ray at two o'clock and coming right on."

"They would've been here three hours ago if he did."

She started to smile as she said, "Maybe they were in an accident." In the dimness, but with light coming from the kitchen doorway, her teeth were small and white against the warm brown of her face.

Evan smiled too, looking at his wife and feeling her close to him. "Thank God for small blessings."

"Or Cal forgot the way," she said.

"Or they stopped at a bar."

Her smile faded. "That's all we'd need." She followed Evan into the kitchen and leaned against the white-painted, oilcloth-covered table as he washed his hands at the sink. She liked to watch him as he lathered his hands vigorously, then rinsed them until the callused palms glistened yellow-pink and fresh-looking. She liked what she called his "honest farmer tan": face and arms a deep brown, with a line across his forehead and upper arms where the color ended abruptly. She even liked his "farmer haircut," with too much thinned out from the sides—just as he liked her freckles and the way her hair moved when she shook her head. They had been married less than a year and noticing and liking these things about one another were as important as anything they shared.

"I was beginning to worry about you," she said.

"It took longer than I thought it would."

"A reluctant calf?"

Evan nodded, drying his hands.

"Did he pay you?"

"Not yet."

"He didn't pay for the brucellosis shots either."

"He will, when he gets his wheat check."

"Eight miles both ways and I'll bet he didn't even thank you."

"He mumbled something."

"Ev, that's a sixteen-mile round trip . . . and a messy afternoon in his barn. For what? Eight or nine dollars."

He looked at her curiously. "That wasn't a child I delivered, it was a calf."

"Four years of veterinary medicine to charge eight dollars—"

"Twenty-five. I had to cut."

"It's still too little, with the attention you give."

"Do you expect him to pay more than the calf's worth?"

She shook her head faintly. "Good Sam."

He frowned, moving toward her. "Julie, what's the matter with you?"

"I'm sorry."

"You sound like Cal, talking about money like that."

"I said I was sorry."

For a moment Evan was silent. "You're upset about them coming, aren't you?" He was standing close to her now, and he drew her against him gently. "All of a sudden you sound like a different person. Listen, don't let him get you down like that."

She closed her eyes, her arms going around his waist. "I was afraid they'd come while you were gone. Then I hoped they would because I didn't want you to be here."

"The worrier."

"Ev, this isn't like the little worries. First I thought, *It's better if you and Ray don't meet.* Then I thought, *No, I don't want to be here alone.* And I wasn't sure which would be worse."

"Julie, Ray knows you're married."

"That's just it."

"But you went with the guy for two years. He can't be that bad."

"He was hard to get along with and conceited and . . . I don't know. I can't even think of one thing in his favor."

"Well, maybe he's grown up."

"I think that would be asking too much," Julie said.

They spoke little during supper.

Julie thought of Ray Perris. She had gone with him during her senior year in high school and off and on during her first two years at Michigan State, whenever she came home to Detroit and Ray bothered to call her. Then, in her third year, shortly after Ray was called into the army, she met Evan. There was no formal breakup with Ray, no ring to return, no goodbye. Ray never wrote, only once called her when he was home on furlough; and as far as Julie knew, Ray was still unaware that she was married. Until now. Not long ago she'd heard that Ray was out of the army and had become a professional fighter. This didn't surprise her. He had entered the Golden Gloves in high school, but, it seemed to Julie, more for the sake of wanting to be known as a fighter than for the actual boxing. Since meeting Evan, the only time she thought of Ray was to wonder how she could have ever gone with him. Perhaps only because she had been seventeen.

Then the phone call this morning from Cal, her cousin. Ray was in Detroit and he was bringing him out. And from that moment, suddenly realizing she was going to see Ray again and not wanting to see him, she was afraid.

Evan thought about Cal. How he would pull up into the drive unexpectedly, uninvited, and sit in the living room with them until all the beer was gone. Cal was twenty-three, Julie's age, four years younger than Evan; but aside from that they had almost nothing in common.

The first few times he came, Evan tried hard to like him. He offered to show him around the farm, but Cal wasn't interested. For conversation he brought up the Detroit Tigers, Lions, and Red Wings, in that order, going from baseball to football to hockey. But Cal was a fight fan, and Evan was familiar with few names, none of them current, in the boxing world.

Cal did talk. After a few cans of beer he carried the conversation and invariably his remarks were directed to Julie.

Why would anybody who knew better want to live in the sticks? I mean what do you do for kicks, sit and look at each other? Nothing to do, you work your francis off and all you got to show for it is a one-story house and a four-year-old car. If Ev wants to be a vet—I mean it takes all kinds of people, believe me—why don't he get one of those dog and cat deals? Plenty of them in Detroit and those guys are making dough.

Evan argued with him mildly the first few times, but when he realized his anger was rising he would stop. It wasn't worth it. Cal had more success with Julie. She was easily drawn into an argument, as if she were obligated to talk some sense into Cal, to make him see that living on a farm and not making much money didn't necessarily mean you weren't happy. And when she became angry, Evan would see Cal smile. A number of times he had to restrain himself from throwing Cal out bodily.

Evan would tell himself, *The next time he opens his mouth, out he goes. Even if he is her cousin.* But he sat quietly and put up with Cal, because he couldn't help feeling a little sorry for him.

But it's not the same now, Evan thought. *It's nice to be nice, but you can carry it too far.*

He thought then, *You're feeling sorry for yourself.*

But that wasn't it, for he was almost always completely honest with himself. He was thinking that he and Julie had been married for almost a year and everything was going smoothly, but for one moment this afternoon his wife had sounded like Cal and she had not even been aware of it.

You did not let a man ruin your marriage or even try to or begin to or even have it remotely in mind. That, you did something about.

They had eaten supper and were doing the dishes when the two-tone ivory-and-green station wagon swung onto the drive and came to a sudden, gravel-skidding, nose-down stop behind Evan's car. The horn blew, and kept blowing until Julie and Evan came out on the front porch.

They heard Cal's voice as he got out of the station wagon, almost stumbling, slamming the door, and Julie closed her eyes. When she opened them he was coming toward the porch. "We were starting to worry about you."

Cal winked at Evan as if they were old friends. "That's the day."

"What happened to you?" Julie's gaze went to the station wagon as she spoke. The curved windshield was green-tinted and she could not make out the figure behind the wheel, though she was certain it was Ray Perris.

"We stopped for some hunting," Cal answered. "Ray figured if we're going out in the woods let's have some fun. So you know what the punchy guy does? He stops at a hardware store and buys two .30-30s." Cal snapped his fingers. "Just like that. The guy's loaded."

"You stopped for more than that," Julie said.

"So we picked up a case of beer."

Evan watched him. Cal stood with his hands on his hips, one blunt-toed cordovan shoe in front of and almost perpendicular to the other in a fencinglike pose. "You're a little early for the hunting season," Evan said.

Cal looked up at him. "Is that right, doctor?"

"What were you hunting?"

"I don't know. What lives in the woods?"

Don't let him get you, Evan thought, and he said, nodding to the station wagon, "What about your friend?"

"He's a shy guy." Cal grinned. "Waits to be invited." His eyes went to Julie. "Ask your old boyfriend in for a beer."

"I think you've already had enough."

"Is that right?"

"You could hardly get out of the car."

"Is that right?" Cal turned to the station wagon. "Ray, we're going to get a drunkometer test!"

"Cal, act right today, *please!*"

They heard the car door open and slam closed. Cal said, "There's a real bomb. Two hundred and thirty horses. Digs out from zero to sixty in ten flat. Something?"

Neither Julie nor Evan answered. They were watching Ray Perris rounding the back end of the station wagon, taking his time, his hands in the back pockets of his khaki pants.

He wore a tight-fitting short-sleeved yellow-and-white sport shirt, and both of his forearms bore tattoos: a tombstone with the inscription IN MEMORY OF MOTHER on the right arm, and on the left a dagger with RAY in ornate, serifed letters on the hilt. Air Corps–type sunglasses covered his eyes (though the sun was off behind the trees and it was almost dark), and his dark hair, curling low on his forehead, was thick and combed straight back on the sides. At the nape of his neck his hair ended abruptly in a straight line.

Cal scratched idly about his shirtfront. He was hatless, with light-colored hair that was crewcut on top and long on the sides, and his entire face, pale and angular, seemed creased as he smiled.

"Ray's next fight's in Saginaw," Cal said. "So he figured, hell, train at home for a change."

Perris nodded. "Besides wanting to see Julie." He was staring at her, ignoring Evan.

She tried to smile. "It's nice to see you, Ray. I don't believe you've met my husband—"

It was Evan's turn to smile, but his mouth was set firmly and his expression didn't change as he extended his hand and almost drew it back before Perris eased his from his back pocket.

"Cal said you were hunting," Julie said to him.

"We shot sixteen beer cans."

"You should've had Ev with you." Julie stopped. "I mean, if it was the season. Ev was practically born in the woods—hunts every year, sets traps in the winter." She watched them shake hands briefly.

As they did, Cal said, "Like in the ring, huh, man?"

Perris's hands went to his back pockets again and he stood hip-cocked, looking at Julie. "This cousin of yours, all he wants to talk about is fights."

"He's already notched twenty-three wins," Cal said. "Only lost four and drawed one. Another year and he's in line for a shot at the middleweight title. How about that?" Cal paused. "You know what they call him around the gym? Tony."

"Tony?" Julie said.

"Tony Curtis! You don't see it?"

Julie nodded, not sure if he was serious. "There's some resemblance."

"*Some*—hell, he looks like his twin!"

Perris was studying the house. His gaze moved to the chicken house and, beyond that, the barn. His eyes returned to Julie as he said, "How much land you got?"

"Eighty-five acres, most of it wheat. Some corn. Of course Ev doesn't have time to work it all now, with his practice. A neighbor sharecrops it for us."

"How much money does this Ev make?"

The question startled her and she hesitated before saying, "We get along fine."

"He makes about four thousand a year," Cal said. "Tops."

Perris grinned. "I can lose and make that in one night. Honey, if all you got out of school was him, you should've stayed home."

She glanced at Evan and away from him quickly. "You can't help whom you fall in love with." She smiled as if carrying on a joke.

Cal said, "While Ray is off in the Arm Service."

"Ev and I would've gotten married even if Ray had stayed home!"

Cal shrugged. "That's not the way I see it. Ray turns his back and the horse doctor comes along."

"I don't care how you see it! All you want to do is argue. You've nothing better to do than that."

"Nobody's asking me," Perris said. "I don't think you'd of married him either. What do you think of that?"

Julie hesitated to control her voice. "I think you've had too much to drink."

"And what's Ev think about it?" Perris turned, his expression cold and partly concealed by the sunglasses. "What's old Ev the horse doctor think about it?"

Evan met his gaze squarely. He stood with his feet apart, unmoving, and said, "You better get out of here right now. That's what I think."

"Ray," Julie said quickly. "There was never anything between us. That's what makes this whole thing so silly." She stopped. Perris was not paying any attention to her.

"What was that, Ev?"

"You heard what I said."

"Something about getting out."

"I can't say it any plainer."

Cal grinned. "Man, he's talking now."

"Asking for it," Perris said.

"Sure." Cal nodded. "Why don't you deck him and get it over with."

"I'm waiting for him."

"You got a long wait."

"Stop it!" Julie stared at Ray Perris, her face flushed and tight with anger. "What are you, some kind of an animal that you fight over nothing? Ray, I swear if you even make a fist I'll call the state police!"

Perris glanced at Cal. "Take her inside and open the beers. I'll be right in."

"Ray, I swear—" Cal's hand closed on her arm and pulled her off balance. "Let go of me!" She saw Evan rushing at Cal and then she screamed.

Ray Perris took a half step and drove his fist into Evan's body, stopping him in his stride, and as he doubled over, Perris's left stung against the side of his jaw and he went to his knees.

Perris stood close to him, waiting. Beyond, past his legs, he saw Cal forcing Julie up to the porch. Cal stopped to watch and called out, "Ray, be careful of those hands!"

Evan breathed in and out, getting his breath, then lunged at Perris, swinging his right with everything he could put behind it.

Perris came inside, taking the roundhouse on his shoulder, and threw four jabs pistonlike into Evan's body. Even went back, staggered by the force of the short punches, and Perris came after him. Evan tried to bring up his guard, but Perris feinted him high and drove his left in; and when Evan's guard dropped, Perris threw the right that had been cocked, waiting. It chopped into Evan's face and he felt the ground slam the back of his head and jolt through his whole body.

He felt himself being dragged by his legs, heard his wife's voice but wasn't sure of it. Then he was lying, half leaning against a tree. He felt his shoes being pulled off and he opened his eyes.

Perris was walking away from him toward the station wagon. He saw him look at it, then open it again and take out the two .30-30s. He held both under one arm, the shoes in the other hand, and called to Evan, "You touch that car and I'll break your jaw!"

He turned and walked to the house. On the porch he said something to Cal, who was standing in the doorway holding Julie. Cal came outside. He went to Evan's car and let the air out of both rear tires, then returned to the house. The door closed and there was no sound in the yard.

He was perhaps sixty feet from the porch, not straight out from it but off toward the side where the cars were parked; and as he lay propped against the tree staring at the house, at the lighted living room windows, not believing that this had actually happened, his lips parted with a thick throbbing half numbness, he tried to assemble the thoughts that raced through his mind.

He thought of Julie, forcing himself to remain calm as he did. He pictured himself getting a pitchfork from the barn and breaking down the door. Then he remembered the .30-30s.

They wouldn't shoot. No? You think they're not capable of it? And they're drunk—beyond what little reason they have. This doesn't happen, does it?

He could run for help. Even without shoes he could run down to the highway and stop a car, get to the state police at Brighton.

He pictured the blue-and-gold police car pulling up and two troopers going into the house and Cal and Ray looking up, surprised, and one of the troopers saying, "Don't give your pals so much to drink and they won't get out of hand." He saw Cal wink at Ray, waiting for the troopers to leave.

He was aware of the night sounds: an owl far off; crickets in the yard close to the house and in the full darkness of the woods behind him.

No, he thought. *You do it yourself. You have to get them out. You have to do it so that it's once and for all, or else they'll come back again. They're not afraid of you, but they have to be made afraid. Do you understand that?*

He heard the owl again and he could feel the deep woods behind him.

The woods . . .

For perhaps a quarter of an hour more he remained in the shadows, thinking, asking himself questions and groping for the answers, and finally he knew what he would do.

His hand went up the rough bark of the tree to steady him as he got to his feet. He moved along the edge of shadow until the station wagon was between him and the house, then stooped slightly, instinctively, and ran across the yard to his car.

With his hand on the door handle he noticed the ventipane partly open. He pulled it out to a right angle, then put his arm in, pressing his right side against the car door, rolled down the window, brought out his veterinary kit, and stooped to the ground with it.

The inside pocket, he thought, remembering putting his instruments away after delivering the calf that afternoon. His hand went in, came out with a three-ounce bottle of chloroform; went in again, felt the mouth speculum—*no, too heavy*—then his fingers closed on the steel handle of a hoof knife and he drew it out, a thin-bladed knife curved to a sharpened hook.

The rifles, he thought then. *No, they won't follow you without the rifles. Just bring them out.*

From the edge of the drive he picked up a rock twice the size of his fist, walked to within six feet of the station wagon, and hurled it through the windshield. He waited until the front door swung suddenly open, then ran for the trees, hearing Cal's voice, then Ray's, hearing them on the steps—

"There he is!"

"Get the guns!" Ray's voice as he ran to the station wagon.

Cal came out of the house with the rifles, and Ray said, "Come on!"

"Where'd he go?"

"Not far without shoes."

From the shadows again, but deeper into the trees, Evan watched them for a moment. They stood close together, Perris talking, describing something with his hands, then taking a rifle from Cal, the two of them separating and coming toward the trees. Evan moved back carefully, working his way over to where Cal would enter. Perris was nearer the road, perhaps thirty yards away.

Evan crouched, waiting, hearing the rustling, twig-snapping sound of them moving through the scrub growth and fallen leaves. Cal was coming almost directly toward him.

He let Cal pass—one step, another—then rose without a sound and was on him, one hand clamping Cal's mouth, the other pressing the hoof knife against his side hard enough that he would feel the blade. He felt Cal go rigid and he pushed against him, turning him to make him walk to the left now, broadening the distance between them and Perris.

About twenty yards farther on Evan stopped. His hand came away from Cal's mouth, went to his shirt pocket, and brought out the chloroform.

Cal didn't move, but he said, "Ray's going to beat you blue."

Evan said nothing, putting the hoof knife under his arm. He drew his handkerchief and saturated it with chloroform, then retuned the bottle to his pocket. "How is Julie?"

"She locked herself in the bedroom."

"Did he touch her?"

"Ask him."

"All right, Cal. Call him over."

"What?"

"Go ahead, call him."

Cal hesitated. Suddenly he screamed, "Ray, he's over here!"

The sound of his voice cut the stillness, rang through the darkness of the trees and was loud in Evan's ear as he clamped the handkerchief against Cal's face and dragged him as he struggled into dense brush. In a moment Cal was on the ground, unconscious. Evan picked up the rifle and started running. He heard Ray's voice and the sound of him hurrying through the foliage and he called back over his shoulder, "Come on!"

He kept running, driving through the brush, feeling sharp stabs of pain in his stocking feet, and twice again he called back to Perris, making sure he was following. Within a hundred yards he reached the end of the woods.

The first quarter moon showed an expanse of plowed field and, far off on the other side, a shapeless mass of trees against the night sky. He turned right along the edge of the field for a few yards, then moved silently back into the woods. Not far in, he crouched down to wait.

There was little time to spare. In less than a minute Perris reached the field and stopped. He scanned it, his eyes open wide in the darkness.

"Cal?"

There was a dead stillness now, without even the small, hidden night sounds in the background.

"Cal, where are you?"

Perris turned from the field. Uncertain, he hesitated, then started into the trees again.

Now, Evan thought. He flipped the lever of the .30-30 down and up and a sharp metallic sound, unmistakable in the stillness, reached Ray Perris.

He stopped. Then edged back to the field.

"Cal?"

Evan waited. Through the trees Perris was silhouetted against the field. Watching him, Evan thought, *Now add it up, Ray.*

He saw Perris turn to the field again and without warning break into a run. Evan brought the rifle to his shoulder and fired. Dirt kicked up somewhere close in front of Perris and he stopped abruptly, turned, stumbling, and went down as he reached the trees again.

Then—"Ev, what's the matter with you!"

Silence.

"Ev, we were just clownin' around! Cal says, 'Come on out and see Julie.' I said, 'Fine.' On the way out he says, 'We'll throw a scare into Evan.' You know, for something to do, that's all. We'd had some beers and that sounded OK with me. What the hell, the way Cal talked I figured you for a real hayseed. Then we come here and you get on the muscle. Get mean about it. What am I supposed to do, let you throw me out? I'm not built that way."

He was quiet for a moment.

"Ev, I'll forget about the car. You were burned up—OK, I'll let it go. What the hell, it's insured."

Silence.

"You hear? Answer me!"

Just like that, Evan thought. *Forget all about it. No, Ray, you're not scared enough yet. You might want to come back.* He raised the rifle, aiming high, and fired again, and the sound rocked out over the field.

"Ev, you're a crazy man! They lock up guys like you!"

Now you're talking, Ray.

Minutes passed before Perris spoke again.

"Ev, listen to me, I'm walking back to my car, and if you shoot it's murder. You understand that? Murder!"

Suddenly Perris stood up. "Answer me!" He screamed it. "You hear what I said? I'm coming out, and if you shoot it's murder! . . . You go to Jackson for life!

"I'm coming now, Ev." He started into the trees. "Listen, man, just hold on to yourself. You're burned up, sure, but it isn't worth it. I mean, not Jackson the rest of your life. You got to think of it that way."

Perris started to run.

Evan was waiting. He gauged the distance, crawled to the next brush clump, and came up swinging the rifle as Perris tried to run past. The barrel slashed down against the .30-30 in his hands and he went back, dropping it, trying to cover, but was too late. Evan's fist whapped against his face and he stumbled. He tried to rush, bringing his hands up suddenly as the rifle was thrown at him, deflected it, ducking to the side, and looked up in time to receive the full impact of a right that was swung wide and hard and with every pound that could be put behind it. Evan kneeled over him and pressed the chloroformed handkerchief to Ray's face before carrying him back to the yard.

Julie was on the porch. She screamed his name when she saw Evan, but he talked to her for a moment and after that she was calm. He went back for Cal, then loaded both of them into the station wagon and drove down to the highway, turned left toward Detroit, and went about a mile before parking the station wagon off on the side of the road.

They would come out of the chloroform in fifteen or twenty minutes. If the state police found them first, let Perris tell whatever he liked. Even the truth, if he didn't mind the publicity that might result. It didn't matter to Evan what he did. It was over.

He crossed the plowed field and passed again through the woods, picking up his hoof knife on the way back to the house.

Julie held open the door. “Ev, what if they come back?”

“I doubt if they will.”

“Then we won’t think about it,” she said.

They sat in the living room for a few minutes, then went out to the kitchen to finish the dishes.

EVAN LEWIS

The Continental Opposite

FROM *Alfred Hitchcock's Mystery Magazine*

JUDGING BY THE old man's hands, I'd have tagged him at sixty. The confidence and economy of his movements might shave ten years from that, but the truth was in his eyes. Those eyes had seen Lincoln shot and Caesar stabbed, and were probably watching when Cain killed Abel. Now they were watching me, and chilled me down to my toenails.

I decided that thinking of him as the "old man" was an understatement. At that moment, forever and always, he became the Old Man.

My letter informing the grand pooh-bahs of Continental Investigations that the head of their Portland bureau was in bed with the Mob had brought this stocky old coot to my door, and I'd brought him here to the Boom Boom Room. In this bright new year of 1953, our fair city boasted eight burlesque clubs, seventeen gambling hells, and forty-three houses of ill repute. As the sole establishment qualifying in all three categories, the Boom was pretty much our Grand Central Station of crime.

The Old Man fished a pack of Fatimas from his pocket, got one burning, and examined me sourly through the smoke.

I could imagine what he saw: a punk kid, just back from fighting Commies in Korea, playing at the gumshoe game. A punk kid who'd accused his boss—a man with thirty years of crime-fighting under his belt—of betraying his own kind.

I picked up my drink, Dewar's neat, and rolled some over my tongue. It tasted clean and strong, the opposite of the way I felt.

"You've made serious allegations," the Old Man said. "Have any evidence to keep them company?"

He read the answer on my face.

I slumped in my chair, wishing the bigwigs had sent somebody —*anybody*—else.

He'd told me his name, but warned me not to use it, and with good reason. It was dynamite. In detective circles, this Buddha-shaped relic was a legend. Scuttlebutt said he'd been a real fire-breather during Prohibition—particularly around San Francisco —and the list of swindlers, yeggs, and killers he'd brought to justice would fill a rogues' gallery to the brim. But sometime in the forties the Continental had put him out to pasture, and he'd spent the years since killing a vegetable garden, sneering at golf courses, and not catching fish. The agency's call to investigate my claims had come just in time to save him from a life of perpetual bingo.

Still, the guy intimidated me. I'd never met anyone so confident, so self-contained, so utterly uncaring of other people's opinions. The last thing I wanted was this all-knowing, all-seeing Master of Detectives judging my every move.

I fished for a way to begin. "How well do you know Portland?"

The Old Man's shoulders rolled in a noncommittal way. "We've cuddled," he said, "but never kissed."

At a table near the stage, next to a placard reading THIS WEEK ONLY—LADY GODIVA AND HER PRANCING PALOMINO, five men eyed each other over cards. I pointed my forehead at them.

"That bruiser with the gold teeth and glass eye is captain of the North Precinct. The slick gent sporting the five-carat pinkie ring is our illustrious mayor, and likely our next governor."

The Old Man gave that the attention it deserved: a shrug.

"But here's the kicker. The mottle-faced man peeking at the mayor's cards runs the East County slot-machine racket. The bozo in the rainbow bow tie collects twenty percent every time some john buys a jane. And the sharp-nosed lad with the pince-nez has slaughtered more men than Jimmy Cagney and Edward G. Robinson combined."

The Old Man shrugged again, but this one lacked conviction.

I went on. "This town is a disease. It gets into the blood and rots people from the inside out. And my boss is no exception. He's taking orders from the local crime lord."

The Old Man's lips grew thin as knife blades. "And who's that?"

I was about to name him when a thin citizen with undertaker eyes and a waxed mustache appeared at our table, a highball glass in each well-manicured hand.

He was Nick Zartell, owner of the Boom Boom Room, and one of the five or six most dangerous men on the West Coast. He was also the reason I'd left home at sixteen and joined the army as soon as they'd take me.

I said, "Times must be tough, Nick, you waiting your own tables."

He grinned without humor, displaying the points of sharklike teeth. "Evening, Pete. This your grandpappy? Must be past his bedtime."

The Old Man's eyes glinted like bullets.

"It's his birthday," I said. "He just turned a hundred and fifty. Something on your mind?"

"Thought maybe we had something to celebrate," he said. "You here to accept my job offer?"

He placed one of the drinks carefully on the table in front of me, lifted the other to his lips and downed it.

I turned a tarnished silver ring around my finger, rubbed a thumb over the smooth jade stone. The ring had been my father's, and was all that remained of him.

I pushed the glass away. "Not today."

Zartell nodded at the stage. "You staying for the burly-que? You'd make your ma proud."

A coolness washed over me. "She's here?"

"Not today. But she'd hear about it."

From him, no doubt. And it would give my mother great satisfaction to know I was as human as the next chump. It was a satisfaction I was determined to deny her.

I was hunting a suitable comeback when the Old Man wrapped a stubby hand around the highball glass, made the liquor vanish, and let out a prodigious belch.

Zartell waved the fumes away. "That geezer needs a shot of Geritol," he said, and left.

We watched until he passed behind the bar and oozed through a doorway.

"I take it," the Old Man said, "that you and Nick are well acquainted."

"He wanted to be my stepfather once, but my mother gave him the air."

"A woman of discriminating tastes."

"Not so much," I said. "She lived with him six years before doing it."

If the Old Man had any thoughts on that subject, he kept them to himself.

"Thought you'd like a look at him," I said. "He's the local crime lord."

The Old Man did something with his lips that sent spiders crawling up my back.

It was even scarier when I realized it was a smile.

Rain soaked my hat and made rivers on my overcoat as we strolled down Salmon Street toward the Portland home of Continental Investigations, Inc. Next to me, the Old Man remained relatively dry. Wide as he was, he had a way of sliding between the raindrops. There was no justice in it.

I said, "Sure you want to do this?"

"We're doing it."

The old guy had never met my boss, Harold Abernathy, and wanted to size him up.

"How do I introduce you? As my grandfather?"

"Uncle." There was acid in his voice.

"How about a name?"

He considered that. "Tracy will do."

"Can I call you Uncle Dick?"

He curled a lip. "Make it Sam. Better yet, Samuel. Now spill the dope on Abernathy and Zartell."

I spilled.

For the past three months, I explained, I'd been collecting envelopes from Zartell and placing them in the fat greasy hand of my boss. Zartell insisted I be the go-between, claiming he didn't trust his own men with cash. That was probably true enough, but the real reason was he liked reminding me my side of the fence was no cleaner than his. Three weeks ago the envelopes got fatter—much fatter—and I knew something big was coming. That's when I wrote the agency.

Next time Zartell phoned, I was ready. Abernathy took the call in his office, and I beat it down to the furnace room, where a certain loose pipe funnels sound from the boss's heat vent.

"I didn't get much," I finished up. "I heard Abernathy say, 'That Chinese gentleman is no baby to fool with. This will require extra funding.'"

The Old Man's eyes gleamed. "And this Chinese gentleman?"

"Abernathy dropped no names, but I've had my ears peeled since."

We had half a block of silence before the Old Man said, "I knew your father."

That stopped me flat. My father, known as Slippery Ed Collins, had been a rumrunner during the Roaring Twenties, and worked himself up to Zartell's lieutenant by 1939, when pieces of him started turning up along the banks of the Willamette River. One of those pieces was a bloated hand wearing his trademark jade ring. My entry into the crime-fighting business was based at least in part on a desire to even up with the universe.

Five paces ahead, the Old Man turned, saying, "I can't believe he named you Peter."

I believed it, but I'd had twenty-odd years to get used to the idea. In underworld slang, "Peter Collins" meant "nobody." To my father, it had been a great joke. To me, it was more an indication of what I'd meant to him.

I said, "How'd you know him?"

"Put him away once," he said, "for an armored car job." And despite my cajoling would say no more.

After a stop at a newsstand, where the Old Man shelled out a quarter for a pulp magazine, we risked our necks in the rickety elevator serving Portland's venerable Victory Building. Emerging on the third floor, I led him past the offices of a cut-rate secretarial service, an unlicensed accountant, and a shyster lawyer, stopping at a glass-paneled door.

The inscription—CONTINENTAL INVESTIGATIONS, INC.—brought a grimace.

"That new moniker," the Old Man said, "is the bunk."

I pretended to agree. But hell, the detective agency had been operating since the Civil War, establishing branch offices in every major American city—and plenty of minor ones too. If the head hawkshaws back east wanted to update their image, it was no skin off my butt.

I laid a hand on the latch. "Here we go, then. Through the looking glass." And through we went.

Harold Abernathy, a neckless toad of a man with four eyes and three chins, squatted behind his desk, one hand in the drawer he thought hid his bottle of Canadian Club. He removed the hand, threw me a scowl, and examined the fat Old Man like something he'd found on the sole of his shoe.

I said, "Chief, meet my Uncle Sam."

The Old Man's cheek twitched, but he stuck out a paw and smiled like a halfwit. "Samuel Tracy," he said. "Young Pete here's been singing your praises up, down, and sideways. Makes you sound like the reincarnation of Sherlock Holmes."

Abernathy ignored the paw, saying, "I trust you gentlemen will excuse me. I have a lot to—"

"Say no more. I understand perfectly." The Old Man slid into the chair facing Abernathy and said, "I was in the detective game myself, you know, after a fashion." He tugged a rolled-up copy of *Smashing Detective* from his pocket and smoothed it out on the desk. "Used to write for rags like this back in the day. Pure flapdoodle, of course, but the readers ate it up."

Abernathy gave up getting a word in and slumped back to wait out the storm.

"I'm contemplating a comeback," the Old Man said, "for a better magazine, of course—probably *Collier's*—and doing it up right. I mean to show folks how a real sleuth works, and you're the perfect model. What do you say? Mind if I make you famous?"

Abernathy's eyes said he was sorely tempted. His mouth said, "My apologies, Mr., uh, Tracy, but agency rules strictly prohibit such self-aggrandizement."

"See, Unc? The chief isn't one to toot his own kazoo. You can write about me instead."

This produced snorts from both men. Miffed, I pried "Uncle Samuel" out of his chair, shooed him into the outer office, and stuck my head back through Abernathy's door.

"Anything cooking?" I asked, hoping for something Chinese.

"If you value your job," he said, "keep that old dodo away from me."

"Anything else?"

"Yes. Shut the damn door."

Two days passed. Two very long days, in which the chubby ex-op grew ever more cranky. I spent the second day in the office, wondering what had possessed me to get into the bloodhound business.

What I came up with was this: After my father died, Nick Zartell became a fixture around the house and began grooming me to join his crew. My mother, herself the daughter of a racketeer, was all for it. I wasn't. So when the army wanted soldiers for Korea, I was first in line. They made killing Commies sound like a worthy endeavor, but as it turned out, the Commies were just people, and just like us except they lived in huts instead of duplexes. Still, the army taught me to shoot, and I'd hoped to employ that newfound skill as a member of the Portland police force.

But things had changed. Or maybe I had. I returned to a town ruled by graft and fear, so riddled with corruption that the police force was little more than a private army protecting the rackets. Still, I was determined to fight crime, so I signed on with Continental Investigations. At the time it seemed a swell idea, but in light of recent developments I might as well have followed the paternal footsteps.

I was still moping when Abernathy said, "Get in here, Collins. And close the damn door."

When I'd done both, he said, "You familiar with Hung Lo's Hop House?"

Hung Lo ran the deadliest of the local tongs, and his opium den was reputed to be the most profitable. It was also reputed to have the best police protection money could buy.

"Sure," I said. "Ma always took me there for my birthday."

"Fine," he said. "That's fine. Well, you're going back. In fact, you're going to become a regular customer."

At one time Portland's Chinese temples, restaurants, joss houses, and fan-tan parlors had been sprinkled all over the downtown area, rubbing elbows with like-minded Occidental establishments. These days they huddled together in an area north of Burnside, between Broadway and the Willamette River.

Smack in the middle of that new Chinatown sat the Gilded Duck Restaurant, the legitimate face of Hung Lo's business empire.

Parked across Fifth Avenue in my Studebaker Starlight coupe, the Old Man and I argued. Or, to be more precise, I argued while he ignored me.

"I don't need you nursemaiding me," I said.

"What kind of mileage does this machine get?"

"I know what I'm doing. I've been undercover before." That was a lie, and I half expected him to call me on it.

Instead he said, "Never owned a car myself, but Dinah Shore's been hounding me to see the U.S.A. in a Chevrolet."

I'd filled him in on the job, or at least the version of the job Abernathy had fed me. The grieving parents of a spoiled wastrel who'd been driven to wrack and ruin—and finally to suicide—by his cravings for Hung Lo's hop had hired the Continental to see justice done. With the fix in, there was no chance of police intervention, so the clients insisted we bust the place open and spill its dirty secrets all over the newspapers. The public outcry would force the cops to act.

My assignment was to make myself a fixture in the joint, at least for a few days, so when the time came I'd be on the inside to bop Chinamen on their skulls and open the gates for the Continental army.

Trouble was, the Old Man insisted on tagging along. He wanted the dirt on Abernathy and Zartell and figured he was the guy to ferret it out. This was Wednesday, and the raid was set for Saturday night, so he'd have to ferret fast.

The result was that he followed me into the Gilded Duck, followed suit when I slipped the waiter ten dead presidents, and followed the two of us down three creaky flights of stairs into Portland's fabled underground.

Legend had it the tunnels beneath the streets had once been used to shanghai recruits for smuggling ships, and during Prohibition they'd been a fine place to hide hooch. Now, with crime running wide open, the underground had been pretty much abandoned to opium dens and the white slavery racket.

I wriggled my nose against a hundred unnamed and unnameable smells as the waiter led us through a maze of dark passages and ancient doorways. Sometimes we had concrete underfoot, sometimes wooden planks, and sometimes bare earth. After several conks on the noodle from low-hanging pipes, I wised up and crouched to half my height, inching along like a crab. This gave the Old Man a smirk; he was short enough not to stoop. We turned this way and that, scuttling through a dozen more passageways before halting at a red door I'd have bet my pants was less than fifty feet from where we'd entered the underground.

Following a Chinese variant on shave-and-a-haircut-six-bits, the door opened and the waiter released us to the care of a pinch-faced kid in gold silk pajamas.

At my shoulder, the Old Man said, "Let me. I know how to talk to these people."

He shuffled past, bowed his head, and steepled his fingers beneath his chin. "This low-born mongrel," he said, "begs entry to your palace of heavenly delights."

Pajama Boy rolled his eyes at me. "Your friend's seen too many Charlie Chan movies."

"He's no friend of mine," I said. "If you hear of any crew vacancies, feel free to shanghai him."

After the exchange of a week's worth of junior detective pay, our host led us down a hazy hallway, past a small office where a bald man hunched over a desk, and finally to a dim-lit room lined with bunk beds. Half the beds held immobile shapes that might once have been human beings. The air was heavy with the scent of crushed flowers and unwashed bodies.

Spotting a vacant bed, I made for the bottom bunk, but the Old Man barreled past me, insisting I climb up top. I got my revenge by stepping on his ear.

Almost immediately a skeletal man in a tasseled hat shuffled out of the gloom bearing two wooden trays. Each held a long-stemmed pipe and a small oil lamp. The Old Man had told me what to expect, and the extent of his knowledge made me wonder how he'd come by it.

The idea was to load the pipe with a small dose of hop called a "pill," then hold the bowl over the lamp's glass chimney until the drug was vaporized. To avoid suspicion, we'd each have to burn a few pills, while taking care not to inhale.

I tried one.

Though I didn't inhale, there was no escaping the smell—a sharp, flowery perfume that made me gag. I lay back on the bunk, trying to relax, but my thoughts kept returning to the Old Man.

It occurred to me that if Fate had assigned me an opposite

number, this guy was it. Aside from the fact we both were—or had been—Continental operatives, we were as different as two male humans could be.

I was young. He was old. I was tall. He was short. I was thin. He was fat. I was at the beginning of my career. His was already over. I believed in concepts like hope and justice. He'd surrendered to the harsh realities of judgment and law. I trusted my feelings and wasn't afraid to act on them. He considered feelings a nuisance. If he accidentally experienced an honest human emotion he'd probably dig it out with a pocket knife. My greatest fear was I'd turn out just like him.

I burned a couple more pills.

This business of not inhaling was all well and good, but the flowery scent was so thick there was no escaping it. Before long I was sitting on a cloud, bouncing Lauren Bacall on one knee and Veronica Lake on the other.

That's when the Old Man kicked my bunk and whispered, "When the ruckus starts, watch the Chinese."

I did my best to keep Lauren and Veronica from scooting off my knees, but both vanished and I was left saying, "Huh?"

"The Chinese, dammit. See where they go."

I chased the brains around in my skull, wondering what he meant, and was still chasing when someone shouted, "Fire!"

That someone was the Old Man. He was a ghostly bear blundering about in the darkness, yanking dreamers from their bunks and creating pandemonium.

Watch the Chinese, he'd said. *See where they go.*

Slipping to the floor, I joined the befuddled mob and spotted one of the employees swimming against the tide. I moved to intercept him, but at the rendezvous point found nothing but bare wall.

I was scratching my head when the bald gent squirted from his hall office and danced past me. I felt a breeze at my back, turned, and watched his shirttails disappear into a gap in the wall. I followed the shirttails. They led me down a narrow tunnel.

Three crooked passageways and two flights of stairs later, I emerged into the basement of a Chinese laundry.

So this was what the Old Man wanted me to find. An escape route.

I was grateful, but not nearly grateful enough to worry what had become of him.

As it happened, he was fine. I found him camped on my doorstep Thursday morning when I left for work. A purple mouse clung to his face beneath his right eye, but he appeared otherwise unscathed. The bad news—or good, depending where you sat—was that he'd been spotted as the false-alarmer and was no longer welcome at Hung Lo's.

Unfortunately, that didn't stop him from following me to the office and regaling Abernathy with more of his mystery-writing claptrap.

Abernathy escaped him long enough to say, "We'll need extra guns for Saturday's party. See what Seattle and Spokane can send us."

Borrowing men from other Continental branches made sense, since I was one of only three operatives on Portland's regular roster.

When I told the Old Man he practically salivated. "That's my meat," he said. "Leave it to me."

Another night of pretend opium smoking—this time solo—went by before I found out what that meant. The occasion was a Friday-morning powwow in the Old Man's hotel room, attended by four men twice my age.

"Mike, Alec, and Rufus," the Old Man said, shooting the first three with his finger. He nodded at the fourth. "And we'll call him Bob."

I didn't like that so much. "Don't they have real names?"

"Sure," the Old Man said. "But names are overrated."

He then pronounced mine, producing a round of sniggers, but whether his pals considered it his joke or my father's I couldn't tell.

There was a lot of talk about people I didn't know, places I'd never been, and cases I'd never heard of. I smiled when they laughed and frowned when they swore, trying to be one of the gang, but I might as well have been wearing short pants and a beanie. The only one who addressed me directly was Mike, and that was to offer me bubblegum.

I learned things, though, including that all four belonged to the San Francisco branch, and had ridden the red-eye up the coast. All knew the Old Man well enough to kid him, but only to a point. Beyond that they treated him with the deference due a powder keg.

At last the Old Man explained the job, saying that Abernathy was too damn cozy with Nick Zartell, that we were putting both men under the lens, and that they may or may not be cooking up something involving opium. The Old Man wanted all the dirt that could be had on all concerned, and he wanted it ten minutes ago. One way or another, he said, we'd be participating in a raid on Hung Lo's Hop House, but how we'd play it was yet to be determined.

When Alec asked the source of the dirt on Abernathy, the old Judas nodded my way, and if the heat in those men's eyes had been real I'd be nothing but a soot stain on the woodwork. To his credit, the Old Man then launched into a barnburner of a speech starting with *Rally 'round the flag,* building up to *Win one for the gipper,* and bringing it home with a taste of *Give me liberty or give me death.* And it worked, after a fashion. By the time he finished, three of the four were able to look me in the eye without spitting. Clearly, they hated corruption in the ranks only slightly more than the rat who squealed about it.

The number of women who'd visited my apartment could be counted on one hand—with three fingers change—and the last had promised to return when hell got frosty. So when I keyed myself into the dark living room and smelled perfume, I knew something was up.

I had a fistful of .38 when I snapped on the lights and said, "Show yourself or eat lead."

"My God, Petey. Have you been reading Mickey Spillane again?"

A middle-aged woman with sharp features and a sharper figure emerged from my bedroom. She wore a red dress decorated with poker hands and a hat that belonged in a birdcage.

I put the gun away, saying, "Why the long face, Ma? No skin magazines under my mattress?"

"You needn't be nasty," she said. "I was worried about you."

"And lizards have wings. Did Zartell send you?"

She peered at the sofa, brushed off an invisible speck, and perched on the edge. "What does a girl have to do to get a drink around here?"

I shrugged out of my overcoat, mixed up her favorite—gin and bitters—and filled her hand with the glass.

"Now give. What do you want?"

"You know how I feel about Nick," she began.

"Sure," I said. "Same way you feel about dung beetles."

She smiled and sipped her gin. "It's more complicated than that."

"Don't I know it."

"I'm sorry for that, Petey. I'm sorry for a lot of things, but I can't undo them."

"You were saying what brought you."

"You've been spending time at Hung Lo's. Don't ask me how I know—I have my sources. And men from San Francisco have been nosing around the Boom. I know what you're up to, Petey, and I want it to stop."

I mulled that a moment. She'd always had her sources. Barmaids, strippers, hookers, women from every class of lowlife who worked on the periphery of the rackets. To their bosses they were just part of the scenery, but their eyes and ears let my mother put the squeeze on men of all stripes. What I hadn't known was that she had contacts in the Chinese community too.

I said, "What am I up to?"

"You're going after Nick. God knows why, but I won't have it. You're both too important to me."

"You're telling me Nick's involved with Hung Lo? I thought they were enemies." I knew better than to expect information from her, but it cost nothing to try.

"I'm telling you, Petey, I don't want you going up against him. Promise me you won't."

I tried to see around all the angles. Had Zartell sent her to find out how much I knew? Was she really worried about me—or *him*? Or was I somehow a threat to her own operation? The possibilities waltzed me around until I was dizzy.

I said, "No promises."

She stood, clamped hands on my lapels, and shook me. "Promise me you won't hurt him, and won't give him cause to hurt you. You're both lousy, and I don't really have either of you, but you're all I've got. Can't you understand that?"

I could, sadly, but I wasn't telling her that.

"No promises," I said. "But I'll tell you this. Zartell's not the target. As long as he doesn't interfere he'll come out smelling no worse than he smells already."

"Is that what your fat little overseer told you?"

That stopped me. She knew about him too?

"I suppose you think you can trust him. Others have thought that, and most of them are dead." Her eyes glistened. For a moment I thought she might cry. "You're a bastard. Just like your father. Just like Nick. And just like every other man I ever met. To hell with all of you."

And while I stood there empty of words, she left.

Next morning I told Abernathy the auxiliary had arrived. He bought the story that Seattle and Spokane had no operatives to spare, but was half inclined to take the train fare from Frisco out of my salary. His chief concern was that I'd lined up a newshound to accompany our raid. Once we pried the lid off Hung Lo's, he wanted publicity and plenty of it.

"Not to worry," I told him. "I have just the guy." And I did. A high school pal of mine was now a cub reporter for the *Oregonian*, and I hoped to hand him a pip of a story. It just wouldn't be the story Abernathy expected.

"We pop the cork Saturday at midnight," he said. "Just in time for the respectable element to get the news with their Sunday funnies."

I spent the rest of the day trying to guess the Old Man's intentions and finished up dumber than when I began. That night at Hung Lo's I was hard-pressed not to inhale.

On Saturday afternoon the Old Man called another chinfest at his hotel. The attendees were Mike, Alec, Rufus, Bob, and me.

"We got the lay on this Zartell bird," Mike said. "He's a tough nut, but his number-two man looks ripe for shelling."

"That would be Jablonsky," I said.

Mike looked at me like I'd puddled on the carpet.

"Name's Jablonsky," he said. "From what we could pick up, all his brains are in his biceps. Guy's got ambition, though. Told one of his floozies he plans to wrangle his own racket someday."

The Old Man said, "Know where we can lay hands on him?"

They did.

Thus it was that at eight-thirty that night I slouched behind the wheel of my Studebaker in a convenient shadow behind the Boom

Boom Room. The Old Man filled the seat beside me. He'd declined all invitations to explain his plan.

"Watch," he said, "and grow wise."

At 8:52 Jablonsky banged out of the Boom's back door and craned his neck as if expecting to see something. The only thing to see was an old panel truck near the door.

When he peered into the truck's cab, Mike and Rufus stepped out of the shadows with guns in their fists. Jablonsky's hands rose and he allowed himself to be prodded into the back of the truck.

I said, "How'd they know he was coming out?"

"We forged a note from a skirt he's been chasing. Said she was waiting to slip him some sugar."

"That's lesson one," I said. "What's next?"

My education resumed in a dark hotel room, one that did not belong to any of our party. Mike and Rufus had Jablonsky on a sofa in the adjoining room, and stood shooting words at him.

The Old Man and I watched through a partially open doorway.

"It's a frame," Jablonsky whined. "A lousy, stinking frame."

Mike said, "You know that, and maybe we do too. But the grand jury won't. And because counterfeiting is a federal rap, Zartell's pet prosecutors and judges can't help you."

"Bull. No one would think I'm dumb enough to walk around with stacks of funny money in my pockets."

Rufus smiled benignly. "You're right. No one could think you're dumb. Not you, the guy who got three years in stir for parking a getaway car in his own driveway."

Jablonsky's sneer was something to look at. "Since when do feds dish out the third degree in a fleabag hotel?"

"See?" Mike said. "You're not all dumb. We got a proposition for you."

Jablonsky's eyes grew sharp. "I can't stop you from talking."

And he didn't.

The proposition, as delivered by Mike, was that if he ratted out Zartell, they'd send the racketeer up for a long stretch and leave Jablonsky free to take over the operation. The alternative was far less enticing.

"We know he has something going in Chinatown tonight," Rufus said. "Something with the head dick at the Continental agency. We want the whole lay."

"And for that you'll give me Zartell's rackets? Hell, you should have said so."

Jablonsky gave them the whole lay.

Zartell, it seemed, had been horning in on the smuggling end of the opium business. Being a greedy soul, he had a yen for the retail end as well, and wanted Hung Lo's hop house empire. Hung Lo was too well protected for Zartell to show in a takeover, but if an outside outfit like Continental Investigations happened to send him to prison, no one could blame Zartell for filling the void.

When Jablonsky ran out of details, Mike said, "Sit tight while I call Mr. Hoover."

He slipped into the adjoining room, closed the door, and looked proud as a bird with a worm.

The Old Man wiggled a finger at me. "You've learned enough for one day. Go hold Abernathy's hand while he gets ready for the raid."

I consulted my watch. Nine-forty-seven. I had plenty of time before reclaiming my bunk at Hung Lo's.

I said as much.

The Old Man's flat stare lay heavy on me. "Did that sound like a suggestion?"

I kept hearing my mother's words. *I suppose you think you can trust him.*

"Tell me this," I said. "That stuff about taking Zartell down was just for Jablonsky's benefit, right? Just a way to get the goods on Abernathy."

The Old Man looked at me so hard I thought his eyeballs would crack. Finally he said, "Go."

I went. But all the way to the office, I wondered what I wasn't supposed to know.

Abernathy was in a snit because his reinforcements were out doing God-knows-what instead of hanging around waiting for pearls of wisdom to drop from his lips. I assured him they'd arrive soon, and he assured me my job depended on it. I was pretty sure he was right.

My two fellow Portland ops were on hand, pretending to look interested as they cleaned their guns and counted their ammunition. Though I'd worked with them half a year, I knew neither man well, and neither showed any inclination to remedy that.

I knew their names, but rarely had occasion to use them, and had taken to thinking of them as Mutt and Jeff. Mutt, as you might expect, was lanky and slope-shouldered, while Jeff had stubby legs and no more hair than a billiard ball. They might have been good detectives once, but their time with Abernathy—five and eight years respectively—had taken its toll. Mutt spent afternoons snoring on a bench in the Greyhound station, while Jeff could usually be found holding up a stool at Kelly's Saloon. I'd never been able to decide if they were on the take with Abernathy or just rotten on their own hooks.

In any case, I'd never trusted them, and wasn't starting now. If the Old Man wanted them clued in, he could clue them himself.

Knuckles on the door announced the arrival of a big-eared, wide-mouthed young man with a notebook in his pocket and a camera in his hand. This was my old pal Harvey, now penning obits and lost-dog stories for the *Oregonian*.

"This had better pan out," he told me. "I cancelled a date with Loose Lucy Morrelli to join this shindig."

We were still commiserating over this misfortune when Mike, Alec, Rufus, and Bob ambled in, and Abernathy called a council of war.

"Pete has to leave," he told the crowd, "so we'll start with him." He tossed me a smug look. "Your part is simple, kid. When both of Mickey's hands point straight up, take the gun out of your pocket and persuade Hung Lo's lackeys to answer the knock at their door."

Averting my red face, I slipped out into the hall.

And tripped over the Old Man, who was listening at the keyhole.

We both went down, but he bobbed up none the worse, while I lay stunned. The old guy might be shaped like a teddy bear, but he was tough as a grizzly.

He helped me up, saying, "Keep your wits handy tonight."

"Should I expect surprises?" I tried to adopt the look of someone worth confiding in.

"Always."

"What are your plans for Zartell?"

He did that horrible thing with his lips.

"You remind me of your father," he said.

"Is that good or bad?"

He remained as inscrutable as the Sphinx.

"With any luck," he said, "our problems should be over tonight."

"I don't believe in luck."

"It happens," he said. "But not as often as people like to think."

It was probably nerves talking, but the fisheye Hung Lo's doorman hung on me seemed fishier than usual, and the .38 felt like a Tommy gun in my pocket.

Reclined on my moldy mattress, I tried to convince myself all was swell. Tonight's doings would expose Abernathy for the snake he was, and he'd soon be residing in the state pen. The agency's honor would be restored, and I'd be the shining knight who made it all possible.

But a niggly little feeling kept after me, telling me all was less than swell. There was something the Old Man wasn't telling, and there had to be a reason. Maybe he didn't trust me to keep my mouth clamped. Maybe he thought I'd disapprove. Maybe he even thought I'd gum the works.

What was that chubby codger up to?

Time went so slowly I feared my watch had stopped and held it close to my ear. It was still ticking, but I was certain whole generations were born and died between each tick.

By the time midnight arrived I was lost in a secondhand opium dream and thought the pounding I heard was some sinner banging on the gates of heaven. But men shouting unheavenly things in two languages brought me out of my bunk with my pistol in my hand.

My big moment had arrived.

The Chinese half of the shouting came from the reception area, so no one bothered me as I cat-footed down the hall and peered out at the shouters.

Four celestials in gaudy pajamas clustered about the door, debating matters with their hands as much as their mouths.

I followed my gun into the room, tried to point it at all four at once, and said, "Hoist 'em!"

They might not have understood my words, but they understood my gun. They hoisted 'em.

The pounding on the door continued apace, accompanied by English demands for admittance.

I edged to one side, bared my teeth to show I meant business, and herded my hosts away from the door. While they jeered and jabbered, I fumbled with the locks and tossed aside the two-by-four barring the entrance. Then I flicked the latch and stood aside to admit the troops.

Alec and Rufus entered first, followed by Bob and Mike. They stepped aside two by two as Mutt, Jeff, and Abernathy paraded in, leading Harvey the boy reporter.

Abernathy set fire to a Cuban cigar and let the Chinese get a look at him.

"You boys," he told them, "are screwed."

While they goggled, he clarified: "You savvy screwed? Pinched. Busted. Behind the eight ball. Up the Yangtze without a paddle."

They goggled some more.

"Somebody put the nippers on 'em," Abernathy ordered. "The rest of you start gathering evidence." He raised a hand, rubbed thumb across fingertips. "Especially the folding kind." Then he strode down the hallway toward the office.

Mutt and Jeff were on the move when Bob and Rufus clamped hands on their shoulders, drew them close, and started whispering. Alec did the same to Harvey.

I looked a question at Mike.

"Time to amscray," he said softly. "Zartell and his goons are on the way."

My niggly feeling grew into a full-body funk. My mother's face rose before me, scowling.

No promises, I told it.

"Who invited Zartell?" I demanded.

"Answers later," he said. "Time to go."

Mutt, Jeff, and Harvey were already convinced and retreating out the door after Alec, Rufus, and Bob. I followed far enough to see them scatter into every tunnel but the one leading back to the Gilded Duck. That one was full of bobbing flashlights and tramping feet.

Mike made to slip past me, but I swung a hip and pinned him to the door frame.

"Answers now," I said, "or we greet the goons."

He struggled against me, swore like a stevedore, and said, "We gave Jablonsky a message for Zartell. Told him Abernathy and Hung Lo had gathered evidence against him and stored it here in a safe. He's coming for it."

I tried to digest that. It gave me a bellyache.

"There's more," Mike said. "The Old Man tipped Hung Lo that Abernathy and Zartell were staging a raid. This place is about to become a war zone."

The flashlights came closer. I could now make out shapes among the shadows.

"And what happens to Abernathy?"

Mike swore some more. "What do you care? You're the one put the evil eye on him."

The bellyache spread through my body. He was right, and maybe that's why I cared. I wanted the bastard canned—or maybe caged—but trussing him up for slaughter was out of my line.

Shouts from the Zartell crowd announced they'd seen us. Their steps quickened.

Mike said, "Happy? Now we're dead too."

The four Chinese had done a disappearing act. I grabbed Mike's lapel and hurried after them. He growled, but offered little resistance. The approach of Zartell's army was loud behind us.

Down the hall we went. The smoking lounge looked much the same, except that several beautiful dreamers had stumbled out of their bunks.

I kicked the secret panel open, pushed Mike through, and said, "Tell the Old Man I wish him a short and sour life." Then the wall clicked shut and I went in search of Abernathy.

Gunfire erupted in the outer room. Above the din, a high-pitched voice screamed orders in Chinese. Hung Lo's troops had arrived.

I found Abernathy in the small office, rifling a desk. One hand clutched a wad of greenbacks.

"There's more here," he said. "There must be. Help me look."

I lunged across the desk, grabbed his tie, and hauled him toward the doorway.

The hall was full of men—Zartell's men, firing back toward the entrance. They blocked our route to the secret exit.

Abernathy kicked my shins, tried to bite my hand.

"Behave!" I batted his nose with my gun barrel. "In case you don't know it yet, both sides want to boil you in oil."

Bullets zipped up and down the hall. Muzzle fire illuminated passing hatchets and knives. Men yelped, grunted, screamed, swore.

Abernathy quivered so hard he made my teeth rattle.

"We have to surrender!" he cried.

"Be your age. They're taking no prisoners."

But the idea stuck in my skull. Maybe he had something.

I put my lips close to the doorway and shouted, "Wait! Hold it!"

The barrage slowed to half its fury, a mere ten shots per second.

"We give up!" I roared. "We surrender!"

My reasoning, such as it was, went like this: the Chinese would think the Zartell faction was folding, and Zartell's men would think the surrender had come from one of their own.

The shooting dwindled to single pops and bangs. While everyone's brains were scrambled, I yanked Abernathy into the hall, pushing through the gangsters in search of the exit.

Gangsters, as a rule, don't like to be pushed. They pushed back, cursing as they did, and Hung Lo's men assumed the cursing was meant for them. We were still a yard and a half from the panel when the battle resumed.

Gunpowder scorched my cheek. A knife blade stole my hat. Lead thwacked into meat all around us. Abernathy squalled like a baby. A bullet slammed into my hindquarters, and I felt like squalling too, but I kicked and clawed my way through the dead and dying, bruised my shoulder on the secret panel, and shoved Abernathy through.

The only sensible thing was to follow. I wasn't Zartell's keeper. I'd resented him my entire life, and for all I knew, he may have been responsible for my father's death. The world would be a better place without him. The only sensible thing was to let him die.

I stood there telling myself these things until my mother's face swam up again.

No promises, I repeated.

But I kicked the panel shut and bawled, "Nick! Where the hell are you?"

A flying tomahawk took away part of my ear. Before I could check how much was left, a heavy slug tore through my leg. I sat down hard, damning Zartell, my mother, the Old Man, and half of mankind.

When I tried to get up, it was no-go. I damned the rest of mankind and had progressed to the animals and little fishes when a dark shape loomed above me.

"Hello, Pete," the shape said. "You rang?"

I thumped the wall with my foot. "Secret panel."

Zartell leaned against it, trying twice more before he found the sweet spot. The air buzzed with lead and cutlery, but nothing touched him. He bent, grabbed my ankles, and dragged me through. The door clicked shut behind us.

"I suppose I should be grateful," I said.

"You should at that, but I know it's against your nature."

He hauled me up and duck-walked me down the passageway. Muffled explosions hurried us on our way. If I hadn't known better, I'd have thought it was Chinese New Year.

I awoke with a head full of visions and a snootful of disinfectant. In the visions, I saw myself stagger into the basement of the Chinese laundry, saw the astonished face of an old woman boiling shirts, and collapsed as Zartell scurried away. The disinfectant represented the here and now, where I lay sidesaddle on a hospital bed.

My leg and hindquarters hurt like hell.

From a chair beside the bed, the Old Man studied me as if measuring my neck for a noose.

I broke the silence. "My ass hurts."

"Thanks to you," he said, "so does mine."

Lacking a suitable reply, I said, "Where's Abernathy?"

"In the wind. Trying to outrun Zartell's bounty hunters and Hung Lo's hatchet men."

I did my best to look displeased.

"Feeling pretty full of yourself, are you? I wouldn't. When they catch him, he'll wish he'd died in the opium den."

"If they catch him."

"When. And you may have won a reprieve for Zartell, but his time is coming too."

I had no more argument in me. "What about Mutt and Jeff?"

"They have their walking papers. They'll never work for the agency again."

I felt the noose slip around my neck.

"And what about me?"

The Old Man tugged the pack of Fatimas from his pocket, shook one free, scowled at the NO SMOKING sign above my bed, scowled at me, and lit the cigarette anyway.

A shape darkened the doorway and a man strode in.

I said, "Hello, Mike."

He grinned at the Old Man. "You tell him yet?"

"No." The old guy scowled at me some more.

The noose tightened.

"I saw three alternatives," the Old Man said. He ticked them off on his fingers. "One—fire Abernathy and let him leave unpunished. Two—have him arrested and drag the agency's name through the muck. Or three—make the problem go away permanently." He grimaced as if the words pained him. "You saw a fourth option, and acted on it."

My ears stretched. This resembled the beginning of a compliment.

"Disobeying orders was rash," the Old Man went on, "and it was stupid. But you caught a break, and your stupidity paid off, at least in the Abernathy matter. Saving Zartell was something else entirely."

So much for the compliment.

"What he's trying to say," Mike put in, "is that you remind him of himself when he was a fine young hellion. And if the worst that happens to you is getting shot in the ass, you might live long enough to become a decent Continental op."

"I'm already a decent op," I told him, "but I'm nothing like old Beelzebub here, and never will be. If he has an ounce of human feeling in him I'll butter my hat and eat it."

The Old Man did that terrible thing with his lips.

"Your hat is safe enough," he said. "As to how different we are, it may interest you to know I once had a mother. She even tried to tell me how to do my job."

I held his gaze until my gums began to bleed.

"So what'd you do?"

"Framed her on a bunko rap. She got three to five in Joliet."

I was deciding whether to believe that when he said, "Mike is transferring up from San Francisco. He'll be training you."

My brain did a somersault.

Mike executed a mock bow. "Charmed, I'm sure."

"I still have a job?"

"It won't be all wine and roses," the Old Man said. "This office still needs a manager. And this town needs someone to shave its fur and dig the leeches out of its hide."

I stared at him, hoping I'd misunderstood.

I hadn't.

"The agency gave me the option of staying retired or becoming your new boss. Guess which I chose?"

ROBERT LOPRESTI

Street of the Dead House

FROM *nEvermore!*

WHAT AM I? That is the question.

I sit in this cage, waiting for them to come stare at me, mimic me as I once mimicked them, perhaps poke me with sticks, and as they wonder what I am, so do I.

I don't think Mama had any doubts about what she was. I don't think she could even think the question. That is the gift and the punishment Professor gave me.

I remember Mama, a little. We were happy and life was simple, so simple. Food was all around us, dangers were few, and there was nothing we needed. When I was scared or hungry Mama would pick me up and cradle me to her furry breast.

I was never cold. It was always warm where we lived, not this place, called *Paris* or *France.* Goujon cannot talk about anything without giving it two names. Sometimes he calls me an *Ourang-Outang,* and sometimes an *ape.*

Mama called us nothing, for she could not speak like people, or sign as I have learned to do. That did not bother her. She was always happy, until she died.

The hunters came in the morning, firing guns and shouting. Mama picked me up and ran. She made it into the trees but there was another hunter waiting in front of her. He made a noise as if he were playing a game, but this was no game. He fired his gun and Mama fell from the tree. I landed on top of her but she was already dead.

My life has made no sense since then.

I remember the first time I saw Professor. He tilted his head when he looked at me and spoke. We were in his house. The smell of the hunters was finally gone.

He gave me food and tried to be kind but I was afraid. The food tasted wrong and soon I got sleepy, but not the kind of sleepy I knew with Mama.

I know now something in the food made me sleep. Things were confused after that and I would wake up with pain in my head.

He did things to my head. Each time I woke the room looked different, *clearer* somehow. And one day when Professor spoke I understood some of his noises.

"Ah, Jupiter. You are with me again. And you are grasping my words, aren't you? The chemicals are working just as I predicted."

He held out a piece of fruit. "Are you hungry, Jupiter?"

I was. I reached for it.

He pulled it away and moved his other hand. "Do this, Jupiter. It means *orange.* Tell me you want an orange."

After a few more tries I understood. I copied his hand and he gave me the orange.

That was my first lesson. That was my first surrender.

Many more sleeps, many more words, many more pains in the head.

Soon I knew enough gestures to ask Professor questions.

Where is Mama?

"Dead. Hunters killed her. When I heard they brought back a baby I bought you from them."

Do you have a mama?

"I did, Jupiter. Everyone does. I will show you a picture of mine. I grew up in a place called Lyon. It is far from here, and full of men like me."

Where is your mama?

"She died when I was young."

Killed by hunters?

"No, Jupiter. She got sick. Not sick like you did last month. Much worse."

Where did you live?

"With my papa. Oh dear. A papa is something like a mama. You had one too but *Ourang-Outang* papas don't live with their children. I don't know why. My papa was a baker. That means he made bread, like I eat with my meals."

I tried bread once. It had no taste.

Did your papa die?

"Yes, but that was much later. There was an accident, he was hit by a wagon. You've seen pictures of wagons." His face changed again. "I had to go to the morgue to fetch him. I knew then I would leave Lyon, because it made me so sad."

What is that?

"What is . . . oh, morgue? It is a house where they put the dead."

Did they put my mama there?

"No, Jupiter. Only men."

Why?

"Well." He scratched his head. "I think it is because men think that only they have souls."

What is that?

Professor waved his arms. "I was afraid you would ask! I know nothing about souls. We would need a priest to explain that—and don't bother asking me what a priest is, because I can't explain that either. Let's say a soul is what makes men different from animals."

A soul lets you speak?

More head scratching. "I'll have to think about that one, Jupiter."

I lived in the middle of the house, where there were trees to make nests in. It was surrounded by white walls, and Professor lived on the other side of the walls. There were some windows, spaces in the walls with bars, through which I could see into his rooms. There were also bars on the top of my part of the house.

One day Professor came to me, excited. "We are to have a visitor, Jupiter! A man who speaks French."

What is that?

"The words I speak, that I have been teaching you. Men from different places use different sounds, and French is how they speak where I was born. Most men here speak English, or Dutch, or Malay."

He made the playing noise. "So many ways to talk, Jupiter. But until now none here have spoken as I do."

Is that why they are afraid of me? Because they cannot speak to me?

His face changed. "Why do you say they are afraid?"

I can smell it on your helpers. The men who clean and cook.

"Have any of them bothered you, Jupiter?"

No. But they peek in my room when you are not there. Some of them speak but I do not know what they say. And when I tried to sign back they did not understand.

Professor got quiet. "I am sorry they are afraid of you, Jupiter. Men fear what they don't understand. Perhaps I should have let my helpers visit you, but I didn't want to confuse you with many kinds of words."

He stood up. "We will see how things go with the sailor, yes? Maybe we can find more friends for you."

What is that?

"What, friend?"

No.

"Hmm. Then . . . sailor? A sailor is a man who travels on boats. I have shown you pictures of boats, yes? We need a sign for sailor, I see."

Boat man.

His face changed. "Very good, Jupiter. You are getting better and better at thinking of signs."

I want to see the sailor.

I smelled him as soon as he came into the house. The sailor smelled like the fish Professor sometimes eats, and like the smoke some of the helpers smell of.

I heard them while they ate.

"So, where are you from, Monsieur Goujon? Is that a Norman accent?"

"It is, professor. I was born near Caen, but I have lived most of my life with my uncle near Paris. That is actually why I am here in Borneo. He asked me to supervise a load of precious cargo, so I left my ship and will take another back."

"Excellent. I trust you will visit me often while you are here. It is a rare treat to chat with someone who speaks the mother tongue."

"How can I resist such a charming host? Not to mention this wonderful food."

It didn't smell wonderful to me. Mostly bread and burnt meat.

"I am amazed that you can survive here in this primitive land. Pirates, natives, opposing armies . . . and yet here you sit in this beautiful villa! How do you do it?"

"Ah well, it is a little miracle, I suppose. The English assume I am a French spy, and would root me out if they could, but this end of the island is run by the Dutch and the Dyaks, and they have no desire to lose the only physician in their territory.

"When I first reached Borneo some of the Malay pirates tried to take me as their personal physician, but I told them I couldn't work that way. If they wanted my services they would have to set me free—and they did! I suspect they feared I could make them sick as well as heal them. But they come by cover of darkness, when they need me."

"Professor, if I am not being rude, may I ask what a scholar like yourself is doing out in the wilderness? It amazed me to hear about you."

"Hmm." Professor's voice got quieter. "What *did* you hear, exactly?"

The sailor made the playing noise. "Oh, you know what the locals are like. The natives are pagans and the Dutch aren't much better. They say that you have turned animals into servants!"

"I suppose that is better than if they thought I turned my servants into animals." They made the playing sound. "In fact, my friend, they are closer to the truth than you might imagine. But they are far away too."

"Really? I am fascinated! Please explain."

"Very well. I should tell you I was trained as a doctor in France. I found myself working in a rural area, and, alas, there were many feeble-minded people there."

"Very sad, but I have heard that that condition runs in families."

"It does. And often a healthy member of such a clan will produce feeble-minded offspring, even though both parents seemed completely normal."

"Perhaps the family is cursed by God."

"I know nothing of curses, my friend. As a natural philosopher I can only deal with *this* world. But my breakthrough came when a fever struck our village and, alas, killed a number of small children, both the normal and the feeble-minded."

"Death makes no distinctions, I know."

"Very true. But it occurred to me that I had a great opportunity here that for the sake of all mankind I could not let slip away. As you know, what we call the mind is contained here, in the skull."

"The brain, yes. I saw one once, when a man was killed by an explosion."

"Ah. Then you understand that there is nothing magical about the brain. It is just a pile of meat, one might say. And yet all art and literature and wisdom spring from it, yes? So I decided to see if there was a difference between the healthy and feeble-minded brains."

I heard nothing for a moment. When the sailor spoke he sounded different. "You cut open dead children? Is that *legal*?"

"No. Autopsies, for that is the word, are not legal in France. But they should be, or how can medicine advance? My so-called crime was discovered and I had to flee the country. How I wound up in Borneo is a long story. But the important thing is what I learned. The feeble-minded brain looked different; there were variations in shape. It did not smell like a normal brain, and I became convinced that there were chemical differences. I thought perhaps it might be possible to improve the little ones."

"Surely you have not been experimenting on living children, professor!"

"No, my friend. Not even on feeble-minded ones, although I hope I will get the chance to do so. Out here I was able to try my ideas out on apes. Have you seen them?"

"I have, here and in Africa."

"And what do you think of them?"

"I hardly know. They seem like a joke the devil played on mankind. A satire."

"Hmm. I think they are more likely a rough draft, if I may call it that. The Bible tells us God made animals before man, after all. I have worked on almost a dozen of them over the years, trying to improve their brains."

"With what goal, professor? To turn them into men?"

"No, my friend. That would be neither possible nor moral. But if I can improve their ability to think, imagine what I can do for the feeble-minded children!"

I heard a chair scrape back. "That is the most fantastic scheme I have ever heard! Has there been any success?"

"Ah! There has indeed. The latest subject has been a marvel. Come with me, my friend, and you can meet my greatest triumph. He lives in my courtyard."

I heard them coming so I backed away from the door.

The sailor was big, higher and wider than Professor or his servants. He had fur all around his face, and where there wasn't fur his skin was red.

He stared at me, eyes and mouth wide.

"Jupiter, this is my guest, Goujon. Goujon, let me introduce you to Jupiter."

I am happy to meet you.

"What is it doing?" said Goujon quietly. I smelled his fear.

"The gestures? That is how Jupiter speaks. You will notice I sign while I speak to him. What is it, Jupiter?"

Is he the sailor?

"Yes, the boat man. Boat man. You see, Goujon, he invented this combination of signs to mean *sailor* when he heard you were coming."

"This is amazing, professor! I wouldn't have believed it possible. How long have you had him?"

"I purchased him almost three years ago. He was a baby and hunters had killed his mother. He is by far the brightest and most trainable subject I have been lucky enough to encounter."

Goujon said more and I got angry. He backed up, toward the door.

"What is it?" Professor asked me. "What is the problem?"

Can not understand.

"Oh. The sailor has an accent. He learned to speak far from my home. I am sorry, Goujon. Jupiter gets frustrated when he can't understand what is said to him."

The sailor looked at me. His face changed. "You know what? So do I."

Professor made the playing sound. "Ah, very good!"

"Could you teach me to sign, professor? I would like to speak with your amazing friend."

It was exciting to be teaching instead of learning.

The sailor came every day. He would say a word and I would show him the sign, then he would copy it.

Professor sat and watched. He helped when I could not understand, or when there was a word there was no sign for.

"Gold," said Goujon.

What is that?

"Ah!" Professor said. "It's a metal, Jupiter, like iron, but yellow and heavier. It shines. How about this for a sign? *Yellow metal.*"

"You leave out the most important thing about gold, professor," said Goujon. "It is valuable."

What is that?

"Valuable? You can get things with it. Here." Professor pulled flat metal things from his pocket and handed them to me. "These are coins. Here's a sign for coin, yes? I give these to the fruit man and he gives me fruit. Then he can give them to, say, the fish man, and get a fish."

Are they gold?

"No, Jupiter. Gold coins are very valuable. That means you would have to trade a lot to get them."

"Or trade something very valuable," said Goujon.

One day the sailor told us he would be leaving soon. A boat had come that would take him and the things his uncle wanted away. After that he kept coming over, but not for lessons. I heard him and Professor talking. They sounded angry.

"You can find another one. My God! With the money he would fetch in France you could hire armies to hunt the deep woods for them."

"What do you think he is, a circus act? This is a great experiment. My greatest! I may never find another I can train so well. And when he starts to decline I will examine his brain and see how my chemicals altered it. Then I can apply what I learned to the children—"

"That's another thing. Do you think anyone, *any* civilized country would let you cut up people the way you have done with that thing in there? That is madness."

"Get out of my house! You are not welcome here! Go back to France, or to the devil!"

After a few minutes Professor came into my room. "How are you, my friend?"

Well. Where is the sailor?

"Ah. He is gone. He is going home. I am sorry he couldn't come to say goodbye to you. Did you like him, Jupiter?"

I liked teaching him.

Two sleeps later and I woke, hearing screams and smelling blood.

I screamed too.

I left my nest and climbed to the top of the tallest tree. I heard more screams. Professor's helpers were running away from the house.

The door opened and the sailor ran in. "Jupiter! Where are you? Come down!"

I stayed in the branches.

"Jupiter! The hunters are here! The professor says I must take you away or they will kill you. Hurry!"

I came down and followed him out of the house, the first time I was outside since I was a baby.

There was a cart at the door with many men. I screamed and tried to back away, but Goujon was behind me. "It's all right, Jupiter. They are my friends. They will help us get away from the hunters. Climb into the cart."

I did, but Goujon did not. The door closed and I saw that the walls were bars, like the top of my room. I screamed.

"Shut the brute up!" said one of Goujon's friends.

"Let him prattle. Go!"

I could smell animals I had only had hints of before. Those must be horses, I thought. Professor had shown me pictures of horses pulling carts.

And then there were so many smells and sights that nothing made sense.

There were many sleeps on the boat. I was never out of the box of bars and I was too sick to eat. No one came except Goujon.

"How are you, Jupiter?"

Sick. Where is this?

"We are going to France. That is where the professor was born."

Where is Professor?

"He died. The hunters killed him."

Is he in the dead house?

"The dead house? I suppose he is. But don't worry. You will be safe from the hunters in France. There are many people there who will want to see you. No one has ever seen an *Ourang-Outang* who could talk before! They will pay a fortune."

What is that?

Goujon called the place where we lived a *barn* and a *house.* It did not look like Professor's house. It was dark and cold and there were no trees to sleep in.

Trees wouldn't have mattered, because he did not let me out of the box.

Two sleeps after we arrived Goujon came in, excited. "Good news, Jupiter! Some professors from the university want to meet you."

Professor is dead.

"Yes, yes, but these are other men like him. You will sign for them and they will want you to come live with them in a beautiful house full of trees and fruit and people. You will be famous, Jupiter!"

What is that?

As usual, he didn't answer.

I heard the professors arrive. I was excited to meet them. Perhaps they would be my friends like Professor was.

But I heard Goujon talking on the way up the stairs. "The man who trained him was mad, gentlemen, quite mad. He wanted to experiment on children! I don't pretend to understand what he did to this poor beast. The scars on his head have healed. But we had to stop the professor before he engaged in more such crimes. I'm afraid he fought to the death."

Then I knew how Professor died.

Goujon entered the room with two other men. They had white fur like Professor and one wore circles that made his eyes look big. They stared at me.

"He can't speak, gentlemen," said Goujon. "You will have to learn the signs he uses, but it is not hard. Even I can do it. Jupiter!" He started signing. "Here are two new friends for you. Say hello."

I looked at them.

"Come, Jupiter," said Goujon. "Show them the sign for your name. Or for sailor! You created that yourself. Boat man! Remember?"

I hooted.

"He's a fine specimen," said the man with the circles. "The Jardin des Plantes would be pleased to have him, but not at the price you are asking."

"He's not a zoo animal," said Goujon. "He can talk! Or sign, anyway. Ask him about life in Borneo."

The younger man came closer to my box. "Oh, why not? We've come this far. Jupiter, my name is Pierre. Are you hungry?"

I said nothing. I did nothing. Soon they left.

Goujon was angry. "What was that for, you brute? They would have taken good care of you!"

You killed Professor.

He backed away. "How—? Oh. You heard what I told them. I didn't mean that, Jupiter. It was just . . . just . . . Well, they wouldn't have understood about the hunters."

You killed Professor.

He made the playing sound. "I'm afraid your evidence would not hold up in a court, even if you knew what a court was. You don't want to set a quarrel with me, Jupiter. The sooner you cooperate, the sooner you can live with someone you prefer."

I will not help you.

"No? We will see about that."

He took the lamp and left.

Two sleeps passed. I had no food. No one cleaned my box.

On the third morning Goujon came in with a basket of fruit. "Are you ready to be sensible, Jupiter?"

You killed Professor. I will not help you.

He waved his arms. "If you starve to death it won't help anyone! The professor is dead, Jupiter. What do you want?"

Home.

"Where do you think that is, exactly? You think you can go back to the professor's house and live there again? Will the Dyaks bring you food and clean up your mess? You could never survive in the forests. In the name of the good god, let me help you."

What is that?

He didn't answer. He took the food away.

The next morning Goujon came back with more fruit. "Don't eat so fast. You'll get sick."

When I was done he said, "All right. You want to go back to Borneo, do you? Very well. It will take money."

What is that?

"Money? The professor told you about that the first time I met you. Remember? Gold coins?"

Why do I need them?

"Because the captain—the big boat man—won't take you to Borneo without them. Now, my uncle keeps an eye on all the important things that happen here in Paris, and he knows of a caper that is perfect for us."

What is that?

Goujon said his uncle knew of an old woman, a fortuneteller, who was going to buy a shop. I didn't know what most of those words meant, but Goujon just waved a hand.

"Never mind. All that matters is this: on Friday she will have a big bag full of gold coins in her house. If we get them there will be enough to send you back to your Malayan hellhole and for me to live here for many years."

He told me that the woman was a mama and her child lived with her, but the child was grown. They lived on the fourth floor of a house.

"My uncle says there is no way to get into the building but through a window on the fourth floor that can be entered from the yard; I have seen it and you could do it easily." He made the playing sound. "Easy as climbing a tree."

That night he let me out of the cage. We went outside, where he had a closed wagon waiting. Two horses pulled it. The man in front was so frightened I could barely smell the horses.

"Come inside, Jupiter," said Goujon.

I didn't want to. It was dark and small and the air was cold.

"If you run away, you will never get home. Do you understand that? You can't get home except by boat, and only I know which boats go there."

I will go.

Goujon turned to the driver. "Rue Morgue. Jupiter, what's wrong? Calm down."

Why are we going to the dead house?

"The dead . . . the morgue? No, Morgue is just the name of the street. We won't be going to the morgue at all. Just calm down and get in the carriage. Please."

We traveled through the place Goujon called Paris, although

sometimes he called it France. The windows were shuttered but I could hear and smell. It was like the boat ride; too much to remember.

The house where the woman lived was not the dead house. Goujon told me the dead house was far away and I shouldn't think about it.

This house was bigger than Professor's had been.

"The door is always locked."

What is that?

"Locked? Closed so no one can get in. Like your cage or your room back in the professor's house in Borneo." He led me to a yard at the rear of the building. "Look at the windows on the top floor. The woman lives there with her daughter. Could you get in?"

I looked up at it and felt happy. I had never been able to climb so high.

I can.

"Are you sure, Jupiter?"

I can. Now.

Goujon put a hand on my arm. "Not now. She will not have the coins until the end of the week. Let's go back home."

I pulled my arm away. *Practice.*

"Practice? That makes sense. But not here." He leaned out of the box and spoke to the man who helped the horses.

"We will go to an empty building I know. You can climb there without being seen."

We went. The building was not as tall as the one where the woman lived, but it was still wonderfully high. I stretched out my arms and began to pull myself up the outer walls.

I felt my heart beating. I had done nothing like this in my life. I had only climbed the trees and walls in Professor's house. I never wanted to stop. I swung from one piece of wall to another. Swung again and caught a window with my leg. I could have gone on forever.

Goujon yelled, "Jupiter! We have to get going! It will be morning soon."

I wanted to ignore him. He said we were going home, but where was home? The cage?

"Jupiter! There's no food here. If you don't come with me, you will never get back to Borneo!"

He was right. I climbed to the top once more and then rushed all the way to the street beside him.

Goujon's face changed. "You liked that, didn't you?"

Yes.

"It was very cruel of that professor to keep you locked up like that. Jupiter, what's wrong?"

I never thought Professor was cruel to lock me up. Why didn't he let me climb the trees outside his house?

I got in the wagon. When we went into the house Goujon said, "I won't ask you to get in that cage again, Jupiter. We have to trust each other, yes?"

Yes.

Each night Goujon took me out to practice at a different empty building.

"That metal tree is a lightning rod, Jupiter. There is one on the roof of the fortuneteller's house, near the chimney. It is much higher. Can you climb it? Yes? Very good!"

I enjoyed the practice so much I did not want it to end, but on the third night Goujon said, "I think you are ready, Jupiter. Tomorrow the old woman will buy another house. So tonight we must move, eh?"

Yes.

I didn't know why the old woman wanted another house. But I was sure she didn't need it as much as I needed to go home.

When the carriage arrived, the street was empty and silent. I could hear that no one moved inside. I could smell how nervous Goujon was.

"Ready, Jupiter?" he whispered. "Excellent, excellent. I will be down here waiting. I'm sure the women are asleep by now."

I climbed the tall lightning rod. It was easy. The shutter was open against the wall. I grabbed it with both hands and swung across to the open window. That was easy too.

Inside the room was one bed, the kind Goujon sleeps on, the head against the window. I squeezed through the window and landed on the bed.

The old woman sat in a chair beside the bed, a metal box full of papers on the table beside her, and she slept. Her eyes were closed, and she growled.

I crept to her. The bags of gold coins Goujon described were lying on the table beside her. I tried to pull one but there were strings on it, and they were wrapped around her wrist.

She growled again. What could I do?

I went back to the bed and stuck my head out the window. I tried to sign my problem, but Goujon didn't understand. Finally he climbed up the pole, badly, and reached the top.

I crawled out the window, hanging on to the sill, and when our heads were as close together as they could get he looked up at me and whispered, "What's wrong?"

Woman asleep. Bags tied to hand.

Goujon took one hand off the pole and almost fell. He pulled something from his pocket and held it up to me. "Razor. You know how to open it?"

Yes. I had seen him shave.

I reached down to take it. I opened the razor and made sure I knew how to hold it. Then I crept back to the woman. I took hold of the first string and started cutting. The woman kept growling.

I caught the bag so it didn't make a sound. I put it on the floor. Then I started to cut the other string.

I heard a door close. A young woman had come in. Her back was to me and she was doing something to the door.

What could I do?

She turned and saw me. She screamed.

The old woman woke. She saw me and screamed.

Now I was scared. I wanted to scream too.

Before I could back away the old woman hit me in the face. Then she grabbed me by my fur. I tried to push her away, but the razor caught her in the throat. Her eyes went wide and blood squirted out, poured down.

I smelled blood. I was scared. I dropped the razor and jumped back. The old woman fell to the floor.

The daughter screamed louder than ever.

Outside from below the window I heard Goujon shouting, "My God! You devil! What have you done?"

The daughter would not be quiet. I put a hand over her mouth. She bit me.

I put my hands on her throat. I made her quiet. She fell down.

"Get out of there, Jupiter! Take the coins and come!"

I was scared. I had never done anything so bad before.

I tried to pick up the old woman by her fur, but pieces of it came out. I grabbed her by the middle and rushed up the bed to the window. I held the woman outside so Goujon could see her. Maybe Goujon could help her?

His eyes went wide. "What have you done?" he yelled, frightening me. I lost my grip, and the old woman fell out the window to the yard below.

"My God! What have you done?" Goujon slid down the lightning rod. He ran from the yard. I heard the carriage with the horses pull away.

I lifted the daughter and looked for a place to hide her. The door was locked. I didn't want to throw her out the window.

There was no fire in the fireplace. I hid her in there.

I heard people running up the stairs, banging on the door.

I left the coins on the floor and climbed out the window, and it slammed shut behind me. I climbed up to the roof.

I kept going from roof to roof until I could not hear the screams, or smell the blood.

Before the sun rose I found a forest. There were many trees and a grassy place with a path where people walked. I climbed into a tree and hid.

I had not meant to hurt anyone, but I think those two women were dead. I had killed them like the hunters killed Mama. Like Goujon killed Professor.

Professor whipped me once for hurting one of his helpers. This was worse. What would happen now?

I stayed in the tree all day. People walked by on the path but they never saw me. I don't think they were looking for me.

After dark I went down and searched for food. I found a place where there had been many kinds of food and carts. I found bins where old food was piled and found fruit I could eat. Then I went back to the trees and made a nest.

That's how I lived for many sleeps.

The food was bad. It was making me sick. Professor could make me better but he was dead. Goujon killed him, but maybe he did it to help me.

One night I knew I couldn't stay there anymore. I climbed down and followed the smells back to the place where Goujon lived.

The door would not open, but I knew what to do. I climbed in a window on the top floor. Goujon was in a bed growling like the old woman had done.

That made me sad.

I touched him on the arm. He woke with a jerk and sat up. He was afraid.

"Jupiter! Is that you?"

I touched his hand.

Goujon leapt out of the other side of the bed. "Wait, just wait." He lit a lamp.

"It is you! I thought you were lost forever. Where have you been?"

Food and water.

"Of course! Where are my manners? Come with me."

I ate. He drank something that smelled spoiled.

I told him what happened.

"What an amazing adventure, Jupiter. I never would have thought you could survive for so long in this city. I am glad to have you back."

Are the women in the dead house?

"Yes. You know you killed them, don't you?"

I didn't mean to.

"Yes. But I doubt anyone else would believe it." He put down his glass. "Listen, Jupiter. There was one man clever enough to realize that only an animal like you could have broken into that house. A strange fellow named Auguste Dupin who lives in a ruined house with his boyfriend, I suppose. You should see the place! Nothing but moldy furniture and books, hundreds of books.

"This Dupin is both a genius and a fool, I think. He tricked me, convinced me that he found you, but he wasn't clever enough to realize that you are an animal who *thinks.* And that's the point, Jupiter. Do you know what they do to murderers in France?"

What is that?

"A murderer? Someone who kills people, like you did. They kill murderers—chop off their heads. Do you want them to chop off your head, Jupiter?"

My hands trembled as I signed *no.*

"And I don't want them to cut off mine either. Understand me, Jupiter. If you are a mere animal, then you are not a murderer. But if you are smart enough to help me *steal,* then you are smart enough to *kill,* and they will kill you for it. Do you understand, Jupiter?"

No.

He sighed. "If they see you signing, they will know how smart you are. Then I will be killed as a thief and you as a murderer. But if you don't sign, if you can keep from ever letting anyone see you do it, then they will think you are just a brute, and neither of us will be punished. What do you say, Jupiter? Can you keep the secret?"

Could I? Could I pretend to be as empty and silent as the horses and the dogs?

"Jupiter?"

I didn't answer. I have never answered.

Goujon had no money to send me home. I understood. This is my punishment.

He couldn't sell me as a talking beast, but he sold me to the Jardin des Plantes. There are many animals here.

I live in a box of bars in a big house that is always cold. That is my punishment too.

There are other apes, but they don't like me. Professor made me different and they can tell. So I live in another building, alone.

Goujon came once and talked to me. I didn't answer.

He thinks I am afraid. He thinks I pretend to be an empty beast because they will kill me if they find out I can think.

I am not afraid. But after I killed those women I knew I had to decide.

What am I?

Professor tried to turn me into a man. I am not a man. I will not be part of a man.

So I must be a beast. I have decided.

Beasts do not speak. Beasts do not sign.

Yesterday there were a lot of excited men in front of my cage. They were all facing one man, who was pointing at me and talking. I couldn't understand what they were saying until one of them called him by name: *Dupin.*

That was the man Goujon told me about, the one smart enough to realize an *Ourang-Outang* killed the women, but not smart enough to know that I was also smart.

Now he was telling everyone how he figured out that it was me and the men were telling him how clever he was.

He looked at me and I thought, If I sign now and he is so clever, he will know that I am signing, even if he cannot understand the words. Would he tell everyone, or would he be ashamed that he was mistaken?

My fingers itched to sign *You are the fool.*

But I am a beast. Beasts are silent. I let him pass me, still thinking that I cannot think.

There are more people outside my box now. They yell at me and make the playing sound. I do nothing.

They look at me and I look back. I look back.

DENNIS McFADDEN

Lafferty's Ghost

FROM *Fiction*

IN THE BED of another woman was by no means unfamiliar ground for your man, but this time there was a twist. This time, he could reasonably argue, it was in the interest of the missus, not merely his own (not that herself would be much persuaded). This time, in the service of their marriage, he'd proved beyond a doubt that their counselor could not be trusted, the same counselor she'd demanded that he accompany her to see if he harbored any hope at all of keeping her roof above his head. He'd demonstrated conclusively that all the rubbish their counselor had been spouting about trust, communication, sharing, that indeed her Ten Golden Rules for a Great Marriage, were nothing but a load of fluff and dander. By Lafferty's way of reasoning, any marriage counselor worth her salt must be honest, trustworthy, and above reproach, attributes he defined to include being above the temptations of the flesh, particularly when the flesh in question is hanging from the bones of one of her very own clients. And so he'd put her to the test. And so she'd failed utterly, the proof beside him here in her bed. Of course, how to frame the proof for Peggy, the missus, without jeopardizing his roof or his life and limb was the challenge with which he was now faced, even in the warm throes of postcoital bliss, those of himself and the counselor in question, Katherine Flanagan, LPC, IACP.

"I suppose I'll regret this," she said, though something in her tone suggested to Lafferty amusement more than regret.

Lafferty said, "I get that a lot," and sure enough, she laughed. A handsome lady she was, a lady who, unlike most of them Lafferty had known, seemed to become less exposed and vulnerable the more naked she became. She was plenty naked now. She'd a polished smile like that of a shark, and eyebrows painted like breaking waves. The short part like a scar at the front of her slippery black hair showed a root or two of indeterminate color.

"Don't be so hard on yourself," she said. "That's my job."

"And I've noticed, Mrs. Flanagan, you're bloody good at your job."

"Please. Katie."

"Katie? I'd have thought Katherine."

"Katherine, Kathy, Kate, Katie-bar-the-door. Take your pick. I *love* the variety."

"I think Katherine the Great, given the grandeur of your position."

"And which position did you find most grand?"

Lafferty considered. "The one hanging by your heels from the trapeze, I think."

"Sure, the blood rushing to your head enhances the sensuality."

"*Keep romance alive.* Is that not one of your ten golden rules?"

"It is. And now you've had your lesson, you and Peggy can find your own trapeze, and I'll claim another victory in the war against the disintegration of the traditional marriage as we know it."

Lafferty ran a finger down her ribs like a keyboard. "What's this?" He'd encountered a scar scarcely visible to the naked eye, a gouge on her side in the shape of a crescent.

"That," she said. "That's my emergency smile. I take it with me wherever I go."

"How did it happen?"

"This skinny fella was asking me too many questions one day, and I had to bump him off."

A moment of musing on Lafferty's part. "And how did that result in a scar?"

"Who said it did?" She smiled, eyes simmering.

"I see. We'll just settle for emergency smile. A scar by any other name. Curiosity is overrated at any rate."

"There's a good lad," she said, rewarding your man with a squeeze and a snuggle, though he found the bones of her a bit sharper now than they had been before. Lafferty allowed his God-given tendency to retreat in the face of confrontation, of any class of unpleasantness, to shut his gob for him, though a bit of the curiosity lingered still. The mysterious Katherine Flanagan, whatever else she was, was evidently good at her job all right, her propensity for the odd lapse in judgment notwithstanding. For that he had to allow her a bit of leeway, he supposed, given the nature of his own charms, compounded by the dimple in the middle of his own chin. Her success was apparent in the opulence of the place, the breadth and depth of the bed, the silkiness of the sheets, the shine of mahogany everywhere, the grand sweep of crimson drapery covering the wall of windows overlooking the village of Kilduff down below. The office in the front of the house was furnished in teak and brass and warm, soothing hues. And the bathroom, when he'd gone there earlier, had been like nothing he'd ever encountered before. He'd been almost reluctant, in fact, to defile the place by doing his business there.

It was back to the bathroom his daydreams took him when the woman slipped into a dreamy quiet and he thought he heard a wee snore. For didn't he have to pee again. And he thought about Peggy, his own wife and her niggardly ways, particularly with the hot water, which she seemed to think required the burning of banknotes to heat. And he imagined luxuriating in steamy water and bubbles in the sunken tub of the blue-tiled room just beyond the polished doorknob there across the poshness of carpet. Decadent and delicious to be sure, the perfect complement to a day such as this.

As Katie dozed he slipped away for his pee, the bed so fine and firm there was never a squeak to betray him, the carpet soaking up his footsteps like a sandy beach. And doesn't your man himself succumb to temptations of the flesh, though of a different class altogether, soon finding himself in the tub, up to his chin in hot water. Snug as a fist in a mitten. The flow of the warm water burbling in his ear, the piquant scent of the bubbles tickling his nose, he allowed himself to surrender to the comfort, having earned it, having performed so admirably in the service of his wife and their marriage, and on the other hand, so splendidly in the service of Katherine Flanagan, LPC, IACP, a widow with needs and wants of her own. Whose other hand, after a while, he heard on the knob of the door, whose footstep on the blue of the tiles, in perfect harmony with his dream of a balmy beach in the south of Spain, a dark-skinned girl in a white kimono, and a pitcher of green margaritas. Warm washcloth soothing his eyes, he showed her the dimple in his chin, which he lifted for a smile. "Come join me, love, the water's grand."

But Katie only shuffled her feet.

"Plenty of room in here for a pair," he said, his invitation enhanced and made all the more sincere by the stirring of his nether part, the blood flowing again, the buoyancy of the lovely hot water lifting him up, the thoughts of her nearby accessibility making him randy as a pup.

But Katie made no reply.

Removing the cloth, Lafferty opened his eyes. To lay them on two of the ugliest men he'd ever seen, standing there gaping down at him as though he were a two-headed donkey in the circus. Though it wasn't the pure ugliness that first caught his eye, to be sure; it was the gun in the fist of the first one, the cluster of yellow daffodils in that of the other.

No stranger to tight spots, Lafferty had indeed found himself naked in tight spots before, although tight spots such as those had generally been occasioned by a jealous lover, never before by two calm and ugly men. And seldom before had weaponry been involved, except for the once near Ballyjamesduff, the weapon in question having been a sailing cookie jar (the jealous lover in question having been of the female persuasion), a far cry indeed from a nine-millimeter pistol.

They brought him to the lounge, where he stood naked, dripping into the carpet. The nakedness was the worst of it and no place to hide, his heart wanting to jump from his throat. The man with the daffodils was the older and fatter of the pair, with lips and ears as thick as your thumb, his jacket brown and stained and two sizes too tight. "Where's the woman?" said he.

"What woman?" Lafferty said.

"What woman says he," said the fat man.

"The woman whose name is on the fucking sign out in front of the fucking house," the other man said. He was skinny and pink and jumpy, twitching the gun as he spoke. The black eyes of him never rested on any one object too long, and his checkered jacket was yellow and baggy and blue.

"Did you look in the bed?" Lafferty said.

"Did we look in the bed says he," said the fat man.

"Of course we looked in the fucking bed," said the skinny man.

Lafferty said, "She was there when I slipped in for my tub."

"She was there when he slipped in for his tub says he," said the fat man.

"Listen," said Lafferty, "could you quit repeating everything I say?"

"Could I quit repeating everything he says says he," said the fat man.

"Well, it is bloody fucking annoying," the skinny man said.

"That's your problem," said the fat man. "No appreciation of irony whatsoever. Everything's black and white to you."

"We got a job to do, and last I looked irony wasn't in the job description."

"That's your problem, right there," said the fat man, the tips of his ears turning red. "No appreciation of irony whatsoever."

"Can I put on my clothes?" Lafferty said.

"Fuck no," said the skinny man.

"The nakeder you are," the fat man explained, "the less likely are you to run. And the less likely you are to run, the less likely your man here will have to put a bullet in you."

Lafferty's knees gave a lurch, his stomach a roll. "Can I sit?"

"Can he sit says he," said the fat man.

They regarded the sofa beside them, deep and plush and beige, five oversized sections arranged in the shape of an L. "That's one L of a sofa," Lafferty said.

It took a moment or two till the skinny man sniggered. Didn't the fat one chortle as well. "One L of a sofa," exclaims he, and they both gave in to the laughter. "One L of a sofa!" said the skinny man. They laughed for a minute or more, Lafferty standing bewildered behind his smile. The fat man wiped his eye. "Good one."

"I like this fucking guy," said the skinny man, jabbing his pistol toward Lafferty.

"Sit," said the fat man, waving his daffodils toward the sofa.

"What are the flowers for?" Lafferty said.

"Ladies love the flowers, sure they do," the fat man said. "And we deliver."

"Special delivery," said the skinny man.

"Here," said the fat man, "you can hold 'em over your oul hooha there."

Thankful for little kindnesses, Lafferty took the flowers, holding them over his oul hoo-ha. He sat on the sofa, the fabric prickling his naked arse. The two men made no move to do likewise, hovering above him, feet planted apart. Only now, the shock of it sinking in, was Lafferty beginning to wonder where the hell Katherine Flanagan had got to, how indeed she'd managed to get away at all. Had she spotted them coming up the road and made off through the back? Was she hiding somewhere in the house? And of course the deeper mystery, why two desperate specimens such as these had come calling in the first place. When the fat man put his hands on his hips, Lafferty saw the holster peeping out from under his stained brown jacket, the wee wink of a pistol. Across the room, the curtain was parted on the wide front window, and outside the gloaming was going deeper, the rusty leaves of the rowan tree in front giving a shiver to a white panel truck passing down the road toward Kilduff.

Lafferty, with little to lose, pushed at his luck. "Can you put down the gun?"

"I can, of course," the skinny man said, "but I won't. Mrs. Dunleavy didn't raise a fool."

"Good job," said the fat man. "Why don't you give him your bloody address too?"

"And why would I do that?"

"You just give him your bloody name."

"He wouldn't have known it was my fucking name if you hadn't just fucking said so."

"And who was your bloody Mrs. Dunleavy then? Your bloody nanny?"

The skinny man shrugged. "For fuck's sake, let's just get on with it."

They looked down again at Lafferty sitting on the sofa, daffodils over his oul hoo-ha. "One L of a sofa," the fat man said. "Good one." He wasn't smiling. "One more time then. Where's the woman?"

One more time then Lafferty told them. All he knew was she was in her bed when he went in for his tub. "What are you doing here in the first fucking place?" the skinny man wanted to know. "How do you bloody well know her at all?" asked the fat man. "How much do you know about her fucking business?" the skinny man said, and the fat man said, "How bloody long have you been dipping your toe in her tub?" Lafferty talked till his mouth was dry. His missus, he told them, contemplating throwing him out of her house for no good reason at all, had bullied him into marriage counseling in the person of Katherine Flanagan, LPC, IACP, a newcomer to the area, chosen because the missus, noticing the spanking new sign by the road every day on her way to work—a nurse over at St. Christopher's she was—judged it to be of the finest professional quality. And hadn't Lafferty merely chanced upon Katherine Flanagan at Connor's News Agent, just across the street from his turf accountant Mickey G's, and hadn't one thing led to another. In his desire to come clean, to make a clean breast of it, to throw himself on the mercy of the court as it were, didn't the words come gushing out of Lafferty in a rush. How he attributed his extraordinary compatibility with members of the opposite gender not to the dimple in his chin, nor to the playful unruliness of his light brown hair—though those qualities certainly couldn't hurt—but rather to his innate ability to detect the tiniest, most subtle signal, such as when Katherine Flanagan, immersed in a session with himself and Mrs. Lafferty, had slowly drawn her eyes away from his and laid her bright red fingernail on the tip of her lip. So not at all surprised was he then, when following their chance encounter he merely wondered if she might be willing to show him what he was doing wrong in his marriage, and she proceeded to do so, in a manner quite eager.

"Let me get this straight," the fat man said. "You're shagging your bloody marriage counselor."

Lafferty shrugged. "Not habitually."

The skinny man jabbed his pistol toward Lafferty. "I like this fucking guy."

The fat man's thick lips curled into a reasonable facsimile of a grin. "Me too. But then again, some of my best friends are stone-cold liars."

"What do you mean by that?" the skinny man said.

"What's your name?" said the fat man.

"Lafferty. Terrance Lafferty."

"You sound like a Dub," the skinny man said. "Any relative to Denis Lafferty from Summerhill?"

Lafferty seized the moment. He lied. "He's my brother."

"Small world," said the skinny man.

"Small indeed," said the fat.

"Do you know him well?" Lafferty said.

"Do we know him well says he," said the fat man.

The skinny one's black eyes finally settled, latching on to Lafferty's. "Well enough to know he's one of the grandest fucking liars ever to breathe Dublin air."

"A trait known to run in the family," the fat man said. "Tell us where the woman is. Tell us now. My manners are wearing thin."

"Did you look under the bed?" Lafferty said, his mouth as dry as a camel's arse.

"Did we look under the bed says he," said the fat man. The skinny man didn't answer. The fat man looked at him. "*Did* we look under the bloody bed?"

"Did *you* look under the bed?"

"How am I to look under the bed with my bloody knees? *You* didn't look under the bed?"

"For fuck's sake," said the skinny man, sulking toward the bedroom door.

The fat man never budged, the tips of his ears turning red. Hovering over your man, staring down at him, he drew his pistol out from beneath his stained brown jacket two sizes too tight. Lafferty, his stomach in full riot, puckered up his arse, fearful of soiling the sofa. The flowers over his oul hoo-ha wilted and trembled from the heat and shaking of his hand, and his heart clambering in his chest like a hamster in a heated cage. He wished he was anyplace else. He felt the color fleeing his face like rats from a sinking ship. He wished he'd never been there.

Never there. Wasn't that the reason he was here in the first place. The first words out of Peggy's mouth at the first session the first time he ever laid his eyes on Katherine Flanagan, LPC, IACP: "He's never been there for me. Even when he's there, he isn't really there."

Through the wide window behind his wife that afternoon, Lafferty saw the broad sweep of fields dotted with sheep grazing among the hedgerows and stone fences leading down to the village tucked in the hillside. He saw the steeple of the church in the mist, the blue façade of the Commodore Hotel, and in his mind he calculated just where the Pig and Whistle would be, down the street, beyond the green. How he wished he was there with his fistful of jar. Of course it wasn't the first time he'd heard the words out of Peggy, not at all, but he'd realized, seated in upholstered splendor in the office out front, gazing down at Kilduff, that he'd grown immune to them. Hearing them again, Lafferty disagreed, and disagreed emphatically. He never thought of himself as never there. Wasn't he someplace all of the time?

The time they'd been evicted from their Dublin flat, hadn't he been at the Curragh, trying to win back the price of the rent. The time of the miscarriage, lamentable, tragic to be sure, but hadn't he been at the Pig and Whistle celebrating his impending paternity, and him with no earthly way of knowing. Any number of other times she'd complained he was never there, hadn't the cause of it been that she'd told him to get the hell out of her sight. Though Peggy's ears were deaf to his persuasions—her brown eyes indeed feigning pain and disbelief as they stared at him across the broad and pricey teak tabletop—Lafferty thought he detected a glimmer of understanding in the eyes of Katherine Flanagan, LPC, IACP.

Didn't it run in the family after all. Lafferty's oul man had never been there either.

And at the end of the day, didn't absence make the heart grow fonder. Hadn't Lafferty himself witnessed as a youth the grand reunions, his oul man and his oul wain on any number of occasions, him waltzing her across the narrow kitchen floor between the table and the stove, and her with her head back to let out the laugh. Hadn't he seen with his own eyes the pair of them, arm in arm, making their way up Drumcondra Road in a zigzag stagger, half blind with the song and the drink and the joy.

Didn't never being there have its sweet side as well.

No sooner did the skinny man walk into the bedroom till a ruckus of noises broke out. The fat man over Lafferty bounced back a step, raising the gun toward the door of the bedroom. Lafferty, shrinking on the sofa, hunkered over his daffodils. There was a shout, a thump or two or three, the sound of a scuffle, another shout and a gasp and a curse, the fat man starting for the bedroom door just before the explosion, the bang of the gun.

Then the silence holding nothing.

"Eamon!" called the fat man. "Eamon!"

More of the quiet. The ears of the fat man the color of raw beef.

Katie-bar-the-door. Standing there suddenly, the gun in her hands in front of her face, looking down the length of her arms over the pistol pointing straight at the fat man, like a right proper soldier, if not for the hot-pink housecoat hanging down, gaping open. "Drop it!"

The fat man in the same proper stance, feet wide, staring down both his arms over the pistol pointing at Katie, the sleeves of his brown jacket up to his elbows. "You drop it!"

Lafferty, slippery with sweat, caught a sweet scent of daffodil.

That was how they stood, squirming closer, squinting down their barrels. It seemed a long time passing. Lafferty off to the side, out of the line of fire, out of the line of vision, out of the picture altogether, might as well have never been there. A chill caught the sweat, and his back ached at how he was hunkered over and he sat up a bit, fearful of making himself too big. But nobody noticed.

"Drop it!" Katie said.

"You drop it!" said the fat man.

Katie creeping closer, her housecoat peeping open another inch, Lafferty staring at the glimpse of her nakedness, the shadows of the woman's body, the navel, the hair down below it, astounded at how it left him cold, at how utterly irrelevant was the clothing and the nakedness and the flesh at the end of the day. Invisible, didn't he keep growing bigger. The daffodils spread out flat and dead over his oul hoo-ha, the one part of him getting smaller.

"Drop it!" said Katie. "Drop it now!"

"You drop it! Now!"

It occurred to your man he could rise slow and easy and creep away, leaving them to their own devices, to settle it however they might, leaving them pointing their pistols at one another ad infinitum, or at least till tomorrow morning when Katie's first clients arrived to find the pair still standing there pointing their pistols yelling drop it. The skinny man he supposed was dead or mortally wounded, and he wondered where this warrior woman called Katherine the Great had come from, though he wanted nothing at all to do with it, whatever it was that it was. He wanted only to never be there. What he wanted, the only thing, was to be someplace else altogether where he could shake himself like a dog climbing out of the water and make it all fly away. He wasn't quite ready yet to stand up naked and tiptoe off, not yet, but the idea having planted itself in his mind was rooting around, searching for purchase, and was this close to finding it when the guns went off, *bang, bang,* one after the other within the span of the blink of an eye. The sound like a wind that boxed his ears, blowing his hair back, causing the sweat on his back to chill and dry in the instant.

Lafferty looked up blinking. Katie and the fat man were gone.

The scent of gunpowder bitter in his nose, the wind of the blast had sucked away all sound, leaving nothing but pure silence in which Lafferty sat for a while. When finally he heard a gurgle and a distant chirp of bird, he stood. Wobbly he was, his muscles like pudding. He dropped the flowers to the table. Katie and the fat man both lay on their backs, the fat man just off the L of the sofa, Katie's head in the doorway of the bedroom. The fat man, his stained brown jacket up past his elbows and squeezing the tips of his shoulders, was lying with his arms and legs flung out, looking at the ceiling with wide-open eyes, a patch of blood in the middle of the untidy white mound of shirt on his belly. Lafferty like a ghost in the quiet. Katie was lying the same, staring up at the top of the doorway, hot-pink housecoat spread open across the carpet, her naked body splayed, the scar, her emergency smile, smiling out from her bottom rib, the hole between her breasts still oozing. In the bedroom lay the skinny man humped up on his stomach, the eye on the side of his face wide open as well, staring under the bed.

Does nobody ever die with their eyes closed anymore?

In the bathroom, he put on his clothes. Without an ounce of consideration, with no premeditation at all, as though it were instinct, he took a small bath towel from the polished brass rail and wiped down the tub and the faucet, then all about the toilet. Taking the towel with him to the bedroom, he wiped off the doorknobs, the nightstand, the headboard, the shade of the lamp he'd admired. Then, in the lounge, the coffee table where he'd braced himself standing up. The back of the chair he'd grasped passing by. Any place he might have touched. Then he folded the bath towel, hanging it back proper on its polished brass rail.

Outside it was nearly dark, air clean and sweet. Lafferty shook his face into it, washing off the scent of the gunpowder, the smell of the blood, the odor of fear. Making it all fly away. He made his way down the road toward Kilduff, scarcely aware of his legs as they marched, nor his arms as they swung, exchanging nods with the odd sheep at the side of the road. Into Kilduff he walked, past the green where the Kilduff Cross stood, its once intricate Celtic design having been washed away by decades of Kilduff rain. It had been erected in loving memory of someone, but the inscription had long since vanished, and no one remembered the identity of the dearly departed, a sad anonymity. Lafferty strolled into the dark and friendly confines of the Pig and Whistle.

There sat Pat Gallagher in the heat of battle, the complexion of him like that of a boiled lobster, arguing with Francie Byrnes, a bald and bitter barber, and a clutch of others. Pint in hand, arse on stool, Lafferty entered the fray. His opinion was as strong as the next man's when it came to how realistic the mechanical contraption that portrayed the great shark in the film *Jaws* had been, and when the argument escalated to the question of whether or not Elvis had ever been in the employ of the CIA, and then on to the British conspiracy responsible for the disappearance of Amelia Earhart, Lafferty was able to hold his own there as well. They argued well into the night.

He was there next morning with Peggy in the kitchen, her roof yet over his head, a fine splash of sun coming in through the green of the curtain. Wasn't he there. Her hands were shaking. He made her tea, rattling the spoon in the cup. Listened to her tall tale. She bit into her muffin, and he watched the buttery crumb on the edge of her lip in a mesmerizing state of flux as the words flowed out of her. She was still excited, still in shock, still incredulous over the goings-on at St. Christopher's.

We sat there, in the same room with her, Terrance, you and me.

Sure, the IACP never heard of the woman. It was all a bloody hoax.

Nobody knows who she is. They're saying all kinds of things. They're saying she was a supergrass and the IRA clipped her. They're saying she was IRA and it was MI-5 took her out. They're saying she was Colombian cartel and it was a Mexican hit squad done her in.

There's no record of her at all. Nothing, nowhere.

Can you imagine if we'd been there? Can you just imagine?

MICHAEL NOLL

The Tank Yard

FROM *Ellery Queen's Mystery Magazine*

THE WOMAN WHO could have been the love of my life lived in a duplex with a black metal railing held to cement steps by loose bolts. I was nineteen years old and out of my league with a tall blonde who'd already graduated from community college. I wanted to hold the door and let her walk down the steps first the way a gentleman is supposed to do—or that's what I'd heard, what I knew about dating—but she came outside too fast, purse in hand, on the move, and if I wanted to be polite, it would have meant leaning against the rail to make room for her, and how would it look to fall into a bush before you'd even sat down to dinner? So I cut ahead of her and kept moving all the way to my truck so that I could at least hold that door open. She had on black pants and a sparkly shirt of sequins all sewn together, like she'd been dancing on a stage somewhere and then walked behind the curtain and straight into our town. I tried to sweep the seat clean. All it did was send a dust cloud in the air.

"Well," she said, "my mom always said not to shoot for the moon."

Then she said, "I'm kidding." The maple trees were red and vast over the street. She could have painted every breath I took. "So, what's the plan?"

I'd given this some thought, which meant I'd asked Rob where to go, and he'd explained that there was only one place in town worthy of a date. "You've got those glass lamps and sparkly cups." Which was true. And also the photos of old people in Italy.

"Pizza Hut," I said, which made her laugh, and so I laughed too, until she stopped.

"No, really."

I stopped the truck right in the middle of the street. "Hey," she said, but I hit the gas and took the next corner too sharp. "Did you, um"—she edged toward the door and gripped the handle —"forget something?"

"Yeah," I said. "My brain."

I didn't want her to jump out and I didn't trust that I could explain myself, so I sped up. At Walmart, I got out of the truck and threw the keys at her. "You stay here," I said. "I'm just going to run in and—" I almost said, "get some things," but part of me knew that if I said that, she'd drive away and leave me there, so I just came out with it. "I'm going to buy a charcoal grill and some charcoal and lighter fluid, and I'm going to buy two steaks and some peppers and onions and a loaf of some kind of bread and some spreadable butter and a bottle of some kind of wine, and then I'm going to come back and we're going to drive—" I almost said, "to City Lake," but I was slowing down, listening to my own thoughts and how I'd sound like a rapist, so instead I said, "to the courthouse and we'll park on the street and put the grill in the back and I'll cook up that food and then we'll eat on the tailgate while looking at downtown. Because one thing we've got here, if you haven't noticed, is a pretty nice-looking downtown. Does that sound okay to you?"

We ended up going into the store together. Afterward, we parked on the post office side of the courthouse because the kids don't drive back there when they're cruising, which means the cops wouldn't find our grill, and we cooked everything up and sat on the tailgate in the dark and watched the shadows of the trees and buildings grow long in the dark. You could see the outline of the town clock against the sky.

Nobody was using the word *steady* anymore, not even me. I don't even know where it came from. Sure, I was nervous. I'd been going on dates with Marissa and hanging out with her for a month. We were sitting in her backyard, drinking beer because it turned out neither of us knew what to do with wine.

"Did you just call it going *steady*?"

"Or whatever it's called. Are we a thing?"

"That depends what kind of thing you have in mind."

"You know," I said, and she shook her head.

"You'll have to do better than that."

"A together thing."

"You mean marriage?" she said, and I blushed so hard that even if I'd turned around, the hair on the back of my head probably would have been red. "I'm just messing with you," she said. "I'm never going to get married."

"Why?"

"Because my parents got married, and look at them. My dad's gone, and I don't talk to my mom."

"Why?"

She reached into the cooler for another beer but took out a piece of ice instead and threw it at me. "What are you, Barbara Walters? Because when it was time for me to go to college, there wasn't any money left. That's why."

"Times get tight," I said, and she shook her head.

"It wasn't like that."

This was an unheard-of idea, this not talking to someone. In my world, you stuck with people. You sat in the same room, watching the same TV show, and never spoke a word—not talking still counted as talking. But this was something different. "Does she live in town? Does she try to talk to you?"

"She tries."

"And what do *you* do?"

Now she threw a bottle cap at me. "You know what I like? Things. Do you like things?"

Sometimes you can feel something happening. You can even see it, I've learned, like a thread of spider silk hanging between you, and if you lean forward, and if she leans forward, the thread grows into a window that you can duck into. Other times, someone just barrels you over. I said, "That depends. What kind of things?"

She raised her eyebrows. "Maybe we should find out." She got up, went to the back door, and turned around. "You coming?"

She asked me, of course, what I did for a living, and I told her about delivering pizzas and newspapers, going door-to-door with vacuum cleaners. "I guess you could say I'm into sales."

"A real go-getter," she said, and I smiled.

"I'm actually picking up a fourth job. Seasonal work at an elevator."

"You saving up for something?" she asked. "Like, maybe, a ring?"

"Or baseball cards," I said. "You never know."

She leaned over, nibbled on my ear, and whispered, "I bet a baseball card can't do this."

The elevator job started with unloading grain trucks, but grain wasn't the point, not to me. The elevator was in one of the small towns out in the country, the kind with a closed grocery store, closed post office, and closed school. The only business left was the elevator, and for six months out of the year there was just one guy working, the foreman. During harvest, he hired another guy to help and kept him on through the first part of winter, when farmers applied anhydrous ammonia to their fields.

Anhydrous is a liquefied gas that, when released from the tank, immediately bonds to the first water it can find: in the ground, ideally, or, less ideally, in your eyes or lungs. It comes in big white tanks that slosh around when you're pulling them and come to a stop. The foreman showed me how to connect the tanks to the blue applicators that we rented out, like plows with hoses that injected the ammonia into the ground as fertilizer. He said farmers sometimes sent their kids to pick up the tanks, and the kids could barely walk and chew gum, so you had to make sure they didn't get themselves killed in case their dads told them to hook the tanks up to the applicator. "If you value your life, you won't mess around with this stuff." He went through the whole process again. "You think you got it?"

"Don't get myself killed," I said, and he clapped me on the back. "Good boy."

The tank yard wasn't next to the elevator but instead miles away, in a square of dirt carved out of a field, with a temporary chain-link fence set up around it and a little tin shed with a stack of forms I was supposed to check off for every trade, empty for full. I'd sit in the shed until the farmers showed up, and when they did arrive, just before dawn, there'd soon be a line of them, pickups idling and me doing the work of an automated machine: bending over, pulling the pin, dropping the tongue, walking to a full tank, lifting the tongue, dropping the pin, stepping back, waving. At the end of the day, I'd lock up. The first day, the foreman came by to make sure I'd done it right. He shook the gate and then reached up and grabbed the points where the wire was tied off around the top bar. He had to stand on his toes to do it. When he was done, he looked sad and beat down.

"How much you want to bet we come out tomorrow morning, there'll be part of somebody's pants caught up here." He looked at me. "Meth. They steal the gas and put it in those little propane tanks that are on your grill."

I asked what I should do if I noticed something like this happening.

"Oh, you won't," he said. "See it, I mean. Maybe you'll smell the ammonia if they don't close the valve all the way, and if that's the case, keep away. And if you see a body on the ground, definitely stay back. I don't want to have to call the morgue for you too."

"What a bunch of idiots."

"Oh," he said, "you'd be surprised. Some of them you probably know."

The sun was setting as we drove away, and when he turned down his road, I went another mile before turning around and driving to the culvert where I'd stashed the half-dozen propane tanks that Rob and I used. I took them to the yard, filled them, and drove through the dark to Rob's house, where he was waiting to cook.

In the evenings, when I got off work and before I went over to Rob's, I'd meet up with Marissa, and we'd walk. She knew all the neighborhood kids and dogs from the loops she'd made on her own, in the time before she met me. Dogs would run up, wagging their tails, sniffing her hand, which she'd let them do once and just once. Then it was my job to scratch their ears so they'd leave her alone and not get her hands smelly. All of her clothes looked like somebody's thoughtful mother had ironed them. She filed paperwork at the hospital, which meant she had to look professional. It also meant she knew private things about people I knew. I'd say, to make her laugh, "Tell me something I won't believe."

"Like what?"

"Like, who's got an STD?"

"Everyone. You should never have sex."

"You sound like my mom," I said.

"She's one of them that I'm talking about."

One night I asked if the hospital ever saw meth addicts. Maybe cooks who'd gotten themselves hurt?

"Hurt how? You mean burned up? I've heard of that, but not here."

"Or blinded."

"Blinded! What do they do, shove it in their eyes?"

"It's just something I heard once."

"I think you're keeping the wrong kind of company."

"The life of sales," I said. "There's people out there you'll never set eyes on unless you're in line for the Tilt-a-Whirl at a carnival. Try selling them a vacuum cleaner, and they have to go get a dictionary to look up what you're talking about."

"They have dictionaries?"

"Self-preservation," I said. "Otherwise they'd just grunt at each other."

"Must be scintillating conversation."

I said, "Oh, there are other ways to be—what'd you call it? Scintillating. Besides conversation."

Rob and I had gotten into the meth business together when we were seventeen. For a long time he'd lived with his grandmother, a brittle old woman who threw saltines at you when you walked in front of her soaps. When she died, Rob stayed in the house and nobody thought much of it. In those days, a sixteen-year-old could be his own guardian, and so he dropped out of school and spent the day dreaming up bad ideas.

I was still in school, a B to C student but vice president of the business club, which was where I picked up the lingo. I'd go up to kids between classes, shake their hands, and say, "I'd like to discuss an opportunity with you." Or, "Have you considered investment plans for your hard-earned cash?" The language caught on—there's no thrill like euphemisms that teachers don't understand: mission creep and hostile takeover. We'd do the deals after school, in somebody's house, and eventually I expanded the market. I'd go out, find the worst houses, and knock on the door, unlock my briefcase, pull out a small amount of crystal, and say, "Try this." Because we had a surplus, we didn't need to cut it. "If this is detergent," they'd say, "you know I'm going to kill you, right?" Then they'd snort it, and their eyes would roll back.

"Exactly," I'd say. "Now, I'd like to discuss an opportunity with you."

Afterward, Rob and I would throw our money in the air and hump the furniture and walls. That last part was his thing, his trademark. He came up with it before he dropped out, and he stuck with it for a couple of years, humping the lab and the propane tanks full of stolen anhydrous and the Maxwell House can where he kept his money. Sometimes he'd hump me, and I'd have to push him off. "Rob, you know they put dogs down for that." He'd laugh and laugh. He was a funny guy. He didn't take showers a lot, didn't eat regular meals, didn't wear shoes. He picked at the dead skin on his heel while the lab bubbled away. He didn't go out in the world, and so seeing him was like seeing a fox. You stopped what you were doing and watched until he was gone. I'd be delivering meth and guys would ask, "Who cooks this stuff, you or that filthy partner of yours?" and I'd say, "Oh, look, it's the world's first fussy addict." I knew they'd fork over the cash. Even if I'd said that the stuff they were snorting had little bits of dead skin mixed in, they'd have paid me and begged me to come back with more.

Between deliveries, I'd stop by Marissa's house. We'd fool around, watch some TV, eat something, and then I'd have to go.

"Why? What could you possibly have to do right now?"

"Those newspapers won't roll themselves."

It was like going off to war, an act, sure, but too dramatic for my taste. She'd grab a wad of my shirt, and I'd have to pull her along with me to the door, smiling and being serious about it at the same time. It was hard not to think about Rob, alone on his couch in his underwear, thumbing sack. Once Marissa kept giving me crap even after I'd got out the door, and so I said, "You know what? After I leave, call your mom. It's not okay to give up on people." She slammed the door, but I was already down the sidewalk, figuring this was one of those moments that tell you something. We'd make up, or we wouldn't, and that'd be the end of it. Either way, I told myself I was fine with what I'd done.

After six months with Marissa, I drove to Topeka, to the mall where the white people used to go, and bought a ring outright, with cash.

I thought the clerk might give me some flak, but I guess he was used to such things. I carried the ring everywhere, all of the time. When I was making deals, I'd think about it, tucked away in my left pants pocket, and when the door closed and I was walking back to the car I used for deliveries, I'd reach in to make sure it was still there. Sometimes it felt like a ticking clock: I'd have to introduce Marissa to my parents, and both of us would have to answer their questions. What were we going to do with our lives? What are you going to *be*? I'd answered them plenty of times on my own, and it wasn't a big deal: "I'm going to be an astronaut. Or a baseball player, not sure which."

"You deliver pizzas," my dad would say, and my mom would chime in. "You're too smart for this. You need a career. You've got to pick one. What are your skills?"

"Talking," I'd say.

"There you go. You should go into sales."

But that was beyond what my dad could abide. He'd slap his head and say, "Jesus, anything but that."

"Why?" she'd ask. "Someone has to do it."

While they debated the merits of sales, I fingered the ring in my pocket and thought about drugs. They were like cars—you tried to find that fine line, the moment where the trouble they'd give you was mostly in the future and not in the past. You never wanted to hang on too long. You didn't want to spend more on them than they were worth. I had about thirty thousand dollars saved up in cash that I'd stuffed in a sun-tea jar and rolled under the front porch of the house I was renting. This was a sizable amount. I could make more, but how much more? For all our business acumen, Rob and I hadn't figured out a better system for what to do with the profits. He kept his money buried somewhere in his backyard. We'd talk about what to do with it: buy cars, buy houses, leave the country and never come back.

"I'd have to come back," Rob said. "Can you imagine me in England, in some castle?"

"I don't think all the Brits live in castles."

"You know what I mean."

"Or," I said, waving generally at the travesty of an abode where we found ourselves. "You could do something about this."

"Do what?" he asked, and for a moment I thought he was joking. The roof leaked in the bathroom. Half the windows had long cracks running diagonally across the panes. One in the bedroom was broken out entirely, and Rob had covered it in tinfoil, just like all the windows in the kitchen, where he cooked. He squinted at me and stuck his hands in his underwear. He kept squinting and rubbed his balls.

"Fix up the house. Upgrade from shithole to hovel."

"Why would I do that?"

Some things you just can't explain. I gave up. "No reason," I said.

Unlike me, he used our product. I'd told him it was unprofessional, and he said, "You never eat Pizza Hut?" Of course I did. "Well, there." He'd gotten thin and edgy, had picked up a gun somewhere. He wanted me to get one too, and he was right. A drug dealer needs a gun like a car owner needs a mechanic. But whenever I held the pistol, it felt heavy and potent, as if it had already made its mind up to go off. I worried about shooting myself in the foot. So when customers called on the phone, I made it clear that I was like the cashier at a convenience store. I didn't carry much cash or product. And in case that didn't work and they robbed me anyway, I made it clear that Rob was the heavy. "He'll crack your eyeballs on your forehead like they're eggs," I said. Mostly I hoped that everyone would play nice.

"They won't play nice," Rob said over and over again. "And I won't dig out their eyes. I'll just shoot them."

"What difference does it make?" I asked. "The point is that we don't want to shoot anybody."

This was when he got pissed. "It's got nothing to do with *wanting*," he said. "You do what you have to do."

It was a pretty fundamental disagreement, and it wasn't going to get solved in one argument or probably ever. But he put up with me—the latitude you give a friend. The truth was, he was just biding his time until the inevitable happened and I quit.

Sometimes I'd call in sick, and Rob would say, "Drug dealers don't get sick."

"Lovesick," I'd say, and then I'd spend the evening with Marissa, talking and dreaming and naked.

One morning I woke up to find her showered, dressed, and curling her hair in the mirror. "Big plans?" It was Sunday. She was going to church.

"Why?" I asked, but this wasn't an argument she wanted to have.

For some reason, I did. "Is this something your mom got you into? Is she going to be there?"

She didn't take the bait. "You can come if you want." Then she left, and I realized that it really didn't matter to her if I came or not. So I ran home and got dressed. The choir was singing when I walked in. The whole church got a good look at me stopping beside each row, looking for Marissa. Afterward people I knew by name only, bankers and doctors and other important Methodists, came up to us and said hello. The women smiled, and the men put their arms around Marissa. "Been awhile. We were worried about you," they said, staking their claim to her. They were her community. She was on her own in life, trying to make great things on a small inheritance, and they weren't going to let anyone get in her way. "And who is this?"

"Oh," she said, "just somebody I met."

"Do you think we'll be seeing him here again?"

She shrugged and bumped her shoulder into mine. "You never know."

That was on Sunday. On Monday I went back to work. Rob was pissed. "You know how much money we lost last night? You know we just drove good customers into the arms of the competition?"

I said, "God didn't mean for us to work every hour of every day. You've got to enjoy life."

Rob said, "You don't know shit about what God wants."

I made a plan. When there was thirty-five thousand dollars in the jar, I'd quit. It'd be the start of summer, a good time for new beginnings. I wanted the change to be neat and tidy. So I started hanging out with Rob more. He'd go for a day without eating, and I'd say, "Don't get up. Let me get the groceries. Let me get toilet paper. Really. It's no big deal." In a way it was the right move, because if anyone had seen him, they might have asked around: Is he okay? Is he sick? He looked like a corpse. He was meth-ly ill. His eyeballs were starting to stick out. When he looked at you, it was like he could see all the way around his body. He knew things, those eyes said. Can't sneak anything past us.

"This lady friend of yours," he said once, "when you going to bring her around here? If there's going to be a wedding, shouldn't I meet her first?"

I reached for the ring in my pocket but stopped myself. He was sprawled out on the couch, no shirt, no pants, in just his stained white underwear, the leg holes so stretched out that his balls fell through.

"I know you're going to ask her," he said. "It's not a secret. You got that puppy-dog look all the time. You're even going to church with her." He winked at me. "What? People talk. It's a wonder they don't walk up and pat your little puppy head, scratch your ears. C'mon, bring her around."

There was no good answer to this. So I didn't give one. He looked down at himself, at his balls, and held out his arms. "Afraid she'll like this too much?"

Some nights I prayed for a delivery just so I could get out of there. We had our regulars, people who called like clockwork every night or every other night. They'd have a nice little routine set up, particular ways they'd rub their hands before they took out their money, a certain kind of music playing on the tape deck. Those were the good ones. Other times I'd get called out to a place I'd never been. Once it was a competitor, another cook, and he opened the door and stuck a steak knife in my face and said, "You're not going to come around here anymore." This was early on. We were encroaching on his territory. I said, "Okay," stepped back, tossed the meth at him, shut the door, and ran. I kept looking back, and he wasn't chasing, so I slowed down, gave it some thought. That guy, I thought, he's probably not even for real. He probably just wanted some free drugs. So I slashed his tires, broke his windshield with a rock, bashed off his side-view mirrors, cut his seats open and gave them a good piss. He must have come out not long after that. Maybe he decided to hunt me down. I don't know. Wherever he was going, on his way there, the highway patrol pulled him over for driving a car that was all beat to hell. He was high. He had a gun without a license. He went to jail. Sometimes I thought about him when I was fingering the ring in my pocket. I'd do some quick math: three thousand to go. Two thousand eight hundred. Two thousand.

"Thank you," I started saying at the end of a delivery. "Be sure to call us again." Given my math, if we had enough nice customers, I could take a pass on the bad ones.

One lady was particularly regular. Like clockwork, every Friday night she'd call, and I'd come by her place. There were some soft boards on the porch and no doorbell, but if that's the worst a person can say about your place, you're doing okay. She always looked nice: recently showered, trim and put together. I wouldn't have been surprised if she was a first-grade teacher—she just had that look, like my mom but on meth. A weekend warrior. She didn't even need to call. Her needs were understood. So one night I pulled up like usual and knocked on her door. It was late, and no lights were on except for one deep inside her house. In the moonlight filtering through the bare tree branches, you could just make out the car and the Pizza Hut sign on top.

The door opened, and I put on a smile.

"Well, hey, stranger." It was Marissa, peering at me and then throwing the door open. Both of us looked at the box in my hands, and she gave me this funny look before yelling back into the house, "Mom, did you order a pizza?"

From way back down a hallway came the reply. "Oh, shit."

"What is this?" Marissa said, and I could have pointed at the box with its cold pizza and my shirt and hat. I could have said, "Pizza delivery, ma'am." But instead I just stood there too long. Even after her mom came out and things got ugly, I just watched it all like an idiot. I'd never seen Marissa so mad. Her mom kept apologizing and asking how Marissa knew me. "I don't," Marissa said. "I have no idea who he is." Then she went inside and screamed, "Well, might as well get what you ordered."

Even then I didn't move.

Her mom held up one finger, stepped into the house, and then came back outside. "When you leave," she said, "just be sure to drop it in the bushes where I can find it." Then she tucked some bills in my pocket.

I drove around town for a while, pounding my fists on my steering wheel, worried that Marissa might call the cops. So I switched out the delivery car for my truck and drove out of town. I probably covered half the county, maybe more, until I wound up at the tank yard, dark except for a single utility light that shone from a pole over the tin shed. I hadn't come with a plan, but one came to me when I saw a blanket spread over the top of the fence and a guy sprinting away into the fields. I waited for his partner, the one inside the fence who would lift the full tank over. I got out of the truck, slammed the door so he'd hear it, and walked right up to the fence. "Did you get yourself killed? Either way, I want you out of there now."

When there wasn't an answer, I banged the fence good and yelled, "I'm not the cops. I work here, so get over to this fence now. And bring the tank with you."

The guy skulked out from behind the tank where he'd been hiding. He came up to the fence. Even in the moonlight, I could see the sickly color of his skin and his rotted teeth. He smelled like he hadn't showered in a year.

"You're really not going to turn me in?" His wedding band shone in the utility light. So did the burns on his hand. "I've got kids."

"Give me the tank," I said. He flipped it over the fence, which isn't easy with seventeen gallons of anhydrous, and then scrambled over. I gave him the tank back, and he stared, incredulous.

"You're giving it back?"

I said, "That's right, I am. What am *I* supposed to do with it?" I followed him to his car. When he was over the hill, I jumped back in my truck and drove after him. I kept my lights off. The gravel had a soft gray light under the moon, and I stayed right in the middle of it, watching the dark for the man's headlights.

He pulled up to a farmhouse and went inside, the screen door slapping the wood frame behind him. I parked on the road so that I wouldn't have to back out of the drive and crept through the yard, past a dozen or so cars on blocks, the grass dead and tall around them. Through the window I saw the living room, the TV, and two kids lying on the floor in blankets. A woman was standing in front of them, yelling into a room out of sight. I couldn't hear her. Those old farmhouses are soundproof: storm windows, plaster walls. It was a good place that they were letting go down the drain. I walked up to the porch and knocked. The guy's wife answered.

"Your husband here?" He must have recognized my voice, because from inside the house I heard the sound of footsteps and then a slammed door. I went inside and shut off the TV so that the wife could hear me crystal clear. I was standing close enough to the kids that I could have kicked them.

"Nice kids," I told the wife. They were asleep. I held my shoe over the fingers of the smallest one. "Tell your husband I said so."

Then I walked out the door. I stopped at the guy's car and dug around until I found an empty bag of meth. It was the sandwich kind with the opening that you had to fold over. The idiot didn't even use a Ziploc.

Rob was awake and cooking when I came in. He didn't jump or start when I let the door slam, just turned around with the gun tucked in his underwear. I went to the fridge, got a beer, and sat down in a chair that had materialized in the living room, one of those old-fashioned wooden kinds.

"Nice chair," I said. "Where'd it come from?"

He shrugged.

I said, "I met some of the competition tonight."

"That's not what I heard," he said. He didn't look at me when he said it. Instead he acted like he was busy with the lab, but it was running. He wasn't fooling me.

"Well?" I said.

"Your girlfriend called. She wanted to give you a message." He turned around, and whatever look was on his face made me stop looking at it and start watching his hands and their distance from the pistol.

"Expecting somebody dangerous?" I asked, nodding at it.

He took the gun out of his waistband and held it up so we could both have a good look. "You mentioned some competition. Did you mess him up?"

"He had kids."

Rob said, "We sell to kids."

"Small kids."

"So you're saying you let the guy get away." He batted the gun barrel in the palm of his hand, like he was thinking something over, and then he walked back into his room. He came out in a pair of jeans. "I've got to go back and take care of what you should have done. Otherwise, everybody's going to think we're weak."

I stepped in front of the door.

"I can't let you do that."

He put his hand on the butt of the gun.

"Or what?"

"Or nothing. You don't know where he lives, and I do. It's going to stay that way. Now tell me what Marissa said."

We were standing eye to eye. The gun was there, in his pants, and I could have grabbed it. I wanted to. I was stronger than him, and he was grinning at me. He shook his head. "You can ask her yourself."

"Okay," I said, and he smiled in a way that I didn't like.

"Well?" He looked at the door. "You've got work to do."

It was three in the morning when I drove past Marissa's house. The lights were out, but her car was gone. I went to her mom's next: lights on, at home. No Marissa, but maybe she'd gone for a drive, gotten mad, and walked back here. Or maybe she'd parked out of sight so no one would know she had a tweaker for a mom. I parked down the street and planned out my strategy: "I quit. Done," I'd say. "And you"—I'd point at her mom. "You're done with meth. I'll make sure that every cook around knows that if they sell to you, I'm coming at them." Then I'd point to Marissa. Maybe I wouldn't point. I'd lower my voice, get softer. "I'm sorry," I'd say. "I should have told you."

"Goddamn right you should have told me."

Whatever grief she wanted to throw at me, I'd take it. I wasn't a Methodist, but I'd gone to church as a kid, and I knew how it went: there was an angry God and a forgiving God, and you had to go through the first to get to the second. I'd just have to sit there and listen and nod and agree. Eventually she'd get tired. It was already so late. She'd slump over. By that time, maybe light would be coming through the windows. The birds would start chirping. "You need to eat," I'd say. "I'll make breakfast."

Just in case Marissa wasn't there, I grabbed a ski mask that I kept under the seat and stuck it in my pocket. This time I didn't knock. I tried the door. "Hello?" No answer, but there was a body on the floor. Her mom. The bag of meth was on the floor beside her, so I picked her up and carried her to my truck. The hospital would ask questions, and besides, she was still breathing. So I took her to the only place I could think of.

The tank yard was quiet at this late hour. Marissa's mom was still unconscious but starting to mumble as I taped her to a chair with a roll of duct tape I found in a drawer. I thought about gagging her but didn't want her to suffocate. Her eyes rolled in their sockets. She twisted her head around and found me, sitting on the floor against the wall, but she couldn't hold her head steady.

"Pay up," I said.

She struggled at the tape but gave up almost immediately. "Who are you?" she demanded.

"Somebody you owe."

She said, "I don't owe anyone. Now let me go. I've got to take a piss."

"Not till you pay."

Her eyes got wide. "I really have to go."

I didn't want a puddle of piss in the shed. It wasn't a big place, and even if I opened the windows, the smell would be terrible. If I opened the windows, we'd both be cold. So I dragged the chair outside, pulled her pants down. She screamed, and I said, "That is not what's happening here." I tipped her forward and said, "Now, go."

She pissed in the gravel and then I pulled up her pants and dragged her back inside. "You want something to eat?"

She shook her head.

"Thirsty?" She nodded, and I went out to the truck and got the jug that I kept in it. Luckily there was some water inside, and I let it run into her mouth.

"Anything else?" I asked, and she nodded.

"Let me out of here."

But that wasn't going to happen. I said, "I'll be back in a while. If you try to escape, I'll kill you."

Then I went to find Marissa.

It was seven o'clock. The sun wasn't up, but there was enough light to see to drive without headlights, which I did. I pulled right in her driveway. It went along the side of the house, where her car was parked, and I blocked her in. She'd deadbolted the door, but I gave it a good kick.

"Go away," she said, through it.

"Hear me out first."

"Don't want to. I'm calling the cops."

"I've gone straight. No more drugs, I promise. I'll be such a straight arrow you'll think I've gone native." She didn't laugh. "Sorry," I said. "No more jokes. Just give me a chance."

"Never come back here again. That's your chance."

"Do you remember how we met?" I asked.

"I'm not messing around here," she said. "Get out."

"It was only seven months ago, but it feels like forever. You know?" Of course she remembered. It was only seven months ago. It was at the courthouse, on the lawn. Saturdays in the Park, the city called it, even though there was no park, just grass and marble. Some kids from the high school jazz band were playing up by the courthouse. People had set up lawn chairs. They were lined up at tables where some organization of old ladies was selling homemade ice cream. Marissa was lined up. She ordered peaches and cream, and I came up to her and I said, "You should have picked vanilla. Always pick vanilla when it comes to homemade."

"Says who? You?"

She dipped her spoon in the soft ice cream and took a bite. She made a face and spit out a chunk into her cup.

"The peaches are like rocks, aren't they? It always happens."

She said, "Are you an ice cream salesman?"

"Nope, just an interested party."

Now I stood back so that I could kick in the door. "Seriously," I said, "do you remember that? Are you there?" When she didn't answer, I kicked as hard as I could, right under the knob, and felt the jamb crack—not all the way, but enough. I got ready to kick again, and she screamed at me to stop. Please, just stop.

So I stopped. I put my mouth right up to the door so she'd be sure to hear me.

"You know what I was doing that day? I was on my way to a delivery, and I had my windows rolled down. I rolled through downtown, and I heard the music and saw all those people there and the old buildings around them and the trees. And I said to myself, 'What would it feel like to be like them?' So I stopped and got out. And I met you."

I waited for her to say something.

"I've made a lot of mistakes," I said, "but that wasn't one of them. I can be a good person if you'll let me. Now, are you going to let me in so we can talk?"

"I'm holding a knife. Go ahead. Kick the door in the rest of the way."

It was a relief, in a way. It's good to know where things stand.

"Fine," I said. "But I should probably tell you where your mom is right now."

Marissa drove her own car and followed me. At the tank yard, I told her to wait at the gate. "Not until you tell me what's going on," she said, but she'd followed me this far. She wasn't going anywhere. I held a finger to my lips and crept up to the office, listened at the door, and then opened it. Her mom was still tied up as I'd left her except that she'd tipped the chair over and was lying on her side. She had a bruise on the side of her forehead that you could see as soon as I set her upright again. I went back out and called Marissa over. When she saw her mom, she ripped off the blindfold and the gag.

"Apparently she owed some other dealers money. They weren't as nice as me."

Marissa stood with her back to the wall, next to the door, as far from her mom as she could get. "How did *you* know that?"

I sighed. "Because I'm a caring person who looks out for his customers." She opened her mouth to tell me what she thought of that, and I said, "Because I know things. That's why. After I heard, I went by her house to check on her, and I found this." I held up the sandwich bag. "This had meth in it, now it doesn't. And I didn't leave it there. Now, you want to get her out of here or what?"

Together we carried her to Marissa's car and slid her into the back seat. I followed her back into town, to the hospital, though I didn't go in. I had thirty-three thousand dollars in a jar under my porch, and that was what I could do, I realized. I could pay for her mom to get clean. So I went home, got down on my hands and knees, and reached under the porch. I reached as far as I could but felt only dirt. I went and got a flashlight. Only dirt. The jar was gone.

I waited until after dark, way after, closer to sunrise than sunset. I wanted to make sure Rob was done cooking, that he was asleep, that he was alone. First I went back to the tank yard, filled up a propane tank with anhydrous, and put it on the floor on the passenger side of my truck, close enough that I could hold on to it around curves so it wouldn't roll around. When it was almost morning, I went over to Rob's. I carried the tank to the back of the house, where his bedroom was. With my finger, I poked a hole in the tinfoil covering his window. There was some old tubing in his backyard, stuff we'd thrown out because of wear and tear, but it was good enough for this. I slid the tubing through the hole until I felt it hit the floor. I connected the other end to the tank and turned the valve. The smell of the ammonia was unbearable, even from twenty feet away, where I stood listening for him to wake up, which he did. He thrashed and threw himself against the wall. He screamed. But he couldn't see, and so he never did find his way out of the room.

When it was over, I went to the back porch to start looking for my money. It wasn't much of a porch, not much bigger than a bathroom floor. He'd moved the new chair onto the middle of it, and I stood there looking at that chair. Somebody had spent a lot of time on that chair. The owner probably had a flower garden with a trellis and a climbing rose, and maybe there were kid toys in the yard and a basketball hoop and one of those lawn-art road-runners with legs that spin in the wind. You work hard, pay your property taxes, paint your siding when it peels or invest in vinyl, and somebody runs off with whatever isn't chained and bolted to a concrete slab. I climbed on top and stuck my hand up through the soffit hole where there should have been a screen but now was open. I reached around until I found my jar and the Maxwell coffee can. I took both back to my truck, and then I came back for the chair. He didn't deserve something so nice, and neither did I, but I intended to one day, so I took it.

The woman who could have been the love of my life got her mom straight again. She went to college. After three years, she graduated and got a job at a bank in Overland Park, a nice suburb of Kansas City where no one is poor and everyone looks cut out of a magazine advertisement for IAMS dog food. She met a man, married him, had three kids, and sometimes her mom comes to stay with them. Her mom, so far as I know, doesn't use drugs anymore. I'd like to take credit for the change, but it turns out that lots of people give up drugs, alcohol, cigarettes, candy, dairy, gluten, poor choices, dead-end jobs, bad partners, the places they live, their pasts, their futures. There's no end to what willpower can achieve. You just have to want things, I guess. Every year, around Christmas, I send her a card. I just write my name. The message is whatever the Hallmark people dreamed up.

A lot of people are able to become exactly the kind of person they want to become, good and upstanding, pillars of the community, a benefit to all who know them. There are gifts in life to those who deserve them. And some people are there to take it away. I like to think that they get exactly what they have coming.

TODD ROBINSON

Trash

FROM *Last Word*

TWENTY-FIVE TONS OF garbage truck made a sharp left onto Mott Street. Will stood on the back runner, his fingers laced through the railing. The summertime stink of Chinatown started polluting his sinuses from three streets away. Those blocks were the worst of the run; the smell of rotting seafood was one that wouldn't leave his nose for a few hours. It roosted inside his nasal cavity like an Alphabet City squatter.

It was worse than Will could have imagined. Even worse than the detailed descriptions his old man had given him about the bad old days.

The elder Mr. Pokorski had warned Will long before he'd set his son up with the job for the summer. The trash route Will was on was the same that his father had done up until his retirement three years ago. It was a soft scam going back generations. A lot of union guys, especially the ones who worked the roughest summer runs, would pay the sons of other union members ten bucks an hour and pocket the rest of their salary for the additional days off. Some guys, like the one Will was covering, were willing to sacrifice the money for the entire summer so long as it meant they wouldn't have to deal with Chinatown at all for the season.

Will absolutely understood the reasons now.

Even though the sun had set a full five hours ago, the heat that had been absorbed deeply into the concrete radiated up in waves, cooking the filth like a convection oven. What sat at the bottom of the black garbage bags had been slow-cooking from the ground up.

Like he tended to do, Antoine made the left hard and fast, disregarding the fact that the light had turned full red a good three seconds before he accelerated into the turn. Two cars let loose with a horn blare as they screeched to short stops.

Will was trying to keep the fetid air at bay by keeping his nose and mouth covered with the crook of his elbow as they sped down the street. When Antoine made another attempted Tokyo Drift move with the garbage truck, the centrifugal force nearly tore Will off the back. "Slow down, you freakin' lunatic!"

Antoine haw-hawed his ass off in the driver's seat. Will could see his fat frame bouncing up and down in laughter through the big side mirror. Just the day before, a hard turn onto Canal nearly turned a middle-aged woman's labradoodle into slurry under the truck's thick wheels.

When he started the job at the beginning of June, Will asked Antoine what was up with the New York City garbage trucks' disregard for traffic laws and public safety in general.

"Fuck 'em," was all Antoine answered with.

Back in the day, Antoine was one of the summertime kids, just like Will. Antoine had done the route with his old man, now a lifer with the Sanitation Department..

Will had no intention of being a lifer. Even though he was sorely jealous of his friends who'd all thrown in for a rental down the shore for the summer, Will wanted the money. When he started the criminal law program at Long Island University in the fall, he had no intention of doing so while commuting out of his parents' home. Will was getting his own place with his girlfriend, Cara. His buddies would still be living in their tiny childhood bedrooms with their Eli Manning posters and high school track trophies. Will was going to finally have his own space to bang his girlfriend without the threat of either his mother coming in or, worse, Cara's dad, the NYPD sergeant.

It was this promise of carnal freedom that kept Will hanging on to his sanity, kept him from seething at the thought of missing what was probably the last hurrah for high school on the shore.

It'll be worth it. It's all going to be worth it, he told himself over and over, every night.

The truck pulled up in front of Lucky Star Restaurant, and Will hopped off. He moved double-time while in Chinatown, wanting to get the hell gone before his gag reflex kicked in. He hurled the trash bags as quickly as he could into the rear of the truck.

One night after grousing about the run at the one bar in Staten Island with a bouncer dumb enough to accept his shitty Times Square fake ID, another customer had asked him how bad could the smell be? He was a garbage man, after all.

"How bad can it be?" Will replied. "I'm a goddamn garbage man, and the smell makes me want to puke. Every goddamn time. That's how bad the smell is."

He'd tried to use a facemask for a while, but after a couple of breaths it only felt like the stink was trapped underneath the thin sheet of cotton, pressed even closer to his face.

There was nothing he could do about it other than hope for short summer months or for something inside his olfactory system to finally give up and die.

Will grabbed the last bag off the pile, the plastic drooping sadly next to a mostly disassembled chest of drawers. On the upswing toward the compactor well, the bag caught on an exposed screw and burst open like a ripe cyst, viscous liquid splattering along the front of his jumpsuit.

"*Fuck,*" Will yelped as the warm fluid soaked through his clothing and boots. He stepped back and felt it squishing wet inside his socks. He was about to reflexively put his hand over his mouth in order to suppress the gagging that he felt rising inside him when he realized that his gloves were covered in what looked like rotting calamari in gelatin.

By the time all his senses could coordinate which aspect to be horrified at (the answer being all of it), Will's vision swam.

On top of everything else, Will had to worry about fainting out of sheer disgust. Took him a moment—a terrible, terrible moment—but then he noticed that his vision wasn't in fact swimming. What were swimming, however, were the hundreds of maggots embedded in the fluid that was covering him.

He nearly screamed.

He almost did.

But it's really hard to scream when you're projectile-vomiting all over the side of a garbage truck on Mott Street.

All the way down Mott Street . . .

All the way to Oliver Street . . .

Back up Katherine Street to Henry Street . . .

Antoine haw-hawed so hard at Will that he nearly threw up himself. On the corner of Market, Antoine had to jump out of the truck's cab, heaving and hawing so loudly that a middle-aged Chinese lady started yelling at him out her window.

Will didn't understand the Mandarin that the woman was shrieking, but it was pretty easily translated into the old classic of NYC sentiments: *Shut the fuck up.*

Will found himself lagging on the bag tosses. All of his prior instincts and muscle memory from the job abandoned him as he was filled with a new caution that he'd never had on the job before. Only a couple more blocks after Antoine nearly lost his dinner, he was whining at Will to speed it up. They were already a half hour behind from their usual mark, and at their current pace they were only going to fall further behind.

But despite all sense of self-preservation toward his senses, Will didn't want to have another bag pop open on him. As it was, he was already dreading his girlfriend's reaction when he got home. She already gave him shit for coming into the apartment smelling the way he did after a normal night on the job, with no exploding bags of Chinatown muck in the mix.

And for some reason he kept thinking about the Hispanic lady at the cleaners, who always looked at him like he was the worst person on earth when he walked through the door of her laundromat. If she held him in distaste before, she was going to love the bag he was going to drop off that night.

He didn't know why he feared the woman's ire, but he did.

That said, he carefully eyeballed every bag for telltale rips, lighter areas of plastic where the bag might be stretched to a point of near-breakage. Nor was he cavalierly chucking the bags into the back, either. Each bag he lifted carefully, if not daintily, as far away from his body as he could, then lobbed it in the back with no more velocity that one would underhand a wiffle ball to a toddler.

"You're killin' me, Will," Antoine whined.

Then the loosest of thoughts flittered across Will's mind as the truck pulled up in front of the Lotus Blossom Massage Parlor. It wasn't just that there were more bags in front of the tiny storefront than usual, but straight up, why would a massage parlor have so much garbage?

Lost in that thought, Will lifted the first bag, the weight striking, almost making him miss the two dime-sized holes in the bag.

"Whoa, shit!" Will yelled.

"What is it now?" Antoine said.

"Holes in the bag."

"You're fucking killing me."

"You're mistaking me for heart disease, you tubby fuck."

That shut Antoine up for a second. Then, "That was a little mean."

Will rolled his eyes and put the bag carefully back down onto the sidewalk so he could find a better purchase for his grip. Then, as the bag flattened back out under its own weight, two purple-lacquered fingernails poked out through the holes. Fingernails that were still attached to fingers.

"Oh *fuck!*" Will jumped back like he'd found a live raccoon in the bag.

"What is wrong with you?" Antoine said, with even more exasperation than he'd already had in his voice for the past hour.

"There . . . there's a hand in there."

"What?" Antoine hopped out of the cab. "No way. Just toss it in."

"We have to call the cops."

"No. No, we don't." Even under the poor light of the streetlamps, Will could see the color draining out of Antoine's normally ruddy face.

Then Will made the observation that the bag was way too small to have a whole body in it. But then again, there were more bags than usual.

If Will had anything left inside, he might have thrown up again. But this time he might never stop. "Fuck that. I'm calling the cops."

"You can't call the cops, you dumb little shit. You're gonna fuck me with the union that you're even here. Then you'll fuck yourself, and your old man. Put the bags in the fucking truck."

Goddammit. Antoine wasn't wrong. Will shook his head. "Don't care. You can take off. I'll wait here until the cops come."

"And then what?"

"I don't know! This is the first time I've discovered a fucking body." Will dialed 911.

"Will, listen to me very carefully. Put . . . the bags . . . in the truck."

Will didn't like the sudden change in Antoine's voice. He looked up. Antoine wasn't looking at Will or the bags anymore, he was staring a laser beam into the window of the Lotus Blossom Massage Parlor.

Will followed his stare.

911. What is your emergency?

Will looked at his phone.

"Hang up, Will." There was a tremble in Antoine's voice that gave Will a shiver.

Against his better instincts, Will disconnected from the call, then followed Antoine's gaze.

In the window stood an elderly Chinese man smoking a thin cigarette. His expression was as warm as a marble statue, the only movement in the tableau being his smoke lifting on the breeze and the incessant *tick-tock* of a waving lucky cat statue on the sill.

"Will, no more fucking around now," Antoine said.

Will swallowed a sour lump. "I'm not just going to throw her in the back. She was a person. Let's just go. I'll call the cops later," he said in a harsh whisper.

Will looked back to the window. The old man hadn't so much as blinked. Then he flicked his fingertips toward Will, a long ash falling off the end of his cigarette, urging Will to get on with it.

Will shook his head. "No," he said softly, nearly a croak. He tried to clear his throat, but it was only dryness in there. "No," he said, a little louder.

The old man pursed his lips and looked to his left, nodded.

"Oh fuck," Antoine said. "Who did he just nod to?"

"Let's just go," Will said, hopping back on the truck's runner.

Then Will heard a series of locks disengaging behind the thick door of Lotus Blossom Massage.

"Fucking drive, Antoine!"

"Just toss the bags in! They seen us. They know who we are."

"They don't know who we—"

"Listen to me, kid. Just throw the bags in." Antoine's voice was calmer than it had been for the last five minutes. Deathly calm.

Click.

The sound came from everywhere and nowhere, the sound carrying on the city night air.

Antoine's face went ghost-white. "What was that click?"

Will's skin turned icy. His old man had taught him enough

about guns on the range in Staten Island for him to recognize the sound.

Will couldn't explain the sensation, but he suddenly felt like the back of his head had a target hanging off it.

"Fuck this noise," Antoine said, reaching for the door handle.

"I don't think we should move right now, Antoine."

Even though Antoine might not have recognized the sound of a bullet being chambered, he certainly understood the seriousness in Will's tone. He froze.

With the gentle jingling of a hung bell, the door to the massage parlor opened.

A woman of indeterminate age due to the long shadows under the neon emerged from the parlor. She was dressed in a white T-shirt and jeans cut off at the knees, but moved with a grace one would normally associate with someone in a ball gown.

She walked over to Will, a slight smile on her lips. Closer, and under the streetlights, Will made her out to be somewhere in her midforties, maybe older.

With a dancer's grace, she lifted the first bag, the one with the poke holes in it from the painted fingernails. She walked it over to the truck and dropped it in the compactor well.

Will was frozen. He felt like a mouse trapped in the glare of a cobra.

"Wasn't that simple?" the woman said, just a breath of an accent left in her English.

"You . . . you can't do this. That's a person," Will said, hating the tremor he heard in his own voice.

The woman *tsk-tsked* at him like he was a child who simply didn't understand. "That is not true, young man. What's in these bags is not a person." She picked up a second bag, placed it next to the first. "Not anymore. What's in these bags is an assortment of meat, bones. Nothing more."

"She . . . was."

"Was what? Was, was, was. Why do you even care, garbage man?"

Her question caught Will by surprise.

She stared at him, through him. She waited for his answer.

"I . . . I don't know," he finally said.

The woman picked up a third bag. Will noticed that her fingernails were painted the same color as those on the hand inside that first bag. "We called her Amy. It was the name she'd chosen for herself when she came to America. Did you know that many Chinese adopt Western names when they come here?"

Will shook his head.

"It makes it easier for your kind to remember us, our given names being too exotic for your lazy minds and tongues." She picked up another bag, dropped it in the well with a wet plop. "After a while we forget our real names. Who we were."

The woman tried picking up another, larger bag, but its weight caught her. "Help me with this one, please," she said, her voice dripping with a poisonous honey.

Will could still feel the target on the back of his head. He reached down and grabbed the bag toward the bottom, ignoring the sensation that he was embracing part of a torso, that it was the softness of a breast under the fingers of his left hand.

The two of them tipped the bag over the lip of the truck, where it joined the others.

"Thank you," the woman said. "Was that so hard?"

Will almost replied, but kept silent.

"Her real name was Chao-xing. Do you know what that means?"

Will shook his head.

"In Chinese, it means 'morning star.' Just like the ones we can't see in this city. Too much light pollution. We forget that they're up there, but they are. Just like our old names. I used to look up in the sky, wondering where the stars were. When I was a little girl, I wanted to be an astronomer. But after so many years, I forgot where they were supposed to be."

The woman gave a wave over the bags in the truck.

"Amy never forgot. She never forgot who she once was, that she wanted to be a dancer. She was going to be in the New York Ballet. She should have forgotten, but she couldn't. She cried a lot. Her crying was bad for business. She tried to leave. She tried to forget, but tried to forget the wrong things—forget who she'd become . . . and who Amy owed debts to."

With a light flourish, the woman tossed the last two small bags into the truck.

"Why?" Will asked.

"Why what?"

"Why are you telling me all this?"

The woman beamed. "You said that the flesh in those bags was a person. You were not incorrect. Now you know who that person was. Now you tell me, the ending of the story being the same no matter what you know about who Amy used to be, do you feel any better knowing?"

Will shook his head.

"Didn't think you would." The woman pulled the lever, activating the rear compactor. The bags crunched wetly, disappearing under the hydraulic press. After the machine completed its cycle, she wiped her hands on her jeans, then pulled a few bills from a pocket sewn tightly to her side.

She walked over to Will and slid the money into his chest pocket, the paper crinkling. Her other hand brushed a caress against his hip. In his ear, she whispered, "Best massage in New York, if you're ever back in the Chinatown."

Without his feeling their movement, the woman's fingers were suddenly in front of Will's face, the wallet from his back pocket wiggling between them. She stepped back, opened his wallet, and took out his driver's license.

"Hmmm," she said. "Mr. William Pokorski, 4489 37th Avenue, Queens."

Will swallowed hard as her eyes studied his face intently. A suddenly warm smile spread across her face.

"You must be Lee's son," she said.

Her words hit Will like a gut punch. "How . . . how do you know my father's name?" He realized he'd taken her bait as the words fell out of his mouth.

As she walked to the storefront door, she tossed Will's wallet over her shoulder. Without looking back, she said, "Always nice to see you too, Mr. Gutierrez."

Will shot Antoine a look. "How does she know your name, Antoine?"

Antoine's lips were pursed tight. His eyes dropped and moved around the filthy street, looking anywhere but at Will.

"How the fuck does she know you and my dad, Antoine?"

Antoine silently climbed back into the truck and shut the door.

Will looked at Antoine's face, set like stone, reflecting back in the rearview.

Then, with numb fingers, Will pulled himself back onto the truck's runner.

"Young man!" the woman called to him before Antoine could put the truck into drive.

Despite his better instincts, Will looked back.

The woman was still smiling. "Do you remember what her Chinese name was?"

Will couldn't. His silence hung in the air like the humidity.

"Didn't think so." She waved as she closed the door, wiggling her purple fingernails at him.

Antoine and Will didn't speak again for the rest of their blessedly short route. When they pulled into the depot on Long Island, the sun was already up, the early heat soaking through Will's coveralls. The stink returned to his senses with a vengeance. Will hadn't even noticed the smell for the last hour of the shift.

Before walking into the garage, Will pulled out the money from his pocket.

Four hundred dollars.

He looked up. Antoine was staring at the bills with an odd expression. Will peeled two of the hundreds off the top and offered them to Antoine. Antoine didn't say no, didn't even shake his head. He just pulled his backpack out of the truck's cab and walked inside the garage.

Will looked at the bills in his hand.

Her name was Chao-xing.

Will crumpled the bills and tossed them in the back with the rest of the trash.

He hoped he would forget.

But he didn't.

KRISTINE KATHRYN RUSCH

Christmas Eve at the Exit

FROM *Ellery Queen's Mystery Magazine*

"WILL SANTA KNOW how to find us?" Anne-Marie asked as she hopped out of the van.

"Of course he will, honey," Rachel said, just like she'd said every time they'd stopped.

Anne-Marie didn't answer. She slammed the door hard enough to shake the entire vehicle, and hurried across the empty ice-covered parking lot. Somehow she kept her balance and didn't fall, despite the pink tennis shoes she wore. Her red mittens hung off a string threaded through her pink coat. She'd lost three pairs so far, which Rachel figured had to be some kind of quiet rebellion.

Eight hundred, maybe nine hundred, miles to go, she thought to herself. She hadn't been willing to check the GPS. She wasn't sure if it transmitted the van's location.

Even though she had never even seen the van before she removed it from a storage unit in Winnemucca, Nevada. Even though the van, its license plates, and that storage unit weren't in her name. Even though she had taken a taxi to the units from that weird hotel and casino.

She'd left a trail. It was impossible not to. If someone had followed her, they would have figured it out. She'd had to leave Anne-Marie with the casino-provided babysitting service, which frightened Rachel more than anything. Then the taxi driver kept talking about how unusual it was to have a woman take a cab to a storage unit. He pressed his card into her hand, told her to call him if her ride didn't show up.

I know you're in trouble, little lady, he'd said through teeth broken so long ago the cracks had turned yellow from the cigars he smoked. *So you just call me and I'll make sure you get back to the hotel, no problem.*

She'd thanked him, trying not to cry. She hadn't wanted him to notice her. She hadn't wanted anyone to notice her. She wanted to be invisible, even though she didn't look like she belonged.

She belonged in Boise, with her trendy blue ski parka and $500 athletic shoes, not in small-town Nevada, where she was so obviously a tourist that everyone asked her if she needed directions.

In the end she hadn't needed the cabdriver. She used the key she'd been mailed to open the storage unit, then followed the instructions pasted to the van. Three different identities inside, each with a different credit card, an entire wad of cash, birth certificates for her and Anne-Marie, and directions to their new place.

Plus seven different preprogrammed cell phones, one for each state. They were numbered. Every time Rachel crossed a state border, she was supposed to toss out the phone she had been using and take the next one. She'd thrown the first away near the Bonneville Salt Flats, heart pounding, and somehow that—not the abandonment of her own car, the use of a new identity, the loss of all her possessions—had finally convinced her there was no turning back.

She still had the feeling she was being followed. She liked to attribute that to the fact that all modern cars looked alike, so the dark-blue SUV she saw in Salt Lake might have had nothing to do with the dark-blue SUV that cut her off in Rock Springs. Or the beige sedan that seemed to dog her trip from North Platte to Kearney.

She ran a hand through her wedge-cut dark hair. She'd bought and paid for that wedge cut, as per instructions, at a beauty shop in Cheyenne, where the kind sad-eyed woman there also gave her a pencil for her eyebrows—to thicken and darken them—and taught her how to alter the shape of her face with blush, foundation, and the right kind of lipstick.

The wind blew hard here in Omaha, carrying with it a chill she hadn't felt in a decade. Her brand-new ski parka felt too thin despite its state-of-the-art promises. Of course, the radio had been telling her that she was driving into a holiday "polar vortex" that filled the air with cold that could kill in less than an hour.

She was glad for the van, glad for the clothes she wore, glad for the interstate with its protective traffic, but she hoped to be off the road soon. She was afraid for Anne-Marie and afraid for herself, and the weather didn't help matters.

She shrugged on her gloves and carefully followed her daughter inside. The ice was so thick that it added another layer to the parking lot. The lot had been well tended; the snow from a massive storm two days ago—one that had been ahead of her all the way—was piled alongside the edges of the lot, taking up at least one row of spaces.

Anne-Marie watched her from inside. Her blond hair wisped out of her blue-and-pink cap, her round cheeks were bright red with cold, and her blue eyes twinkled in the Christmas lights framing the glass door. She looked like a child waiting for Santa Claus instead of a little girl who had no idea how much her life had already changed.

Rachel pushed the door open, heard the *bing-bong* of electronic notification, and saw a twenty-something dark-skinned man behind the desk. His appearance momentarily startled her. She'd lived in Idaho so long that she had forgotten how diverse the rest of the country was.

He looked at her and grinned. The expression softened his face and made the red-and-green silk scarf around his neck seem appropriate. "I assume this little one belongs to you?"

"She does," Rachel said with a smile that she had to force. She put her hand on Anne-Marie's shoulder and guided her daughter toward the tall front desk, festooned in garlands.

A real Christmas tree took over a corner of the lobby, filling the air with the scent of pine.

"She and I have been discussing Santa," the young man said. His nametag identified him as Luke.

"She and I have as well," Rachel said. "She thinks he won't find her because we're very far from home. I told her that Santa is magic, and can find everyone."

"Yes, he can," Luke said, leaning over a little so that he could see Anne-Marie on the other side of the desk. "And people like me, we help Santa when he needs it."

Rachel's stomach clenched. She tried not to look frightened by that admission, but it was hard. She wanted to ask Luke who else he would help if need be, but she didn't.

She wanted to seem as normal as she could for a woman who brought her daughter to a chain hotel off I-80 on Christmas Eve.

"What's the largest room you have?" She really couldn't afford it, but it was Christmas, and she wanted the room to be festive somehow.

"We have a choice of everything," Luke said. "We're empty at the moment, although I expect the usual travelers and truckers after ten."

She smiled. His good mood, surprising for a man working on the holiday, was infectious. He smiled back and tapped at the computer keyboard. As he did so, the Christmas lights woven into the garland above him winked off the tiny sparkly red-and-white candy canes in his pierced ears.

"When do you get to go home and celebrate?" she asked as she pulled out her wallet. She was pleased that her hands weren't shaking.

"I'm here all night, ma'am," Luke said, sounding distracted. He was still staring at the screen in front of him.

"Will Santa find you?" Anne-Marie asked, her voice a little shaky.

Rachel braced herself for him to say something disparaging like, *Santa hasn't found me for years, honey.*

Instead Luke reached to one side of the computer and grabbed a real candy cane. He kept it under the lip of the desk, then looked up at Rachel, a question on his face. She nodded her approval.

His smile became real then and he leaned over the desk again, offering the candy cane to Anne-Marie. Anne-Marie took it like it was the most precious thing she'd ever received.

"Santa doesn't have to find me," he said. "I'm one of Santa's helpers."

Anne-Marie clutched it to her pink coat. "Really?" she asked breathlessly.

"Really," he said.

She backed away a little. "Can I put this on the tree?" she asked Rachel softly.

But Luke heard. "It's okay, hon," he said as he tapped the keyboard some more. "The tree has enough candy canes on it. That one's for you."

Anne-Marie frowned. Rachel smiled at her, encouragingly. The last thing she wanted was for her daughter to be this wary. Had she taught Anne-Marie that? Or had Anne-Marie learned it through observation?

"You can put it on our tree when we get upstairs if you want," Rachel said.

Anne-Marie nodded seriously and clutched the candy cane to her chest. Luke was looking at Rachel over the computer.

His questioning gaze startled her.

"We've been setting up a small tree at nights in the hotel rooms," she said, feeling as if she were giving him the secrets of her soul.

He grinned. "That's wonderful," he said. "Great thinking."

She braced herself again for more questions, like she'd had at the other hotels. *When will you get to your destination? Are you spending Christmas with your family? Where's your husband, sweet thing?*

But he didn't ask them, and she didn't volunteer. Her heart was beating hard, the wallet in her hand feeling like an accusation. She had to remember which identification she was using. It was hard, because she looked at them all every night.

The instructions told her to change identification only if she felt she needed to, and she wasn't sure what that meant, especially since she felt like she needed to change identification every minute of every day.

"We have a suite," Luke said. "No one's booked it. I think it's late enough that I can give it to you at a lower rate."

The price he quoted to her made her heart pound harder, but, she reasoned, she'd planned to pay that much anyway, the moment she walked in the door.

All she could feel was the money going out. She wondered how much of it she would owe later.

But she couldn't think about that. Not yet.

"Credit card?" he asked, extending one hand while the other still tapped on the keyboard in front of him.

Her fingers twitched, and she swallowed hard. Then she pulled out the card on top, checked the name, made sure it matched the driver's license in the front of this wallet, and set the card in Luke's hand. He shifted the card so that it fell between his thumb and index finger—clearly a maneuver of long standing—and then slid it through the card reader.

He had to be able to hear her heart. Everyone had to. Even

Anne-Marie, who had moved to the Christmas tree as if it held the secrets of the world.

She hadn't asked after her father. She hadn't even asked where they were going.

That wasn't natural, was it?

Rachel didn't know. She'd never done anything like this before.

All Anne-Marie had asked was about Santa Claus, over and over again. That, Rachel believed, *was* normal.

"Your card," Luke said, still without looking up. He was holding it out.

Rachel's breath caught. She expected him to finish that sentence: *Your card . . . didn't run. Do you have another?*

But he didn't. He was just handing it back to her. He hadn't even asked to see ID.

"Your key," Luke said, holding a little folder with a black credit-card-sized square and a room number handwritten inside. "You're on the third floor. Just take the elevator up. Would you like help with your luggage?"

Rachel didn't see anyone who could help besides Luke himself. She was about to say no when she glanced at Anne-Marie, still staring at the tree.

"Yes," Rachel said. "Yes, please."

The van had a compartment in the back built for the spare tire and for some repair equipment. When Rachel found the vehicle inside the storage unit, she had taken the tire out and placed it flat on the van's carpet, then added the repair equipment on top of it. Later, at the hotel, she had taken out the bag of Santa presents she had bought before leaving Boise and placed them inside that little compartment.

Then she'd added the suitcases she'd bought just that afternoon at the local Walmart, plus the new overnight bags. And stepped back to look at her handiwork.

So much new stuff, such a lack of familiarity. Only Anne-Marie's favorite toys remained, mostly because Rachel hadn't had the heart to toss them out.

She'd bought a little tree too, with the lights already attached.

Even though the two of them were running away, she had vowed that her daughter would have Christmas.

Luke had come out with her, leaving a woman Rachel hadn't seen when she checked in to watch the front desk. And Anne-Marie. The woman was watching Anne-Marie too. The woman looked tired and stressed, and something in her disheveled blouse and wrinkled skirt screamed shift's end, a fact confirmed by Luke just before he left the lobby.

"It's just a minute, Sherrie," he had said to the woman. "I promise. Then you can go home."

"Always just one more minute," Sherrie had said. "I gotta get to the stores before they close."

"Kmart's open until ten," Luke had said, and in his voice was just a bit of contempt. Because he thought Sherrie should shop at Kmart or because she *did* shop at Kmart?

Rachel couldn't tell, and truly didn't care. She just didn't want the woman to see her—at least not much.

Luke, well, Rachel was taking a chance with him. This was the first time since she left Winnemucca that anyone other than herself and Anne-Marie had seen inside the van.

Anne-Marie was still inside the lobby, holding the candy cane and staring at the tree. She wouldn't even sit down. She had asked Sherrie if she believed Santa would find them.

"You'd be surprised what Santa can find," Sherrie had said.

Rachel pulled the Santa bag out of the hidden compartment. "Is there any way to put this behind the desk for a few minutes without Anne-Marie seeing it?"

Luke grinned at her. "No wonder you weren't worried about Saint Nick. He's already been here. Anything good in there?"

"If you're seven, like pink, and have always longed for at least one more Barbie," Rachel said, rather surprised she could banter. She had thought the ability to banter had left her years ago.

He smiled at her. "She'll remember this trip forever," he said, as if that were a good thing.

"Yes," Rachel said. "I suppose she will."

She grabbed the overnight bags and slung them over her shoulders. Then she double-checked to make sure she had the key fob. She grabbed the small tabletop tree before slamming the lift gate shut.

"I'll be down for the bag after my daughter falls asleep. You'll still be here?"

"Of course," Luke said. "You've already had dinner?"

For a moment she thought he was asking if he could join her. Her stomach clenched. Then she remembered that he had said he was working all night. He was just asking for information.

"No, we haven't yet." Her breath fogged the air as she spoke. "I suppose no one's doing delivery tonight."

"Not tonight." Luke sounded apologetic, as if it were his fault that no one else was working. "But most of the restaurants around here are staying open. And there's a church about three blocks away if you're so inclined."

"I think we're too tired," she said. She *hoped*. She didn't want to leave the room after they'd eaten something. It was just too cold.

As if hearing her thoughts, Luke shivered. "I'm taking this in the back, then I'll meet you."

Without waiting for her to answer, he picked his way across the parking lot, slipping more than she liked.

The wind seemed even colder. Cars still whizzed by on the interstate behind her. The lights from the chain hotels and the chain restaurants that hugged this exit should have seemed festive, but they didn't. They seemed like beacons of a past life.

She didn't look at them, instead making certain she got across the slippery parking lot with her burden.

Luke went in a side door, then came back outside without the bag. He truly was Santa's helper. He grinned, took the tree from her, and opened the main lobby doors.

Anne-Marie turned, eyes wide, as if she were expecting someone else, someone she didn't want to see.

Rachel hated how jumpy her daughter had become.

"You brought the tree!" Anne-Marie said to Luke.

"I did indeed," he said, then looked at Rachel. "Will you need help setting it up?"

Rachel was tempted, but she couldn't quite face having a stranger take her to her room.

"Do you have a bellman's cart?" she asked. "That's all we need."

He nodded as if he understood, then disappeared in the back, tree in hand. Anne-Marie watched it go as if he were never going to bring it back.

"Tough traveling on Christmas, isn't it?" Sherrie said to Rachel.

"People are friendlier," Rachel said, and it was true. People *were* friendlier, particularly when they saw her daughter. They assumed that Rachel was on her way to see relatives, that maybe she got behind or needed an extra bit of help.

She never dissuaded them.

"That friendly will end tonight," Sherrie said. "The folks who show up after nine are generally upset because they can't get to Grandma's house or because they got no one to celebrate with."

Rachel gave her a hard look, hoping she'd quit being negative.

Sherrie didn't seem to notice. "Thank the good Lord for Luke, though. Ever since he came here, I haven't had to work a Christmas Day. He calls it his gift to all of us."

"He doesn't have family?" Rachel asked, despite herself.

This time Sherrie did look at Anne-Marie. Anne-Marie was leaning toward one of the ornaments as if she'd never seen anything like it.

Sherrie shook her head. Anne-Marie turned around, as if she expected to hear Sherrie's answer. So Sherrie put on a bright smile.

"He loves New Year's. He takes the days around New Year's off. One year he flew to New York to watch the ball drop. Said he damn near froze his ball—"

"Crudeness on Christmas is not allowed," Luke said, interrupting her. He was dragging a gold bellman's cart, with the tree set on one side of it.

"Where *are* you going this year?" Sherrie asked, as if she couldn't be dissuaded from anything.

"Miami," Luke said. "Party central. And it's *warm*."

At that word, Rachel shivered. She would give anything to live somewhere warm now, but that wasn't in the cards. She had made her choices, and they were good ones.

Or they would be. Once she got to Detroit.

She set the overnight bags on the cart, careful not to knock the tree off it. Her shoulders ached from carrying the bags, and from the stress of driving.

Hours to go, she reminded herself, hearing her fourth-grade teacher intone Robert Frost's most famous poem, just like she always did when she realized she couldn't sleep no matter how exhausted she was.

"There's an in-room Jacuzzi," Luke said softly, loud enough that only she could hear him. "Perfect after a long day. Merry Christmas."

"Thank you," Rachel said. She had done nothing to deserve this man's kindness, and yet he had given it to her.

The one thing she did not regret about traveling at Christmas was exactly what she had said to Sherrie: people *were* friendlier. It was as if a bit of the season had infected them and gave them just a little bit of joy.

"Come on, Anne-Marie," she said, and Anne-Marie scurried to follow her.

Rachel wheeled the cart to the elevators behind the stairs. Anne-Marie didn't even ask if she could ride it. She had in Cheyenne.

"Is Santa really going to find us?" Anne-Marie asked.

"If you fall asleep," Rachel said as the elevator doors opened. "Just like last year."

She regretted the words the moment she spoke them. Anne-Marie had a look of horror on her face.

Without Daddy, Rachel wanted to add. *You don't have to worry about Daddy.*

But she didn't. She'd mentioned last year, and she couldn't take it back.

"I don't like Christmas," Anne-Marie said as she stepped inside, head down.

Rachel's heart twisted. Little kids weren't supposed to say that. Little kids were supposed to plan all year for Christmas, do special things to get in good with Santa, and be so excited that they couldn't sleep the night before.

They weren't supposed to turn off the Christmas specials and keep their faces averted during the commercials. Christmas wasn't supposed to make them *sad.*

That emotion was for grownups, especially the ones for whom nostalgia was not enough.

Rachel put her hand on her daughter's fuzzy little cap and didn't say a single word.

Rachel put the little tree on the round table in the suite's kitchenette. The suite was bigger than anything they had stayed in so far. It seemed like luxury, even though they hadn't been traveling very long. Part of her had already forgotten the wealth in her past life.

She took small presents out of the overnight bag and scattered them under the tree, the first time she had done that. It made Anne-Marie frown.

"I got nothing for you, Mommy," she said.

"It's okay, baby," Rachel said. "This trip is for me."

Anne-Marie's lower lip trembled, and Rachel wanted to curse Gil. He'd thrown a fit last year when he realized he hadn't gotten as many presents as Rachel had. Anne-Marie had thought he was blaming her, when he wasn't blaming anyone. He was just being an asshole, his specialty.

"I didn't buy the trip," Anne-Marie said softly.

"I know, sweetie," Rachel said, making sure she sounded cheerful. "But you came with me."

Anne-Marie let out a little sigh, then went to her toy bag and pulled out the stuffed dog that had become her lifeline. She set it on the bed nearest the kitchen, claiming that bed for her own.

"You hungry?" Rachel asked.

Anne-Marie nodded.

"Then bundle back up," Rachel said. "We have to go outside again."

They couldn't really walk to the nearby restaurants, as much as Rachel wanted to. They had to drive, just because of the severe cold. They waved at Luke on the way out and got into the chilly van.

He had been right; most of the chain restaurants were open. Normally Rachel would have stopped at a super-large truck stop with six restaurants inside it, as well as shops and showers. No one noticed the people who came and went from those places.

But she decided not to because Anne-Marie had mentioned gifts. Rachel didn't want her daughter to attempt to buy something for her.

Instead they stopped at the closest family restaurant chain. They all had a disagreeable sameness to her. They smelled of coffee and grease, even in the evenings. They served pancakes at all hours, and usually had pies that looked a little tired in a glass case near the cash register.

This restaurant had an open floor plan, a busboy wearing an elf hat, a manager wearing a tie covered with reindeer, and a waitress whose brown uniform had no holiday decoration at all.

She waved them to a table, then brought waters and menus before Rachel and Anne-Marie could even get settled. They ordered, got halfway decent food, and some free cookies courtesy of the manager.

Rachel was trying to decide whether she wanted to pay with cash or a credit card when she heard Anne-Marie gasp. Anne-Marie's face had gone a kind of white that Rachel hadn't seen since they left Boise. A look that usually meant Anne-Marie had been doing something she thought her father would disapprove of.

Rachel followed Anne-Marie's gaze and saw a Santa accepting a menu from the waitress. He wasn't wearing any padding under the suit, so it hung loosely, and his beard hung around his chin, as if he'd loosened it. He looked as tired as Rachel felt.

His appearance must have shocked Anne-Marie, who had only seen fat Santas so far. There had been a lot of them. She'd seen Santas everywhere, from the men manning the Salvation Army buckets by every public building to the men standing outside malls, smoking before they went back to work.

"What's wrong, honey?" she asked Anne-Marie.

Anne-Marie shook her head and then scrunched down, as if she didn't want Santa to see her.

Someday, when Rachel got back on her feet, she'd get her revenge on Gil. She wasn't sure what that revenge would be, but her husband had put the fear of God into their child.

And into her.

Or she wouldn't be running now.

The food she had eaten rolled over in her stomach. It had taken a village to get her out of Boise. Her husband was so rich that she'd never thought she could escape him. But a forbidden phone call to her sister had changed her mind.

Helen had begged her to find a pay phone and call back. Helen had asked that before, and Rachel had refused. But this time she would listen to anything. Helen had hated Gil from the beginning and warned Rachel not to marry him. Rachel had resented that once. Later, she wondered what Helen had seen.

Still, Helen's pushing had made her uncomfortable. It had also embarrassed Rachel. She felt so stupid. But that day she had gone past her embarrassment, past her inferiority. She was nearly dead inside. And Anne-Marie's eyes were dying too.

So Rachel had found a pay phone near the ladies' room in the back of a very large, very old grocery store. Rachel had felt naked making that call, standing to one side and watching the employees go by, hoping no one recognized her. She had barely been able to concentrate on her sister's words.

Helen had told her that she knew a group of women who could help her and Anne-Marie, if she only followed instructions.

Rachel needed the help. A shelter couldn't take her in, and she had no money of her own. Plus, Gil had more resources than any women's organization.

But Helen had reassured her: the organization—SYT—had an incredible amount of money, and Rachel was exactly the kind of woman they could help.

The cost to Rachel? One year's work at the organization, helping women just like her escape from whatever bad circumstance they were in. It would mean donating time and energy to a rehab project in Detroit, using old design skills that had led Rachel astray in the first place.

Once upon a time in a land faraway, she had been the best interior designer in Idaho. She had helped with projects from Boise to Sun Valley, and that was when she had met the multimillionaire charmer who would become her husband.

She should have known what a control freak he was right from the beginning. He'd had his fingers in every part of her work on that project. But she had agreed with him—his suggestions were good ones—and she hadn't thought anything was amiss until six months after Anne-Marie's birth, when he'd grabbed Rachel's arm so hard during a disagreement that she'd had bruises for weeks.

She'd always thought women who stayed with men like him were doormats, so she tried to escape on her own. That's when she discovered he had his own private army. He called them security, but they tracked every move she made and everything she did.

They had even asked her why she had used that pay phone on the way to the ladies' room, and she had told them it was pretty simple: her cell had died.

They hadn't double-checked. Nor did they check her purchases the next time she went shopping. She'd bought what her sister called a "burner phone" every time she shopped, and she hid them in the purses she had stacked in her closet like extra shoes.

"Mommy, can we go?" Anne-Marie asked.

Rachel nodded. She decided to stop waiting for the waitress to come back with their bill. Instead she went to the cash register and paid with cash.

The Santa was the only other person in the restaurant. He looked out the window. Then his gaze met hers through the glass. Rachel gave him an uncertain smile, mostly for Anne-Marie's sake, and he nodded at her.

Anne-Marie grabbed her hand and held tightly.

"Let's make sure you're buttoned up," Rachel said. She hated this kind of cold. It required preparation just to walk from a restaurant to the van.

But she had to get used to it. At least a year in Detroit, rehabbing, and getting her credentials back—under one of her new names.

They stepped outside and she sighed. The cold air burned her lungs. Anne-Marie nearly pulled her to the van, making her slide on the ice.

Everyone was nice here. Maybe she would stay one extra day. She wasn't looking forward to a drive on Christmas. Most places were closed, and this arctic blast made travel so treacherous.

She would call Helen after Anne-Marie fell asleep.

They got into the van and drove the short distance back to the hotel. Luke was still at the front desk. He was watching some religious ceremony on television; it took Rachel a minute to realize it was the service from the Vatican.

She waved at him and mouthed, "I'll be back soon," as she and Anne-Marie headed toward the elevator.

They barely made it to the room before Anne-Marie decided she needed to get some sleep.

Rachel wished she could sleep. Ever since she'd fled Boise, she'd dozed, but never slept deeply. Every time a hotel-room heater clicked on, she bolted awake, thinking the sound was someone racking a shotgun.

Gil had threatened to kill her if she ever took Anne-Marie away from him, and she hadn't doubted he could make good on the threat.

But Helen was convinced they could build her a new identity, and that no one would ever find her, if she did the right things. Helen had always worked with women's groups, and this one, SYT (short for Sweet Young Things), seemed more organized and wealthier than anything Rachel had ever imagined.

They had had quite a plan for her, and she'd executed 99.9 percent of it. The hardest was leaving her Lexus SUV in the parking lot of that hotel-casino in Winnemucca and pretending that she actually had a drinking problem.

She had hidden whiskey all over her house before she left, disguised to look like tea or juice or a whole variety of things, as if she had been a secret drunk all along.

Helen had promised her that someone would take the SUV and leave it in the snow on a spur road between Winnemucca and Boise. Tracks would lead away from the SUV, and rescuers would believe that she and Anne-Marie had walked away from the car. There would be a high-profile search, and then nothing until spring, when someone might find a bit of their clothing and Rachel's purse out in the wilderness.

Rachel thought it all a long shot, but she'd lived in the West long enough to know that families went missing there all the time. They took the wrong road, got stranded, and had no cell service. Rather than wait for rescue, like they were supposed to, they'd try to hike out, and generally die of exposure.

Everyone would believe the story, particularly after all that alcohol got found in the house.

Everyone, she suspected, except Gil.

But Rachel had to trust Helen. It was her only shot. Anne-Marie's only shot. Because Gil terrorized his daughter. Mostly he wasn't home, but when he was, just a twitch of his lips could make her turn that horrid shade of white that Rachel had seen in the restaurant.

Anne-Marie was terrified of him. As far as Rachel could tell, only because Rachel was frightened of him. To Rachel's knowledge, he hadn't physically hurt their daughter . . . yet.

But Rachel had known it was only a matter of time.

She sat near the television, turned so low she could barely hear it, and wished she smoked. Or actually did drink. Just to give herself something to do, something that would relax her.

She was on her own until she got to Detroit. Well, sort of on her own. The woman who had cut her hair in Cheyenne told her it got better. When Rachel asked if she was trading services, the woman had gotten very serious and nodded, finger to her lips.

There are women like us everywhere, she'd said. *We're setting up a network. I know it's hard to trust, but you'll be okay, if you just do what they told you.*

And she had. Everything except the toys. And those she had searched over and over. She'd even stopped in a spy shop in Laramie and asked if they had one of those electronic bug-finders.

They did, and she asked if she could see how it worked. She brought in the bag of toys and the man demonstrated, finding nothing. He showed her that it did work with some demo they had, and told her that the toys were tracking-free.

She believed him. And she had seen him before Cheyenne, before her hair and appearance changed, before she dumped yet another coat, before she had done anything to make herself look like someone new.

Helen hadn't said she had to avoid stores and things. Just warned her to be careful, and to leave her old life behind. No friends, no phone calls, no gloating e-mails to Gil.

Not that Rachel would have done any of that. She had no real friends, not ones she had contacted since her marriage, and she wasn't about to contact her husband. Her cell was gone, left in the Lexus with her purse and her old identification.

Since she got on the road, she was a different woman, although she still felt the same inside.

A knock on the door made her jump out of her skin. She glanced at Anne-Marie, to see if her daughter had heard it.

She hadn't.

Rachel got up and almost went to the door, thinking it was probably Luke from the desk. Then she wondered if he would just come up with the Santa bag. Wouldn't he wait for her call?

She swallowed hard, heart pounding.

If something feels wrong, Helen had told her, *then it probably is wrong. Your subconscious sees something you don't. Get out of that situation.*

Only there was no way out of here. Except the window, which was probably blocked against opening, not to mention the jump from the third floor into the damn polar express or whatever the hell that cold was called.

Rachel got up and moved silently away from the kitchen area, finding the house phone. She hit 0 and Luke answered.

"You ready for the presents now?" he asked cheerfully.

"You didn't just knock on my door?" she asked very quietly, and even though she tried to control it, she could hear the fear in her voice.

"No, ma'am—damn. I didn't see him go up there. There's a Santa on security camera. He's outside your door. You expecting someone?"

"No," she said.

"Didn't hire a Santa?"

"No." And now she was chilled. She glanced at her daughter. What had Anne-Marie been trying to tell her?

"Okay." Luke no longer sounded cheerful. He sounded businesslike. "He doesn't belong here. I'll kick him out."

"No," Rachel said. "He might be dangerous."

"A *Santa*?"

"How did he get past you?" she asked. "And how did he know we were here, in this room?"

Luke cursed. "Good point. We don't have security tonight either. I'm going to have to call the cops. You hang tight and don't open that door."

And he hung up before she could tell him no cops. The last thing she wanted was cops.

She reached into the purse she was carrying tonight and took out the stun gun that SYT had left in the van with mace and a few other protective things. Her hand was shaking terribly.

"Open the door, Rachel," said a male voice she didn't recognize. "I'm sure we can find a way to convince your husband that this was all a misunderstanding."

Tears threatened. They'd found her. Gil's army, just like she knew they would.

She didn't go near the door. She turned up the television a little more, so that Anne-Marie wouldn't hear, then crept toward the bathroom, keeping the bathroom wall between her and the little corridor that led to the door.

"I'm thinking we fly back to somewhere near Winnemucca and I bring you and the little one out of the wilderness, saving your lives. It might mean you need to lick your fingers and stand outside in this cold for fifteen minutes, because frostbite would really help the story, but if we do that, Gil won't know a damn thing."

Rachel wanted to ask why he would do that, this mystery Santa, but she didn't. She knew better than to engage. If she engaged, she had already lost.

She held the stun gun like it was a real gun. Helen had told her not to get a real gun, not with Anne-Marie in the van. Because Rachel didn't know how to use it and, Helen said, too many bad things happened around children and guns.

"You're not saying anything," the man continued. "I know you want to."

She peered around the wall. The safety chain was on, and she'd deadbolted the door, plus pushed in that so-called security lock. The only way in was for him to knock the door down, right? Or she had to let him in.

That's why he was talking. He wanted her to let him in.

"Mommy?" Anne-Marie asked.

Rachel put a finger to her lips, and then she covered her ears so that Anne-Marie would too. They used to do that when Gil got home from a long day, angry and wanting someone to take it out on. Rachel would mime instructions to her daughter: remain quiet and don't listen.

"Is Daddy here?" Anne-Marie whispered, and Rachel heard the fear in her voice.

Rachel shook her head. She then indicated that Anne-Marie should join her, because there was protection against this wall, particularly if the man outside wanted to shoot them.

She didn't know if he did. She wasn't sure what the point of that was. But she knew that sometimes Gil could be irrational, and she had no idea who worked for him, or why they felt it necessary to carry so many weapons.

"We can make this work," the man outside the room said.

Anne-Marie grabbed her dog and her slippers, then tucked in behind her mother. Her daughter's warmth made Rachel feel stronger.

"I bet you're wondering why I'm willing to help you," he said. "I've been thinking about it for the last three days as I watched you drive. It's pretty simple, really: you have a big allowance from that husband of yours. You just give me part of it, under the table, and you'll be free and clear. Back in the arms of your family, safe and sound. You don't want to be on the road like this forever, do you?"

She closed her eyes. Maybe a few years ago she would have done that. Maybe. But she'd seen Gil get mad at Anne-Marie too many times. She'd seen him clench his fists and unclench them like he meant to hit her.

And Anne-Marie cringed a lot, even now.

"Open the door, Rachel," the man outside the door said.

God, what would he tell the police? That she had faked her death in Nevada? There were no restraining orders against her husband, no calls to 911, nothing to prove her claims of abuse. There was nothing that would prevent him from flying out here and getting her and Anne-Marie.

Rachel was back where she started, no matter what.

She stood slowly, putting her finger to her lips. She wasn't sure she could shut him up, but she had to try. The stun gun, as Helen had told her, could knock down a man five times her size. And then she could—what? Stab him with a butter knife? Use his gun if he carried one?

This hotel clearly had security video, and if she killed him, it would be recorded.

She shouldn't have listened to Helen. Rachel should have known that this plan would all go to hell.

She was never going to escape Gil, never, no matter who made the promises or how big the network was or how much money they threw at the problem.

It had been a dream all along, and she had let herself believe it.

"Honey," Rachel said to Anne-Marie, knowing that she would be damning her daughter too. "I'm going to—"

Sirens. They got louder and then they cut off. But red and blue lights reflected in the windows.

At least the police had arrived before she could do something stupid. Before she even tried to hurt this unknown man. Not that it would have helped.

Now he was going to the police station, and he'd give them her identity, and—

"I thought you said someone was in the hall," a new male voice said outside her room.

"I did." That voice belonged to Luke. "I'll show you on the security feed. Send your guys out looking. He couldn't have gone far. Some weirdo in a Santa suit. He was menacing my guests."

And then they walked off, still talking.

Rachel's heart kept pounding. Slowly she sank back down, keeping a death grip on the stun gun. After a few more minutes of silence, she put her fingers to her lips again, then quietly, in a crouch, made her way to her purse.

She took out Nebraska's phone and hit the preprogrammed number.

"Hi," she said breathlessly. "I'm Rachel—"

"I know who you are," said an unfamiliar female voice on the other end of the line. "What's happened?"

Rachel told her, in a low voice, then turned away, adding, "He's seen the van. He knows who we are. He knows where we are. I just wanted to say thanks, but I'm going to have to go home now. Because there's nothing anyone can do—"

"You stay put," the woman said. "I'll have someone meet you in fifteen minutes. We'll have a new vehicle for you and a safe place to stay."

"But how can you get here so fast?"

"Omaha, right?" the woman asked. "Thank God you listened and didn't stop in a small town. Then it might've taken hours for us to reach you. But you're okay there. It might take twenty minutes, seeing it's Christmas Eve, but no more than that. You stay on the line with me while you wait, okay?"

"Okay," Rachel said.

She heard the tapping of a keyboard, some voices, and someone say, "We got it."

Then she glanced at Anne-Marie.

"It was Santa," Anne-Marie said like an accusation.

Not *like* an accusation. It *was* an accusation.

Rachel nodded.

"He was *everywhere,*" Anne-Marie said.

Rachel closed her eyes for just a minute. Like that stupid song. *He sees you . . .*

And she had seen him. In truck stops and cafés, smoking outside a gas station in Rawlins. She'd thought him a different Santa every time.

Santa was everywhere this season.

It was the perfect disguise.

The house phone rang and she almost tossed the stun gun into the air. She made herself set it down.

"What's that?" the woman on the other end of the burner cell asked.

"The hotel phone," Rachel said.

It stopped ringing.

"Have you talked to anyone?" the woman asked.

"I called the guy at the desk," Rachel said. "When someone knocked on my door. I wanted to see if it was housekeeping or something."

"Then call the desk," the woman said. "Tell him you're all right. You are all right, aren't you?"

If she didn't think about her elevated blood pressure, then maybe she was. "Yes," Rachel said.

She picked up the hotel phone and hit 0 again. "Sorry, I—"

"It's all right," Luke said. "The police scared him off. I'm the one who should apologize. They couldn't find him, but at least he's not outside the door. They'll talk to you if you want."

"No," she said. "It's okay."

He hadn't been caught. She didn't know if that was good news or bad.

"Tell him that Candy Mills is coming for you," the woman's voice said on the burner cell. "Tell him it's okay to let Candy come see you."

Rachel told Luke that, even though it felt odd.

"I think I see her pulling in," he said. "I'll send her right up."

Then he hung up.

"I don't know anyone named Candy Mills," Rachel said, and she would remember. The name was weird.

"I'm texting a photo and the pass phrase now," the woman said. "She'll give you the pass phrase. You'll recognize her from the photo."

"Okay," Rachel said.

"And I'll be on the phone to hear everything."

The cell vibrated in her hand. Rachel looked at it. A middle-aged woman with a weathered face smiled tentatively at the camera.

There was a knock on the door. "Rachel?"

This time it was a woman's voice.

She said, "There's an awful lot of Sweet Young Things on the road."

The pass phrase.

And the moment of truth.

Rachel walked to the door, then peered through the peephole. A woman wearing a heavy jacket let down the hood, revealing a version of that weathered face from the photo.

Rachel crossed her fingers, regretting the fact that she'd left the stun gun behind. She opened the door slowly, keeping the security chain on.

"Candy Mills," the woman said.

"Rachel," Rachel said, because for the life of her she couldn't remember her fake name. "And this is Anne-Marie."

She turned to point out her daughter, and her breath caught.

Anne-Marie was standing behind them, pointing the stun gun at the woman. She looked fierce. Her hands didn't tremble at all.

But Rachel's did. She nearly dropped the cell. The woman on the line was asking what was going on.

"Give me the gun, Anne-Marie," Rachel said quietly.

"We don't know her," Anne-Marie said.

"I know, honey, but it's okay," Rachel said.

"Do you know Santa?" Anne-Marie asked the woman.

The woman looked confused. She glanced at Rachel, who drew in her breath slowly. She couldn't help. She didn't dare help. But she tried to convey that the usual answer was the wrong answer.

"I've never met him," the woman said after a moment.

Anne-Marie considered that. Then she set the gun down. Rachel hurried toward it.

The woman closed the door. Rachel picked up the stun gun and put it in her purse. Then she wrapped her arms around Anne-Marie. Anne-Marie clung to her.

"We're going to get you out of here," the woman said. "You'll spend the holiday at my house. It's not much, but it'll do. Christmas put a kink in our plans. But by the twenty-sixth we should have a new van for you, and new stuff. You'll have to leave everything behind."

"Except Anne-Marie's toys," Rachel said. "I checked them. They don't have a tracker."

She thought about the Santa bag at the front desk. Maybe they could pick those up on the way out, and she could thank Luke.

The woman—Candy Mills, if that was her real name—frowned. "I'll double-check. I have some equipment."

She didn't seem too concerned.

"Will he find us again?" Rachel figured it was okay to ask. Anne-Marie had been asking for the entire trip.

"No," Candy Mills said. "We think if there was a tracker, it was on the van. We'll know for sure tomorrow. You said he followed from Winnemucca, right?"

"He had a whole plan," Rachel said.

"Well, we'll take care of that now. He shouldn't be hard to find." She glanced at the tree, gave it a once-over that looked a bit sad.

"You sure you can protect us?" Rachel asked.

Candy Mills smiled, which made her seem younger and friendlier. "Yes," she said. "We've helped a lot of women escape situations worse than yours."

"What if he called Gil and told him where we were?"

"That's why we're going somewhere else. He had no idea where you were headed, right? You never told anyone, right?" Candy Mills sounded a bit intent, as if she wanted to make sure.

"I never said a word," Rachel said. Not even to Anne-Marie.

"I'm signing off now," said the voice on the cell. "You're in good hands."

And before Rachel could say thank you, the woman on the other end of the line hung up.

Rachel swallowed. She didn't want to admit it, but she was happy to have help, even for a day or two.

She felt less alone.

Candy Mills looked at Anne-Marie. "Get your stuff. We're going to go."

Anne-Marie hugged her dog to her chest. She didn't move. "Will Santa know how to find us?"

Candy Mills looked at Rachel, smart enough to realize these questions weren't what they seemed.

"No, honey," Rachel said. "Santa will never find us again."

The sentence made her heart hurt. Somehow she was going to have to give her daughter Christmas magic again. But not this year.

This year she was giving her daughter freedom. A real life. A life away from Gil.

"Good," Anne-Marie said, and reached for her clothes. "I hope I never see him again."

"Oh, honey," Rachel said, knowing that wish was impossible. "I hope so too."

GEORGIA RUTH

The Mountain Top

FROM *Fish or Cut Bait*

BRUNCH WAS OVER. Jeff settled into his leather recliner close to the hearth and watched Sally maneuver an iron pot of hot water. She wrapped a towel around the slim handle and removed it from its fireplace hook. She didn't need his help for now.

"Honey, did I tell you that I saw Walter Bailey at the barbershop last week?"

Sally carefully stepped across the cherry hardwood with her load. "The state senator?" She poured the water into the sink in the kitchen corner of the great room.

"Yeah," Jeff said. "Instead of suit and tie and Italian loafers, he was wearing some kind of uniform under the barber's cape. And work boots. Still trading jokes with the old-timers. It's hard to tell the difference now between him and the farmers who voted for him."

"A shame he lost his house." She added a spot of detergent to the hot water.

Jeff struggled out of his chair to put another log on the fire. And to replace the screen that Sally had shoved aside. "Let's get into the co-op again this year. Trading eggs for produce worked well for us."

"I'm glad my grandmother taught me how to can vegetables." Sally set rinsed dishes in a rack, dried the plates with a towel, and put them into her treasured china hutch.

"I'd like to barter for a few goats," said Jeff. "What do you think?"

"I'd rather have sheep. But there'll be plenty of possibilities now that more people have booths at the marketplace."

"Neighbors helping neighbors." *Yes, this is one of her good days.*

A familiar squabble outdoors captured Jeff's attention. He smiled in anticipation and stepped over to the window. Seventy feet down the hill, a gang of turkeys raced across the clearing, necks outstretched, wattles jiggling, competing for position.

"Wildlife onstage," he announced, putting his magnifiers to rest on Robert Burns's poetry. Jeff climbed to the loft for a better view.

Sally removed her homemade apron and laid it next to the cast iron pot that dried on the useless electric stove. She joined him upstairs, and through the chalet windows they watched the huge birds stuff themselves on the corn Jeff had scattered earlier that morning. The bright face of the sun briefly overcame gray clouds, peeking into the woods, warm fingers touching pockets of crusty snowdrifts and hundreds of animal tracks.

"What a life, my love." Jeff cuddled his bride of fifty years.

"Yes, it is. Atlanta was the right place to raise our boys, but these North Carolina mountains are perfect for me."

"That's good, because we can't afford to move. Not many folks can even travel."

"I'm happy watching water freeze into icicles that thaw the next day." She smiled.

"Very inspirational." Jeff squinched his eyes.

> Come live with me and be my love,
> And we will all the pleasures prove
> That hills and valleys, dale and field,
> And all the craggy mountains yield.

"Very impressive." Sally chuckled. "High school English?"

"That's all I can remember from last week. Christopher Marlowe." He tugged the faded red braid that lay halfway down her back.

"I like it when you remember to be romantic." She tilted her head back to cock an eyebrow.

"I'm a Renaissance man." He smiled into her pale blue eyes.

"We do all right by ourselves, don't we?" She spoke softly. "Jeff, I don't ever want to go to one of those old-people homes."

"We'll take care of each other, honey. I promise." He hugged her close, his eyes misting.

Time stood still as they watched the fluttering attendance at the bird feeders.

"I do wish that Daniel and Chad could be here with us."

"They were always big-city boys, honey." He swallowed hard and looked to the mountains. "They never spent a day reading a book."

"Or walking deer trails." She sighed deeply. "I know, but I worry that they're not getting enough to eat."

The turkeys abruptly took flight.

"Something spooked them," he said.

"Probably the fox casing my hen house. And if I see him, I'm going to shoot him." Sally reached for the binoculars from the roll-top desk to examine the outbuildings near their young orchard. "One day I'll be able to trade jars of preserves."

"Unless Mr. Bear or Woody Woodchuck sneaks up on us and confiscates our fruit."

"I won't allow any varmint to steal my food. We worked too hard."

Jeff laughed. He had always admired her spunk.

The scrape of boots on the front deck turned their attention. Over the loft railing they could see a dark face glower through the glass at the top of the mahogany door. Someone else in a black ski mask pressed his nose to the porch window and peered into the cabin's main room.

Jeff felt a spasm of fear squeeze his chest. His wife dropped the binoculars on a chair and hastened toward the steps.

"Be careful, Sally. Looks like trouble, those slackers from the bottom of the hill."

She hesitated. "They can see we're here."

"Stay with me."

Jeff sought options of self-defense. His pistol was tucked away at the top of the closet in the downstairs bedroom. Out of reach. The penknife in his pocket would be slow to open. *Need something with a sharp point.* He glanced at the letter opener on the desk, the scissors, a ballpoint.

The knob turned, and a huge shaggy head loomed around the door. "Hallow, anyone ta home?"

"We're up here in the loft," shouted Jeff. "Hang on, we're coming down." *The fireplace poker!*

The two men invited themselves in. "Nice place you got here."

Jeff's heart was pounding as he descended the open staircase,

Sally behind him. He steeled his intention to be cordial as long as possible. "Come in by the fire."

"Thank ya kindly." The husky intruder in the camouflage bibs clumped to the hearth, leaving wet tracks on the oval braided rug. "Shoar looks like another snow headed our way."

His sidekick stood by the door, looking around the large room. He rolled his stocking cap off his face up to the top of his head, uncovering short brown hair and stubbly beard. Denim cuffs partially hid the burn scars on his chapped hands.

"Aren't you from the cluster of mobile homes in the valley?" Jeff asked.

"Yep, my family all lives together. Like the Kennedys." His laugh revealed a cavern of sparse teeth stained by the bits of tobacco wedged among them.

Jeff didn't see any bulges suggesting concealed weapons. He forced a smile. "What can I do for you?"

The stranger turned away from the blazing warmth. "Friend, times are tough. We ate our last chicken for Christmas dinner. I see you still got some."

"Yes, we do. We've hatched a few eggs and made our own flock."

"We ate ours, didn't have nothin' else." He picked up the beach photo from the mantel. "Big boys. They live here? Or you two all alone in these woods?"

"We have friends and relatives nearby." Jeff claimed the family memory and replaced it below the grapevine wreath. He didn't mention both sons had been killed in Afghanistan.

"Sounds like the good life." The behemoth called out to his hostess, who stood behind the island sink. "What do you think, honey? You like it here?"

"I certainly do." Sally picked at a button on her sweater.

"Forgot my manners, darlin'. My name's Boyd. What's yourn?"

Jeff interrupted. "What brings you boys up the mountain?" He stationed himself between his wife and the two strangers. He expected Sally to follow his lead, whatever it would be.

"Well, like I said. We need meat, and we're mighty tired of squirrel. I seen them turkeys in front of your place, and it 'pears to me that they'd make a right tasty dinner. Course they scattered when we come up the drive."

"If you follow the tracks, you could catch up to them. They poke along."

"I know that." Boyd glanced upward at the thick exposed beams. "Yep, real nice place." He reached out a dirty fingernail to touch the photo again. "We need some firewood too. I seen you have a big pile out there."

"Work at it all winter," said Jeff. "The stack closest to the back door is seasoned. Behind that is what I cut this year from the trees damaged by the ice storm."

"Too cold to go out in that stuff." Boyd wrapped his large paw around the fireplace poker, swiped the screen to the side, and nudged a flaming log. Sparks flew.

Jeff picked up the coffee mug next to his chair and clutched it tightly.

"Would you boys like some vegetable soup? I could heat it up real quick." Sally pulled a jar from the pantry.

Jeff nodded at her. *Smart idea—appear neighborly, nonthreatening.*

The younger man at the door perked up. "Sounds good, don't it, Boyd?" His thin frame looked as though it could use another meal.

"Shoar. We'll stay to eat. We're not in no hurry." Boyd shed his jacket, tossing it across a tartan footstool. A tiny snowball from the sleeve melted on Sally's knitting. "C'mon, Cooter. Make yourself ta home."

Sally poured the soup into the iron pot. "Would you care to wash up first? We could turn on the pump."

"So you got your well water, do ya?" Boyd moved directly to the table, rubbing his palms on his barrel chest. His hunting cap still covered tangled strands of long black hair. "We can't 'ford no generator."

"We tried to get prepared last year when the government looked shaky. We put back a few extra groceries each month. Installed a woodstove downstairs." Jeff took the kettle from his wife, hung it on the fireplace crane, and swung it over the blaze. "I'll warm up some coffee."

"I reckon you lost a bundle in the stock market crash."

"Everyone did." Jeff retrieved the coffeepot from the hutch, where Sally had misplaced it.

"I didn't." Again the toothless grin.

"Me neither." Cooter burst into squeals.

Boyd slapped his thigh and hooted at him. "You was in prison."

"Oh, yeah." And they both laughed rabidly until Boyd abruptly stopped. Cooter closed his mouth immediately, eyes on his companion.

Jeff smiled indulgently while he positioned the ceramic pot close to the fire.

Sally stood motionless behind the kitchen island.

"Honey, do we have any bread?" Jeff squeezed her arm as he passed. When he got a serrated knife to place near her cutting board, he secreted a paring knife in his cardigan pocket. He handed Sally her apron.

"Seen any deer?" Boyd scraped a ladder-back chair into position as he sat down. Cooter sat across from him, imitating his friend's table manners.

Sally opened a cabinet door. And a drawer.

"Not recently. I was hoping our little herd would grow." Jeff studied his guests from his stool at the granite countertop, away from the greasy animal odor trapped in their clothing. "Someone shot the two bucks last month."

"That was me. Got one, anyway. Big ten-pointer, wadn't it, Cooter?"

"Shoar was, Boyd. A rack this long." He held his hands three feet away from each other. Cooter bumped Boyd's hand with his over and over. "Too bad we couldn't use his head. Remember that, Boyd? 'Member that?"

"You're my buddy, ain't ya? You helped plant that salt lick and all."

Cooter sat up straight and nodded. "I followed that trail of blood to finish him off, too. I'd do anythin' for you." He smiled. His tiny eyes burned brightly. "Buddy."

While their guests jawed about dressing deer meat, Sally placed a plate of thick-sliced bread on the table. Boyd watched her cleavage rise and fall as she leaned forward to serve soup to her guests. Jeff watched Boyd.

"I ain't never et at a rich man's table. Looks good, don't it, Boyd?" Cooter leaned both forearms on the oak table, bread in one hand, spoon in the other. He hunched close over his bowl and quickly slurped every drop. Belching loudly, he leaned backward, balancing on two legs of his chair. "Yessir. That was extry good." He swiped his mouth with his sleeve, napkin still in its decorative holder.

Sally poured coffee for the men and then retreated behind the counter.

Boyd pushed away his empty bowl and lit a cigarette. "So you got a big pension comin' in? You must be one of them guys with a sweet retirement package. I heard about it when they was bailin' out all them companies with hard-earned money from us little folks. You one of them?"

"I don't have a pension, but I don't think it should concern you." Jeff used a checked napkin to dab a coffee drip from his neat gray beard.

"You're wrong about that, mister. Everything you do concerns me. You live in my backyard." He nodded at Cooter. "Ain't that right?" Boyd flicked an ash into the soup bowl. "Our grandpappy used ta own all this land afore the developers got hold to it. I know every creek and holler."

"No doubt your grandpappy got paid for it. You should be the rich one," remarked Jeff.

"Well, I ain't. My folks bought a restaurant, and we all worked at the family bizness. We tried to make a go of it, but neighbors quit eatin' out. Nothin' to be done but shut 'er down." Boyd pushed back his chair and stood up. He gave Cooter what was left of his cigarette. "What kinda work did you do?"

Jeff got to his feet. "I'm an electrician."

"You musta owned your own bizness. You got some mighty fine things here." Boyd winked at Sally. "And a fat diamond ring for the missus."

She frowned and put her hand in her apron pocket.

"I saved what I could in the good years. And didn't go into debt. We retired on Social Security, but since there's no longer any of that, we just make do." Jeff hoped to move them toward the door.

"You're making it better than me and my family."

"We live a quiet life. It was hard to get used to kerosene lamps, but at least we can read at night. One day they'll get the power up and going again in this area."

"It just ain't right for some people to have so much and others to have nuttin'." Cooter rhythmically slapped his spoon on the table until Sally snatched it to wash in the sink.

"The guv'ner said we should share. You ready to share with me, neighbor?" Boyd moved closer to Jeff, forcing him to look up or step back.

Jeff looked up.

"Sure. I'll tell you what. You can take half of my woodpile."

"That's a start." Boyd slapped Jeff on the back, unsettling him.

"What are you going to trade? Share means helping each other." Jeff was determined to show some strength.

"I don't have nothin'."

"Do you have any beer?" Jeff asked.

Cooter sat up straight.

"I ain't givin' up my beer," said Boyd.

"Maybe you have something stronger in that shed in the woods? The one where I've seen smoke?" He had to show strength or they would run right over him.

Boyd narrowed his eyes at the stooped man in front of him.

"I don't think that concerns you," Boyd mocked.

"Tell it, Boyd." Cooter twisted a stalk of baby's breath from the dried centerpiece and crushed it slowly between thumb and forefinger.

"Sounds like you're mad at us because we prepared for hard times. You could have done the same thing," said Jeff. He clenched and unclenched his fists.

"I lost my job when all the furniture companies went to China. That ain't right."

"Companies moved where they could have lower operating expenses. No union jobs."

"My girl would do better in a union. She works at a nursing home, and they cut her hours. She can't pay her car note."

"You're right." Jeff nodded. "People all over the country are struggling."

"Yep. Fifteen teachers at the high school were let go."

"Ain't so many prison guards left, neither." Cooter giggled. He swiped the crumbs from the table with his sleeve.

"No way I can get work. But a man's gotta take care of his family," said Boyd, his voice sharp and loud.

Cooter stood, sucked in one last mouthful of smoke, and threw the cigarette butt into the fire as he ambled past.

"I think we agree on that." Jeff spoke softly. "It's power and greed that'll ruin us. All of us." He took shallow breaths now. He put one hand into his sweater pocket.

"You don't seem to be worried." Boyd snorted.

"Worrying won't change things. We're too old to work, and too old to revolt."

"You're right. You're too old. What use are yunz?" Boyd grabbed his jacket and brushed Sally's knitting to the floor.

"Not for you to say." Jeff eased the paring knife out but kept it hidden at his side.

Sally started out of the kitchen area, her forehead furrowed. Jeff stopped her with a shake of his head.

"Well, grandpa. Let me tell you how it's gonna happen. First off, I'm takin' all your wood. We're gonna load it on my pickup right now." Boyd motioned at Cooter. "Then tomorrow I'm takin' all your chickens. And I'm sendin' my young-uns up here to get all your canned goods. Whacha got to say about that, old man?"

"I say you're stealin'." Jeff raised his voice and stepped closer.

Sally slipped out of the kitchen. Jeff heard her lock the bedroom door. She was safe.

"Hey, Cooter, look at that there recliner. Help me move it to the porch. We'll carry it on top of the wood."

"I worked hard for my possessions. You have no right to them," Jeff shouted. He made his decision. "You will not take them."

"Who's gonna stop me?"

"Me." Jeff thrust his knife at Boyd's chest.

The men guffawed. A titanic arm brushed him aside. Jeff banged his shin on the footstool.

As he fell toward the hearth, he caught a glimpse of a determined Sally returning to the room. "No! Go back!"

"You will leave," said Sally. "Now."

Jeff watched in horror as she charged the visitors.

"Boyd, she got a gun!"

"Honey, give it to me."

Sally fired.

At daybreak the doves fluttered off in different directions at the sound of knocking on the log cabin door. With every muscle in his body complaining, Jeff limped over to peer through its glass at two teenage boys. One wore a ski mask. "Sally, we have visitors."

Jeff unlocked the door and opened it.

"Good morning, sir. We're looking for our pa."

"Well, I haven't seen anyone today. Two men stopped to visit yesterday."

"Our big brother found Pa's truck down by the creek but no sign of nobody," said the shorter boy. "He had to go on to work, so me and Danny are out lookin'."

"That's strange. They said they were going to hunt for turkeys." Jeff peered past them into the frozen forest. The crows roosted noisily. "Do you boys want to come in? You must be cold."

"Thanks, we are. The sun don't feel too warm when the wind goes right through ya," said Danny. They entered, stomping their snowy boots on the clean mat at the door. "Pa's shotgun was missing from over the back window. I think mebbe he and Cousin Cooter have a deer stand close to the creek." His adult baritone contrasted with the teenage acne erupting on his forehead. "Sweet place you got here, mister."

"Could you eat some livermush with eggs?"

The teenagers exchanged bright-eyed looks. "We sure could. That sounds great." They hung their jackets next to Jeff's parka on the pegs by the door and removed their boots.

"We were just about ready to sit down to breakfast." Jeff went to the kitchen to help Sally. She stood motionless at the sink. She stared at the boys.

"One day I'm gonna have me a log cabin like this." Danny surveyed the room as he moved in holey socks toward the fieldstone fireplace.

The younger one made a sliding approach to the roaring fire.

"Careful, Brad."

"This feels good, don't it?" He put his hands toward the heat.

Danny examined the beach photo on the mantel.

Jeff pointed out the basin of water at the antique washstand, and the boys rinsed their hands. Sally set places for them at the table.

"Fine boys like you need plenty of food." Jeff sat with them, sipping his coffee as Sally served their plates with unsteady hands. Her hair stuck out like eagle feathers.

"Have you guys been out of school long?" Jeff asked.

"I'm tryin' to get on at that military gear factory in Fletcher," said Danny. "Might hafta join the army to get me a job."

"You're a smart fella." Jeff offered a smile.

"Ma says I need to go back to school." Brad grimaced. "But Pa says I don't."

"Y'all eat up now," said Sally. "Tell you what. I'll fix a basket of canned goods for you to carry back. And it just so happens I made a pie yesterday. Chocolate. Your favorite."

"Yes, ma'am. Thank you."

Jeff studied the boys as they quietly gobbled down their breakfast. "I'll share a couple chickens with you too."

"When the chicken farmer down the road went out of business, he gave us some. But we ate them all," said Danny.

The boys pushed back from the table. Brad followed the lead of his brother, wiping his mouth with a napkin.

"Have to keep a rooster around, you know," said Jeff.

"Pa wanted to eat him first, 'cause he woke us up so early." Little brother grinned.

"C'mon Brad, daylight's burnin'." Danny went toward the door to put his boots on. "If we don't find Pa and Cousin Cooter, Ma hasta go tell Uncle Walter. He's the new deputy sheriff."

Jeff wobbled as he stood, holding on to the table for balance.

"Mister, you okay?" Danny shoved one arm into a coat that was too large for him.

"Yeah, thanks. I did some heavy lifting yesterday and threw my back out. Nothing that a few hours of rest won't cure." He paused. "But I could use a hand in planting my garden this spring. You boys know anyone who would work for me?"

The boys glanced at each other.

"Sure thing. We can do it." They talked as one, with bobbing heads.

After they zipped their coats under Sally's prodding, she handed one a sack of groceries and the other a pie carrier.

"I believe you've got a load to carry today, but you come back to get those chickens anytime you want." Jeff shook their hands. "We'll make our plans then."

"Thanks. And thanks for breakfast." Brad's grin lit up the room. "Was nice to meetcha."

"I'm so glad you came to visit your old folks." Sally kissed their cheeks.

The two boys exchanged blank looks.

The door closed.

"It was nice to see Daniel and Chad. I worry that they're not getting enough to eat." Sally tracked them from the window.

Jeff pulled her close, tears in his eyes. "It's all right, honey. Come sit here with me."

Sally watched the gift-laden teenagers until they were out of sight, making their way through the pines in the swirling snow. "I hope those horrible men don't hurt them."

"The men are gone, honey. They won't be back."

He adjusted the lamp wick and eased into Sally's rocker with his banjo. The instruction book was propped up on the footstool.

"Wonder where those turkeys are today." She shuffled over to Jeff's recliner to wait with bowed head for his new song, "The Ballad of the Mountaintop."

This is going to be a good day.

JONATHAN STONE

FROM *Cold-Blooded*

THROUGH RAIN, SNOW, sleet, hail, gloom of night, fog of morning, and torpor of afternoon; through cutbacks, and post office closings, and diversity initiatives, and reorgs, and a bureaucratic succession of postmasters general; through truck breakdowns, and snow-tire flats, and post office shootings and bombings, and the holiday rush; through the rise of FedEx and UPS with their swashbuckling, gym-pumped young drivers swerving at high speed arrogantly around you; through the days, weeks, months, through time itself, George Waite has delivered the mail. Thirty-five years now. Through American invasions and wars, and famines and genocides, and tsunamis and earthquakes and volcanoes, George Waite's red-white-and-blue mail truck has lurched from mailbox to mailbox with the utter predictability of a brightly painted figure on a cuckoo clock.

And not only that—he's delivered the mail for all these years to this same neighborhood. Well, the same, and different. The original, simple, unprepossessing capes and ranches had now transformed into McMansions, some expanding gradually over the years, growing as if through a painful adolescence; others literally scraped from the face of the earth and replaced with something grander and prouder, looming and spanking new. But he has delivered it with the same smile and wave to the neighbors watering their lawns, pushing their kids in strollers, heading out on or back from bike rides. The same exchange of pleasantries.

He knows these people, and they know him.

Hiya, George. How's everything?

He's actually—arguably—saved two of their lives. He watched Jimmy Swale—special needs/autistic—stroll right into the pond, and George jumped out of his truck, splashed into the water after him, pulled out the already flailing kid. His uniform was soaked. The pond turned out to be shallow, so did he really save him? And in his rearview mirror he saw eighty-year-old Mrs. Ostendorf, shuffling back from her mailbox to her house, suddenly grip her chest and drop her mail, and George sprinted from the truck, carried her into her house, called the ambulance (this was before cell phones), and she survived.

For both, George was thanked profusely. The neighborhood threw him an appreciation party. Just a half hour or so—he couldn't take more time than that from his route. John Tepper made a speech—"Honorary Member of the Neighborhood." Gave him a plaque they'd had made. What a day.

Here was the unspoken little secret of being a mailman: he loved it. He loved the routine and the predictability. He loved how even today, despite the Internet and smartphones, people still looked forward to their mail. To the surprise and excitement of good news or bad.

The other unspoken little secret was that he *knew* their mail. By this time George pretty much knew who was getting what. Who had which banks and which brokerage accounts (statements delivered monthly; most of them hadn't switched to paperless yet). He knew where their kids and parents lived by the birthday cards and letters; he knew the good news and the bad news of the households by the obvious look of a condolence card or colorful birthday card envelopes. He knew the acceptance and rejection letters from colleges, even the paycheck stubs from which employers, until pay stubs largely stopped. He saw the legal-size documents which still went by mail for signatures—for real estate closings, divorces, wills, life-altering events. He often knew what was in the packages he delivered by the size and shape and weight of the box—books, or DVDs, or specialty foods, or even what article of clothing it was from a given retailer: sweaters, or a coat, or slacks, or shoes. (He would also see the FedEx or UPS package waiting at the garage or at the front door, and could often tell what it was in the same way, and often would do the favor of bringing the box in for them if not already at the front door along with the rest of their mail.)

You couldn't *help* knowing. You had to sort it all; you couldn't help seeing who was getting what. In some lives, there was lots of mail. In some lives, there was very little.

He had seen many residents grow old with him, and you couldn't help but note all the change, all the years, evident in their bodies and faces. He'd watched their kids grow. Tricycles, to training wheels, to sleek racing bikes, to reckless teenage driving as they passed his truck, and soon enough adopting the responsible waving and greeting they'd observed all their lives, addressing George with the same postures and cadences as their respective mothers and fathers, the stupefying power of genes.

New people moved into the neighborhood and old people moved out, and occasionally, of course, passed away. Wistful, inevitable, proof of life. An undertone of transition that the neighborhood yards and gardens and routines did their collective best to belie.

Then the Muscovitos moved in. And then, by god, there was change.

No one ever saw them. Any of them. Doorbell rung, casseroles and homemade cookies left on the front steps, no thank-you notes or calls or acknowledgments.

"Seen the new neighbors, George?"

"No, you?"

Shake of head. Shrugs. But people are busy. The neighborhood has always had its absentees: dads who travel, couples in Florida or Georgia for half the year. Jim O'Brien, a trader in Asian currencies, went in to work at 3 a.m. You never saw him—until the weekends, when he lived in his yard, happily planting and trimming and mowing, waving his shears like a television neighbor, tossing a Nerf football with his kids.

George did see Alberto Muscovito's shadow a couple of times, just inside his front door. His silhouette. Arms crossed. Like a criminal or convict interviewed on TV, not wanting to reveal his features or voice. Obviously waiting until George's truck moved down the street, and then heading out quickly to get the mail—focused, not looking up, making no eye contact with any part of the neighborhood.

First came the walls.

Stone walls; elaborate fencing. Nine feet high, three feet over code. Offhand grumbling to George from the neighbors getting their mail. (George was safe to grumble to, always merely passing through, always merely a visitor.) Construction vehicles, crews of Nicaraguan masons and laborers, issuing friendly uncomprehending shrugs when a neighbor wandered by and asked about the new owner. George caught wind of some neighborhood debate about filing formal complaints about the (possible) height violation. But it was the man's own property, after all, and nobody wanted to spend on a legal battle, and it was an aesthetic judgment after all, so, grumbling, they let it go . . .

Little bits of gossip. The two Muscovito boys, nine and twelve, were in boarding school. Muscovito worked in financial services.

And George, you still haven't seen them?

No, haven't.

Pretty mysterious. And all this construction—pretty annoying.

Of course, George knew more than he was saying. He couldn't share the information. Privacy of the U.S. mail; he'd taken an oath and respected it.

But right off, almost immediately, Alberto Muscovito had piles of mail—yet no personal mail at all. Envelopes addressed to both Muscovitos' P.O. address, and to this new house of theirs, so it was a little confusing for the postal system. From senders who obviously wanted to be very sure it got there—putting the P.O. box *and* the home address to be double certain.

Yes, piles of mail. Contracts from individuals and firms George had never heard of. Legal documents from a law firm in the Cayman Islands and from outfits in New Zealand and Malaysia and Micronesia. The Maldives. Mauritius. None of the conventional standardized brokerage and bank envelopes that the rest of the neighborhood got. And the numerous legal and financial documents required no signatures, George noticed, which would have necessitated his actually meeting Mr. Muscovito.

Even though he shouldn't have, even though it came dangerously close to the line on respecting and safeguarding the privacy of the U.S. mail, George jotted down and Googled a couple of the firms.

He was surprised—and then again, not surprised at all—by what he found. Firms with numerous ethics violations. Fraud warnings from various business and trade associations. Warnings from an international watchdog group. And in several cases, no website, no contact info, no information, no Web presence at all. No evidence of existence beyond an address on an envelope. A return address that was just a post office box—on an island overseas.

After the walls and the fencing came satellite dishes. Weird lines to the house. Unmarked small white vans pulling in at night, parked there for hours, sometimes even overnight, then pulling out, the drivers in sunglasses.

Jeez, what's he doing there, George? Tracking satellites? Going off the grid?

The annoyance of the neighbors shifts to a much higher gear with the hammering, drilling, noise, activity at two in the morning. Can't tell what it is, behind the high new walls. And by the time a neighbor frets and paces and fumes and finally calls the police, the sound has stopped, and the police do nothing. It happens a few nights in a row. The neighbors come to anticipate and dread it.

(Soon there's a police cruiser driving slowly through the neighborhood. Drifting slowly past the Muscovito residence, circling lazily—and doing nothing. Even more infuriating, in a way, because of its obvious impotence. The neighbors shake their heads—incompetent suburban cops.)

George hears more anecdotes. Muscovito's Cadillac SUV, with the blacked-out windows, driving in and out at unpredictable hours—midnight, three in the morning, 5 a.m.—and always too fast, way too fast for the neighborhood lanes. The other morning Muscovito almost hit the two Miller kids on their bikes at the corner, up early catching worms. Never even stopped to look and see if they were OK! Tommy Miller fell back into the rhododendrons in terror, crying, poor kid was so scared . . .

And finally, of course, an electric locking gate and—symbolically, inevitably—a new mailbox with it. A large locking mailbox built like a strongbox into the elaborate gate's left stone pillar. Stark contrast to the rickety, rural-route-style mailboxes along the rest of the lanes—cheap, casual, periodically knocked over by a delivery van or snowplow and propped up, dented and brave, their hinged tongues opening and closing with a squeak and falling wide open half the time.

The Muscovitos' new mailbox, a narrow, tamper-proof slot to slip mail into methodically. For George to collect any outgoing mail, a special key issued through the post office and now an official part of the route, forms properly filled in, the whole key-issuing procedure processed through the mail, so George, once again, never sees Muscovito in person.

George gets it all in bits and pieces. Hearing the anecdotes of misery, of mystery. Many of them wrapped in the bland manila envelope of resignation: "The neighborhood is changing, I guess. The world is changing . . ."

George ponders this from the worn, duct-taped driver's seat of his truck. Isn't that what all the resentment is really about? People resent change, they're suspicious of it, they're wistful and nostalgic for the familiar. Doesn't Muscovito have a right to his weird mail? A right to alter his residence and property? A right to his privacy and his odd hours? He's a symbol, a lightning rod of change, in the neighborhood, in the world. A reminder of nature's cycle of decay and replacement, the myth of stasis. Life is change; death comes to all eventually—people, neighborhoods, political systems, nations. All of it. All of us.

George would come to wonder in the days ahead how much this line of thinking had taken hold of him.

He starts small, and quickly. George slips the next Caymans document out of its envelope, snaps a shot of each of its eight pages with his iPhone, slips the document back into the envelope, and reseals it. All postal carriers know how to reseal. They carry special glue in the truck for items that have opened in transit. It takes less than twenty seconds. If you see him in his truck, it looks as though he is sorting mail.

He prints the photos at home.

Overseas account statements. Offshore investments—no doubt unreported and untaxed. Clearly illegal—there in black-and-white. You didn't have to be a genius to see it. Exhibit A.

The only thing more clearly illegal? Opening someone's mailed financial documents. So this is evidence that can be officially used exactly nowhere. Revealed to no one. It serves only as evidence to George.

Across the street from the Muscovitos: the lovely old Davidoffs. Now with their canes and osteoporosis and skin drooping from necks and arms, full lifetimes etched and stretched on them, but smiles of greeting unchanged for all the years since they had moved in as spry newlyweds. And they are a walking mirror, of course. George isn't much behind them. Mandatory retirement with full benefits at the end of the year. Not something he can afford to jeopardize with illegal behavior.

Next door, the Schumans. Doctor Schuman, an old-fashioned GP. Four Ivy League kids: two Harvard, a Yale, a Princeton. He remembers their acceptance letters. Now two physicians, one cancer researcher, one oceanographer. God, he remembers all their bikes. The color of each one.

The neighbors he has grown to love, the neighbors who have grown to love him.

George feels their frustration, their sense of powerlessness. He feels identity with them. It isn't just their neighborhood. It is *his* neighborhood too.

One option: he can simply stop delivering the Muscovito mail. Just kind of lose it. What would that do? Create a disruption, a delay certainly. But eventually Muscovito would simply get on the phone with the overseas entities he is dealing with, they would resend, and the disruptions and delays would ultimately trace back to the U.S. Postal Service, and ultimately to George. No, that would accomplish nothing, except temporary mischief and permanent dismissal.

But what if Muscovito were to begin to receive contracts where the details of the deal were different? Where the terms were slightly altered? Certainly that would rattle Muscovito, infuriate him, sow seeds of paranoia and mistrust. Or what if the return documents that Muscovito sent back had different deal terms, the agreements had been altered, the documents had been changed, retyped, forged, as if trying to slip in more favorable terms for himself? Clearly his overseas business partners and entities—when they discovered the changes—would not be pleased about that. Could hardly continue to do business with someone so capricious, so unsteady.

Clearly that kind of elaborate forgery and fraud would not originate from a meek veteran postman on his daily rounds. It was too involved, too outrageous for that. Fraud like that would come from a longtime practitioner—such as Muscovito himself. Finally going a little too far. After all his caution and cleverness, he would become a little too risky and too bold.

George is no longer simply slipping documents out of and back into their envelopes. Now he is looking into everything, reading through it all, really getting to know Muscovito's businesses.

Lots of overlapping bank accounts. Shell financial companies inside shell financial companies, a shiny nautilus of dummy corporations and paperwork, echoes upon echoes in dark empty chambers. George sees some themes and patterns—schemes so complex, so cross-border, that it would be hard for legitimate investors caught in the maze to ever get their money back.

He studies some of them closely. Tries to follow all the steps. Like a land purchase, 1050 acres of what at first appears to be an Indonesian atoll in the Pacific. With the help of Google Maps and GPS coordinates and a little further investigation, George ascertains that there is no such atoll, no corresponding piece of geography. So the money is being sheltered somehow, to be funneled somewhere else.

The money for that purchase, George sees, comes partly from a wire transfer out of an account at a bank in Montevideo, Uruguay. George digs further: there is no such bank. So—a transfer from a bank that doesn't exist to buy land that doesn't exist. Laundering the money twice, George tentatively concludes. Making it squeaky clean, for some further expenditure.

On the one hand, he doesn't follow a lot of it. On the other hand, he follows it enough.

Then there are the names of the corporations: Parcel 666, Devil's Bluff Partners, Black Hole Trust. How arrogant.

No, George can't follow it very well—hell, that is the idea in a lot of cases—but retyping and altering the terms of the contracts and forging the signatures—*that* he can do. If the signatures on these "new" contracts look forged, give themselves away, well, that would be even better. Because that would tell Muscovito that his partners are trying to pull a fast one on him—or tell his partners that Muscovito is trying to put one over on them. Either way, it would be an ugly development in any prospective partnership. Courtesy of George.

An intensive Internet search on Muscovito himself turns up nothing. Which tells George something: Muscovito has managed to scrub himself. When George checks the government databases open to government employees, he finds nothing. No mention of Muscovito.

He can report Muscovito for mail fraud. With all the documents he's photographed and copied, everything he's learned, he can practically present the case himself. But prosecutions take forever. Years, probably. At any point, with the right lawyers, an operator like Muscovito could manage to wiggle out of it and slip away. Plus, after all these opened envelopes and copied documents, George is now guilty of repeated, systematic mail fraud himself. No different from Muscovito, probably, in the blindfolded eyes and impartial scales of the law. He could be charged and prosecuted in the same courtroom. No, reporting the fraud is too risky, and maybe useless. Dealing with the fraud directly is the best, the only course of action—if action is what one wants.

The neighborhood has always had a rhythm. Men leaving in early morning for the commuter train, then the buses and carpools for school, then the garbage truck, then the household repair vans—plumber, carpenter, electrician, appliances, the store delivery trucks, the dry cleaner's van. And at half past two in the afternoon, the mailman. Part of the rhythm. Like the phases of the moon or the seasonal shifting of the sun. Ingrained in the nature of the place.

Squirrels gathering nuts from beneath the shedding oaks, a wild turkey or a fox darting across the lane. The autumn rain pattering on the fallen leaves, the snow's coating of white silence, the rich warm smell of spring. A primal orderly march, a deep rhythm, that Muscovito has tampered with.

Or is it bigger than that? Is Muscovito simply guilty of . . . modernity? Personifying an atomized, disconnected age. An age without social connection. An age of complexity. An age that leaves neighborhoods behind. Is George's tampering with Muscovito and his mail simply, at some level, a rebellion against that age?

Which leads to a broader philosophical question: in wanting to preserve the world around him, is *George* the one tampering with the rhythm of things, inserting himself into their natural processes? Is he the one creating change, just as guilty as Muscovito? Overstepping—a highly unfamiliar position for a U.S. postal employee.

Playing god, or superhero?

Superman. Batman. Mailman.

*

George works on the documents late at night. Lights burning brightly in his little dining room. Spreading them out at his dining room table. Retyping and spell-checking sections of the documents on his old Dell desktop. Downloading font libraries from suppliers around the world to let him match typefaces perfectly. Choosing printing paper that matches the weight and color of the originals, from the wide selection of papers he has purchased for just that purpose. Checking his handiwork with a magnifying glass, to scrutinize the telltale edges of the letters where ink meets page. Getting the appropriate international stamps and markings (which proves easy for a postal employee).

He has been alone in the little ranch house since Maggie's passing three years ago. All the retirement magazines recommend a hobby. George's current activity isn't what they mean, but it does keep him occupied, after all. Something to do. A craft. Focusing his mental energy. He can only take a day with each document so that Muscovito still receives it in a timely manner. The swift completion of his appointed rounds—with a slight detour.

It adds up to a primer in white-collar crime. Mail fraud. He is a student of it, cramming assiduously at night.

Making Muscovito, in a way, his partner in crime. Probably sitting at his own dining room table late at night—or in his locked home office, or wherever—cooking up a scheme for George to slightly, subtly modify.

Why is he doing this? Why really? Retirement is approaching fast, Maggie is gone, and once he is no longer behind the wheel of the truck, making his way through the neighborhood, he will lose his last connection to the world. He'll have no focus, nothing to do. So is this a last act, a desperate bid for preserving not a neighborhood's way of life but his own? The neighborhood of his route is *not* his own neighborhood, after all. But after thirty-five years, it *is* his past, his existence, his tie to daily life, and perhaps he is doing everything he can—even something completely crazy—to avoid at all costs the total, annihilating disconnection to come. Is keeping the neighborhood intact really about keeping himself intact? Doing something crazy to head off the aloneness he faces? Doing something uncharacteristically risky, utterly insane, as an alternative to utter quiet, utter resignation, utter loneliness?

One day, as he delivers Muscovito's mail, the gate opens. A disembodied voice comes on a speaker built into the gate: "Can you bring the mail in today? I want to ask you something."

George's heart accelerates, pounds as if on cue. *Does he know? Does Muscovito know?*

George watches himself, observes it from outside himself: backing the truck out, in a screeching-rubber retreat, hustling the truck down the familiar lane, guilt on plain display, abandoning his bright trusty vehicle in a commuter lot by the highway just as he's imagined for years, disappearing into a new life. A flash of extreme action, of clear procedure, shooting through his brain.

But George is George, with a mailman's temperament and a mailman's soul, and he drives his bright, cheerful mail truck obediently through Muscovito's new front gate and up the drive.

Muscovito is there in the driveway to meet him.

Squat, thick. Skin pale, almost translucent. Clearly a man who spends an inordinate amount of time in front of computer screens. An ungroomed mop of black hair. Big, fleshy arms folded across his considerable, Buddhistic chest and stomach.

George rolls the truck to a stop. Takes out the pile of Muscovito's mail. Holds it out to him with a friendly smile.

The smile is not returned, making George's smile hang there, awkward, unacknowledged.

Muscovito: No greeting. No niceties. Going right to it. "I've got a question."

George: "Yes, sir?"

Muscovito: "Could anyone be tampering with my mail?"

George frowns with concern.

Muscovito: "At any point in the process?"

George (pausing, considering): "When you say tampering, what do you mean?"

Muscovito (irritably): "I mean tampering. Opening it somewhere."

George (leadenly): "Well, where exactly?"

Muscovito (irritation rising): "Somewhere! Anywhere! That's what I want you to tell me."

George (shaking his head): "I can't imagine that happening, sir. That kind of thing is very rare. I've been on this route for thirty-five years, haven't had a problem. But it's not unheard of. I can file a report if you want."

Muscovito (looking somewhat alarmed, shifts on his feet a little, looks out past George to the gate): "No, that's OK. Just wondering if it's possible."

George: "Well, if you change your mind, I can have it looked into. You let me know."

And pulling out of the driveway, a huge exhalation of relief. His relief fills the truck cabin. But he is wistful, philosophical, as well.

Because the man never imagines that it might be George. Based on the immutable, unchanging, common perception that George —after thirty-five years—knows he can utterly rely upon: not that mailmen are honorable and above reproach, but that mailmen are stupid. Why else would you be *just* a mailman?

Presumably Muscovito is calling the various parties. Either accusing them of changing the contracts or apologizing for the bizarre changes in the contracts coming back to them. If he is accusing them, that tone of accusation is undoubtedly not going over very well with his overseas partners. And if he is apologizing, he is raising their anxiety about being involved with such a reckless, untrustworthy party. And if he is apologizing, then they will be doubly irritated when the alterations and forgeries continue. Either way, his partners aren't going to be happy.

At the very minimum, it is producing an atmosphere of suspicion and mistrust. And phone calls, normally a recommended mechanism for clearing the air, might in this case only heighten that mistrustful atmosphere, hearing the annoyance, frustration, and suspicion in each other's voices. So go ahead, call away. Talk as smoothly and reasonably as you like to each other. You're only going to amplify each other's suspicions and dark alertness that a few weeks ago existed not at all.

George continues to deliver the mail. Through rain, snow, sleet, and hail. And at night he continues to inspect Muscovito's mail and make small alterations and amendments. George drives toward some ultimate action, but what action he does not know.

It turns out he does not know at all.

On a gray afternoon, George is sliding Muscovito's mail into the locking box in the stone pillar when the gate opens.

The disembodied voice comes over the speaker again. "Could you come in the gate for a minute? I've got a package to go out that didn't fit in the box."

George hears both the heightened friendliness and interest in the voice and the little edge to it, and he once again imagines throwing the truck into reverse, hitting the accelerator, screeching the tires, exiting the neighborhood one last time, and disappearing into the world. But he doesn't, of course. He does instead what he knows how to do, what he has done for thirty-five years. He heads in to deliver and pick up the U.S. mail.

Muscovito is standing in the same place in the driveway, arms crossed.

"Hi again," says Muscovito, with a thin smile, eyes steady on George, with evident fresh interest.

George gives a friendly nod hello. "Where's the package?"

Muscovito uncrosses his arms to reveal he's holding a Walther 9mm. "Right here." He points it at George, the black muzzle only two feet from George's chest.

The slamming into reverse, the screech of tires, is no longer an option.

George feels himself going dizzy. He blinks hard to keep from passing out.

"Into the house," instructs Muscovito.

Dazed, blank-brained, George steps gingerly out of the truck and walks up the steps and into the house.

The living room is rococo, ornate. A huge, glittering chandelier, big deep couches, heavy Empire mirrors, bold commanding patterns on the couches and throw pillows, a fanciness and high decoration and vibrancy of color entirely out of character with the gruff, grim Muscovito.

The furniture is not the most attention-getting feature in the room. That honor goes instead to the two men sitting on a couch and chair in the middle of it. Men several years younger than George or Muscovito. Younger, and tan, and fit, with healthy white teeth and big smiles. And each of them, like Muscovito, holding a weapon.

"Sit down, mailman," says one of them, the one with the slicked-back hair, gesturing casually with the gun to a chair opposite them. A mild accent of some sort, unplaceable—Eastern European?

George sits. His body, his brain, are in a mode they have never experienced—a fog, a haze, in which he can barely process what is going on around him, can barely hear or see—and yet he feels a hyper-alertness to everything. Like being a disembodied observer of your own fate, your own approaching destiny. A destiny approaching fast.

There is silence for a moment, while the men study him. Then the one with the slicked-back hair says, "It's illegal to tamper with the U.S. mail."

An accent, yes, but clearly fluent and at ease with English.

George is silent.

"Of all people, you should know that," says the second man—a shaved head, a deeper, more curt voice than the first.

"You can be punished for something like that," says the first man, circling the gun lazily, almost casually, in his hand.

There is obviously no one else in the house. Kids away at boarding school. Wife traveling.

"We've been waiting for you, mailman. But not for very long. Your schedule is extremely reliable," says the one with the shaved head.

"Our partner, Muscovito, he didn't think a mailman could be doing this. Never even occurred to him," says the one with the slicked-back hair, who looks momentarily annoyed—as if personally offended by Muscovito's provincialism. "You're about to retire, aren't you, mailman? Aren't you, George? Whose Maggie has died? Who now knows our business, inside and out?" He shakes his head of slicked-back hair and pretends to ask the rococo ceiling, "What are we going to do with you, George? What are we going to do?"

But George knows it is merely a rhetorical question.

He knows it is the last rhetorical question he will ever hear.

The last question of any sort.

'Well, we do have an answer, mailman. Here's what we are going to do."

An answer, not a question, thinks George, and the thought cuts bluntly through the thick haze of his terror.

His world will end with an answer, not a question.

All obedient, cooperative George can do is watch as the second one, the shaved-head one, grimly, matter-of-factly, with no evident glee but only focus on the task, checks his weapon, levels the gun, and applies the answer.

He fires a single shot.

Unerring. Professional. Passionless. Corrective.

Right where he aims it.

Right into the brain.

Right where all the troublesome scheming and illegal solutions and overreaching hubris began.

Right into Muscovito's forehead.

George is paralyzed. He has stopped breathing. He is only eyes. He is panic, terror personified.

The man with the shaved head silently, immediately, begins attending to Muscovito's body. Solemnly, like a mortician, folding arms, shifting him. But first, of course, handing Muscovito's fallen Walther to the man with the slicked-back hair, who watches the proceedings while addressing George.

"He never fit into the neighborhood, did he, George? Built walls, gates, drove his car with blacked-out windows too fast, never even introduced himself to the neighbors. That's not how you make yourself welcome. That's not how you blend in, is it? You've got to ingratiate yourself. Make yourself part of the scenery. You garden. Play some tennis and golf. You host a party or two. Everyone knows that's how you conduct yourself, right?"

He shakes his head with pity. "He never even thought that a mailman could be doing all that to the contracts. That's not a very alert or interested view of life, is it, George? A pretty prejudiced, unenlightened view of the postal service and its employees, don't you think? You've probably observed that view all your life. When the fact is, in our business, the postal service is one of our best friends."

The man stops watching the proceedings with Muscovito's corpse and looks directly at George. Demanding, it seems, that George look directly back at him.

"We knew it was you. We could tell. So we looked a little further. Did some research. Just like you did, George. And George, you have been utterly reliable." Smiling for a moment. "Someone to count on through rain, snow, sleet, and hail. And now you've studied our businesses, and what you don't understand, and I'm sure there's still plenty, we can teach you. You are about to retire, you live alone, you're healthy and alert and skilled in the subtleties of the mail services. You are ready for the next phase, the next challenge in life, yes? So you are now our partner. And of course you have no choice. If you refuse, Muscovito's murder will be tied to you, very easily in fact, with your truck in his driveway at the time of death, which Muscovito's security camera clearly shows on the tape we will take from it shortly. The murder weapon, which will in a moment have your handprints on it, will be sitting for all time in a post office box that you have already requested and paid for with cash and will have mailed the weapon to for safekeeping."

"We'll take care of everything from here, partner," says the other man, the one with the shaved head. He gestures to Muscovito's body, already wrapped in plastic sheeting and taped up, a package ready for transportation and disposal. "We'll load it in the truck for you. We have instructions for where you will dump it. Don't worry, no one will see. But we'll be taking photos of you doing it, for our own insurance."

The man with the slicked-back hair jumps in, as if to set George's mind at ease. "We'll have plenty of use for your skills and your knowledge. We'll compensate you very fairly. We'll be in touch."

And then, more philosophically, the man says, "Listen, we all need something to occupy us. A hobby, a focus in life . . ."

"Continue your appointed rounds," instructs the second man.

The first man smiles. "The neighbors will be so happy, won't they, George? Good job! You did it! Muscovito is gone."

"Welcome, mailman . . . ," says the second.

"Yes." The first one smiles wider, as if with sudden inspiration. "Welcome to *our* neighborhood."

ART TAYLOR

Rearview Mirror

FROM *On the Road with Del & Louise*

I HADN'T BEEN thinking about killing Delwood. Not really. But you know how people sometimes have just had enough. That's what I'd meant when I said it to him, "I could just kill you," the two of us sitting in his old Nova in front of a cheap motel on Route 66 —meaning it figurative, even if that might seem at odds with me sliding his pistol into my purse right after I said it.

And even though I was indeed thinking hard about taking my half of the money and maybe a little more—literal now, literally taking it—I would not call it a double-cross. Just kind of a divorce and a divorce settlement. Even though we weren't married. But that's not the point.

Sometimes people are too far apart in their wants—that's what Mama told me. Sometimes things don't work out.

That was the point.

"Why don't we take the day off?" I'd asked Del earlier that morning up in Taos, a Saturday, the sun creeping up, the boil not yet on the day, and everything still mostly quiet in the mobile home park where we'd been renting on the biweekly. "We could go buy you a suit, and I could get a new dress. Maybe we'd go out to dinner. To Joseph's Table maybe. Celebrate a little."

He snorted. "Louise," he said, the way he does. "What's it gonna look like, the two of us, staying out here, paycheck to paycheck, economical to say the least"—he put emphasis on *economical,* always liking the sound of anything above three syllables—"and suddenly going out all spiffed up to the nicest restaurant in town?" He looked at me for a while, then shook his head.

"We don't have to go to the nicest restaurant," I said, trying to compromise, which is the mark of a good relationship. "We could just go down to the bar at the Taos Inn and splurge on some high-dollar bourbon and nice steaks." I knew he liked steaks, and I could picture him smiling over it, chewing, both of us fat and happy. So to speak, I mean, the fat part being figurative again, of course.

"We told Hal we'd vacate the premises by this morning. We agreed."

Hal was the man who ran the mobile home park. A week before, Del had told him he'd finally gotten his degree and then this whole other story about how we'd be moving out to California, where Del's sister lived, and how we were gonna buy a house over there.

"Sister?" I had wanted to say when I overheard it. "House?" But then I realized he was just laying the groundwork, planning ahead so our leaving wouldn't look sudden or suspicious. Concocting a story—I imagine that's the way he would have explained it, except he didn't explain it to me but just did it.

That's the way he was sometimes: a planner, not a communicator. *Taciturn,* he called it. Somewhere in there, in his not explaining and my not asking, he had us agreeing. And now he had us leaving.

"Okay," I told Del. "We'll just go then. But how 'bout we rent a fancy car? A convertible maybe. A nice blue one." And I could see it—us cruising through the Sangre de Christos on a sunny afternoon, the top tipped back and me sliding across the seat, leaning over toward him, maybe kicking my heels up and out the window. My head would be laid on his shoulder and the wind would slip through my toes and the air conditioner would be blowing full-blast since June in the Southwest is already hot as blazes.

Now *that* would be nice.

"No need to waste this windfall on some extravagance," he said. "No need to call attention to ourselves unnecessarily. Our car works fine."

He headed for it then—that old Nova. Flecks of rust ran underneath the doors and up inside the wheel well. A bad spring in the seat always bit into my behind. Lately the rearview mirror had started to hang a little loose—not so that Delwood couldn't see in it, but enough that it rattled against the windshield whenever the road got rough.

He'd jury-rigged a hitch under the bumper and hooked up a flat-as-a-pancake trailer he'd rented to carry some of the stuff that wouldn't fit in the trunk. A tarp covered it now.

I stood on the steps with my hip cocked and my arms crossed, so that when he turned and looked at me in that rearview mirror, he'd know I was serious. But he just climbed in the car, then sat there staring ahead. Nothing to look back at, I guess. He'd already packed the trunk and the trailer both while I slept. The mobile home behind us was empty of the few things we owned.

"A new day for us," he'd whispered an hour before, when he woke me up, but already it seemed like same old, same old to me. When I climbed in beside him, I slammed the passenger-side door extra hard and heard a bolt come loose somewhere inside it.

"It figures," I said, listening to it rattle down. The spring had immediately dug into my left rump.

Del didn't answer. Just put the car in gear and drove ahead.

When I first met Del, he was robbing the 7-Eleven over in Eagle Nest, where I worked at that time. This was about a year ago. I'd been sitting behind the counter, reading one of the *Cosmo*s off the shelf, when in comes this fellow in jeans and a white T-shirt and a ski mask, pointing a pistol.

"I'm not gonna hurt you," he said. "I'm not a bad man. I just need an occasional boost in my income."

I laid the *Cosmo* face-down on the counter. I didn't want to lose my place.

"You're robbing me?" I said.

"Yes, ma'am."

I bit my lip and shook my head—no no no—just slightly.

"I'm only twenty-eight," I said.

He looked over toward the Doritos display—not looking at it, but pointing his head in that direction the way some people stare into space whenever they're thinking. He had a mustache and a beard. I could see the stray hairs poking out around the bottom of the ski mask and near the hole where his mouth was.

"Excuse me?" he said finally, turning back to face me. His eyes were this piney green.

"I'm not a ma'am."

He held up his free hand, the one without the pistol, and made to run it through his hair—another sign of thinking—but with the ski mask, it just slid across the wool. "Either way, could you hurry it up? I'm on a schedule."

Many reasons for him to be frustrated, I knew. Not the least of which was having to wear wool in New Mexico in the summer.

He glanced outside. The gas pumps were empty. Nothing but darkness on the other side of the road. This time of night, we didn't get much traffic. I shrugged, opened the cash register.

"You know," I said, as I bent down for a bag to put his money in, "you have picked the one solitary hour that I'm alone in the store, between the time that Pete has to head home for his mom's curfew and the time that our night manager strolls in for his midnight to six."

"I know. I've been watching you." Then there was a nervous catch in his voice. "Not in a bad way, I mean. Not voyeuristically." He enunciated both that word and the next. "Surveillance, you know. I'm not a pervert."

I kept loading the register into the bag. "You don't think I'm worth watching?"

Again, with the ski mask, I couldn't be sure, but he seemed to blush.

"No. I mean, yes," he said. "You're very pretty."

I nodded. "There's not much money here we have access to, you know? A lot of it goes straight to the safe. That's procedure."

"I'm a fairly frugal man," he said. "Sometimes I need extra for . . . tuition."

"Tuition?"

"And other academic expenses."

"Academic expenses," I repeated, not a question this time. I thought that he had a nice voice, and then I told him so. "You have a nice voice," I said. "And pretty eyes." I gave him my phone number, not writing it down because the security camera would have picked that up, but just told him to call, repeating the number twice so he would remember it. "And my name is Louise."

"Thanks," he said, "Louise."

"Good luck with your education," I called after him, but the door had already swung closed. I watched him run out toward the pumps and beyond, admired the way his body moved, the curve of his jeans, for as long as I could make him out against the darkness. I gave him a head start before I dialed 911.

I know what you're thinking. You're thinking I was some bored, bubblegum-popping, *Cosmo*-reading girl, disillusioned with the real world and tired already of being a grownup, and along comes this bad boy and, more than that, literally a criminal and . . . Sure, there's some truth there. But here again you'd be missing the point.

It wasn't exciting that he robbed convenience stores.

It was exciting that he was brave enough to call me afterward, especially in this age of caller ID, when I had his phone number and name immediately—Grayson, Delwood—and could have sent the police after him in a minute.

That *Cosmo* article? The one I was reading when he showed up in the ski mask? "Romantic Gestures Gone Good: Strange but True Stories of How He Wooed and Won Me."

Not a one of those stories held a candle to hearing Del's voice on the other end of the phone: "Hello, Louise? I, um . . . robbed your 7-Eleven the other night, and I've been percolating on our conversation ever since. Are you free to talk?"

That takes a real man, I thought. And—don't forget those academic expenses—a man who might be going somewhere.

But it had been a long time since I believed we were going anywhere fast. Or anywhere at all.

We took the High Road down from Taos. That figured: two lanes, forty-five miles per hour.

"Afraid they'll get you for speeding?" I asked.

"One thing might lead to another," he said. "And anyway, the rental place stressed that it was dangerous to exceed the speed limit while pulling the trailer here."

As we drove, he kept looking up into the rearview mirror nervously, staring back across the sweep of that trailer, as if any second a patrol car really was gonna come tearing around the bend, sirens wailing, guns blasting. He had put his own pistol in the glove compartment. I saw it when I went for a Kleenex.

"If we get pulled, are you gonna use it?"

He didn't answer, but just glanced up again at the mirror, which rattled against the windshield with every bump and curve.

I was doing a little rearview looking myself.

Here's the thing. Even if I had become disillusioned with Del, I don't believe I had become disappointed in him—not yet.

I mean, like I said, he was a planner. I'd seen my mama date men who couldn't think beyond which channel they were gonna turn to next, unless there was a big game coming up, and then their idea of planning was to ask her to pick up an extra bag of chips and dip for their friends. I myself had dated men who would pick me up and give me a kiss and ask, "So, what do you want to do tonight?"—none of them having thought about it themselves except to hope that we might end up in the back seat or even back at their apartment. I'm sorry to admit it with some of those men, but most times we did.

On the other hand, take Del. When he picked me up for our first date, I asked him straight out, "Where's the desperate criminal planning to take the sole witness to his crime on their first date?" I was admiring how he looked out from under that ski mask—his beard not straggly like I'd been afraid, but groomed nice and tight, and chiseled features, you'd call them, underneath that. Those green eyes looked even better set in such a handsome face. He'd dressed up: a button-down shirt, a nice pair of khakis. He was older than I'd expected, older than me. Thirties maybe. Maybe even late thirties. A touch of gray in his beard. But I kind of liked all that.

"A surprise," said Del, and didn't elaborate, but just drove out of Eagle Nest and out along 64, and all of a sudden I thought, *Oh, wait, desperate criminal, sole witness.* My heart started racing and not in a good way. But then he pulled into Angel Fire and we went to Our Place for dinner. (Our Place! That's really the name.) My heart started racing in a better way after that.

Then there's the fact that he did indeed finish his degree at the community college, which shows discipline and dedication. And coming up with that story about his sister and why we were moving, laying out a cover story in advance, always thinking ahead. And planning for the heist itself—the "big one," he said, "the last one," though I knew better. Over the last year, whenever tuition came due, he'd hit another 7-Eleven or a gas station or a DVD store

—"shaking up the modus operandi," he said, which seemed smart to me, but maybe he just got that from the movies he watched on our DVD player. He'd stolen that too.

That was how we spent most of our nights together, watching movies. I'd quit the 7-Eleven job at that point. It was dangerous, Del said—*ironically*, he said—and I'd got a job at one of the gift stores in town, keeping me home nights. Home meaning Del's mobile home, because it wasn't long before I'd moved in with him.

We'd make dinner—something out of a box because I'm not much of a cook, I'll admit—and I'd watch Court TV, which I love, while he did some of his homework for the business classes he was taking over at the college or read through the day's newspaper, scouring the world for opportunities, he said, balancing work and school and me. Later we'd watch a movie, usually something with a crime element like *Bank Job* or *Mission: Impossible* or some old movie like *The Sting* or *Butch Cassidy and the Sundance Kid* or all those *Godfather* movies like every man I've ever been with. I suggested *Bonnie and Clyde*, for obvious reasons, but he said it would be disadvantageous for us to see it and so we never did.

"Is that all you do, sit around and watch movies?" Mama asked on the phone, more than once.

"We go out some," I told her.

"*Out* out?" she asked, and I didn't know quite what she meant and I told her that.

"He surprises me sometimes," I said. "Taking me out for dinner."

(Which was true. "Let's go out for a surprise dinner," he'd say sometimes, even though the surprise was always the same, that we were just going to Our Place. But that was still good because it really was our place—both literally *and* figuratively—and there's romance in that.)

"He loves me," I'd tell Mama. "He holds me close at night and tells me how much he loves me, how much he can't live without me."

Mama grunted. She was in North Carolina. Two hours' time difference and almost a full country away, but still you could feel her disappointment like she was standing right there in the same room.

"That's how it starts," Mama would tell me, "'I can't live without you,'" mimicking the voice. "Then pretty soon 'I can't live without you' starts to turn stifling and sour and . . ."

Her voice trailed off. *And violent,* I knew she'd wanted to say.

And I knew where she was coming from, knew how her last boyfriend had treated her. I'd seen it myself, one of the reasons I finally just moved away, anywhere but there.

"I thought you were going to start a *new* life," she said, a different kind of disappointment in her voice then. "You could watch the tube and drink beer anywhere. You could date a loser here if that's all you're doing."

I twirled the phone cord in my hand, wanting just to be done with the conversation but not daring to hang up. Not yet.

"Frugal," Mama said, making me regret again some of the things I'd told her about him. "Frugal's just a big word for cheap."

"Are things gonna be different someday?" I'd asked Del one night, the two of us lying in bed, him with his back to me. I ran my fingers across his shoulder when I asked it.

"Different?" he asked.

"Different from this."

He didn't answer at first. I kept rubbing his shoulder and let my hand sneak over and rub the top of his chest, caressing it real light, because I knew he liked that. The window was slid open and a breeze rustled the edge of those thin curtains. Just outside stood a short streetlight, one that the mobile home park had put up, and sometimes it kept me awake, shining all night, like it was aiming right for my face, leaving me sleepless.

After a while I realized Del wasn't gonna answer at all, and I stopped rubbing his chest and turned over.

That night when I couldn't sleep, I knew it wasn't the streetlight at all.

For that big one, that *last* last one, Del had roamed those art galleries in downtown Taos after work at the garage. He watched the ads for gallery openings, finding a place that stressed *cash only,* real snooty because you know a lot of people would have to buy that artwork on time and not pay straight out for it all at once, but those weren't the type of people they were after. He'd looked up the address of the gallery owner, the home address, and we'd driven past that too.

I liked watching his mind work: the way he'd suddenly nod just slightly when we were walking across the plaza or down the walkway between the John Dunn Shops, like he'd seen something important. Or the way his eyes narrowed and darted as we rode through the neighborhood where the gallery owner lived, keeping a steady speed, not turning his head, not looking as if he was looking.

We had a nice time at the gallery opening itself. At least at the beginning. Delwood looked smart in his blue blazer, even though it was old enough that it had gotten some shine at the elbows. And you could see how happy he was each time he saw a red dot on one of the labels—just more money added to the take—even if he first had to ask what each of those red dots meant.

I hated the gallery owner's tone when he answered that one, as if he didn't want Del or me there drinking from those plastic cups of wine or eating the cheese. He had a sleek suit, and his thin hair was gelled back dramatically, and he wore these square purple spectacles that he looked over when he was answering Del. I couldn't help but feel a little resentful toward him. But then I thought, *Square Specs will get his,* if you know what I mean. And of course he did.

"I like this one," I said in front of one of the pictures. It was a simple picture—this painting stuck in the back corner. A big stretch of blue sky and beneath it the different-colored blue of the ocean, and a mistiness to it, like the waves were kicking up spray. Two people sat on the beach, a man and a woman. They sort of leaned into one another, watching the water, and I thought about Del and me and began to feel nostalgic for something that we'd never had. The painting didn't have a red dot on it, but it did have a price: three thousand dollars. "With the money," I whispered to Delwood, "we could come back here and buy one of them, huh? Wouldn't that be ballsy? Wouldn't that be ironic?"

"Louise," he said, that tone again, telling me everything.

"I'm just saying," I said. "Can't you picture the two of us at the ocean like that? Maybe with the money we could take a big trip, huh?"

"Can't you just enjoy your wine?" he whispered, and moved on to the next picture, not looking at it really, just at the label.

"Fine," I said after him, deciding I'd just stay there and let him finish casing out the joint, but then a couple came up behind me.

"Let's try *s* on this one," the woman whispered.

"*S*," said the man. "Okay. *S*." They looked at the picture of the beach, and I looked with them, wondering what they meant by "trying *s*." The man wrinkled his brow, squinted his eye, scratched his chin—like Del when's he's thinking, but this man seemed to be only playing at thinking. "Sappy," he said finally.

"Sentimental," said the woman, quick as she could.

"Um . . . Sugary."

"Saccharine."

"No fair," said the man. "You're just playing off my words."

The woman smirked at him. She had a pretty face, I thought. Bright blue eyes and high cheekbones with freckles across them. She had on a gauzy top, some sort of linen, and even though it was just a thin swath of fabric, you could tell from the texture of it and the way she wore it that it was something fine. I knew, just knew suddenly, that it had probably cost more than the money Del had stolen from the 7-Eleven the night I first met him. And I knew too that I wanted a top just like it.

"Fine," she said, pretending to pout. "Here's another one. Schmaltzy."

"Better! Um . . . sad."

"No, *this* is sad," she said, holding up her own plastic wineglass.

"Agreed." He laughed.

"Swill," she whispered, dragging out the *s* sound, just touching his hand with her fingers, and they both giggled as they moved on to the next picture. And the next letter, it turned out.

T was for *tarnished*, for *trashy*, for *tragic*.

Del had made the full circuit. Even from across the room I could see the elbows shining on his blazer. Then he turned and saw me and made a short side-nod with his head, motioning toward the door. Time to head back home.

I looked once more at the painting of the couple on the beach. I'd thought it was pretty. Still did.

I'd thought the wine had tasted pretty good too.

But suddenly it all left a bad taste in my mouth.

A bad taste still as we continued south now.

The steep turns and drop-offs that had taken us out of Taos had given way to villages, small homes on shaded roads, people up and about, going about their lives. I saw the signs for the Santuario de

Chimayó, which I'd visited when I first moved out this way, picking northern New Mexico just because it seemed different, in every way, from where I'd grown up. I'd found out about the church in Chimayó from a guidebook I'd ordered off the Internet, learned about the holy earth there and how it healed the sick. When I'd visited it myself, I gathered up some of the earth and mailed it off to Mama—not that she was sick, but just unhappy. I don't know what I'd imagined she'd do with it, rub it on her heart or something. "Thanks for the dirt," she told me when she got it.

"Do you think they've found Square Specs yet?" I asked Del.

"Square Specs?"

"The gallery owner," I said. "Do you think the cleaning lady found him, or a customer?"

We were nearing another curve and Del eased the Nova around it slowly, carefully.

"Probably somebody will have found him by now. Like I told you last night, I tied him up pretty good. I don't think he'd have gotten loose on his own. But by now . . ."

He sped up a little bit. I don't think he did it consciously, but I noticed.

A while later I asked, "Are we gonna do anything fun with the money?"

"What kind of fun?"

"I don't know. Clothes, jewelry . . . a big-screen TV, a vacation. Something fun."

He scratched his beard. "That's just extravagance."

"Are you gonna make *all* the decisions?"

"All the good ones," he said. He gave a tense chuckle. "Don't you ever consider the future?"

But again he missed what I was saying. The future is exactly what I was thinking about.

After we bypassed Santa Fe proper, Del had us two-laning it again on a long road toward Albuquerque: miles and miles of dirt hills and scrubby little bushes, some homes that looked like people still lived there and others that were just crumbling down to nothing. The Ortiz Mountains stood way out in the distance. We got stuck for a while behind a dusty old pickup going even slower than we were, but Del was still afraid to pass, especially with that trailer stretched out behind us. We just poked along behind the truck until it decided to turn down some even dustier old road, and every mile we spent behind it, my blood began to boil up more.

I know Del was picturing roadblocks out on the interstate, and helicopters swooping low, waiting for some rattling old Nova like ours to do something out of the ordinary, tip our hand—picturing it even more after I asked about that gallery owner getting loose. But after a while I just wanted to scream, "Go! Go! Go!" or else reach over and grab the wheel myself, stretch my leg over and press down on the gas, hurl us ahead somehow and out of all this. And then there was all the money in the trunk and all the things I thought we could have done with it but clearly weren't going to do.

Once or twice I even thought about pulling out that pistol myself and pointing it at him. "I don't want anybody to get hurt," I might say, just like he would. "Just do like I ask, okay?" That was the first time I thought about it—not even serious about it then.

Still, it was all I could do to hide all that impatience, all that restlessness and nervous energy. None of it helped by that *tap tap tap tap tap* of the mirror against the windshield. I felt like my skin was turning inside out.

"I need to pee," I said finally.

"Next place I see," said Del, a glance at me, one more glance in the rearview. I looked in the side mirror. Nothing behind us but road. I looked ahead of us. Nothing but road. I looked around the car. Just me and him and that damn mirror tapping seconds into minutes and hours and more.

We stopped in Madrid, which isn't pronounced like the city in Spain but with the emphasis on the first syllable: MAD-rid. It used to be a mining town back in the Gold Rush days, but then dried up and became a ghost town. Now it's a big artists' community. I didn't know all that when we pulled in, but there was a brochure.

We parked lengthwise along the road by one of the rest stops at one end of the town—outhouse, more like it. Del waited in the car, but after I was done, I tapped on his window. "I'm gonna stretch my legs," I said, and strolled off down the street before he could answer. I didn't care whether he followed, but pretty soon I heard the *scuff scuff* of his feet on the gravel behind me. I really did need a break, just a minute or two out of the car, and it did help some, even with him following. We walked on like that, him silent behind me except for his footsteps as I picked up that brochure and looked in the store windows at antiques and pottery and vintage cowboy boots. Fine arts in the mix as well. "Wanna make one *last* last job?" I wanted to joke. Half joke. "Get something for *me* this time?"

I walked in one store. Del followed. I just browsed the shelves. The sign outside had advertised "local artisans and craftspeople," and the store had quirky stuff the way those kinds of places do: big sculptures of comical-looking cowboys made out of recycled bike parts, close-up photographs of rusted gas pumps and bramblebush, hand-dipped soy candles, gauzy-looking scarves that reminded me of the woman at the gallery the night before. I browsed through it all, taking my time, knowing that Del was right up on me, almost feeling his breath on my back.

One shelf had a bowl full of sock-monkey key chains. A cardboard sign in front of the bowl said, HANDCRAFTED. $30.

"Excuse me," I called over to the man behind the counter. He'd been polishing something and held a red rag in his hand. "Is this the price of the bowl or of the monkeys?"

"Oh," he said, surprised, as if he'd never imagined someone might misunderstand that. "The monkeys," he said, then corrected himself. "Each monkey," he said. "The bowl's not for sale at all."

I turned to Del. "Why don't you get me one of these?" I asked him, holding up a little monkey.

I tried to say it casual-like, but it was a challenge. I felt like both of us could hear it in my voice. Even the man behind the register heard it, I imagine, even though he'd made a show of going back to his polishing.

"What would you want with a thing like that?" Del said.

"Sometimes a girl likes a present. It makes her feel special." I dangled the sock monkey on my finger in front of him, and Del watched it sway, like he was mesmerized or suspicious. "Or is the romance gone here?"

"It's kind of pricy for a key chain."

I leaned in close for just a second, whispered, "Why don't you just slip it in your pocket then?"

Del cut his eyes toward the man behind the counter, then turned back to me. His look said *hush.* "I told you last night was the last time," he said, a low growl.

I just swayed that monkey back and forth.

A woman in a green dress jingled through the door then and went up to the counter. "You were holding something for me," she said, and the man put down his polish rag, and they started talking.

You could tell that Del was relieved not to have a witness anymore. "C'mon, Louise," he said. "Be serious."

But me? For better or worse, I just upped the ante.

"Suppose I said to you that this monkey"—I jerked my finger to make his little monkey body bounce—"this monkey represents love to me."

"Love?" he said.

"The potential for love," I clarified. "The possibility of it."

"How's that?"

"Suppose I told you that my daddy, the last time I saw him, me only six years old, he comes into my bedroom to tuck me in and he gives me a sock-puppet monkey, bigger than this one, but looking pretty much the same"—because the truth is they all do, handcrafted or not—"and he says to me, 'Hon, Daddy's going away for a while, but while I'm gone, this little monkey is gonna take care of you, and any time you find yourself thinking of me or wondering about me, I want you to hug this monkey close to you, and I'll be there with you. Wherever I am, I'll be here with you.' And he touched his heart."

I wasn't talking loud, but the man behind the counter and the customer had grown quiet, listening to me now even as they pretended not to. It was a small store, they couldn't help it. Del wasn't sweating, not really, but with all the attention—two witnesses to our argument now—he looked like he might break out in one any second.

"And Mama was behind him, leaned against the door watching us," I went on. "Anyone probably could have seen from her face that he wasn't coming back and that it was her fault and she felt guilty, but I was too young to know that then. And I dragged that monkey around with me every day and slept with it every night and hugged it close. And finally Mama threw it away, which told me the truth. 'Men let you down,' she told me when I cried about it, because she'd just broken up with her latest boyfriend and had her own heart broken. 'Men always let you down,' she told me. 'Don't you ever fool yourself into forgetting that.' And I stopped crying. But still, whatever Mama told me and whether my daddy came back or not, I believed—I *knew*—that there had been love there, there in that moment, in that memory, you know?"

Del looked over at the wall, away from the shopkeeper and his customer, and stared at this sculpture of a cowboy on a bucking bronco—an iron silhouette. The tilt of his head and the nervous look in his eyes reminded me of the first night we'd met, at the 7-Eleven, when he'd called me "ma'am" and I'd told him my age. Seemed like here was another conversation where he was playing catch-up, but this time he seemed fearful for different reasons.

"And maybe," I said, helping him along, "just maybe if you bought this for me, I'd know you really loved me, for always and truly. Now," I said, "would *that* get it through your thick skull?"

Out of the corner of my eye, I saw an embarrassed look on the storekeeper's face—embarrassed for Del and maybe embarrassed for me too. His customer, the woman in green, cleared her throat, and the shopkeeper said to her, "Yes, just let me find that for you."

Del shifted his lower jaw to the side—another indication, I'd learned, that his mind was working on something, weighing things. He really was sweating now, and still staring at that bucking bronco sculpture like he felt some kinship with the cowboy on top, like staring at it might give him an answer somehow.

"What was your monkey's name?" he asked me.

I gave out a long sigh, with an extra dose of irritation in it. He was missing the whole point, just like always. "I don't know," I told him. I sighed again. "Murphy," I said.

His look changed then, just a thin crease of the forehead, a tiny raise of the eyebrow. "Murphy the monkey?" he said. He wasn't looking at the sculpture now, wasn't looking afraid anymore. "Louise," he began, "I don't really think that this monkey represents the love we share, and the truth is that thirty dollars seems like quite a bit for—"

But I didn't hear the rest of it. I just put that monkey down, then turned and walked out the door, slamming it behind me the way I'd slammed the Nova's door that morning.

I can't say whether I wanted him to call for me to come back or rush out after me, something dramatic like that, but if I did, I was indeed fooling myself, just like Mama had warned. That wasn't Delwood. When I got in the car, I saw him through the window, slowly coming back—those sad footsteps, *scuff scuff scuff.* No hurry at all, like he knew I'd be waiting.

We rode on in silence after that—a heavy silence, you know what I mean. More ghost towns where people used to have hopes and dreams and now there was nothing but rubble and a long stretch of empty land. I wasn't even angry now, but just deflated, disappointed.

"Men will do that to you," my mama told me another time. "After a while you feel like it's not even worth trying." I'd known what she meant, theoretically. Now I knew in a different way.

Soon the two-lane widened, and the strip malls started up, and fast-food restaurants—civilization. I saw a Wendy's and asked if it was okay to stop.

"I'll pick from the dollar menu," I said, sarcastic-like.

Del didn't say anything, just pulled through the drive-thru and ordered what I wanted. He didn't get anything for himself. I think it was just out of spite.

Late afternoon, we cruised through Winslow, Arizona, which I guess would get most people in the mind of that Eagles song. Standing on a corner and all that. But it had me thinking of the past and my old high school flame. Winslow was his name—Win, everybody called him—and I couldn't help but start indulging those what-ifs about everything I'd left behind. It was a fleeting moment; Win and I had had our own troubles, of course, but it struck me hard, discontented as I was with things and people—thinking myself about running down the road and trying to loosen my own load.

Then toward evening we stopped at a motel in Kingman, one of those cheap ones that have been there since Route 66 was an interesting road and not just a tourist novelty—the ones that now looked like they'd be rented for the hour by people who didn't much care what the accommodations were like.

Del checked us in, pulled the Nova around to the stairwell closest our room, and parked sideways across several spaces, since that was the only way we'd fit.

"Get your kicks," I said.

"Kicks?" he said, baffled.

"Route 66," I said, pointing to a sign. "Guess we couldn't afford the Holiday Inn either, huh?"

He stared straight ahead, drummed his fingers light against the steering wheel. He curled up his bottom lip a little and chewed on his beard.

"You know those court shows you watch on TV?" Del said finally. "And how you tell me some of those people are so stupid? You listen to their stories and you laugh and you tell me, 'That's where they went wrong' or 'They should've known better than that.'"

"Do you mean," I said, "something like a man who robs a convenience store, then calls up the clerk he's held at gunpoint and asks her out for a date?" I felt bad about it as soon as I said it. Part of why I fell in love with him and now I was complaining about it.

"There were extenuating circumstances in that instance," he said, and this warning sound had crept into his tone, one that I hadn't heard before. "I'm just saying that we need to be fairly circumspect now about whatever we do. Any misstep might put us in front of a real judge, and it won't be a laughing matter, I can guarantee you that." He turned to face me. "Louise," he said, again that way he does. "I love you, Louise, but sometimes . . . well, little girl, sometimes you just don't seem to be thinking ahead."

It was the *little girl* that got me, or maybe the *extenuating* or the *circumspect,* or maybe just him implying that I was being stupid, or maybe all of it, the whole day.

"Del," I said through clenched teeth, putting some bite into his name, same as he always did me. "I love you, and when I say that, I mean it. But sometimes, Del, sometimes, I could just kill you."

He nodded. "You'd go to jail for that too," he said, slow and even as always, but still with that edge of warning to it. He handed the room key across to me. "You go on in. I want to check that things haven't shifted back in the trailer."

"Fine," I said, toughening the word up to let him hear how I felt. He stared at me for a second, then went back to get our bags. In the rearview, I watched him bending open the tarp covering the trailer, but still I just sat there.

I don't know how to describe what I was feeling. Anger? Sadness? I don't know what was running through my head, either. What to do next, maybe. Whether to go up to the room and carry on like we'd planned, like he seemed to expect I'd do, or to step out of all this, literally just step out of the car and start walking in another direction.

But then I knew if I really did leave, he'd come after me. Not dramatic, not begging, but I knew he wouldn't let me go. Can't live without you, that's what he'd said, and like Mama said, sometimes that kind of love could turn ugly fast. I'd seen it before.

"You just gonna sit there?" Del called out.

He'd opened the trunk now, blocking my view, just a voice behind me. More rearranging.

"No. I'm going up," I called back. Then just before I stepped out of the car, I opened up the glove compartment and slipped the gun into my purse.

In the motel room, I locked the door to the bathroom, set down my purse, and turned the water on real hot before climbing in. I stood there in the steam and rubbed that little bitty bar of soap over me, washing like I had layers of dust from those two-lane roads and that truck we'd followed for so long.

I thought about what would happen after I got out. "Sometimes people are too far apart in their wants," I could say. "I do love you, Del, but sometimes a person needs to move on." It was just a matter of saying it. It would be easy to do, I knew. I'd done it before, back with Win all those years ago, and I hadn't needed a gun then. But the gun showed I was serious in a different way. More than that, it was protection. "I'm not taking all the money, Del," I might say. "That's not what's going on here. That's not the point." As if he had ever got the point.

I took both towels when I got out of the shower. The steam swirled around me while I stood there drying myself off—one towel wrapped around me and one towel for my hair, leaving him none.

Would he try to talk me out of it? Would he try to take the gun away? Would I have to tie him up the way he'd left that gallery owner back in Taos? Even thinking about it made me sad.

He was sitting there when I came out of the bathroom, sitting on the one chair in the room, staring at the blank television, the screen of it covered in a light layer of dust. I hadn't taken the gun out but just held my purse in my hand, feeling the weight of it. Thinking that I might have to use it. I suddenly wished I'd gotten dressed first. I mean, picture it: me wrapped in two towels and holding a gun? Hardly a smooth getaway.

Del's face was . . . well, *pensive* was the word that came to mind. He taught me that word, I thought. I wouldn't have known it without him. And that kept me from saying immediately what I needed to say. I just stood there, feeling a single drip of water sneak past the towel around my head, race down my back.

"You never talked much about your daddy," he said, breaking the silence. "He really leave you when you were six?"

"Yes," I said, and I realized then that I felt like I was owed something for that.

Del stared at the blank television. I turned my own head that way, toward the gray curve of the screen. I could see his face there, reflected toward me, kind of distorted, distant.

"He really give you a sock monkey when he left?"

I thought about that, but I was thinking now about what I owed Del.

"No," I told him, and I could hear the steel in my own voice. "But what Mama said, she did say that."

I stared hard at the dusty TV screen, at his reflection there. I saw then that his fists were clenched, and that he clenched them even tighter at my answer. I could feel myself tighten. I knew then that he knew the pistol was gone. I didn't take my eyes off that reflection as I pulled up the strap of my pocketbook, just in case he stood up quick and rushed me. But he dropped his head down a little, and I saw his profile in the reflection, which meant he'd turned to see me straight on.

"You lied to me, then?" He was clenching his hand hard, so much that if I'd been closer, I might have backed away. But there was a bed between us. And the pocketbook was open now.

"If that's what you want to take from it."

His eyes watched me hard. Those green eyes. First thing I'd really noticed about him up close.

"Do you believe Cora was right?"—meaning Mama. That's her name.

"I don't know. Do you?

Those eyes narrowed. Thinking again. And it struck me that I could just about list every little thing he did when he was pondering over something: how he sometimes stared hard at the wall or other times stared off into space with this faraway gaze, running his fingers through his hair or through the tip of his beard, biting at his bottom lip or chewing on that beard or just shifting his jaw one way or the other. Usually left, I corrected myself. Always to the left. And sure enough, just as I thought it, he shifted his jaw just that way, setting it in place.

I almost laughed despite myself. *Men always let you down,* Mama had said, but Del had come through with his jaw jut exactly like expected. At least you could count on him for that. And all of a sudden I felt embarrassed for having taken that gun from the glove compartment, just wanted to run out in my towel and put it back.

"Do you want a surprise?" he asked, and I almost laughed again.

"It's a long drive back to Our Place."

"A new surprise."

"Sure," I said.

"The story we told back at the mobile home park, about me having a sister out in Victorville," he said then. "I really do. Haven't talked to her in a while. We were estranged." He stretched out the word. "She's in real estate. Got us a deal she worked out on a foreclosure. A house. Said she'd let me do some work for her, at her company, now that I have a degree. It's all worked out. I needed to get the down payment on it, so I figured, one more job. One big one and that'd be it." He tapped his hand on the side of the chair, like you would tap your fingers, but his whole hand because it was still clenched. I think it was the most words he'd ever said in one breath. "That's my surprise."

Part of me wanted to go over to him, but I didn't. *Don't you ever fool yourself into forgetting,* I heard Mama saying. I stood right in the doorway, still dripping all over the floor, all over myself.

"I stole that painting you wanted too," he said, as if he was embarrassed to admit it. "We can't hang it in the house, at least not the living room, not yet, not where anyone might see, but you can take it out and look at it sometimes, maybe, if you want. It's out in the trunk now if you want me to get it." He gave a big sigh, the kind he might give late at night when he was done with talking to me, done with the day. But something else in his face this time, some kind of struggle, like he wanted to go quiet but still had more to tell. "But I was serious about that being the last one," he said finally. "This is a fresh start and I want to do it right. That's why I paid for this."

He opened his fist then. The sock-monkey key chain was in it. Crushed a little in his grip, but there it was.

"I knew that story wasn't true, about your daddy," he said. "I knew it while you were telling it. But it being true or not, that wasn't the point, was it?"

I smiled and shook my head. No no no, that wasn't the point. And yes yes yes too, of course.

Needless to say, I didn't kill him. And I didn't take my half and hit the highway.

When we got in the car the next day, I almost didn't see the rust along the wheel well, and I closed the door so soft that I almost didn't hear that loose metal rolling around inside. While Delwood packed the trunk and rearranged stuff one more time under that tarp, I slipped that pistol into the glove compartment, just like it had been in the first place. I didn't touch it again.

As Delwood drove us along 66 and out of town, I rolled down the window and kicked up my heels, leaned over against him.

You might imagine that I was stuck on that three-thousand-dollar painting in the trunk and that house ahead, and partly I was, but again you'd be missing the point. It was the sock monkey that meant the most to me. Light as a trinket but with a different kind of weight to it. When I hung it from the rearview mirror, the rattle there died down almost to a whisper, and it all seemed like a smoother ride ahead for a while.

SUSAN THORNTON

Border Crossing

FROM *The Literary Review*

A YOUNG GIRL stood in a desert canyon just north of the border between the United States and Mexico. She was wearing a short, tight black skirt and a low-cut red blouse of soft, clingy material. On her feet were high-heeled shoes.

She was thirsty.

It was just before dawn on a Wednesday in mid-March.

To the south was Mexico. The girl stood on U.S. territory. The canyon was in Imperial County, California. The nearest city was Imperial Beach, only a few miles to the west.

A fence separates the United States from Mexico. It runs from Imperial Beach for fourteen miles into Tecate. The fence ends at Colonia Nida de las Águilas, a riverbed, now dry, which crosses the border. The girl was standing well east of that point.

The land to the north of the border is four hundred square miles of dry and barren hillsides.

The girl had regular features and smooth, unmarked brown skin. Her eyebrows had been plucked into a careful, artful line. As she looked at her surroundings she bit her lips gently together, then opened them and lightly ran the tip of her tongue along the back of her upper teeth, in a reflexive, thoughtful gesture.

Her eyes were brown and her long dark hair was held back from her face with a red ribbon.

She stood at the bottom of the dry riverbed. Along the riverbed stood or sat other young girls, dressed like herself, in short skirts and high-heeled shoes. There were perhaps fifteen girls altogether. At the head of the canyon stood a man with a rifle. He was looking away from the girls, to the north. With him was another young man. The men wore blue jeans and sturdy leather boots. The man with the rifle wore a white T-shirt and an open tan jacket. The two men were talking to each other. A third man stood some distance away. He cradled his rifle, an expensive American make, loosely with one arm as he smoked a cigarette.

The girls were being marched through the canyon. They had started two hours before, in the dark, and had walked seven miles in the desert to get to this point, just north of the border. They had crossed the border without incident, as the area was not well patrolled. It was cool in the canyon, and the sky over its eastern rim was beginning to turn pink. Soon the real heat of the day would begin.

The girl was thinking. She stood apart from the other girls. If the guards were looking away, she could run. She looked down the canyon, the way they had come. The dry riverbank had taken a sharp curve as the water that formed it had found softer rock to carve through. That created a natural wall, and a limit to the sightline of the men holding the guns. If she ran back the way they had come, south, she would have a chance. Once she was behind the wall, she could climb up to the top of the ridge and escape down the other side.

She was only one girl. They had other girls to watch, and they were hurrying to meet someone, someone with a truck, further north. If there was a diversion, a moment in which to run, she could get behind the wall. She tensed her calf muscle. Her feet were still callused and hard. Once she discarded the crippling shoes, she could run. She knew she could.

II

Altagracia Guzman was fourteen years old. Until nine weeks ago she had lived in a suburb of Delicias, a city south of Chihuahua, Mexico. She had been a student in middle school and had won the school prize in geometry the previous quarter. She was studying English and could count to one hundred and exchange simple greetings. Her father and mother were preparing for her Quinceañera, the party to mark her fifteenth birthday. Her mother ran a sewing and tailoring business out of their home, and Altagracia could sew a straight seam by hand if she had to but preferred the sewing machine. Her mother depended on her for simple tasks —shortening trousers, letting out a waistband—and was teaching her how to make a satin evening jacket for a high-paying customer.

Altagracia could also make perfect tortillas that never tore in her hands and never burned. She made arroz con pollo and corn tamales. When her mother was occupied with her little twin brothers, Altagracia did the cooking and had supper ready when her father came home from his maintenance job at the factory.

All this had changed when two men grabbed her on her way home from school on a Friday. By habit she walked with her friend Edelmera, but that day Edelmera's mother had called for her early at school; her grandmother had become ill and the girl was needed at home.

Altagracia had been alone on the two blocks that skirted the edge of the industrial park in the southern part of the city. When the white panel van pulled up to block her path, she thought the driver meant to ask her directions. Then she saw the look on his face, but it was already too late. Someone grabbed her elbows from behind, and the first man put a cloth with a strong-smelling chemical to her face. She was aware of being lifted off her feet and she heard the opening of a metallic door.

She came to in the back of the van, hearing the engine and smelling the diesel fumes. There were seven other girls in the van.

The first part of her journey ended in Calle Santo Tomás in the La Merced section of Mexico City.

This neighborhood has been a home to low-end prostitution since the 1700s. She fought and was beaten, resisted and was starved. When she decided to quit eating and starve herself to death, she was force-fed. At last she submitted. She was forced to parade in the square in front of them, display herself in her skimpy garments. Allow them to view her, to select before purchase, to walk with them back through the warren of rooms to the space allotted her. It was a mockery designed to make her feel complicit, to provide a pretense of agency where there was none. Each man bought fifteen minutes. Four men in an hour. Eight men in two hours. The nights began at ten p.m. and ended at three in the morning. Twenty encounters in each night's work.

Altagracia kept track of the nights by ballpoint-pen marks on the edge of her mat. When she was alone in the early hours of the morning, she closed her eyes and counted to one hundred in English, recited the conjugations of the English verbs she had been taught: to have, to be, to be called, to play, to eat, to love. She remembered garments she had sewn for her mother; she recited the prayers she had been taught in church. She whispered her street address and pictured the white tablecloth with the blue embroidered edge she had made when she was nine as a gift for her mother. She remembered the silver chocolate pot her father had purchased for her mother and recalled how her mother stirred the chocolate for the family.

The nights had followed one another for sixty-one nights. Then another panel van and another journey in the jolting darkness with the smell of diesel. They were being driven north this time—she was being taken into the United States. The forty-eight states were big. She knew that from her geography lessons. Once she was in that big place she would be lost forever. She wanted to go home.

III

The sun had not yet come up and the light had an obscuring quality that she hoped would be to her advantage.

The two men at the head of the ravine were still talking. The third man put down his cigarette and turned behind a rock to relieve himself.

Then, a scream. And another. *"Culebra! Culebra!"* A girl had seen a snake. They were all terrified of rattlesnakes. A knot of confusion, more screams, a scuffle; the men were looking away. She saw her chance, she ducked, she ran. South, as they would not expect. East toward the sheltering wall. One shoe fell off as she pelted forward, then she stepped out of the other just as easily. Her feet felt sure on the hot flat rocks of the stream bed. Overhead she felt the air cool as the shadow of the rock wall came over her. In a moment she would be underneath it and then she would have a chance.

Behind her she knew the guard was raising his rifle, but she could not spare him a thought. Her entire being was focused on forward motion. She pumped her arms, reaching for the next foothold with her long legs. Her lungs were burning and there was a sharp pain in her side. She ignored it and breathed hard, in through her nostrils, out through her open mouth, keeping her lungs full so that she could continue running.

Now she was behind the outcropping of rock and she began to climb. Another stream had come down to join the main canyon where they had been. She found easy footing suddenly in softer, moister soil that was clustered with smaller pebbles. She climbed rapidly upward into the heat of the sun, then turned south again with the rising sun on her left-hand side, along the top of the ridge. She kept running, looking forward, never back, the canyon now behind and below her. The land sloped rapidly downward to a road. They were this close to a road! She could hardly believe it. She feared the road because she would be exposed, but she could run so much faster. The road was blacktop, with clear white lines painted at the margins and a double yellow line down the middle. She didn't know this, but the road was California State Route 94, which parallels the northern border of Mexico.

She stumbled down the last bit of the slope, bruising her ankle on a rock, landing on her buttocks, and sliding down; the sheer black fabric of her skirt rode up and the rocks scraped and cut her long brown legs. She couldn't think about what she looked like; she had to keep going.

At the margin of the road she looked again for the sun. South, she wanted to run south, home was south. She kept the sun on her left side and settled into a steady jog. No one was shouting, no one was shooting, she would not look back; she would only look forward.

The sun had risen higher when she heard a car. She glanced backward, fearful. It wasn't the van. It wasn't the white panel van. Suddenly she felt close to tears. She saw a boxy square shape, a large sedan. With sudden hope and desperation she stopped, turned to face the car, and stood in the middle of the driving lane, waving her arms.

The car slowed and stopped. It was a red Subaru, dusty from off-road driving, with a man driving and a woman passenger. Altagracia ran to the side of the car. The blond woman lowered the window on her side. "What's the matter? Are you in trouble?"

The words didn't mean anything to Altagracia, but she could read the woman's expression. Intelligent, cautious, maybe helpful.

"Please," said Altagracia in English. "Please . . ." Her English deserted her. She switched to Spanish. "Help me. Help me please. I must go south."

The man spoke. He had close-cropped dark hair and was wearing a blue polo shirt. "What's going on? What's she doing out here dressed like that?"

"She needs help." The woman spoke, in English, suddenly decisive. "And we're going to give it to her." She spoke to Altagracia in Spanish. "Get in. We will help you."

Altagracia pulled the door open and collapsed on the back seat.

"I don't know where she's coming from, Michael," said the woman. "But we're getting out of here. Let's get going."

Michael put the car in gear and stepped on the gas. Altagracia burst into sobs.

"Here, here, it's all right now." The woman spoke in English, then in Spanish. "*¿Quieres agua?*" She handed Altagracia a narrow water bottle. At first all Altagracia could do was hold it next to her face, then she got her breathing under control, opened the bottle, and took a long drink.

"*¿Cómo te llamas?* What's your name?"

Altagracia looked directly at this surprising woman who spoke to her in her own language. She didn't answer.

The woman continued in Spanish. "My name is Elizabeth. I am a translator. I work for the court system in Imperial City. Are you in some kind of trouble?"

"No trouble," Altagracia lied. "I want to go home."

"And where is your home?"

"Delicias, near Chihuahua."

"What's going on? What's her story?"

"She says she's not in trouble. She just wants to go home."

"Not in trouble? Dressed like that? In the desert at five-thirty in the morning? She's in trouble."

"Just drive, OK?"

"Is anyone following us?"

"Us?" Elizabeth turned around, scanned the empty highway behind them. "No, no one's following us."

"Good." Michael looked in the rearview mirror and then again at the road. He wore glasses with silver rims.

"Are you hungry?"

Altagracia managed a small nod.

Elizabeth reached into a cooler by her feet, found a sandwich in a plastic wrapper, and handed it to Altagracia. The girl took it warily. It was thick, homemade bread, with cheese and some kind of spicy filling. She took a bite and chewed carefully. As she ate she became hungry.

"How did you get here?" Elizabeth asked.

Altagracia shook her head. "Some bad men. I just want to go home." She pictured her mother's kitchen clearly, the table with the white tablecloth and the blue embroidered lace border that she had made when she was nine. "I live in Delicias," she repeated, and gave the address. "Is it far? Please?" She said *please* in English.

"We will help you," Elizabeth said.

"Help her do what?"

"Help her get home."

"Home? To Delicias? South of Chihuahua? That's far. That's not in Baja. That's in mainland Mexico."

"You understood a lot for someone who says they don't speak Spanish," Elizabeth said.

"Whoever brought her out to the desert is going to be looking for her," Michael said. "I'm just looking at the larger picture here."

"I don't think so," Elizabeth said.

"You don't?"

"I think if they were looking for her she wouldn't have gotten this far. And if she's a trafficking victim like I think she is, they won't be chasing her; they'll be trying to get the rest of the girls across. The thing to do is to take her to the police."

"No!" Altagracia shouted. "No. Not the police. No police." She remembered the police who had been her customers in La Merced. She grabbed Elizabeth's arm and began to shake uncontrollably. "No police. I just want to go home."

"We'll get you home, I promise."

"And what about our trip?" They were on their way to land they owned in Baja. They had left their home early that morning. It was a vacation they had planned for weeks.

"Peter has those dental clinics in Mexicali. He can take her back into Mexico."

"Smuggle an illegal back into Mexico? Are you kidding me?"

"Peter has never so much as smuggled a candy bar in all the years he's been running those clinics. He crosses the border twice a day. They give him a free pass. He's the perfect person. Then she can get a bus to Juarez and go south from there. It's possible. It can happen."

"And who's going to buy the bus ticket?"

"That's not important now. Just drive, OK? There's no one following us. I'll call Peter in an hour or so when he's up."

Altagracia had been listening with wide eyes. Elizabeth explained rapidly in Spanish. Home, Altagracia was thinking. She could get home. She relaxed against the back of the seat and fell instantly into a deep sleep. In a dream she heard a girl's voice. *You're just going to leave her here like this?* It was a voice she knew. Who was the girl talking about? Leave her where? When the car changed speed and slowed down she snapped awake. "What is it? What's happening?"

Elizabeth's voice was soothing. "We're stopping at a rest stop. It's OK." The car slowed more, and stopped.

"I can give you some different clothes if you want them," Elizabeth said.

"Yes, please." Altagracia spoke in English.

Elizabeth took clothes out of a small bag in the back of the car. She walked with Altagracia to the rest stop, but Altagracia didn't feel the same psychological hold from Elizabeth that she had felt from the madam in La Merced. She changed clothes in a stall in the restroom—a pair of jeans, a clean white shirt with long sleeves that she could button as high as she wished. A tan windbreaker that was slightly too large. She looked at herself in the restroom mirror. There was nothing to show where she had been, what she had done, who she had been. She looked as she always had, only older. With luck, she could pass for eighteen.

"Do you want to discard the old clothes?" Elizabeth asked.

Altagracia put them in the trash container and they walked back to the Subaru side by side. Altagracia looked around. No one was watching them.

Michael joined them at the car. He looked at Altagracia. His look was neutral, not charged with possession or calculation. "All set?"

In the back of the car, Altagracia fell asleep again. She awoke again at dusk. They were in a residential neighborhood. "This is where our friend lives. Peter. He can help you. He can take you back into Mexico."

Altagracia nodded. Somehow she knew she could trust these

people. "We will leave you here," Elizabeth said. "Peter is ready. He can take you in his car. You will have to lie on the floor of the back seat. We will cover you with a blanket and put some boxes next to you. He crosses the border regularly for his businesses in Mexicali. He is a trusted person. No one will question him. He speaks Spanish too, but not as well as I do. Here is money." Elizabeth put folded money in her hand; it was pesos. "This is for the bus." Then she gave her different money. "This is dollars. In case you need them."

Peter was small and stocky. He looked like an accountant on a TV soap opera she used to watch at home with Edelmera. He was waiting by his car, a Kia sedan. Altagracia lay down on the floor in front of the back seat. She was between two large boxes packed with glass bottles. Elizabeth touched her shoulder. "Peter will take you to the bus station. Good luck."

Elizabeth pulled a blanket over Altagracia and shut the door of the car. The car started and drove from the quiet neighborhood into an area of heavy traffic. The sounds of the city were all around her. The car slowed and stopped. She breathed shallowly, through her mouth.

"Across again?" A male voice. Spanish. It must be the border control.

"Emergency surgery at the clinic." Peter's voice was light. His Spanish was good, but mispronounced: a strong American accent. "Got a panicked call. The technician needed some supplies. You know how it is."

"Is that what's on the floor in the back seat?"

"Yeah, it's surgical kits, a new sterilizer, slides for the X-ray machine. Unless I've got lucky and it's a teenage girl."

Altagracia stopped breathing.

The guard laughed. "You, get a girl? With that face?"

"Come on, it's not that bad."

"Crossing back to the States again tonight?"

"As soon as I deliver the goods."

"All right, then."

The car accelerated again, and Altagracia breathed. She was in Mexico, she could go home. Again she pictured her mother's kitchen table; the white cloth with the blue embroidered edge, the stove, and the kettle; the silver pot for making chocolate, her father's gift to her mother.

They drove for several blocks. Peter stopped the car, got out, and opened the back door. "It's the bus station; you can get out now."

Was she still asleep? She could hardly believe this had all gone according to plan. Peter walked next to her and stood aside as she bought the ticket she needed with Elizabeth's pesos.

"Are you hungry?"

Peter bought her a tamale and a Coca-Cola. He sat with her as she ate and waited with her until her bus was called. He stood at the bus station watching as the bus pulled out. She waved to him from the window.

No one on the bus paid any attention to her. No one took the empty seat beside her. It had all happened with such an easy logic: Elizabeth and Michael slowing to pick her up, driving her to Peter's place; Peter taking her across the border. Now she was on the bus, going home.

In Delicias, outside the bus terminal, she held out her hand for a cab. At first she was afraid. She was young and alone. Would he stop? Would he question her? Perhaps it was the American clothes that made her look older. The cabdriver nodded as she gave him the address, the address she had repeated to herself over and over in those rooms in Mexico City.

As she approached her neighborhood she felt a tightness in her chest, a sensation that she could not breathe deeply enough. She was going home; she could see her mother, her two brothers, her father. Would he be home from the factory?

The cab turned down the familiar street. The cab stopped; she paid the driver and got out. The house looked the same. But of course it would, she had not been gone all that long. She walked toward the door. The street seemed steep to her suddenly, as if in her absence she had indeed aged, had become an old woman, an old woman with weak legs, weaker lungs.

The door stood open; it was a warm day. She hesitated at the threshold. "Mama," she said, "Mama." Her mother looked up, startled, from her work at the sewing machine. Altagracia seemed to see everything with preternatural clarity. There it was, the table, covered by the white cloth with the blue embroidered edge that she had made when she was nine. Her mother's sewing machine, the table piled high with shirts to be altered, with trousers to be hemmed. She heard her brothers playing in the other room. Her mother stood up, stepped forward to embrace her, her face open and smiling. But the scene changed, the light on the silver coffeepot suddenly blinding.

"Mama," Altagracia said again, and then she stopped, puzzled. An exploding pain was beginning in the back of her head; her vision went away in a searing heat of white light. "Mama," she cried again, and fell forward.

IV

Altagracia lay on her face in the stones of Cottonwood Canyon. The bullet had caught her in midstride and her limbs now lay still in the terrible disarray of death. The rifleman lowered his gun. He had seen her turn just as the other girls had shouted *"Culebra! Culebra!"*

He inspected his work. It was a good clean shot in the back of the head, exiting through the eye. He had spent many hours practicing his marksmanship over long distances and was justly proud of his well-made American rifle. Still, given the difficulty of hitting a moving target, it was an extremely lucky shot. He had hoped to bring her down with a bullet between the shoulder blades. The loss of the girl was regrettable. In the nine weeks at La Merced she had earned the syndicate almost nine thousand pesos, less the costs of her upkeep—food and clothing—since she had been a slave and had earned nothing for herself. And his bosses would have realized two thousand dollars for her from her purchaser in Arizona, but that would now not happen.

He stood and turned away from the body. "OK. Let's get going."

A girl stepped forward. "You're just going to leave her here like this?"

Without a word he lifted the rifle and sighted down the barrel. The girl looked at her shoes and took a step back. He lowered the rifle.

The girl turned and followed the other girls. The footing was bad and the sun was hot as they made their way north, into Los Estados Unidos.

The rifleman followed. His boss had told him to expect losses in this part of the journey. Some girls died of exposure, some of snakebite. So far he had prevented that. And now the other girls would be more tractable. He reminded himself of a central fact of his business. More young girls were born and matured every day: this meant an inexhaustible supply of product. And there was an equally inexhaustible demand. He considered himself a fortunate man. He had found a place in the best business opportunity in the world.

BRIAN TOBIN

Entwined

FROM *Alfred Hitchcock's Mystery Magazine*

ON SEPTEMBER 12, 1994, in my second week of college, I killed Russell Gramercy.

In the last eighteen years, how often have I gone over it all? Pearl Jam, the orange traffic cones, the young woman in white short shorts, the sound of kids playing, and then . . .

I had been driving alone back to my dorm from the lake. Despite what people claimed later, I had not been drinking—not one drop. I want to be clear about that. Even though there were coolers full of beer at our blanket, I was not intoxicated. It was about five-thirty on a beautiful balmy afternoon, the last twinge of summer in upstate New York. I wasn't speeding, nor was I driving in a "careless, reckless, or negligent manner," which is the criteria for negligent homicide.

A song I loved, Pearl Jam's "Alive," came on the radio, and I took my hand off the two position of the ten-and-two driving stance I had so recently been taught in driver's ed. I reached down and turned the volume up from loud to *really* loud. I was barely aware of the pedestrians on the sidewalk; they were indistinct, background. Vaguely I registered the sign ROAD WORK AHEAD. However, my registering Daria Gramercy's ass was anything but vague. She was wearing white short shorts; seen from behind, she was breathtaking. This figure of lust (I can't describe it in any nicer way that reflects better on me) was walking with two males. All three had been forced to abandon the sidewalk that paralleled Beach Road because of construction—for fifty yards the sidewalk had been jackhammered and it was cordoned off with orange traffic cones and yellow caution tape. Later, when I went back to the scene, I saw the clearly marked signs that warned pedestrians to cross to the other side of the road, that clearly told them not to walk on the shoulder. Weren't those signs implicit—no, definite—warnings that to proceed was dangerous?

At the time, I have to admit, I didn't notice those signs. Even though the radio was blaring "Alive," I could also faintly hear children playing: a Pee Wee League soccer match was just beginning.

If only it could have stopped there. If only I could go back in time and slam the brake pedal, so that nothing more would have happened except Pearl Jam, the orange traffic cones, the young woman in white short shorts, the sound of kids playing. Then it all would have just faded, one of millions of trivial sense memories that disappeared.

But time didn't stand still.

My car—actually, the 1979 Impala my father had handed down to me—was going around forty miles per hour. I know I lied about it later to the police, telling them that I was doing the posted thirty-five, but I can honestly say I was going about forty. At that speed, a car travels fifty-nine feet a second. (In my support group, *everyone,* every last person regardless of education, has done the calculations, the feet per second, the reaction times.) The three figures on the road outside the cones and caution tape, one with an extremely sexy sashay, were approaching rapidly. (I know they weren't approaching, that in fact I was overtaking them, but that's how it seemed to me.) And then the largest of them, a man in khaki shorts, a navy blue T-shirt, and Chuck Taylor Converse sneakers, stumbled beyond the white line into the road. Into the path of my thirty-five-hundred-pound lethal weapon going fifty-nine feet per second.

What happened took only milliseconds. There was a sickening jolt to the car; Russell Gramercy flew up over the hood. His shoulder and head shattered my windshield, then he disappeared over the roof of the Impala. I did not slam on the brakes until he had already landed on the highway behind me.

There was a faint whiff of something burnt—my tires on the asphalt—and Pearl Jam was still playing on the radio. Behind me someone was howling in pain and grief. "Oh, my God! Oh, my God!" Daria Gramercy.

Everything seemed in a heightened sense of unreality. I got out of the Impala, but immediately someone yelled, "Hey, put your car in gear." So I got back in the car, which was slowly rolling, and did so, also turning off the engine. I noticed glass on the passenger's side seat; in the next moment I realized that little shards of glass, almost festively decorative, covered my shirt as well.

The body lay in the road fifty yards away—I had traveled half a football field *after* hitting him. Another pedestrian stood in the middle of the road behind Daria and the victim, waving a hot-pink beach towel to stop oncoming traffic.

Racing back, I thought, He'll have some broken bones. He may have to go to the hospital. Daria was leaning over her father, whimpering.

Then I got a clear view of Russell Gramercy's body. This wasn't a case of some broken bones. His entire body was broken. One shoulder and arm were tilted at an impossible angle away from the rest of him. Blood was pooling behind his head, which also seemed . . . broken. Daria said, "Hold on, Dad. Hold on." But it was obvious to me that he could not hear, would never hear again.

And . . . I'm not proud of this, but I want to tell you exactly what it was like. Daria, in an attempt to stanch the ever-expanding pool of blood behind her father's head, took off her pale green sleeveless T-shirt and used it to compress the wound. She wore a white bikini top underneath. My eyes were drawn to her full breasts.

I had just killed a man, and I was ogling the daughter I had made an orphan.

There was probably a gap of time, but it seems to me now that the police cruiser arrived very quickly with short yelps of the siren and strobing of the Visibar. Walkie-talkies squawked, an ambulance came; someone shifted the cones from the sidewalk construction to the road. Daria was sobbing in the arms of her older brother, Chris. With a start, I realized I knew Chris; I had played baseball against him. Which meant I knew the victim as well.

Russell Gramercy was the coach of the Verplanck American Legion League baseball team of which his son, Chris, was the star pitcher. Russell Gramercy was also a chemistry professor at Howland College, the school I had just started two weeks earlier, though I wasn't in any of his classes. The previous year, the American Legion team I was on had played against Verplanck. Chris had been pitching, and he struck me out twice. He was by far the best player in our area, and scouts from the majors as well as LSU and Arizona State had shown interest in him. His father coached him that day, and I remembered Russell Gramercy putting his arm around Chris's shoulder with pride as he came off the field with another victory.

"Are you okay?" the paramedic asked me at one point. "Are you injured?"

"No, I'm fine," I replied, knowing even then that it was a lie, though there was nothing physically wrong.

Later, as the first ambulance took Russell Gramercy away, I asked the same paramedic, "He's going to be okay, isn't he?"

He stared back at me, then, masking his true feelings, said, "Well, we can only pray." After that, on instructions from one of the cops, he took my blood for a blood alcohol level test.

I gave my statement to three different police officers. The last one, a detective named Dave Pedrosian, interviewed me for a long time.

Pedrosian also questioned Chris and Daria. She had not seen the actual impact because she had been walking a few feet in front of her brother and father on the narrow shoulder. "I just heard this awful crunch, and by the time I turned around my dad was landing on the pavement," I overheard her say. And then she lost control and gave loud gasping sobs. Her brother put his arms around her.

At some point I also heard Chris being interviewed. "We were walking and my father sort of stumbled. I don't know if he twisted his ankle or what. But he veered into the road. I reached out to grab him, but then . . . just this unbelievable impact with that car . . ."

What I remember most were his next words. "The car just slammed him. It was so fast. My dad never had a chance. And neither did the driver. It would have been impossible to react. It wasn't his fault."

Right after a cop gave me my second field sobriety test and first Breathalyzer, Chris came up to me. I was wary and I half expected him to take a swing at me. But in a dazed voice he told me, "There was nothing you could have done. Don't beat yourself up. It was just a horrible accident." He turned and walked back to his sister, who glared at me with eyes filled with anger and hate.

Detective Pedrosian came by in a while and said, "You're not going to be charged at this time. All the preliminary statements support yours. A collision-reconstruction unit will continue to investigate. If everything holds up, you will not be charged. Your father is here to drive you home."

On the ride home, back to my childhood bedroom, not my new dorm room, I kept saying, "It happened so fast. There was nothing I could do."

Russell Gramercy was declared DOA at Verplanck Hospital at about that same time.

The next few days I spent in my bedroom or, when my parents went to work, roaming the house. I couldn't eat, sleep, watch television. Both my parents kept telling me that it wasn't my fault, that it had been an accident. I shouldn't blame myself.

My father initially insisted that I go to the Gramercy family home.

"And do what? Upset them more? Apologize for killing their father?" I did not want to face them, in particular Daria.

"Just tell them how sorry you are for their loss," my mother replied.

I had already put on my suit and was waiting for my parents to drive me to a condolence visit that I wasn't sure I could endure when the phone rang. A few minutes later my father came into the living room and said, "We're not going."

The relief I felt was immense.

"Of course we are," my mother said.

"The insurance adjuster just called. He said we're not to have any contact with the victim's family."

The victim. His name was Russell Gramercy. He was a beloved father, a husband, a coach, a teacher. And we weren't using his name. He was the victim. And I was the person who had killed him.

"That's just not right," my mother complained.

"He's on our insurance policy," my father said, nodding toward me. "We could lose the house, our savings. Everything. Even a frivolous case could cost us hundreds of thousands of dollars."

So in the end we didn't go. And I did not apologize.

The funeral was private, so I didn't go to that either. But when I returned to Howland College two days later, one of the first things I noticed was a flier about a memorial service.

Howland College is a small liberal arts college in Verplanck, New York, twenty miles from my hometown. Its academic reputation is slight, its campus charmless—buildings of red brick and glass, dormitories that look like singles' apartments. In my area it was the ultimate backstop school, the place you wound up when your other scholastic plans didn't pan out.

That next weekend hundreds of students milled about in the quad. I was handed a slender white candle that reminded me of a fencing foil. People kept glancing my way, it seemed to me with disgust or pity. Right before the service I overheard two students in front of me talking.

"I heard the kid who ran over Gramercy goes to school here."

"Yeah," his companion replied. "A freshman. Apparently some pathetic loser."

Hymns were sung. Speakers came up to a makeshift stage and talked about *Russ* or *Professor G.* It was heartfelt, moving, filled with the inadequate words we use when confronted with death. Some were amazingly articulate, others spoke badly, but their clichés and boilerplate emotions were overlooked because of a collective goodwill and understanding. One person read a poem that somehow felt familiar, and it was only years later that I realized he had cribbed the W. H. Auden work from the movie *Four Weddings and a Funeral.*

One speaker stood out for me. "I'm a doctor," he began. "And last week, on the day that Russell died, I saved a life." He went on to recount that if it hadn't been for the extraordinary work of Russell Gramercy, he would never have passed his organic chemistry course, the bane of all premed students. Gramercy had tutored him, made clear the obscure, gone way above and beyond for him. "It's a simple calculus for me. If it wasn't for Professor Gramercy, I wouldn't be a doctor. If I wasn't a doctor, that patient would not have been saved. That spared life, and everything good in it, can be toted up to Russ.

"There are connections in our lives that we're often not aware of. We're entwined. We intersect, like chains, or strands of DNA."

I did not speak at the service.

By November I had left college. I eventually moved to New York City; it is a place where not driving a car is the norm. My driver's license expired when I was twenty-one; I did not renew it, nor have I ever driven a car again after that day I killed Professor G.

Nightmares plagued me for a decade, though they diminished over time. For years I had to wear an orthodontic device because I ground my teeth in my sleep.

In my early twenties I aimlessly worked boring, dead-end jobs. Then, when it became clear that I was not going to resume my education, my father gave me the fifty thousand dollars he claimed he would have spent on tuition. So I started a small business, a frozen-yogurt shop in the West Village that I can walk to. It is a modest success.

I never married. Relationships never seemed to survive the moment I had to confess to the accident. The fault for these failed courtships, I'm sure, is mine. For the most part, the women I've been involved with were understanding, compassionate. (Though one woman got so angry that she slapped me.) But no matter the degree of their empathy, I always sensed in their eyes a change. In how they viewed me.

Years ago, at one of my lousy, mind-shriveling jobs, a coworker asked all the people gathered around the break table, "What's the most memorable or important moment of your life?" The answers were predictable: *When I met my husband; When I gave birth to my daughter.* Or humorous: *When I felt up Gina Simmons in sixth grade,* or *It hasn't happened yet, but it will be when I get fired from this job.* When it was my turn, I was set to lie: *It was when the Giants won the Super Bowl.* Instead, I shocked myself by replying, "When I killed a man."

There was laughter around the table, and my questioner added, quoting Johnny Cash, "When you shot a man in Reno, just to watch him die?"

"Yeah," I answered, relieved. Although I knew that, unlike most people, I actually had a moment in my life that had irrevocably changed me.

So that was my existence. Constrained, nowhere near having fulfilled a potential. I always thought that there had been more than one victim that day, though I would never say that aloud. And certainly not to the family, not to the woman who had whimpered and sobbed by the side of Beach Road. Nor to her tall, athletic brother, who had once struck me out.

In April 2011 the first body was discovered.

Russell Gramercy's widow had sold the lakeside cabin months earlier. In upstate New York, the small vacation homes that dot the many lakes are called camps. The Gramercy camp, sheathed with cedar clapboards, was small, only sixteen by twenty-four, and had a half loft. It had been in the family for generations. Russell Gramercy winterized the structure himself early in his marriage. He liked to go there to unwind, he said, to write academic articles and prepare lessons and presentations. Except for a week or two in the summer when he was accompanied by his family, he went to the camp alone.

The new owners had no interest in rustic simplicity or outdoor showers. An architect drew up plans for some garish monstrosity. It was a backhoe operator digging trenches for the McMansion's new septic system that had uncovered the skeleton.

(A rumor went around that the new owners, with visions of construction delays and permit problems, tried to talk the construction workers out of reporting the discovery. I'm not sure I believe this. What is true is that they sued the Gramercy family.)

In the weeks after the grisly find, the police dug up eight other corpses. All but one were identified, and I can reel off the eight names by memory. I find it ineffably sad that the ninth victim could not be named. Had nobody in his short life felt connected enough to report him missing?

There were eight male victims and one female. Four of them were runaways. Two were thought to have been hitchhiking, a boyfriend and girlfriend, who had been on their way to a bluegrass festival. One was reported to have been a male hustler at truck stops, though his parents vehemently deny it. But one of the victims had also been a National Merit Scholarship winner. So there didn't really seem to be a pattern except the youth they had all shared.

Forensics teams found traces of dried blood inside the cabin. Most of it was too degraded, but one sample proved a DNA match with one of the victims. I've heard that incriminating and very disturbing photos were found, though I don't know for a fact that they exist. But other objects that had belonged to the victims were discovered in a hiding place in the cabin.

The conclusions were inescapable, and a grand jury agreed. The victims had all been murdered by Russell Gramercy. They had been murdered by *Russ*. By *Professor G.* By the man I had killed with my car.

On the hottest day of the following summer, my phone rang just as I was about to go to work. "Hi, this is Daria Gramercy. Do you remember me?"

Startled, I replied, "Yes, I remember."

"Your parents gave me your number. I hope I'm not disturbing you," she said uncertainly.

"No, you're not."

"I'd like to talk with you. About the accident and everything. If you don't mind. I'd prefer in person, but if you'd rather we could do it over the phone."

I had been hoping for and dreading this call for decades. We made plans to meet at a coffeehouse around the corner from her midtown hotel.

Daria had changed from the sexy teenager I had encountered briefly one fateful day. She had gained considerable weight, I saw as she entered the Starbucks. And her hair was cut in an unflattering style and frizzy from the equatorial humidity that day. Immediately I felt guilty and somehow disloyal for forming these unkind impressions. Given what she had been through, it was an achievement just to be walking around at all. I searched her eyes for anger or recrimination. My entire body seemed clenched with tension.

"Thanks for seeing me," Daria said, shaking my hand and sitting down. She took a deep breath and seemed set to start a prepared talk.

"I want to apologize to you," I interrupted. "I never did . . . back then."

"You sent a sympathy card," she replied noncommittally.

"I wanted to visit your family, but our legal advisers told us not to. They were afraid of liability." *Legal advisers?* Some insurance company guy and my father's fraternity brother who was the family lawyer?

She nodded. "I understand."

"I wanted to," I repeated, protesting too much. Then I blurted out, "Actually, that's not accurate. I was dreading the visit; there was nothing I wanted to do less. When my father told me we couldn't, it was like I had gotten a reprieve."

Daria gave a knowing sigh. "Believe me, I understand how you felt."

And then I let everything out. I told Daria exactly what I remembered. Everything: my inattention, the lies about my actual speed, my creepy, lascivious stares as she comforted her dying father. I'm not a Catholic, but I imagine it was like the sacrament of confession. "I'm just so very, very sorry," I ended, and then, to my horror but yet relief, for the first time since the accident I broke down and cried.

She gave me a few moments, then said, "It wasn't your fault. Even with everything you've told me, there was nothing you could have done to prevent it. You didn't have time to react. I understand that." Daria handed me a tissue.

When I had regained my composure, she gave me a rueful smile and said, "Well, you've sort of stolen my thunder. The reason I'm here is to apologize to you."

Daria had been going to the families of all her father's known victims and asking forgiveness. From how she described it, it sounded a bit like making amends in a twelve-step program. "After I had seen all the victims' families, I knew I also needed to talk with you. My father caused so much pain and horror. If I can do anything to lessen that legacy, then I want to."

We talked for a while. For years I had imagined just this, I told her. In my daydreams I had talked with her: I had explained, I had been succored. And remarkably, something like those fantasies had just happened.

Near the end of our conversation, I asked, "How is your brother, Chris?"

She was momentarily taken aback. "Oh, I thought you knew," Daria said uncomfortably. "Chris died in 2004."

"I'm so sorry," I replied, mortified. "How?"

"A traffic accident."

I flinched.

"He was living in Arizona. It was a one-car accident, late at night. Alcohol was involved."

I must have seemed shaken.

"It had nothing to do with you," Daria said. "Believe me. If you're tempted to see this as some sort of delayed collateral damage from what you did, don't. My brother had his own demons."

We were silent a moment, then I said, "I went to the memorial service for your dad at Howland. The one speaker I remember most was a former student who your father helped become a doctor. And what he said was that our lives are inexplicably entwined. That many of the good things that the doctor had done could be added up in your father's column in this sort of cosmic ledger. I thought about that when I heard about the . . . incidents."

"You thought that by killing my dad," she said gently, "even though inadvertently, you had saved other young people from being brutally slaughtered . . . Let's call it what it is."

"Once again, it's not something I'm real proud of. But yeah."

"I understand. More completely than you'll know. And I think you're right. I think what happened that day did spare others from my father's . . . evil."

We stared at one another for a moment, then she stood. There ensued one of the most awkward hugs in the history of farewells. Then she went out into the street and disappeared.

I discovered the tape by a fluke.

For the first time in years, I returned to Verplanck. A cousin was getting married. At the rehearsal party at my aunt's house, a bunch of my younger cousins were watching videos of their childhood in the family room. I was barely paying attention: the charms of children mugging for the camera is quickly lost if you're not the one doing the mugging.

"Oh, let me show you this one of Barry playing soccer," the brother of the groom said to the bride. "He falls right on his face."

Suddenly my aunt strode into the room from the kitchen and said, "Tim, that's enough of the videos." Her tone was brusque.

Tim seemed confused. "What?"

Flustered, my aunt said more insistently, "I asked you to do something. Turn off the TV. Not *all* our guests may be as enthralled as you."

Her last words seemed to have some special meaning, one that her son belatedly understood.

"Okay, Mom, sorry." He darted a glance my way, then looked away, embarrassed.

It was only an hour later that it clicked. I took my aunt aside and asked. "That videotape of Barry playing soccer. It was taken that day, wasn't it?"

Pained, she sighed. "I'm sorry. Tim just wasn't thinking. I could smack him sometimes."

"I'm not upset," I assured her. "But I'd like to see that tape. Not now, not this weekend."

I returned to New York with the DVD transfer of the VHS tape. It was in my DVD player even before I had taken off my coat.

Seven-year-olds are playing soccer. *Way to go, Kyle. Way to go,* some woman keeps calling out. Another faint but discernible conversation is a woman telling a friend about what a bitch her boss is. And then.

A small *thunk.* The tinny sound of screeching brakes. *Oh, my God, did you see that?*

The first time I watched the tape, I didn't really notice the accident at all. But on the second, I could see the tiny figures in the upper left corner of the frame. Pedestrians walking, a hazy blue car approaching. Then one of those figures flying high into the air, over the car. One detail, however, didn't quite fit.

Obsessively, I watched the tape over and over, at times my face just inches from the screen. And every time I thought I saw that troubling blur.

You can find almost anything on the Internet. Two days later I was in Irving Beckstein's workshop in Astoria, Queens. Beckstein is a forensic video analyst. He has worked for the Defense Department and often testifies as an expert witness at trials.

Beckstein had cropped and blown up the footage of the accident. "Forget what you see on TV. Our software can't miraculously sharpen an image so it looks like a thirty-five-millimeter movie. But we can do quite a bit." He went on to explain what he had done. His words seemed well burnished, as if he had given them many times in front of juries.

Then he played the images for me on a large, sixty-inch monitor. Though heavily pixilated, it showed Chris Gramercy shoving his father into the path of my oncoming car.

Over the years I've attended a number of support groups. Most of the people there are like me: someone who has caused a fatal accident. Most have not been charged because it was determined that they were not at fault. That it was all a tragic accident. A few of the group members had slightly different stories. One was a police officer who had been involved in a suicide-by-cop incident. Another was a train engineer who ran over and decapitated a suicidal man who had just been diagnosed with Alzheimer's who threw himself in front of his train. You would think that they would somehow feel less guilty. But they didn't. Maybe, the cop said, it was because it brought home how vulnerable, how much at the mercy of unseen forces, we all are.

As far as I know, no member of the groups ever was an unknowing instrument of a murderer. Except me.

I did nothing with the information I discovered from the tape. But a month ago Daria Gramercy called me late at night.

"I've been thinking about you," she said after apologizing for calling. "I somehow feel that we have unfinished business."

"And why is that?" I asked carefully.

"I have nothing definite to go on, but my brother may have been more involved in the accident."

"How?"

"I really don't know. It was just this impression . . . After the accident, Chris was never really the same."

"Were any of us?"

"I remember times when he was drunk—and he was drunk a lot near the end. He kept coming back to one theme. Was it ever justified to kill someone? Stupid stuff about would you go back in time to kill Hitler. Would I kill my husband to protect my children?" She sighed, then added plaintively, "My husband is the kindest, gentlest man in the world."

There was a long silence on the line, then I heard, "When everything came out about my father, Chris's words gained a different meaning."

"I'm not sure I follow," I said, though of course I did. "Are you saying that Chris somehow caused your father to fall in front of my car?"

"I don't know what I mean," she wailed. "I hope to God that's not what happened. But I thought you had the right to know."

I considered what she had told me, then said, "I really appreciate your calling me. And your contacting me has helped me in countless ways, so I'm grateful to you. But I can tell you definitely that your brother did not cause your father's death. I could clearly see them both, and Chris was a good two or three feet away from him. Your father stumbled. That image is etched in my mind permanently."

I heard her crying softly and then, "Thank you."

Did I do the right thing? I like to think I did, but who knows?

The nightmares and my obsessive thoughts about that day have lessened. I don't know. Maybe I'm getting better.

SARAL WALDORF

God's Plan for Dr. Gaynor and Hastings Chiume

FROM *Southern Review*

DR. GAYNOR WAS on the move again, walking briskly into town on her lunch break, just what she did most days in the dry season. She wished to pick up the blouse being made for her by Mr. Pherri, who held two jobs, one as tailor running his old foot-pedal Singer sewing machine on the raised wooden porch of Mrs. Tsembe's general store, the other as scrivener, or *mlemba,* who, moving to a rickety table at the other end of the porch, wrote letters or filled out documents for those illiterate.

As Dr. Gaynor moved along, wondering if Mr. Pherri had finished her blouse as he so earnestly promised to do, she had no premonition that today in town, on the way to her tailor, she would have a brief encounter with the young man who would kill her two weeks later.

Some of Dr. Gaynor's staff, watching her leave through the small hospital's back gates—gates seldom used because of the morgue next to them—also had no premonition of their boss's impending death. At best, they had noted some blackbirds chattering in a tree, which might mean visitors coming, and that could include death and his minions. However, since the three-times-a-week bus was always dropping off visitors or relatives in Chitipa, these sightings of blackbirds seldom reached an ominous level. On this day, no one saw anything unusual about Dr. Gaynor's decision to go into town; they only thought her quite crazy as usual, quite *kerezeka,* to want to walk anywhere when, as boss, she had at her disposal the hospital's Land Rover, her driver growing fat as he sat in the tiny transport office eating and drinking and waiting to take her somewhere.

The very fact her staff members made these same remarks about their boss and her noon walks into town showed how, in general, nothing much *did* happen in Chitipa, this the last district town in the mountainous northwest corner of Malawi before the Zambian border, a town reached only by a wide and winding bulldozed-dirt road the government kept promising to pave.

In truth, it was this main dirt road from the lakeside town of Karonga to Chitipa, high on a plateau, that offered the best chance of excitement, because even during the rainy season, when bushes and wild grasses sprang up in its middle, the three-times-a-week, blue-and-white government-owned bus always got through—sometimes on time, most of the time not, but it got through. Gears grinding, up it made its way, goats, sheep, and suitcases piled on its top, batteries and auto parts packed inside, as well as expensive items, like toilet paper, for the local elite. There were also the days-old newspapers in both English and Chichewa, the cooking oils and salt and sugar, the many cartons of cigarettes and matches that vendors bought to resell in allotments of one, two, or three, the large bars of yellow lye-looking soap sold in wholes or halves, and always at least two sacks of incoming mail, for electricity was still too irregular for people to depend on the new cell phones used in the cities or even the old land phones, of which the hospital had three.

Most importantly, the white-and-blue bus brought people, people returning from *matoling*, from visiting relatives or friends elsewhere, or from attending marriages and funerals—especially funerals, because all government and privately employed workers got three paid days off for any family funeral, wherever in the country. It also brought people the police might be looking for, or people who could turn dirt into gold, and its arrivals and departures were pretty much the biggest events of the week, coming Mondays, Wednesdays, and Fridays, leaving the next day on Tuesdays, Thursdays, and Saturdays. Usually the same bus, usually the same driver.

Of course events happened locally too, people being born, people dying, people getting sick, some brought immediately to the hospital but most waiting it out at home or seeing Mr. Chimbalala, the traditional healer, at his camp nearby. For not until about to die did people actually go to the hospital, because no one wanted to die at home. Dying at home meant pollution and ghosts and the home had to be abandoned or purified in elaborate rituals, which were expensive and time-eating.

So it went: bus days overlapping with the local birth days, sick days, funeral days, school days, harvest days, church days, and then the big-drama days, the days when someone stole one of the hospital's two motorcycles and tried to sell it in Mzuzu, or when someone snuck into the home of Mrs. Kondowe and took her disabled TV set, or when the young husband in Vwaza killed his wife with his machete because he thought she was having an affair, which she was. Then there was that big-drama day, just six months after Dr. Gaynor had come to the hospital, when a government helicopter from Zomba landed at the now-abandoned airfield near the hospital to deliver the body of a high-ranking government official for transportation to his village, Lufita, his arrival causing much excitement. After harvest days, there was also the drama of the big-fire days, when fields were burned at night, men keeping the fires moving like cattle, penning them on the edges with big flat sticks and brooms. Crime was down on these nights because the town and surrounding farms were so lit up no one was stupid enough to take a neighbor's chickens or beat a wife.

However, this Tuesday, a departure-bus day, was turning into a low-drama day, like the low-drama, arrival-bus day before, and Dr. Gaynor hadn't much on her mind as she approached town, where the bus was waiting for its early-afternoon departure. She walked quickly and efficiently, eyes forward, not swiveling her head side to side slightly as so many of the female vendors did, the women who sat under the large, shady mango trees of the town's dirt parking lot, their wares laid out before them on overturned wooden crates.

Dr. Gaynor felt, as head of the hospital, she had to maintain a professional if not severe air when dealing with the townspeople, and not show, as they so often did through their turned-sideways heads and fluttering eyelids, this *calculating* curiosity, as she saw it, a curiosity ever-vigilant for something from which a profit might be made.

She felt herself no fool when it came to the motives of her fellow townspeople and knew vigilance was needed on her part too. Her demeanor had to be pleasant but professional, her dress modest, her white doctor's coat worn over her black polyester skirt even when she went into town, nothing to inflame the minds of the male locals, as had happened apparently with the low-cut-dressed wife of her expat predecessor.

Dr. Gaynor had no ambition to stir interest in herself, and, as was to be written up at her autopsy, she wasn't the sort who would stir up male interest, being an unexceptional, white-skinned, thin, middle-aged female of thirty-eight years who had borne no children. She had no signs of recent sexual intercourse. She carried marks of two surgeries: one old, perhaps done in adolescence, where the appendix had been removed; the other, on her left leg, more recent: titanium screws holding together the fibula. Maybe she shattered it in some accident. Her body type was recorded as thin, ectomorphic —or what the female vendors called *nkuku,* chickenlike, when the breasts are flat and empty of milk after nursing.

Passing the Ladies of the Ladles, as Dr. Gaynor called them, for the vendors were always stirring or picking things from their boiling iron pots, she knew many disapproved of her. This came with the territory, as her predecessor, the English doctor Jamie Swain, now working at the Queen Elizabeth Hospital in Lilongwe, told her (he later supervising her autopsy, since she was a white woman and he the only white doctor in the city). However, if Dr. Gaynor's mind was anywhere on this day, it was on her assistant, Robinson Tmembo, and the alacrity with which he had just said he would guard over her office—something he often said when she left for hospital rounds or surgeries or for town errands—but this time there had been some added eagerness that made her wonder just how trustworthy Robinson was, given the young man's frequent quest for her office key so, he said, he could come early and sweep, or stay late and clean up. There was no question he was a hard worker and fervent member of his Living Waters Pentecostal Church, telling her how God in his infinite wisdom had led him to her, but was it *her* or her *property*?

She itemized the current status of her office: a laptop she had to run mostly on batteries or have charged up by the hospital's Land Rover's engine, so she didn't use it very much; her green manual Olivetti typewriter, on which she wrote up schedules, requests, and monthly statistics that were then given to the ladies in the typing room who did the official, clean copies on their heavy manuals.

There was also the copier some nonprofit had given to the hospital before she came, and again she used it only occasionally, since it didn't run on batteries and instead relied on the town's erratic electricity. There were also her many medical books and personal medical kit, and the two wooden file cabinets made by the hospital carpenters that contained files by past administrators (others were kept in the small file room near the men's ward, an office piled up to the ceiling with paper folders). Then on her desk rested a framed photo of her father and mother when they were young, for while she was divorced with no children, Dr. Gaynor had so far refused to display photos of her brothers' children, her nieces and nephew, as if she had maternal instincts. Ticking off all these items, she couldn't think what Robinson could steal without the theft being very noticeable, and, in terms of generating income, quite useless.

With these thoughts, Dr. Gaynor walked past the former general store once owned by Mr. Gupta, an enterprising Indian who had now shifted into the up-and-coming video business, as the more prosperous local businessmen and government employees bought home generators to run their TVs. The wooden building of his emptied store had been bought by another new evangelical church, the New Church of the Prophet Hosea, which seemed to be holding a noontime service.

She had paused briefly to listen to the loud, enthusiastic singing coming from inside when out from the storefront came the very recent arrival Hastings Chiume, the only and spoiled son of the widow Mrs. Makela Chiume, also mother of six daughters, four married, two not. Before bumping into the doctor as he escaped his mother's eye and left the service, Hastings had been sitting on one of the wooden pews of his mother's breakaway church with the other delinquent sons and husbands, while across the aisle, in their section, sat his mother, sisters, and fellow women, singing lustily, "O living Lord from heaven, how well you feed your guests!"

It was after the song's end, while everyone was praying with eyes closed under the pastor's exhortations to "God bless everyone, no exceptions," that Hastings exited swiftly, passing Mr. Mwale, who was standing in the rear, head bowed, as he waited to pass the collection basket, in which sat already the two *kwachas* belonging to the pastor to encourage parishioners to do the same. However bowed his head, Mr. Mwale saw Mrs. Chiume's son's defection and would be one of the older men who later nodded sympathetically when Dr. Gaynor's murder was announced on the radio and in the government newspapers, although Mr. Mwale had no reason to link it to Hastings's hasty departure on this day.

Hastings, paying no attention to Mr. Mwale except to note the money in the collection basket, slipped through the front door of the church and out into the sunshine, and this is where he collided with the white female head of the *chipatala*. This forced Dr. Gaynor, on contact, to step back, annoyed. She made a curt motion to indicate he could go ahead of her on the narrow, chipped-cement sidewalk. But in the ingratiating way many of the town's young men had, he bobbed his head up and down, saying, *"Pepani! Pepani!"*—how sorry he was. When he just stood there, nodding away, smiling, as if to indicate she should go first, she did so with a shrug, leaving the young man in his rope-tied khaki pants and secondhand white shirt just standing at the church's door, watching very alertly her continued passage down the sidewalk that paralleled the small, one-room stores.

Dr. Gaynor, unaware of the young man's intense scrutiny, gave no more thought to him, not even noticing he was now following her some paces behind. Hastings, a man of quick decisions, had spotted the slight bulge in the right pocket of the doctor's skirt, one of many locally famous black skirts the doctor wore every day to the hospital and over which she put her white doctor's jacket, kept starched and clean by her houseworker. So, back in stride, some dust getting into her lungs from a passing rumbling truck full of cornhusks, Dr. Gaynor had not the slightest idea that the *"Pepani"* young man was behind her until he suddenly brushed by her to the right, crying out again, *"Pepani!"* He then took the lead, increasing the lengths between them until he jumped down from the cracked sidewalk onto the tree-shaded parking area and disappeared from sight.

Dr. Gaynor showed brief annoyance again and then thought no more about the incident as she arrived at Mr. Pherri's, offering her *muli ulis,* for she had laboriously taken lessons on the local Chitumbuka greetings and other phrases. Mr. Pherri greeted her in kind and then fetched her blouse. It was after he had wrapped it up in newspaper and handed it to her that Dr. Gaynor put her hand in her right skirt pocket to take out her small, brightly embroidered coin purse, in which she kept her local *kwacha* money. It was a Guatemalan-made purse she had bought in a museum gift shop in Philadelphia when attending the University of Pennsylvania's medical school. She was much attached to it, it acting somewhat as a lucky charm and also as a remembrance of herself in a past when she and her about-to-be husband Richard, then also at medical school, walked the city sightseeing, eating cheaply, envisioning themselves in the future: joining a family practice in the suburbs, having kids, making lots of money, taking trips to Paris and other glamorous places.

However, as Robinson would say—and as he did often say about the reversals of fortune so many suffered, including himself—God had different plans for Dr. Gaynor. And so here she was, eight years later, on this Tuesday bus-departure day, halfway across the world from Philadelphia, Richard married to someone else, and she, Dr. Gaynor, looking for the change purse of her past. She patted herself crossly, peered intently at the ground as if the purse might have dislodged itself somehow, but finding nothing beyond the usual sidewalk debris—eggshells from eaten hard-boiled eggs (the vendors sold these from trays balanced on their heads), dog shit, cigarette butts, soda pop tops, used condoms—she apologized to Mr. Pherri. She must have left her purse at the office and would send someone later to pay him. She left, package in hand, feeling very aggrieved by the loss of her purse, and determining its missing either as a consequence of having lost it or having it stolen. If it were lost, it might be found again, and she briefly considered offering a reward. But that might encourage someone to hold on to it longer, until the reward was increased. Also she had enough to do without having to supervise Robinson in writing up signs and posting them on trees.

No, given the most likely scenario, that it had been stolen, the consequence was simply that she would never see it nor the money again. These things happen in both poor and rich countries, so why get upset? But she was upset, for she felt taken advantage of, especially since the locals knew she had come from so far to *help* them.

Back at the hospital, Dr. Gaynor continued to search, in case she was at fault. She opened her desk drawer, rummaged inside, and shook her wastebasket, even putting a hand into it and moving around the balled-up papers. (There was little else in it; Robinson or the others always found a use for anything she wished to discard.) But again no success. She hadn't lost much, at most the amount of five American dollars, but still, the immediate consequence of her loss meant she would now have to lock her office at all times, even when she went to use the hospital's one decent bathroom in the new donor-funded pharmacy. She asked Robinson, who had been looking too, to check under her desk, behind the wooden cabinets, under the neat, unopened package of copy-and-print paper for the brand-new printer another nonprofit had donated, still as shining and mute on its small metal table as the unused copier. However, Robinson came up only with a dropped Biro pen and some scattered papers as he swept away with his little broom the usual dead bodies—cockroaches, ants, and various flying insects—on the floor. Dr. Gaynor was always very liberal with the insect spray. She bought it in lakeside Karonga, where she went once a month to get supplies and to meet with her counterparts at the much larger and better-equipped hospital there.

After watching his hopeless search, Dr. Gaynor asked Robinson if he'd seen anyone in her office, anything suspicious, while she was out, and then, remembering the collision with the man outside the storefront church, she asked if he knew some young man with a dark blue baseball cap on backward that had TIGERS printed on it, probably gotten at the used-clothes stall in the market ("dead men's clothes," everyone called them). The young man had been lean and almost as tall as her, in worn khaki pants, no belt, a limp white golf shirt with short sleeves. She tried to think of something else distinguishing but couldn't, just the baseball cap, which most of the local male youth wore anyway.

Robinson indeed knew Hastings; he had seen him in just such a baseball cap very early that morning, when he and his mother came to visit one of Hastings's uncles in the men's ward. The uncle was dying of AIDS, or *edzi,* as the locals called it, although the nurses told relatives he had pneumonia (something Dr. Gaynor, once she learned of it, did not approve of, but found it was a custom hard to break). After Hastings and his mother's visit, the staff began to complain how things had gone missing. Hastings was a well-known thief, said Robinson, which was why he had to leave Chitipa in the first place.

Dr. Gaynor pursed her lips and told Robinson to go fetch one of the policemen stationed in the tin-roofed, cement-block building up the street from the hospital. Robinson left to do her bidding, but came back almost immediately to say Mr. Myanka, one of the medical officers, had stopped him in the corridor to have him tell Dr. Gaynor that there was a father from Zambia outside in the courtyard and with him, on his back, was his possibly rabid son. The father was asking for admittance. Dr. Gaynor, who was now searching for her missing purse in the hallway, said brusquely that she didn't have time to examine the boy now, for it was imperative to have the police stop Hastings before he left on the afternoon bus, but to have the father and son put in the children's ward until she was free.

Now it is true that Dr. Gaynor, if she had not been distracted by her missing purse, would never have admitted a rabid boy to the children's ward because of the possible spread of the virus. The boy should have been taken to the German-built TB building behind the hospital, a brick structure that had started out for the few remaining full-blown TB patients but now, vaccination programs having been very successful, was used for people with short-term contagious diseases that needed isolation.

Yes, put him in the children's ward, Dr. Gaynor said, and after locking her office, she first went to the men's ward to question the two ward nurses there as to when and how long a Mrs. Chiume and her son had visited. What had the son looked like? Had the nurses noticed anything was missing after the mother and son had left? Then, not finding satisfactory answers and, on her return to her office, not finding Robinson back, she went out the hospital's front gates and walked to the police station herself, but there was no one there. Thinking perhaps Robinson had been successful in his mission, she returned and headed for the children's ward.

There screens had already been put around the sides of the boy's bed, shielding it from the others—a bad sign, meaning imminent death. Dr. Gaynor stood at the end of the empty, blanketed cot and saw the father on the floor, leaning against the bed and holding his young son in his lap. Rabies was so highly prevalent in all the rural areas, she needed only one look to know the boy was in the last stages. She knew she had made a mistake; the father and son should have been in the old TB building, where there were individual small rooms. But it was too late now. The screens would give some protection, and luckily the children's ward had only three other patients. They could be moved to the women's ward while the children's was thoroughly disinfected.

The father, Mr. Chimpimere, when told the head of the hospital was present, bowed his head respectfully, then, speaking good English, told the story of his son. How he, the father, worked in the Copperbelt west of Lusaka, leaving his wife and four children back in their village near the border, and when the dog bit the boy, the mother said she had washed off the arm wound, bound it with a rag, and after a while it stopped bleeding. The boy, once over his initial fright and crying, went back to playing with his siblings and friends. After that, the mother decided to wait for the husband to come home, which he did every six weeks.

They had been in the fields when the dog attacked the boy, the wife weeding along with the older children. No one knew to whom the dog belonged, but some of the older male villagers working in nearby fields came when the mother cried out and they ran after the emaciated dog, finally beating it to death with their hoes and machetes. It had been a female, starving besides being rabid, her teats long and thin from nursing, his wife had told Mr. Chimpimere when he returned two weekends later, the boy by then running a fever and talking silly. The mother had given the boy some paracetamol tablets she bought at the open-air market, but her son's arm kept festering, and she tried washing the wound again, then binding it up in a poultice the medicine healer at the market said would help.

The father said he knew there were shots they gave nowadays for the dog sickness, but the hospital in his district had closed a year ago, as had the missionary one, so he had strapped the boy to his back and begun walking. It was twelve kilometers to the border and another twenty kilometers into Malawi to where Dr. Gaynor's hospital was. Many of the Zambians near the border came to the Chitipa district hospital, and so far none had been refused help, even though they weren't Malawian citizens.

Dr. Gaynor said as kindly as she could that the boy did indeed have the dog sickness and was very sick; unfortunately, there was not a great deal she and her staff could do at this stage. Even if the hospital had vaccines—which at the moment it didn't, no matter how many times she ordered them—the shots could only be given in the early stages, when someone was first bitten or shortly after.

During this exchange, the boy became very agitated, crying, "Dada Dada," and moving so restlessly that the father had a hard time keeping the boy in his arms. The young boy was smeared with saliva, the father holding fast, crooning in his local language. Dr. Gaynor already had a face shield on, as did the two ward nurses, and Dr. Gaynor asked the taller nurse, Mrs. Kondowe, to give one to Mr. Chimpimere, telling him the virus was very contagious.

But the father just shook his head. So Dr. Gaynor, putting on latex gloves, motioned to the father to move away while the nurse knelt down to hold the boy so she could examine him with her stethoscope.

The boy, however, getting a look at the strange white woman in a mask, threw his head upward, arched his back wildly, and began to keen. The father became agitated, saying he did not want her to touch his son, that his son thought the lady doctor was a ghost and he was frightened. The father did not want his son frightened.

Dr. Gaynor said not to worry, she wouldn't examine the boy for now. She would wait, she said to the father before looking at Mrs. Kondowe, who nodded slightly, confirming Dr. Gaynor's sense that the boy would be dead within the hour. Nothing could have been done; she decided not to give a sedative for fear the boy might choke in taking it.

An hour later the boy did die, his tormented body still at last. Dr. Gaynor supervised the nurses in helping the father to wrap the body in one of the hospital's cotton blankets, then putting the small, shrouded body on the father's back, strapping it with the same piece of cotton *chitenge* skirt material the father had used to bring the boy in. Mr. Chimpimere, now with his son on his back again, seemed stooped—not so much from the slight weight of the dead boy but from the heavy weight of his son's death. He said politely, "*Zikomo,*" the local word for thanks; Dr. Gaynor said she would try to see if their ambulance had returned from taking a body to its village for burial, and if so, it could take the father and son to the border. She was very sorry they couldn't have done more, but the father came too late. He must tell his wife that when children are bitten by a dog or a bat, they must be brought to a hospital immediately. Also, once home, Mr. Chimpimere should tell his wife not to try to wash or hold the body, but leave it wrapped up for burial so as to prevent possible contamination. If his wife or any of his other children got sick, he must bring them here quickly. Dr. Gaynor suddenly heard herself saying all this in her lecturing manner, and so stopped, adding—again in a softer tone—how sorry she and the staff were.

The hospital's ambulance was not back, so Dr. Gaynor, along with Robinson and some of the staff, watched Mr. Chimpimere set off by foot with his dead son on his back, leaving through the hospital gates and turning left to reach the main dirt road.

"It is God's plan," said Robinson, who was standing behind the silent doctor on the steps. "God's plan!" he repeated in his young, knowing voice that often drove Dr. Gaynor to aggravation. "We must accept God's plans, whatever our fate."

"Robinson, you are so naive!" said Dr. Gaynor exasperatedly.

However, the little boy's death did upset Dr. Gaynor more than the other deaths she had witnessed since being there. The children were the hardest, but the others had been mostly silent, just watching the doctor from fevered eyes, exhaustedly placid before they stopped breathing. But this boy had been so young, so frightened, and so beautiful! However, her face showed nothing as she led the others back into the hospital.

Her stolen coin purse now forgotten, she suddenly thought she should call her mother in her nursing home in the States, although Dr. Gaynor usually only did this on the last Friday of every month. Her mother, after her stroke, had a special aide who was supposed to stay in the room at all times, but often during the day the aide wheeled the old woman out of her room and down halls into the TV room or social room, more for her benefit than for her patient's. But she always knew to be in the room for Dr. Gaynor's once-a-month call.

Well, Dr. Gaynor would just have to take the risk of not finding her mother in her room. She went to the telephone room, where calls, if reserved, were made by one of the two clerks on one of the three rotary phones. The lines were kept busy, but as boss, she was not refused. While waiting for the connection, Dr. Gaynor debated whether or not to tell her mother about the dead boy. In the old days she told her mother about all her various patients and their problems. But now her brothers insisted she didn't upset her mother any more than she had already done by taking these overseas assignments, especially this one in Africa.

So Dr. Gaynor usually only spoke to her mother in her professionally cheerful voice, spoke in this voice which had gotten more hearty in the last two years, because even before the stroke her mother spoke about Africa as if it were still the heart of darkness, both literally and biblically.

Dr. Gaynor also suspected that her mother, when first widowed and then stroked, thought her daughter would come home and care for her in the family house, for her daughter was a doctor, wasn't she? Isn't this what doctor daughters should do? her mother seemed to signal again as her hand clung like a ferret to her daughter's during Dr. Gaynor's last visit, yes, clung like a ferret, this cruel comparison popping then into Dr. Gaynor's head. Dr. Gaynor had never entertained the idea of staying home with her mother. Now here she was, finding herself calling her mother for solace as if she were a hurtful child.

"Mother?" said Dr. Gaynor as she heard pips, some crackling, the tinny sound of a phone ringing far off across oceans, then a click and someone answering, her mother's aide no doubt.

"Mother?"

"Wait a minute, Dr. Gaynor," and then there was her mother's voice, soft but querulous, "Who's this? Who's this?" speaking in an unpleasant tone she had developed after her stroke.

"It's Helen, Mom. It's not Friday, but I had some free time so how are you, did you have a good week?"

"Edward Allen?"

"No, Mother, Helen, your daughter."

"I don't have a daughter, I have two boys, Christopher and Kevin, do you know my sons?"

"Mother, Kevin was our father, you mean Chris and Ted, are they there with you? Put Chris on . . ."

But the phone made a banging noise and went silent. The aide's voice came back on. "I'm sorry, Dr. Gaynor, your mother dropped the phone. She's been very agitated recently. Also very incontinent." Incontinent? That was new.

Suddenly the line disconnected, and Dr. Gaynor decided not to try to call back. She felt very disturbed by the call, considered for a brief moment flying back to check on her mother, then thought she had best wait for December, when her annual holiday came up.

But scarcely a week later Dr. Gaynor found herself flying back to Pittsburgh to attend her mother's funeral. She was now sitting with her two brothers on folding chairs in the sanctuary room of the funeral home. She was far from Chitipa, far from her missing purse, far from the rabid dead boy, and now, finding herself so quickly here in the States, a small part of Dr. Gaynor worried that her phone call from Africa may have triggered some final insult to her mother's fragile mind that had killed her. But Dr. Gaynor's guilt hardly found root, for she immediately said to herself that her mother hadn't even recognized her voice, so how could this have set off anything?

Dr. Gaynor looked around. Attendance was sparse. Her brothers, Chris and Ted, sat with her in the front row of chairs, while behind were Chris's latest wife and two of his four children. Ted had come with his partner; there were also several aides and colleagues from the nursing home. Their mother had put resuscitation orders on her advance directive, because, she wrote, she was Catholic and not to do so was a sin. Where she picked up this idea, her sons didn't know, for she had only been an Easter-and-Christmas Episcopalian most of her life.

"Catholic?" Dr. Gaynor said in a tone of bemusement to her brother Chris, who had picked her up at the airport in his SUV that he was going to get rid of because of the gas, because of the bad times, because of his wife ruining its gears. As they drove directly from the airport to the funeral home, he went on and on in his explosive, bad-tempered way. Dr. Gaynor just repeated, "Catholic? Whatever put that in her mind?"

"At least she didn't leave everything to the church!" her older brother snapped. "She was really getting loony at the end."

"They had her on a lot of antidepressants and other medication," Dr. Gaynor said, intending to explain how these affected the elderly, but Chris had already moved on to fulminate about some oxygen therapy expense the home had ordered for their mother without his consent.

Now, in the sanctuary, as the taped music poured over them, Dr. Gaynor said again to her brothers that she found it odd how her mother had died so quickly. It had been less than a week since Dr. Gaynor had called her; it had been the day that a rabid boy came to her hospital and died and she felt like calling her mother. Her mother hadn't seemed herself then. Was the doctor visiting her on schedule? The nurses checking her vitals and giving her meds?

"Listen, we should be thankful!" said Chris, her older brother, testily. "They were going to have to move her up to the Alzheimer's floor, and that would have cost us all double what we've been paying."

Dr. Gaynor did not like her older brother's complaining tone, which had begun to sound so much like her now-dead mother's. "Why was that a problem? I was willing to pay. You know I've always been good for that!" she said curtly.

"You're always good for the money. It's the heavy hauling you run out on." And on that sharp note, still resonating after the funeral and reception and after more sibling bickering, Dr. Gaynor flew back to Lilongwe, the capital. *Yes, God bless everyone, no exceptions, as you would say, Robinson,* she said to herself angrily as she thought about her brothers and thought about her mother and looked at the blank landscape of gray clouds from the plane window.

She had already made an international call to Michael, a fellow expat doctor working in Zomba, that she was stopping over in Lilongwe to pick up some supplies before going back to Chitipa and could he come up to see her. Michael and Dr. Gaynor had met at a medical symposium in Lilongwe a year ago and saw immediately they were kindred spirits; it had taken a while for them to sort out the personal aspects, the carnal side of the relationship lasting less than six months. Now they were just best friends, as they told one another, the best of best friends. And Mike *was* Dr. Gaynor's best friend. She felt she could tell him anything, and had already told him about her stolen purse by someone called Hastings—Hastings! How the locals loved these English names!—and she had told him about the rabid boy and his fear of her, and how that somehow made her call her mother, who then died, not right after the call, but two days later. Michael had just laughed at her concern that these events could in any way be connected. None of her assistant Robinson's God's plan here, he said, just life as usual.

This Dr. Gaynor was thinking about, yes, life as usual, as here she was back in a cat's whisker to the heat and bustle of Lilongwe, when she turned down Chilembwe Road to the newly refurbished Capital Hotel at the northern end of the city. It was a major hotel, with a long tree-lined driveway and portico under which taxis let out their customers, a doorman in white gloves opening the doors.

Lilongwe, even though the biggest city in Malawi, didn't really have a center. Like many African cities, it had grown this way and that, from being no more than a cluster of vendors along the side of the road in precolonial times to an open-air market that added a craft market, then morphed into Asian-owned shops next to bus stations and Spar markets, finally now a jacaranda-lined, spread-out capital city, with glassy high-rises and grand-looking stone-and-brick government buildings, all interconnected by small shopping malls, so one either had to find a bus or grab a *matola* taxi to get from one part of the city to another.

It could become something like Calcutta in time, Dr. Gaynor thought as she walked back to the hotel, her large backpack now filled with boxes of real Band-Aids she had bought at the pharmacy in the small mall she had just visited. Her backpack also contained twelve boxes of rubber gloves, ten boxes of disposable needles, and other ordinary items taken for granted in stateside hospitals, items like the newer type of paper tape instead of the old-fashioned adhesive tape, which was an insult to the skin.

Pleased with her day's shopping, and the small mall being so close to her hotel, she had decided to walk back instead of taking a taxi. So when the attack came, she was furious with herself. Everyone knew muggings were frequent near the fancy hotels and restaurants, where the *mzungus* came to spend money. However, since she could see the hotel's driveway right ahead, she had no expectation that anyone would dare to mug her so close.

But they did, three young men, one of them behind and pulling her by the backpack straps so she fell down backward to the ground while another began cutting the straps to take off the backpack. A third, now that she was down, was on top of her and feeling her across her waist, where, from practice, he must have known most tourists still used money belts for their cash, credit cards, and passports.

"I'm a doctor!" she cried out. "I don't have anything but medical supplies in the backpack!" And she aimed a fist at the nose of the young man on top of her, scoring such a hit the nose began to bleed, and Hastings Chiume, yelling in pain, felt to see if the slag had broken it, then took out his knife even while she kept yelling, "Listen, for God's sake, you idiots, I'm a doctor, I'm here to help you people!"

But it wasn't until he was trying to cut, then yank off the chained purse around her neck that he recognized the woman in her T-shirt and sunglasses as the bitchy doctor who ran the hospital in

Chitipa, whom he had bumped into that day two weeks ago in the town. The stupid lady with the bulging purse in her pocket! Then the doctor, suddenly thrusting her head up as she tried to shake him off, said with surprise, "You're the one who stole my purse!" and, flattered, Hastings wanted to say something boastful to her, like, *Hey, Doktorama, you'd better learn not to carry purses and backpacks when I am around, because see what could happen.*

But people were beginning to run out of the hotel and down the driveway, and a taxi driver, stopped to let someone off, got out of his car, so Hastings and his friends knew it was time to go. After a few more yanks and jabs with the knife until the chain came apart, Hastings and his friends ran off, the loot later distributed in the rented room they shared with two others.

Meanwhile Dr. Gaynor—arterial blood spurting out from Hastings's knife cuts, blood she was trying to stem with her hands—kept calling out more and more feebly, "Help me, call an ambulance, for God's sake! I'm bleeding to death! I can pay! I can pay!"

The next morning Hastings was at his stand at the huge outdoor Wall Market, a place filled with hundreds and hundreds of tables and stalls, around which people milled and bargained. Hastings was squeezed on his left by Mr. Swembe, a *sing'anga* or witch doctor from Tanzania who was selling bat's blood as a cure for AIDS. On the other side was Mrs. Champire's stall; she ironed items brought to her by customers from the secondhand clothes market, using one of her three flatirons kept heated over a charcoal brazier.

On this day Hastings had laid out on his small table, two crates put together, the profits from his gang's raids the day before, which included wallets, purses, and Ray-Ban sunglasses, as well as a lot of capsule containers that the others gave Hastings because they had no use for them. He also got most of the stuff they got off Dr. Gaynor, who had really tried to hurt him. Let her suffer now like everyone else!

But she had been right. Her possessions were almost all practical and medical. He could sell the Band-Aid boxes and syringes, but maybe not the rolls of funny paper tape, because when he had tried using some of the tape for his bruised face, the tape broke too easily. There had also been bottles of pills that Hastings had never heard of before but decided to push as the newest brand to help men with problems down below.

Hastings was proud of his table, for he catered mostly to clients searching for things to make them feel better. He had a lot of stuff he got from the chemists' shops, pills and cough medicines that had expired a long time ago, so they sold them cheap to vendors like him. Other wares came from tourists like the doctor. Tourists always carried a lot of pills on them to ward off death. Besides his medical supplies, Hastings also sold food cans—especially condensed milk cans whose expiration dates were long past—paperbacks either stolen or discarded by tourists, and stolen credit cards, which had to be used fast, before their owners reported the thefts.

A woman carrying a screaming baby on her back came and looked over Hastings's wares. After a while Hastings couldn't take it and asked her why was her baby yelling so, did it need to be fed? It wasn't good for his business. Something had hurt her son on his head, the mother replied, unconcerned, examining the bottles, shaking one of them and watching it cloud up. So Hastings came out from his table and looked at the baby, who was trying to work himself out of the *chitenge* material holding him fast to his mother's back. He could see the baby had been bitten by something on the head, causing a big ugly red abscess to fester above his left ear.

Hastings, who considered himself as knowledgeable as anyone about sicknesses, told the mother she should take the baby to see a doctor to have the abscess opened up and the poison let out. If a dog had bitten the baby, the mother should take it to the hospital to see if the baby had rabies, which would kill him and maybe her too if she didn't act fast. Meanwhile he would use one of his powerful cleaning fluids on it, then bandage it with one of the new Band-Aids he had in stock. Some were Band-Aids for children and had little smiley faces on them.

"A doctor gave them to me to sell," Hastings told the mother. "But I'll let you have it free!" And as he painted the baby's sore with the red stuff out of one of his bottles and put a yellow Band-Aid over the wound, he whistled cheerfully.

Let the Chitipa doctor see him now! *I'm a doctor!* Hastings mimicked to himself as the mother thanked him formally. Yes, God was good! No exceptions!

Later, did Hastings repent? Did he become a changed man, turn himself in, especially after the American Embassy offered a large reward of five thousand *kwacha* for information that led to the perpetrator or perpetrators of this unconscionable crime, the murder of Dr. Helen Gaynor?

Of course not. Hastings, after a year's stay in Nairobi—until interest in the doctor's death died down—moved on from his medicine table to a small pharmacy, then expanded to own several more, not just in Lilongwe but also in Blantyre, in the south. He married the daughter of a highly placed government official and had many children, for his life wasn't some work of fiction. His life, and Dr. Gaynor's, they were part of God's great plan at work, as Dr. Gaynor's former assistant Robinson said often and indignantly to the doubters, even back when he, with his now-dead boss's office key finally in hand, swept and kept Dr. Gaynor's office safe until the new doctor from Holland arrived.

Contributors' Notes

Other Distinguished Mystery Stories of 2015

Contributors' Notes

Megan Abbott is the Edgar Award–winning author of seven novels, including *Dare Me, The Fever,* and her latest, *You Will Know Me.* Her stories have appeared in several collections, including *Detroit Noir, The Best American Mystery Stories 2015,* and *Mississippi Noir.* She is also the author of *The Street Was Mine,* a study of hardboiled fiction and film noir. She was the 2015 winner of the International Thriller Writers and Strand Critics awards for best novel. "The Little Men" was nominated for a 2016 Edgar Award. She lives in Queens, New York.

• The idea for "The Little Men" sprang from real life, a decades-old bit of Hollywood lore. Years ago I read about the sad fate of one of the most successful and charismatic booksellers of Tinseltown's golden age. His untimely death in 1941 took place in his apartment in one of those lovely courtyard bungalows that loom so large in Hollywood tales, from *In a Lonely Place* to *Day of the Locust* to *Mulholland Drive.* Over the years I remained haunted by the real-life story, and I'm generally a sucker for Hollywood tales anyway—especially ones with dark twists. So when Otto Penzler asked me to set a story with a bookstore/bookseller focus, I finally had my chance to dive deep into that jacaranda-scented world of golden-age Hollywood where everything is beautiful and, quite possibly, deadly.

Steve Almond is the author of eight books of fiction and nonfiction, most recently the *New York Times* bestseller *Against Football.* His short stories have appeared in the Best American and Pushcart anthologies. His most recent story collection, *God Bless America,* won the Paterson Prize for Fiction and was shortlisted for the Story Prize. His journalism has appeared in the *New York Times Magazine,* the *Washington Post,* and elsewhere. Almond cohosts the podcast *Dear Sugar Radio* with Cheryl Strayed. He lives outside Boston with his wife and three children.

• "Okay, Now Do You Surrender?" emerged from one of those thought experiments endemic to the domesticated suburban husband: what would happen if one's spousal missteps were monitored by mafiosi rather than marriage counselors? It would be idiocy to deny that personal authorial guilt played a formative role. I had no intentions of writing a whodunit, but the moment the mobsters waylaid our hero outside his workplace, the die was cast. We're all living under surveillance at this point—and always have been. Our conscience does the legwork. It's what sets us apart from the serpents and the badgers and the whatnots. I'm just happy to have found an unorthodox way to write about marital anguish. It remains one of the essential human mysteries.

Matt Bell is the author most recently of the novel *Scrapper,* a Michigan Notable Book for 2016. His previous novel, *In the House upon the Dirt Between the Lake and the Woods,* was a finalist for the Young Lions Fiction Award and an Indies Choice Adult Debut Book of the Year Honor recipient, as well as the winner of the Paula Anderson Book Award. He is also the author of two collections of fiction and a nonfiction book about the classic video game *Baldur's Gate II.* His next story collection, *A Tree or a Person or a Wall,* is a fall 2016 publication. A native of Michigan, he now teaches creative writing at Arizona State University.

• The finding of the boy in "Toward the Company of Others" came to me after a couple months of writing about Kelly scrapping metal in the abandoned buildings of Detroit. I'd wanted to write about metal scrapping and about the urban abandonment in my home state for a while, but I knew very little else when I started. For most of those early weeks, Kelly didn't even have a name: he was simply "the scrapper," and I knew very little about him other than his occupation, his deep isolation and loneliness. I went forward with two rules: I would keep him acting, describing the work he did, and I would try to learn who he was by the way he saw the empty schools and churches and houses he gutted for steel and copper. (Most revealing in those days was the habit he had of seeing the abandoned parts of the city as *the zone.*) I wrote this episode much the way the reader experiences it: I wrote Kelly scrapping the house, unaware there was a boy held in the basement; I then wrote a few sentences where it seemed that Kelly had already found the boy, splitting him into a person who had and had not yet done so, an awareness the reader (and the writer) would share for a moment; and then I wrote the saving of the boy. It was a surprise, but it changed everything else I wrote about Kelly: How would this loner be transformed by saving another person? What new responsibilities would he take on, and how would he discharge the duties they suggested? And if he came to love the boy in the days to come, might he learn that the boy was still in peril, and then how far would he be willing to go to keep the boy safe?

Bruce Robert Coffin began writing seriously in 2012, several months before retiring from the Portland, Maine, police department. As a detective sergeant with twenty-eight years of service, he supervised all homicide and violent crime investigations for Maine's largest city. Following the terror attacks of 9/11 he worked for four years with the FBI, earning the Director's Award (the highest honor a nonagent can receive) for his work in counterterrorism. Coffin's short fiction has been shortlisted twice for the Al Blanchard Award. He is the author of the John Byron mystery series. He lives and writes in Maine.

• I wrote this story several years ago while trying to finish my first novel. As so often happens, ideas creep in and take hold of the creative reins. I've learned not to fight it when this happens. Setting the novel aside, I began to write the tale of an ill-contrived escape attempt from the former Maine State Prison in Thomaston. The story was written in only two sittings, followed by untold hours of rewrites and edits, until eventually it became "Fool Proof."

Lydia Fitzpatrick was a Stegner Fellow at Stanford University from 2012 to 2014. She received an MFA from the University of Michigan, where she was a Hopwood Award winner, and she was a 2010–2011 fiction fellow at the Wisconsin Institute for Creative Writing. She is also a recipient of an O. Henry Award and a grant from the Elizabeth George Foundation. Her work has appeared in *One Story, Glimmer Train, Mid-American Review,* and *Opium.* Lydia lives with her husband and daughter in Los Angeles. She is working on her first novel.

• "Safety" came from a mix of memory and fear. The first line came from a memory: the gym in my elementary school had skylights and high ceilings, and all this dust floating up there in the light, and I remember being little, lying on my back during the wind-down, staring up into space, and feeling completely relaxed and safe. I wrote the first couple of lines hoping to tap into that emotion and transfer it to the reader before it's broken by the sound of the gunshot.

There's that Donald Barthelme quote about writing what you're afraid of, which is, I think, usually an organic process. As the story evolves, the writer's fears surface, and her job is not to shy away from them. With "Safety" that relationship was reversed: it began as a fear that I felt compelled to write about. I began writing it just after the one-year anniversary of the shooting at Sandy Hook Elementary School, when that tragedy was very much in the public eye. I'd just had a baby, and all of a sudden my fears all involved this new person and the safety of her current self, over which I had some control, and her future self, over which I have no control. I didn't have any connection to the victims at Sandy Hook, but I couldn't stop thinking about them, and this story was the best way I could find to express those fears.

Tom Franklin, from Dickinson, Alabama, published his first book, *Poachers: Stories,* in 1999. Its title novella won the Edgar Award for Best Mystery Story and has been included in *The Best American Mystery Stories of the Century* and *The Best American Noir of the Century.* It is currently optioned for film by James Franco. Franklin's novels include *Hell at the Breech, Smonk,* and *Crooked Letter,* which was nominated for nine awards and won five, including the *Los Angeles Times* Book Prize for Best Mystery/Thriller, the UK's Golden Dagger Award for Best Crime Novel, and the Willie Morris Award for Southern Fiction. Franklin's latest novel, *The Tilted World,* was cowritten with his wife, Beth Ann Fennelly. Winner of a Guggenheim fellowship and, most recently, a fellowship to the American Academy in Berlin, Franklin lives in Oxford, Mississippi, where he teaches in the MFA program.

• Once in a while a story comes to you from an outside source. "Christians" found me several years ago, when Alabama writer and folklorist Kathryn Tucker Windham called to say she'd read my novel *Hell at the Breech.* This novel is based on a dark, little-known chapter in Alabama history known to locals as the Mitcham War. It took place in Mitcham Beat, the worst voting beat (district) in one of the poorest, most rural, most violent sections of one of the poorest, most rural, most violent counties in a poor, rural, violent state. There have been books other than mine about these events, which, in some circles in Clarke County, are still contested because a lot of truths are (and likely always will be) hidden, unknown. What's known is that poor sharecroppers and farmers waged a war against less poor townspeople. These countrymen called themselves Hell-at-the-Breech and wore white hoods and did terrible things until county officials, and even the governor, took notice and eventually put a bloody end to it. A lot of people died, some innocent, some not.

Ms. Windham had read my novel and liked it and said she had another Mitcham Beat story for me. As she told me about the young man the Hell-at-the-Breech gang had sent to kill a preacher, as she told how his supporters killed this young man instead, how they took him home to his mother, as Ms. Windham told me, "It was August, so they had to bury him quick," I knew I was being given a gift. I listened, I took notes, I began to write.

Stephen King is one of the world's most famous and popular authors, with more than 350 million books sold worldwide. Noted primarily for his horror and supernatural fiction, he has also written numerous crime and mystery novels and stories, westerns, and cross-genre works. In addition to countless awards for horror, supernatural, and science fiction, King has received the National Book Foundation Medal for Distinguished Contribution to American Letters, the Grand Master Award from the Mystery Writers of America, and a National Medal of Arts from the United States National Endowment for the Arts for his contributions to literature. More than sixty motion pictures have been produced from his work, mostly notably *Carrie, The Shining,* and *The Shawshank Redemption.*

Elmore Leonard wrote more than forty books during his long career, including the bestsellers *Raylan, Tishomingo Blues, Be Cool, Get Shorty,* and *Rum Punch,* as well as the acclaimed collection *When the Women Come Out to Dance,* which was a *New York Times* Notable Book. Many of his books have been made into movies, including *Get Shorty* and *Out of Sight.* The short story "Fire in the Hole" and three books, including *Raylan,* were the basis for the FX hit show *Justified.* Leonard received the Lifetime Achievement Award from PEN USA and the Grand Master Award from the Mystery Writers of America. He died in 2013.

Evan Lewis received the 2011 Robert L. Fish Memorial Award for "Skyler Hobbs and the Rabbit Man," published in *Ellery Queen's Mystery Magazine.* The adventures of Hobbs, who believes himself the reincarnation of Sherlock Holmes, continue in *Ellery Queen,* while an *Alfred Hitchcock* series features a modern-day descendant of Davy Crockett, a man bedeviled by the spirit of his famous ancestor. Lewis also spins yarns of pirates and cowboys, and has contributed articles on such detective writers as Frederick Nebel, Richard Sale, Norbert Davis, and Carroll John Daly. He resides in Portland, Oregon, with his wife, Irene, his pulp collection, and a pack of pint-sized rescue dogs.

• The Portland I know—and have portrayed in my Skyler Hobbs stories—is fiercely proud of its image as a hip, clean, and progressive city on the cutting edge of social and environmental issues. Imagine my surprise to discover that as recently as the 1950s it was a hotbed of racketeering, bootlegging, gambling, prostitution, and political corruption.

That revelation came in Phil Stanford's rip-roaring 2004 exposé, *Portland Confidential: Sex, Crime and Corruption in the Rose City.* I came to the book a few years late, but hot on the heels of my umpteenth reading of Dashiell Hammett's Continental Op series, culminating in his hardboiled masterpiece, *Red Harvest.*

Yikes. The mayor, the police chief, and the judiciary all playing footsie with the Mob. It was as bad as Hammett's Poisonville. So the leap was easy: this was a job for the Continental Op. From there, the plotting and drafting of "The Continental Opposite" was a pure joy, and I am indebted to Linda Landrigan of *AHMM* for giving the story legs. The cleansing of Portland has just begun, so there are more adventures of the Op and the Opposite on the way.

Three childhood moments **Robert Lopresti** remembers vividly: reading the words "They were the footprints of a gigantic hound!"; discovering the Nero Wolfe books while hiding in the mystery stacks from librarians who wanted to banish him to the Children's Room; and seeing *Alfred Hitchcock's Mystery Magazine* on a newsstand. Almost half of his sixty-plus published stories have appeared in *Hitchcock.* They have won the Derringer (twice) and Black Orchid Novella awards. His first novel, *Such a Killing Crime,* was set in Greenwich Village during the Great Folk Music Scare of 1963. His latest book, *Greenfellas,* is a comic crime novel about a top New Jersey mobster who decides it's his job to save the environment—by any means necessary. *Kings River Life Magazine* ranked it as one of the best mysteries of 2015, but he is proudest that a reader called it a book about "ethics as a last resort." Exactly.

Lopresti is a librarian and professor at a university in the Northwest. You can read his multiple blogs at www.roblopresti.com.

• One Saturday evening I tuned in to the NPR show *Says You,* and the goal of the quiz was apparently matching great detectives with their nemeses. (Yes, that's the plural of *nemesis.* It doesn't look right to me either.) When they got to C. Auguste Dupin I thought, *Can they possibly mean the orang-outang?* They did (although the contestant guessed gorilla). It struck me as bizarre to treat the ape, who never physically appears in the story, as if he were an archcriminal—and then the idea for "Street of the Dead House" hit me so hard I stumbled and almost fell down.

It was great fun to give Edgar Allan Poe the steampunk treatment while trying not to contradict anything in the original story. Through dumb luck, I saw a notice that *nEvermore!,* a Poe-themed anthology, was looking for a few more tales. Many thanks to editors Nancy Kilpatrick and Caro Soles for their helpful suggestions.

Dennis McFadden lives and writes in an old farmhouse called Mountjoy on Bliss Road, just up Peaceable Street from Harmony Corners. His stories have appeared in dozens of publications, including *The Best American Mystery Stories* (2011 and 2013), *Fiction, Ellery Queen's Mystery Magazine, Alfred Hitchcock's Mystery Magazine, The Missouri Review, New England Review, The Sewanee Review, The Massachusetts Review, Crazyhorse,* and *The South Carolina Review.* His first collection, *Hart's Grove,* was published in 2010; his second collection, *Jimtown Road,* won the 2016 Press 53 Award for Short Fiction.

• Plot is nice, and necessary, setting is essential, but for me, and for a lot of other writers, story begins with character. And this Lafferty guy is a character. It's been said that if you can come up with a good one, you can use him or her again and again, and though I suspect that's intended to mean in varying guises and disguises in varying stories, I took it a little more literally, no pun intended. Terrance Lafferty has been my main man in multiple stories now, and the next one's already in progress. Other people seem to like him nearly as much as I do—he's appeared in some pretty good places, *Fiction* and *Ellery Queen's Mystery Magazine* among them, and he was first introduced to mystery fans a few years ago in *The Best American Mystery Stories 2013,* when Mr. Penzler and Ms. Scottoline were kind enough to include "The Ring of Kerry." I think people like him because he's harmless. He's by no means heroic. He could be any of us. All the trouble he gets into, all his predicaments, are generally self-inflicted, and happen only because he's on that most elemental of quests—looking for love. Alas (and of course), he's invariably looking in all the wrong places. He didn't make his debut until a few years ago (in *The Missouri Review,* a story called "The Three-Sided Penny"), but he's been with me a lot longer than that. Unlike most of my characters, based on people I've encountered over the years, Lafferty was a seed that grew and grew, inspired decades ago by one Sebastian Dangerfield—J. P. Donleavy's ginger man. A tip of the hat to both of those gentlemen.

Michael Noll edits *Read to Write Stories,* a blog that offers weekly writing exercises and craft interviews. His stories have appeared in *American Short Fiction, Chattahoochee Review, Ellery Queen's Mystery Magazine,* and *Indiana Review.* His book *In the Beginning, Middle, and End: A Field Guide to Writing Fiction* is forthcoming. Noll earned his MFA from Texas State University, lives in Austin with his family, and is at work on a novel.

• I grew up on a hog farm in rural Kansas. Down the road, two old men lived with their mother, their house hidden by dense woods. A van sometimes raced by late at night, and then a little while later drove away again, so fast that the gravel popping under its tires woke us up. This was the 1980s, and not long after, people began getting arrested for cooking meth. My hometown's population is only three thousand, so everyone knew almost everyone else, including the drug dealers. I didn't understand what meth was, only that cooking it could blow up your kitchen and that tinfoil in the windows of a house was a bad sign. As a farmer, my dad applied nitrogen fertilizer to his fields with big tanks of anhydrous ammonia. If I should ever smell ammonia, he taught me in no uncertain terms, I should immediately get away. The tanks were prime targets for meth cooks, and they sometimes sat in our driveway at night.

I wanted to write a story about those innocent days when meth hadn't yet become an epidemic, when meth dealers and users were regular people and not participants in a public crisis. To be clear, meth is terrible, and this story was informed in part by Nick Reding's excellent book *Methland: The Death and Life of an American Small Town.* But it was also inspired by the people in my hometown, kids who rode the school bus and played baseball with me, who were smart and funny and also, perhaps, stealing ammonia from anhydrous tanks, planning to make a little money and hoping not to end up blind or dead from suffocation.

Todd Robinson is the creator and chief editor of the multi-award-winning crime fiction magazine *Thuglit.* He has been nominated three times for the Derringer Award, thrice shortlisted for *The Best American Mystery Stories,* selected for *Writer's Digest's Year's Best Writing 2003,* and lost the Anthony Award both in 2013 (Best Short Story) and 2014 (Best First Novel, for *The Hard Bounce*). His inclusion in this edition joyfully brings his Susan Lucci–like streak to a close. His newest novel, *Rough Trade,* was recently released.

• "Trash" arose from several elements within my personal periphery. Living in New York City, passing by the traditional massage parlor becomes a part of everyday life—a criminal underbelly of sex trafficking that is not only near-impossible to police but that exists just under the periphery of the bright and shiny tourist trap that the city has become. During a conversation with a friend who lives in Flushing, Queens (an area notorious for its numerous shady spas), she talked about the "tells" she'd developed in distinguishing the obviously questionable businesses from those that might actually be offering therapeutic services. Later that night, on the subway home, I saw one of the many "If You See Something, Say Something" posters intended to keep the city safe from terrorist acts. The story about a young man, not jaded enough yet to simply ignore the horrors around him, began to form.

Kristine Kathryn Rusch has published mystery, science fiction, romance, nonfiction, and just about everything else under a wide variety of names. Her Smokey Dalton mystery novels, written under her pen name Kris Nelscott, have received acclaim worldwide. She's been nominated for the Edgar and the Shamus (as both Nelscott and Rusch), and the Anthony, and she has repeatedly won *Ellery Queen's Mystery Magazine*'s Readers Choice Award for best short story of the year. Her short stories have been reprinted in more than twenty best-of-the-year collections, including two previous appearances in *The Best American Mystery Stories.*

Rusch also edits. Her anthology *Women of Futures Past* has just appeared, reprinting classic science fiction by important women writers. Along with John Helfers, she completed the first *Best Mysteries of the Year* anthology, which focuses on worldwide mystery fiction. With her husband, Dean Wesley Smith, she acts as series editor for the *Fiction River* anthology series. She also edits at least one mystery volume per year for that line.

Rusch often writes cross-genre fiction. Her character Miles Flint, from her Retrieval Artist series, has been chosen as one of the top ten science fiction detectives by *io9* and as one of the fourteen science fiction and fantasy detectives who could out–Sherlock Holmes by the popular website *blastr.*

Her most recent pure mystery novel, *Spree,* written under her Rusch name, was published in 2013. Her next Nelscott mystery will start a new series. That book, *A Gym of Her Own,* will appear in 2017.

• I live in a beach town on the Oregon coast. Seven thousand of us live here year-round, but the town has over 150,000 hotel rooms. My daily runs take me past several of those hotels. Two days before Christmas, I ran past a nearly empty hotel parking lot as a little girl, no more than eight, got out of a van. She said loudly, "Will Santa know how to find us?" I never heard anyone answer her. But by the time I had gone to the end of the block, I had the entire scenario for this story in my head. That rarely happens, so I'm grateful to the little girl for her concerns. I never saw her again. I wish I had. I would love to thank her for the inspiration she gave me.

Most of **Georgia Ruth**'s work is gently layered with situations that foster discourse. Because perspective influences behavior, her stories offer a psychological window to examine the motivation for a crime amid tangled relationships. Many of her tales explore historical conflict between cultures. Her most recent manuscript, *Rampart of the Phoenix,* is a historical suspense novel with roots in mythology.

Georgia Ruth lives in the storied gold-mining foothills of North Carolina, where she records and shares the folklore of neighbors who can trace family roots back to Wales and Ireland. Her former careers in family restaurant management and retail sales inspire an endless source of fictional characters and conflicts. Published short stories are listed on her website, http://www.georgiaruthwrites.us.

• In "The Mountain Top," I pivot from a focus on the past to speculation on a future without national structure, where communities slide backward from protected individual freedoms to a lawlessness, dependent upon shared morality but susceptible to the power of a strongman.

When I jumped out of the workforce onto the shaky ledge of retirement, the national debt was out of sight. There were rumors that the Social Security program I had continuously supported for fifty years could not sustain itself. We moved to a log cabin in a remote area where we could reinvent ourselves. My husband discovered a love for gardening, and I was free to exercise latent writing skills. Like many others, I put fingers to keyboard to probe my thoughts. Fear and greed are the roots of "The Mountain Top," but its theme is a fierce devotion to family.

Jonathan Stone does most (but not all) of his writing on the commuter train between his home in Connecticut and his job as a creative director for a midtown Manhattan advertising agency. His seven published novels include *Two for the Show, The Teller, Moving Day,* and *Parting Shot.* His short stories appear in the two most recent story anthologies from the Mystery Writers of America: *The Mystery Box,* edited by Brad Meltzer, and *Ice Cold —Tales of Intrigue from the Cold War,* edited by Jeffery Deaver.

• I'm sure it's easy for a moderately astute reader to guess that George the mailman is based on our neighborhood mailman, also named George, now retired, who delivered our mail with a wave and a smile for as long as I can remember. I'm sure the moderately astute reader can also guess that the neighborhood itself is based on my own—a stable, staid, suburban cul-de-sac where many of us have raised our kids together and now grow old with one another. Even Muscovito is based on a neighbor who moved in, renovated a charming little cape into an architectural monstrosity, disrupted everything, and soon moved out—thank god.

What an astute reader would hardly guess, however, is that the story was written on sunny Caribbean mornings during a vacation on St. John, USVI, with my wife, my daughter, and her best friend, Liza. Writing a scene or two on the patio before anyone else was awake, then joining the girls for breakfast, then sunning, swimming, snorkeling, and snacking the rest of the day away—for a guy who normally grinds out fiction on a bouncing laptop on a cramped, jangling commuter train, *that,* my friends, is the way to write! (Then again, it's the cramped commuter train that makes possible the St. John vacation.) As for such a dark story coming from such a sunny clime? Hey, if you want sunny, you've got the wrong writer—and the wrong story collection.

Art Taylor has won two Agatha Awards, the Anthony Award, the Macavity Award, and three consecutive Derringer Awards for his short fiction. *On the Road with Del & Louise: A Novel in Stories,* his first book, won the Agatha Award for Best First Novel. An associate professor of English at George Mason University, Taylor also writes frequently about mystery and suspense fiction for the *Washington Post,* the *Washington Independent Review of Books,* and *Mystery Scene.*

• More so than with any of my other stories, I'm able to chart clearly the genesis of "Rearview Mirror" and the various factors that led me to write it: a trip with my wife, Tara, to New Mexico that followed much the same path as Del and Louise's travels; a *Washington Post* short story contest whose prompt was a photograph I describe almost exactly in this story's twelfth paragraph; and a challenge from my wife, who's also a writer, for us each to enter that contest, which got me writing this story in the first place. What I've never been able to figure out, however, is where Louise's voice came from. While I admire voice-driven stories (Eudora Welty's "Why I Live at the P.O." and Ring Lardner's "Haircut" jump to mind as favorites), I don't often write them myself. But in this case Louise's voice appeared somewhere in my head and then found its way onto the page, and suddenly that voice was driving the story, with me simply following along the best I could, struggling to keep up.

Another journey I didn't map out beforehand: how these characters, who took their earliest steps in the pages of *Ellery Queen's Mystery Magazine,* would embark on these more extensive, more elaborately developed travels in my novel in stories, *On the Road with Del & Louise*—venturing to Victorville, California, through Napa Valley and Las Vegas, and then up to Williston, North Dakota, before turning toward Louise's home state of North Carolina—adventures that together form the larger story of their evolving relationship, a quest to figure out who they are, what they mean to one another, and where they belong.

Maybe—as Del and Louise learn, and as I've learned myself—you sometimes just need to trust that whatever road you choose might ultimately take you where you need to go.

Susan Thornton is the author of *On Broken Glass: Loving and Losing John Gardner,* a memoir about the celebrated author of *Grendel.* Her fiction and poetry have appeared in *The Seattle Review, Puerto del Sol, The Literary Review, Paintbrush Journal, Dark Fire Fiction,* and others. A former journalist, editor, and technical writer, she now lives in Binghamton, New York, where she teaches French. Visit her blog at http://susan-thornton.tumblr.com.

• While working as an editor at a research institute at Binghamton University, I read a great deal about sex trafficking and thought for a long time about how to dramatize this issue. My goal was to humanize my protagonist and to highlight her blamelessness, her courage, her determination. Because I teach middle school, when I think about victims of trafficking I think about my students—their strengths, their abilities, their weaknesses, their goals—and how they participate in all the drama of the human condition.

I have been to San Diego, Tijuana and Baja Mexico, and El Paso, Texas. I went to AAA for maps of California, Arizona, and Baja Mexico, and spent hours poring over books about the Sonoran Desert, peering at Google Earth, figuring out the setting and plotting the route of my heroine.

My literary model was Ambrose Bierce. I wanted to do an homage to him and his story "An Occurrence at Owl Creek Bridge." Bierce's story ends with the reveal and the death of his character. I added a coda to take the focus off my protagonist and place her drama in a larger social and political context.

I was strongly influenced by John Gardner, who had been my teacher and my lover. At the end of his life, John's last lecture to his students at the Bread Loaf Writers' Conference centered on this message: "if you are not writing politically, you are not writing." In crafting my story I took his challenge to heart: to write politically and to create a vivid narrative.

When I was a child I was surrounded by people who read mysteries and crime fiction: my father, my mother, their friends. Dad had a subscription to *Ellery Queen's Mystery Magazine.* We watched Alfred Hitchcock on television. As a teenager I devoured Sherlock Holmes (we had a two-volume anthology), while Mom and Dad read Margery Allingham, Dorothy Sayers, Ngaio Marsh. I still have Dad's 1957 volume *A Treasury of Great Mysteries.* I remember their delight with P. D. James's creation of a female protagonist for her novel *An Unsuitable Job for a Woman.* Deep in my heart I have always wanted to write a mystery story that would show up in an anthology my mom and dad would have been likely to buy. This dream has now been fulfilled.

Brian Tobin is the author of four novels: *The Ransom, The Missing Person, Below the Line,* and *A Victimless Crime.* His short fiction has appeared in *Ellery Queen's Mystery Magazine* and *Alfred Hitchcock's Mystery Magazine.* In 2015 his short story "Teddy" was nominated for an Edgar Award. He lives in Los Angeles with his wife, Vickie.

• "Entwined" was inspired by an episode of *This American Life* in which the writer Darin Strauss recounted his teenage experience of having struck and killed a bicyclist who swerved into the path of his car. His account was compelling, not only for the quality of his prose but also for the acuity of his self-examination.

Plotting a story is usually difficult for me, involving many false starts and wrong turns. I was listening to *This American Life* during a morning walk. By the time I reached home, I had the story fully formed in my imagination.

Saral Waldorf is a medical anthropologist who has lived and worked in various countries in Africa (Uganda, Lesotho, Cameroon, Malawi, Benin) and elsewhere (Malta, Thailand, Turkmenistan), these places often serving as background for her short stories. She has published stories in *Anthropology and Humanism Quarterly, Commentary, The Hudson Review,* and *The Southern Review.*

• Growing up, I and my two sisters were brought up not on fairy tales but on mysteries, because my parents, Darwin L. Teilhet and Hildegarde T. Teilhet, wrote them jointly, separately, and under pseudonyms from the 1930s to the 1960s, and I am particularly honored to have made this slight contribution to a genre that they so assiduously loved and promoted. I also would like to thank editor Emily Nemens of *The Southern Review,* who took a stab in the dark and published my story, which explores an old theme in literature, the well-intentioned stranger in someone else's "exotic" country who leaves either wiser or not.

The stranger, in this case, is Dr. Gaynor, a female white doctor running a district hospital in Chitipa, Malawi, and tells of her two brief encounters with Hastings, a young, locally born thief back from the capital to visit his mother. There is no real drama between the two—their first encounter is hardly noticeable and simply by chance—yet the deadliness of their final one is dictated, in some sense, by their being from different worlds with different demands and expectations.

I myself did live in Chitipa for two years as a somewhat aged Peace Corps volunteer sent to help set up and run the first AIDS clinic at the district hospital there, which served a population of 125,000. Although Dr. Gaynor and I shared some experiences, I luckily had a much more benign outcome, as related in a memoir kept of these years, *The Condom Lady,* which is now out for publishing review. I should note that one of my neighbors, the accountant Mr. Majonga, in Line #8, the hospital's small row of tin-roofed cinderblock houses for middle management, was a mad mystery story fan who owned and traded almost as many worn and torn street-vendor-bought Agatha Christie and James Patterson paperbacks as I did.

Other Distinguished Mystery Stories of 2015

ALLINGHAM, MAYNARD
The Rostov Error. *Alfred Hitchcock's Mystery Magazine,* October

ALLYN, DOUG
Claire's Mirror. *Ellery Queen's Mystery Magazine,* May

ARDAI, CHARLES
Who Shall Live and Who Shall Die. *Jewish Noir: Contemporary Tales of Crime and Other Dark Deeds,* ed. Kenneth Wishnia (PM Press)

BOURELLE, ANDREW
Event Horizon. *Crossing Lines,* ed. Rayne Debski (Main Street Rag Publishing)

BOYLE, T. C.
No Slant to the Sun. *Harper's Magazine,* March

CALLAHAN, TOM
The Soldier, the Dancer, and All That Glitters. *Dark City Lights: New York Stories,* ed. Lawrence Block (Three Rooms Press)

CARCATERRA, LORENZO
Tin Badge. *The Strand Magazine,* February/May

DOLSON, NIKKI
Our Man Julian. *Thuglit,* September/October

DOOLITTLE, SEAN
Driftwood. *Murder Under the Oaks,* ed. Art Taylor (Down and Out Books)

ESTLEMAN, LOREN D.
The Black Spot. *Ellery Queen's Mystery Magazine,* March/April

FLOYD, JOHN M.
Driver. *The Strand Magazine,* February/May

FOSTER, HAZEL
The End of the Dock. *West Branch,* Fall

FRANKLIN, S. L.
Trip to Reno. *Alfred Hitchcock's Mystery Magazine,* January/February

FREEMAN, CASTLE, JR.
Squirrel Trouble at Uplands. *New England,* vol. 35, no. 4

GATES, DAVID EDGERLEY
A Crown of Thorns. *Alfred Hitchcock's Mystery Magazine,* April

GORE, STEPHEN
Black Rock. *Ellery Queen's Mystery Magazine,* August

HERBERT, FRANK
The Yellow Coat. *Fiction River: Pulse Pounders,* ed. Kevin J. Anderson (Fiction River)

HUNTER, STEPHEN
Citadel. *Bibliomysteries,* ed. Otto Penzler (The Mysterious Bookshop)

KARESKA, LANE
Destroyer Come Home. *Progenitor Art & Literary Journal*

LAWTON, R. T.
On the Edge. *Alfred Hitchcock's Mystery Magazine,* October

LEVIEN, DAVID
Knock-Out Whist. *Dark City Lights: New York Stories,* ed. Lawrence Block (Three Rooms Press)

MADDEN, MIKE
Proof of Death. *Thuglit,* July/August

MOORE, WARREN
Bowery Station, 3:15 A.M. *Dark City Lights: New York Stories,* ed. Lawrence Block (Three Rooms Press)

OATES, JOYCE CAROL
Gun Accident: An Investigation. *Ellery Queen's Mystery Magazine,* July

ROZAN, S. J.
Chin Yong-Yum Meets a Ghost. *Ellery Queen's Mystery Magazine,* March/April

SCHWARTZ, STEVEN
The Horse Burier. *North American Review,* Summer

Todd, Charles

The Heroism of Lieutenant Wills. *The Strand Magazine,* July/October

Tucher, Albert

The Beethoven House. *And All Our Yesterdays,* ed. Andrew MacRae (Darkhouse Books)

Walker, Joseph S.

Pill Bug. *Alfred Hitchcock's Mystery Magazine,* March

Woodrell, Daniel

Joanna Stull, 3/11/18, Blond, Brown. *The Fiddlehead,* Summer